D1685251

MURDER AT THE JUBILEE RALLY

Also by Terry Shames

Samuel Craddock mysteries

A KILLING AT COTTON HILL
THE LAST DEATH OF JACK HARBIN
DEAD BROKE IN JARRETT CREEK
A DEADLY AFFAIR AT BOBTAIL RIDGE
THE NECESSARY MURDER OF NONIE BLAKE
AN UNSETTLING CRIME FOR SAMUEL CRADDOCK
A RECKONING IN THE BACK COUNTRY
A RISKY UNDERTAKING FOR LORETTA SINGLETARY

MURDER AT THE JUBILEE RALLY

Terry Shames

SEVERN
HOUSE

First world edition published in Great Britain and the USA in 2022
by Severn House, an imprint of Canongate Books Ltd,
14 High Street, Edinburgh EH1 1TE.

Trade paperback edition first published in Great Britain and the USA in 2023
by Severn House, an imprint of Canongate Books Ltd.

severnhouse.com

British Library Cataloguing-in-Publication Data
A CIP catalogue record for this title is available from the British Library.

ISBN-13: 978-1-4483-0934-4 (cased)
ISBN-13: 978-1-4483-0968-9 (trade paper)
ISBN-13: 978-1-4483-0958-0 (e-book)

This is a work of fiction. Names, characters, places and incidents
are either the product of the author's imagination or are used fictitiously.
Except where actual historical events and characters are being described
for the storyline of this novel, all situations in this publication are
fictitious and any resemblance to actual persons, living or dead,
business establishments, events or locales is purely coincidental.

All Severn House titles are printed on acid-free paper.

Typeset by Palimpsest Book Production Ltd.,
Falkirk, Stirlingshire, Scotland.
Printed and bound in Great Britain by
TJ Books, Padstow, Cornwall.

For Winter Fate Morvant and the Deuce

.

ACKNOWLEDGEMENTS

As we recover from two years of pandemic life, I want to begin by acknowledging those who kept me going when it seemed as if we'd never be the same again. To David, Geoffrey, and Winter; to Carol, Joan, Mary Ann and Jerry, Anne and Ray – all members of our 'pod,' my deepest love and thanks.

And much love and thanks to the members of the Crime Scribblers Salon, led by the incomparable Craig Faustus Buck. Our Friday night Zoom meetings have been a mainstay of my life for over a year. I also want to express appreciation to the 'Usual Suspects' Zoomers, led by Keith Raffel.

My thanks would not be complete without acknowledging the writers of all the books that I read in the past couple of years, too many to name. Our lives would be impoverished without books, so deep appreciation to those who write them.

And where would I be without readers who continued to send me letters telling me how much they love my books? Thank you one and all.

A special nod to Janet Reid, who over the past few years has taught me how to end a book. She kept saying, 'You're not done yet. You need one more twist.' And she was right.

And finally thanks to my agent Kimberley Cameron for connecting me with Severn House Publishing, and to Carl Smith, Piers Tilbury, Martin Brown, and all the others who work behind the scenes at Severn House to produce such beautiful books.

If you enjoyed the book, please consider writing a review at your favorite review site. To stay in touch with me, you can subscribe to my newsletter at www.Terryshames.com.

ONE

'Let the fireworks begin,' Lester Pierce, the mayor, leans over and whispers to me. You'd think we were about to host the gunfight at the O.K. Corral instead of a town hall meeting. He bangs his gavel and the last stragglers dive for their seats. Although this meeting will probably be as tedious as all the others, at least our new city council meeting room is a lot more comfortable than the old one, with modern folding chairs that replaced the metal ones, and air conditioning that works. The room is painted a nice beige and decorated with vintage photos of Jarrett Creek. There's also a big bulletin board with flyers and announcements, some already out of date.

I'm sitting at the table at the front of the room, because Lester insisted that as chief of police I should be at the head table to help work out a solution to tonight's topic. I note that the unusually large crowd of thirty or so attending the emergency meeting have divided themselves into two sides of the aisle: pro and con. The issue is whether to shut down the town during the yearly Jubilee Motorcycle Rally out at the lake. Proponents of the move say it's a heathen event that brings in an unsavory element. They want to shut down businesses so the bikers have to go to Bobtail, ten miles away, to do their shopping, and stay out of our town with their loud machines and rowdy behavior. It's no surprise that business owners are opposed. As are those who don't want to be inconvenienced. So the 'anti' side of the room is larger.

I don't know why, after years of indifference to the Jubilee Rally, this year people got riled up about it. They actually tried to ban it altogether. Six months ago, Lily Deverell formed a committee to take a petition to the state of Texas, signed by two hundred of our fearless citizens. The state makes a fair amount of money from the rally so, to no one's surprise, they rejected the request. After that Lily came up with the 'Shut Down the Town' movement.

Lester calls on Lily, as head of the committee, to make the

case. About forty, with a round face and hair cut like a helmet, Lily always wears eye-popping clothes. Tonight she's sporting electric green pants and a blinding-yellow sleeveless blouse that buttons to her neckline. Her voice quavers at first, as if she's nervous about addressing the crowd, but passion takes over as she speaks. She concludes by saying, 'There's no reason why we have to put up with their loud music and the roar of those motorcycles, and their vulgar behavior. The way they tear up and down the highway, it's not safe to get out on the road.'

There are murmurs of ascent from the people on her side of the room.

Spurred on, she says, 'Alls I'm saying is that even if the state lets them have the rally out at the lake, we don't have to allow bikers to run wild in our town. It won't kill us to shut down our stores for a week.' She plops down, looking pleased with herself.

There's a smattering of applause, and then Amber Johnson gets up. Amber couldn't be dressed more differently from Lily. She's wearing a short blue skirt that shows off her legs and a white top with a plunging neckline that shows off her ample bosom. Her dark hair is in a ponytail.

'Y'all know I have a family to take care of, and shutting down my store for a week would be a problem,' she says, her voice shaking. 'I don't approve of the way some of those bikers behave any more than you do, but they're not all like that. I know from experience that most of them are good people who just like to get together and have some fun. Bottom line is, I can't afford to lose the money they bring in.' She tugs her skirt down over her shapely hips before she sits down.

Amber and her husband were members of a motorcycle club when, a few years ago, the driver of a pickup truck lost control of his vehicle and plowed into a group of club members riding on a country road. One man was killed; Amber's husband Mike's back was broken and he's on disability now. Amber had broken bones, but she recovered. Since then, she's had to shoulder the burden of running their convenience store.

Lily Deverell jumps up again, without waiting to be called on. 'Amber, it's possible some of them are good, God-fearing people. I don't know. But every year somebody gets drunk and loses their temper and a fight breaks out and somebody gets hurt. If they kept it out there at the lake, it would be one thing, but remember how two years ago they had a big brawl at the Two Dog?' She looks to me at the central table at the front of the room, and I nod. It's true, there was a set-to at our town's only bar, but that was a rare event. My police department hardly ever has any problems with the rally because they have their own security and the highway patrol is out in force.

Lily isn't done. Her face is red as she sputters, 'I'm tired of my kids seeing how they act rude, and the way they dress so vulgar, like they don't have any respect for themselves or anybody else. Drinking, carousing and roaring up and down 'til all hours.' She finally stops to draw breath.

Lily's husband is hunched over as if he wants to be anonymous. When she stops talking, he pulls her down into her seat.

Amber stands up again. Her face is white and her big calf eyes look on the verge of tears. 'I've got to make a living, and you think that's easy?' She looks around the room, meeting people's eyes. 'It's hard. I'm lucky to keep a roof over our heads and supper on the table. And as for you,' she speaks directly to Lily, 'you're upset because your son is a troublemaker and now that he has a motorcycle you're scared he's going to raise hell. And that daughter of yours looks like she's going to be just like him, made up like somebody out of a vampire movie. Maybe it's them you need to worry about and stop sticking your nose into everybody else's business.'

The room is stunned into silence.

Lily gasps audibly. 'How dare you talk about my kids that way! Maybe you ought to look to your own behavior.' She starts to get up and her husband, Harold, grabs her arm.

'Lily, sit down.'

She throws him off and rises. 'I don't have to stay here and be bad-mouthed.' She climbs over people to get to the aisle and heads for the door.

Her husband goes after her.

Amber has grown pale and reaches out to steady herself on the back of the seat in front of her. 'Lily, I shouldn't have said that. Come back.'

Harold catches up with his wife and says something to her.

She lets him lead her to the nearest seat, across the room from Amber.

'Let's all just settle down,' Lester says. 'We'll take a break for a few minutes and partake of some of the coffee and cookies.' We've already done that once, but people rush back there as if they're starving.

I go back to get another cup of coffee and take a couple of sugar cookies. My buddy Gabe LoPresto ambles over to me. I'm surprised he's here. He's a building contractor whose business won't be affected one way or another by the rally.

'What are you doing here?' I ask. 'You don't have any dog in this fight.'

'You know me, though, I like to keep my oar in. Besides, this is one of the stupidest ideas I ever heard and I was sort of curious to know what was going to happen.'

'Well, Lily's got a point, the bikers do cut up and make a lot of racket.'

'You sound like you don't care for the rally. I don't particularly either, but a lot of the businesses in town count on the extra income from this week. Lily doesn't have enough to do with her time, if you ask me.'

Lester rushes over to us. 'Got any ideas?' he says. He's a scrawny guy with a long, horsey face. I didn't give him enough credit when he first became mayor. He was tentative and seemed in over his head. But he's settled in.

'Why don't we just curtail the hours in the evening?' I say. 'A curfew. Won't do much, but it might satisfy the do-gooders.'

'I like it,' Lester says, nodding.

He corrals us back to our seats. No one seems to have sneaked out during the break.

'Folks, I think if we put our heads together we can come up with a compromise,' Lester says.

'What do you mean "compromise"?' Bill Kazinski grumbles from the front row.

'He means everybody gives a little and gets a little, Billy,' Maureen Washington says, with a wry tone, digging her elbow into his side. Everyone laughs, relieved to have the mood lightened, even if just for a minute. A high school teacher with a sharp tongue, she is a close friend of Kazinski's, a guy who normally thinks women should be seen and not heard.

'I know what it means, smart Alec,' he says. 'I just want to know what it means in particular.'

'Now look, y'all,' Lester says. 'We can't stop the rally. They're contracted with the state, and it's happening whether we like it or not.'

'I move that we table the discussion and bring it up again next year.' Gabe LoPresto is reared back in his seat like he's king of all he surveys, with one leg crossed over the other at the knee, showing off his flashy black boots.

Indignant cries at his suggestion break out all over the room.

'No,' Lily yells. 'It's time we took action. Every year we just let it happen. But not this year.' She jumps to her feet again. 'I move that we shut down business the week of the rally.'

Lester has to pound his gavel at the outcry.

'We have two motions. Anybody want to make another one?'

I can see this going on for another hour, so it's time for me to make a move. 'Mr Chairman,' I say, when the noise has died down, 'I'd like to put a proposal on the table and let everybody discuss it.' I feel the sigh of relief running through the room.

'OK, Chief. What's your plan?'

I glance at LoPresto, who's grinning. 'We could have a business curfew. Something like eight o'clock. Post signs at both entrances into town announcing it. Any business found open after that without a good reason will be fined. That might keep bikers out of town in the evening hours.' We're a small town and most businesses like hair salons, real estate offices and the like close at six anyway. Even the few cafes usually shut down by nine.

Lester looks at me, a smile playing on his lips. 'A sound suggestion. Any discussion?'

There are nods and murmurs.

I hope no one in the room actually believes the police will monitor the curfew. Besides me, I have two full-time and two part-time deputies. The town can't afford overtime pay for any of us to be monitoring the town's business habits. But we're here in the interest of taking a stand tonight, and if we can rally enough supporters for the compromise, we can go home.

And that's exactly what we do, with exceptions made for the town's two gas stations and motels. After the decision is made, the Chamber of Commerce president says she'll contact her members and urge them to shut down at eight.

Once the meeting is adjourned, Lester says, 'You know we can't make them do it. Plus we've got businesses that aren't part of the Chamber of Commerce.'

'We'll send out a city-wide notice,' I say. 'That's all we can do.'

Afterwards, I nab Gabe LoPresto and ask him if he'll slap together some signs for us to post at either end of town. He says he'll have them out as soon as he can tomorrow morning.

TWO

For the last thirty-plus years, I've kept a herd of twenty-five Herefords in the pasture behind my house. I never had dreams of becoming a big-time rancher, I just wanted to raise a few cows. My wife Jeanne indulged me, but when my mother heard about it she sneered that I was pretending to be a gentleman farmer. That may be, but I get a lot of pleasure out of spending the early morning hours tending to them.

It's going to be a fiery hot day and I need to be sure they aren't suffering in the heat. People think cows are sturdy, but they can actually be delicate and prone to all kinds of odd illnesses if they're stressed by heat. I used to depend on Truly Bennett to keep an eye on their well-being, but he's been out west in the Lubbock area for several months setting up a ranch for a wealthy man who retired and decided to become a cattleman with a big spread.

My dog, Dusty, doesn't seem bothered by the heat. While I check on the cows, he scares up a squirrel and they keep each other busy until I'm ready to go back up to the house. When I took in Dusty last fall, the vet told me he was a Border Collie, and they tended to be smart. Neither proved to be true, but Dusty's a good dog, a brown and white mutt with a frizzy muzzle. The fact that he doesn't behave well is more my fault than his.

I'm barely back from the pasture before my neighbor Loretta

Singletary knocks on the door and walks in and I can tell by the aroma that she's bringing cinnamon rolls. She makes it her mission to bake for her friends most days. That way she can do a good turn and also catch up on the latest gossip.

'Come on in,' I call out from the kitchen. 'I'm just putting on a pot of coffee.'

She's bright-eyed, a morning person who's up earlier than anybody I know in order to bake. She's dressed for gardening, with her loose slacks and a short-sleeved blouse. Until a couple of years ago, when she decided it was time to modernize herself, she never wore slacks, only dresses, even for gardening. And she always wore her hair in tight white curls. Now it's got a blondish color to it and is cut short like a pixie. It looks good on her.

She sits down with a cup of coffee and a piece of toast, while I have my eggs and one of her rolls. She says, 'Spill it. How did last night go?' She told me last week that she'd like to ban the rally, and was in favor of shutting down the town, 'but not bad enough to go to the meeting.'

Last night's two hours takes me three minutes to recap. 'What I can't figure out is why, out of the blue, a bunch of people decided to make a fuss about the motorcycle rally,' I say. 'You know I'm not a big fan, but the town has had a lot of years to get upset about it. Why this year?'

'I don't know, except that Lily Deverell has been a one-woman campaign. She's in the Baptist Ladies Circle and our president finally had to take her aside and tell her to cool it.'

I tell her about the fight that broke out between Amber and Lily.

Loretta puts her hand to her heart. 'They're both good people, but they've never gotten along. They're like oil and water. Like I said, Lily got too riled up over this, but she's a good person. And Amber! What a cross she has to bear. I guess I'm not surprised she got upset. She's under a lot of pressure. But it seems to me that after what happened to her and her husband, she wouldn't want anything more to do with motorcycles.'

'I'm going out to the lake to talk to the rally organizers and tell them what's going on, maybe get them to ask participants to give the town a break,' I say.

'Humph. That won't do any good and you know it. Even if most of the bikers try to be respectful, there's always that group that thinks the rules don't apply to them.' She picks at a corner of her toast. I stopped serving her the baked goods she brings, because all she does is pick at food. These rolls are too good to waste.

'Are you really going to put up signs?' she asks. 'It's Wednesday, and the first bikers will start arriving tomorrow.'

I tell her I turned it over to Gabe and she's satisfied.

When I get to headquarters, my deputy, Maria Trevino, pounces on me to find out about last night's meeting. She teaches a basic self-defense class on Tuesday nights and couldn't attend.

I fill Maria in. She's my main deputy, a young Hispanic woman assigned to me a few years ago by the state as part of a minority outreach program, with the idea that she'd be here for a year. But despite thinking I'm an old fogey who doesn't know what I'm doing half the time, and despite the fact she's easily riled, she made herself indispensable to me and settled in to life in the town. She's short and compact, with chin-length dark hair, deep-set dark eyes, and what I think of as a stubborn chin.

'How did your class go?'

She frowns. 'I don't know what these girls think is going to happen. The way they talk, you'd think they need to learn how to fend off a zombie invasion.'

The school asked us to give a basic self-defense class to high school girls over the summer, and Maria had so many sign up for it that she has to give two classes.

There's one aspect of the class I've been worried about. 'How about gun safety? What did you decide to do?' She's been trying to decide whether to just talk about gun safety or to actually have the girls bring guns in and show them how to handle them. Most of them already know anyway. In a town where we routinely get poisonous snakes and a lot of people are hunters, guns are a way of life.

'I asked them to bring a gun to class, but to leave their ammunition at home. At least I hope I can teach them not to shoot their friends.'

Before I get down to work, I call my girlfriend, Wendy Gleason. She answers, sounding like she's out of breath. 'I just got in from my power walking class. It's too hot for that. Just a minute while I get a drink of water.'

Wendy is always doing some physical activity – yoga, swimming, or power walking. She's been trying to get me to take up kayaking with her. I've never been a big fan of the water, but I imagine she'll talk me into it sooner or later.

'You want to go to the motorcycle rally Friday?' I ask.

'What? I thought you said you didn't want to go.' We had our first argument about it last week. She said she wanted to go, and I told her it wasn't for me, that she should go with a girlfriend.

I tell her about the town meeting last night and my plan to go to the rally to give the organizers a heads up about the curfew. 'I figure if I have to go over there, we might as well go together. It's only the first day, so it may not be the most exciting.'

'You never know, you might like it so much you decide to go back.'

I'm almost ready for bed when my nephew, Tom, calls. He is my brother Horace's son. My wife Jeanne and I took him in and raised him as our own after Horace and his wife proved to be unfit parents. There were drugs involved, and both of them died within a few years of Tom coming to live with us when he was seven. Although we adopted Tom legally, we never got out of the habit of calling him our nephew, partly because I didn't want him to think badly of his daddy. Tom's an attorney now. He and his family live in Austin and we talk often. I haven't heard from him in a couple of weeks. It's unusual for him to call this late.

'What's going on?' I ask.

It's a beat before he sighs. 'We're having problems with Hailey.'

'Hailey? What's she done?'

'She's started sneaking out and going out with an older guy. She's been drinking and I'm afraid she's going to get into drugs.' Hailey is his younger daughter. I've always had a soft spot for her. When she was little, she was full of curiosity and asked non-stop questions. And she could get the giggles faster than anybody I ever saw.

'I'm sure it's just a phase,' I say.

'Maybe, but I've smelled marijuana on her clothes. You know, with my daddy being the way he was, I worry.'

'I know you do. How did she fall in with a bad crowd?'

'Who knows? We never had trouble with her before. Her

grades have always been good, and she was pretty easy to discipline. But that's changed. At the end of this year her grades fell. I guess we should have realized something was going on, but we didn't. June was the one who alerted us that Hailey was sneaking out at night and dating an older guy.' June is Hailey's older sister; she graduated from high school this year.

'Did her teachers notice a change?'

'They say it isn't unusual for kids her age to act out a little. But she's been belligerent and seems really angry.'

'Have you seen a counselor?'

'We tried to get Hailey to see a therapist, but she refused. Vicki and I have been seeing someone, though. She thinks Hailey is going to be OK, but I don't know . . .' His voice trails away.

'Listen, you remember Wendy Gleason, the woman I've been seeing? She raised two daughters and one of them was a handful. Maybe she has some advice.'

'We don't have time for advice. We've got to act now. We're thinking of sending her to a boarding school for troubled kids.'

'That seems pretty drastic.'

'I'm afraid she's going to get into big trouble. She won't listen to us and she's really nasty to Vicki. We're at our wits' end.'

'Still, sending her away is a big step.'

'Yeah, I know. I don't really want to.' He sounds desolate. I can't stand for him to be so upset.

'I have an idea. What would you think about bringing her down to spend a few days with me? Maybe she needs a change of scene.' As soon as I say the words, I feel like I'm stepping off a cliff.

'Uncle Samuel, that's really generous, but you don't know what you're asking for.'

The thought of trying to corral a teenaged girl scares me, but Hailey and I always got along. When she was little she liked going to the pasture to watch while I took care of the cows. We had an easy way between us. It's hard for me to picture her being out of control, but she's sixteen now, and I know from kids here in town that that's about the age they start acting up.

But this is Tom, and I'm always inclined to help him any way I can. 'Get her down here, and we'll sort it out.'

'Are you sure? Hold on,' he says.

I hear his wife Vicki's voice in the background, but can't hear what she's saying.

'Vicki thinks it's too much. Let me put you on speaker.'

'Hey, Vicki, I'm sorry Hailey is giving you fits.'

'Samuel, we can't ask this of you. She's changed.' She sounds like she's been crying.

'I think we ought to give it a try,' I say. 'If Hailey and I can't work it out, I'll haul her back home.'

There's silence and I can picture the two of them exchanging worried glances.

'You really want to try?' The relief in Tom's voice is evident.

'I do. When do you want to bring her?'

'I'm in a trial right now and can't come, but Vicki could bring her this weekend. What do you think, honey?'

'If I don't get her out of here soon, I'll probably kill her. Do you think I could bring her Sunday?'

Whoa. Not much time to get used to the idea. But also, no time to have second thoughts. 'Sure. Bring her on.'

As soon as I hang up, I call Wendy and tell her I've offered to take Hailey on, and why.

'Oh, boy, that should be interesting.' Her voice tickles me. She always sounds like she's on the verge of laughing.

'I hope I can get some help from you.'

'We'll see. If she's anything like my daughter, I'm not sure how much help I'll be. When is she coming?'

'Sunday!'

'That gives you time to get prepared.'

THREE

Wendy spent Thursday night at my place, and in the morning, after I get back from seeing to my cows, I roust her out of bed. 'Let's go see if we can scare up some action,' I say. 'I might like the rally so much I'll decide to buy a motorcycle. I'll get a side car for you. We can tear around the country.'

She laughs. 'A side car? No way! If you buy one, I'm buying one.'

Wendy dresses in tan Capri pants, running shoes, and a blue sleeveless blouse. Her curly mop of hair is pulled back from her face with two barrettes. She looks terrific.

We get in my pickup, with Dusty next to Wendy, peering out the window as if he knows we're doing something different. He isn't the world's best-behaved dog and I wondered if it was a good idea to bring him, but Wendy insisted.

When we get parked and are out of the car, Wendy says, 'I don't know how long we're going to last in this heat.'

It's got to be close to one hundred degrees, with humidity to match.

All day yesterday, motorcycles paraded down Highway 36 through town headed for the rally. I can't even imagine what it will be like with so many people and motorcycles crammed into this park area, cutting off every hope of a breeze. Why the motorcycle folks think it's a good idea to have the rally in the middle of summer is beyond me. All that leather traps the heat, and the helmets are likely to fry people's brains. Scanning the horizon, though, I see a scattering of clouds to the west. Maybe we'll get rain later to cool things off.

At the entrance, we survey the area to get the layout. There's a wide central lane with camper vans and cars along each side, many with tents set up beside them. A lot of people come early to get the best camping spots. By Wednesday, they'll be crammed in at lakeside. Luckily, some of the people only come for the day, so folks don't usually get turned away.

I clip Dusty's leash on because he can't be trusted to stay out of trouble, and we start strolling along the center lane. With nothing going on yet, most attendees are escaping from the heat by sitting in lawn chairs under portable awnings outside their vans. Beyond the camping area, booths are being set up to sell motorcycle-related goods – T-shirts, helmets, water bottles, saddlebags, leather clothing, souvenir mugs, keychains, and the like.

A couple of hundred yards on, we stop at a trailer with a sign that says 'Rally Headquarters.' Wendy stays with Dusty while I go up and knock on the door. No one replies. I go back to the entrance and ask the guys taking tickets if the honchos are around.

'They've got a lot to do to make sure the setup goes right. I can call them if you'd like.'

I tell them I'll check back later.

We stroll past RVs, trailers, and tents, most of them with motorcycles parked next to them. The bikes are in every size, shape, and color. There are brand new ones in startling shades – chartreuse, bright orange, dazzling yellow – along with vintage bikes that have been lovingly restored, as well as some that look like old workhorses, unadorned and basic. Some of the bikes look like they cost more than my pickup.

We pass food trucks and vendors unloading their goods for the week. At the far end of the area there's a stage, where young guys are setting up sound equipment. A few people hover around it, but nobody seems to be moving fast. In this heat I don't blame them. The entertainment doesn't start until late afternoon anyway. There's a sign set up with the weekend's roster of bands.

On the other side of the sound stage there's a stand advertising 'BEER' in big letters, and next to it is a Sno-Cone truck. Both of them already have lines.

What I don't see are the security forces that are supposed to be patrolling. Not that there's anything to patrol at the moment. It's all pretty quiet, with an air of expectation.

Just then I spy unlikely attendees, my next-door neighbor Jenny Sandstone and her boyfriend Will. Jenny is a big woman, almost as tall as me. In her forties, she has flame-red hair and decided opinions. Will is tall and lanky. I like him because he makes Jenny happy.

'You never told me you come to these rallies,' I say to Jenny.

She hoots. 'It may surprise you to know I don't tell you everything I do.'

'How'd you get off work today?' Both Jenny and Will are public defenders at the courthouse in Bobtail.

'We just closed out a big trial and I have time coming and Will has vacation days. After we leave here, we're going to take off to the beach for the weekend.'

'The beach sounds fabulous,' Wendy says, giving me a side-eye.

Will says, 'Looks like there's some kind of action down at lakeside. Let's go on down there. Maybe there's a breeze.'

Jenny rolls her eyes. 'You just want to drool over the motor-cycles.' To me, she says, 'One of these days he's going to make good on his dream to buy one of these menaces.'

Wendy laughs.

'I'm on Will's side,' I say. 'Let's go down there and see what's up.'

What's up is a bunch of guys doing wheelies in the damp soil at the shoreline. The lake – an eighteen-square-mile expanse – has a beach, of sorts, of sand mixed with gravel. This week the rally will be competing with dozens of vacationers who come here to get out of the heat and into the water.

Some of the riders are pretty good, and we're all entertained.

In the collection of thirty or so onlookers I recognize a surprising number of people from town, including Lily Deverell's son, Steve. I'm surprised she didn't keep him away.

He spies me, peels off from his two buddies and comes over to us. 'Hey, Chief. I didn't expect to see you here. You interested in buying a hawg?' He laughs.

Even though he gets into trouble, and some townspeople think of him as a hooligan, I can't help but like him. He's a goofy kid, with ears that stick out and hair that looks like he cut it himself. But even when I have to give him a ticket for speeding or racing on the dam road, he's invariably philosophical about it, assuring me he deserved it. I expect he'll grow out of his rowdy behavior.

'I'm here to make sure you stay out of trouble,' I say. 'I under-stand you got a bike yourself. How come you're not doing some of these stunts?'

He blushes. 'I'd make a fool of myself out there. I've only had it for a couple of months.'

Jenny and Will have wandered off to get closer to the action, but I introduce him to Wendy. His blush gets deeper. She has that effect on men.

'Do you have your motorcycle here?' she asks.

'Yes ma'am, it's over by that tree.' He points to where a scroungy-looking bike is propped up.

'What kind is it?'

'It's just a used Yamaha. I couldn't afford anything fancy. But I'll get it fixed up.'

'What are you doing this summer?' I ask him. 'You got a job?'

'I sure do. At least a temporary job. I'm helping out here at the rally four to midnight on cleanup crew. It's a three-week gig. Pays pretty good, too.'

I wonder if he got the job before his mom joined the campaign to have the rally banned, or if it's recent.

'Three weeks?'

'Last week we cleaned up and got everything ready for the crowd, then this week I'll be doing cleanup, and then a week to get it back the way it was.'

'It's hard work. Good for you.'

He salutes me and swaggers away.

When the event winds down, Jenny and Will rejoin us and the four of us head up to where we smell barbecue. We buy ribs and brisket and all the trimmings and take our food over to a shady area to eat.

We've hardly settled down when I hear two men snarling at each other and a woman squealing. I can't see what's happening because of the RVs and tents in the way. 'I'll be right back,' I say to Wendy. 'I don't see any security and I want to see what the fuss is about.'

'Be careful,' she says.

'You want me to come with you?' Will asks. I tell him there's no need.

Around the front side of the RVs I find two rough-looking men wearing full biker regalia of jeans off the hips, T-shirts with motorcycle themes and leather vests, squaring off at each other. One is probably forty and the other ten years older. Sweat is pouring off both of them and their cheeks are bright red. A woman stands off to one side, grinning like a fool. She's five feet tall and has on strappy high-heeled sandals, of all things, and a bikini which is almost hidden in her flesh. Her blondish hair cascades down her back and she has on enough lipstick to stock a five and dime.

'What's going on?' I ask.

The older guy, who has a bristly beard and a hefty chest, glances over. 'Nothing to get your undies in a bunch about, old timer,' he says.

'I believe if you'd take off those heavy vests, you'd cool down a little bit,' I say.

Both men turn to glare at me. 'What didn't you understand when I said this is none of your business?' the younger one says.

A couple of people have stopped to watch, eager to be entertained, and not in a good way. The woman traipses over to the older man and pushes herself up under his arm. 'Lonny, cut this out. You're going to give yourself a stroke. Marvin didn't mean a thing by looking at me.'

'Why would I want to look at you?' the younger man says. 'You look like a pig in ribbons.'

At that, the older man snarls and lunges for the young guy. But the younger man sidesteps him and he goes sprawling. He wastes no time scrambling to his feet, his face even redder than before.

'Cut it out!' I yell with all the authority I can muster. Everybody freezes and stares at me.

I look at the onlookers. 'Anybody seen any security here?'

One guys shrugs. 'Somebody said they're on strike.'

Oh, great. Just what we need. I step closer to the two men who look set to start up again. 'I'm Samuel Craddock, and I'm chief of police here in Jarrett Creek. If you two don't settle down, I'll run you in and you'll get to spend the weekend in jail. If that appeals to you, keep it up.'

The younger man spits at the other's feet. 'If Lonny gets in my way again, it might come to that.' He stalks away.

The older man shouts after him, 'You chickenshit!'

As the guy walks past a big RV several feet away, the door opens and Amber Johnson walks down the steps. She has her head down and doesn't see me. She must be visiting some friends who have come in for the rally.

'That was pretty impressive,' a familiar voice behind me says. I turn to see Ralph Tyson standing next to a bike with a 'For Sale' sign on it. He's a red-faced man with a blond buzz cut.

'Ralph, I didn't know you were a motorcycle fan,' I say.

He smiles. 'I didn't used to be, but look at this beauty.' Ralph is a stocky guy. If he wasn't cleaned up and wearing a golf shirt and loafers with his jeans, he'd fit right in as a biker.

The bike is a standard-looking Harley-Davidson, sleek, black with red trim. 'I can see the appeal. Who's minding the store?' Ralph is the postmaster, and is usually working in the post office.

'I've been taking off a couple of afternoons a week and letting

Myra fill in. Not that she loves it, mind you, but it's good for her to learn the ropes.'

'What would she think about you buying a bike?'

He shrugs and shoots a look at the guy standing next to the bike, who I take to be the seller. 'I might have a mind to find out.'

I chuckle. 'Good luck.'

Ralph takes a step toward me, looks past me and nods to where the guys were arguing. 'Was that Amber Johnson I saw coming out of that RV?'

'I think so,' I say.

'Wonder what she was doing there?' he mutters.

'You know she used to be with a motorcycle club, so maybe she's visiting a friend.'

I tell him I need to get back to my party. As I walk away, I hear the guy selling the motorcycle say, 'That's Grant Butler's RV.'

I get back to my interrupted meal, and after we eat, while the others go to buy Sno-cones, I head for Rally Headquarters. This time when I knock someone hollers for me to come in. Inside, there's a tall, rangy bald guy with a brownish-red beard behind a desk.

I introduce myself, and he gets up and comes around the front of the desk and offers his hand. 'Luke Harriman. My partner and I put this show together. He's around here somewhere. Good of you to come out. What can I do for you?'

First, I tell him about the town curfew. 'I'd appreciate it if you'd get on the PA system and tell people to get their business in town done before eight o'clock.'

'I'll sure do that. But I can't really tell people at the rally what to do and what not to do.'

'I understand. Just remind them to be courteous if you would. Now, there's another matter . . .'

Harriman shifts his weight, impatient to see me gone. 'What's that?'

'I hear security didn't come through.'

Harriman squints. 'Yeah. It's not only for the rally. The company we hired decided to go on a general strike. I've contacted another company and they'll have somebody out by tomorrow. Today's the first day and it will be light activity. We shouldn't have any problems.'

I shake my head. 'Not good enough. I've already broken up one fight. You need to get security out here now or call CHP to come out and help.'

Harriman shakes his head. 'CHP won't want to get involved.'

'What do you mean? It's their job.'

'I mean we don't really need them,' Harriman says. 'My partner and I can handle things today.' He snaps his fingers. 'But I have another idea.' He walks past me to the door. 'I'm going over to talk to Gilly Moon and get him and his sons to help.'

'Who's Gilly Moon?'

Luke grins. 'Gilly Moon is a preacher and he's only happy when he's bossing people around. Trust me, him and his sons will be perfect security people.'

When I rejoin my party, Wendy says they've heard about a stunt program being held down by the lake. We go back down there and it's as entertaining as advertised. Bikers propel their machines off the ramps, soar through the air, and every single one of them comes down safely, some of them with more style than others.

It stirs my blood and I remember a few years back my friend Walter Dunn telling me I ought to try riding one.

It's so hot that Wendy and I decide it's time to go. Jenny and Will say they'll stay a little longer. On the way back to the entrance, no sooner have I thought about Walter Dunn than I see him outside a big trailer with its side open, revealing shelves with every kind of part imaginable on them. Walter is crouched down examining a BMW cycle. I walk over and say hello.

'Samuel Craddock, what are you doing here?' He straightens up. He's a big, burly guy with a lazy grin and intense blue eyes. I should have known he'd be here. He and some other Gulf War vets have a motorcycle repair shop out on the road to College Station.

'Good to see you, Walter.'

We shake hands and I introduce him to Wendy. 'I guess I shouldn't be surprised you're here,' he says. 'You've had an eye out for a motorcycle for a long time.'

'No way,' Wendy says, laughing.

'Yeah, that's what my wife says. I had to sell my bike. She

said with two toddlers she has no intention of being left a motor-cycle widow.'

'I see you have a shop set up here.' I gesture to the truck.

'Yep. We make a lot of money at these rallies. What are you doing here if it isn't to get a line on a good bike?'

I tell him about the brouhaha in town. 'I need to tell the organizers to let people know about the curfew.'

He laughs. 'I don't blame them. Some of these guys and gals can get pretty rowdy.'

When we get back, Wendy goes to the grocery store while I check in at headquarters. There's nothing going on my deputy can't handle, so I head back home and watch while Wendy cooks up fried chicken. We like to eat out on my front porch, but the heat hasn't let up so we sit at the kitchen table and are early to bed.

FOUR

Wendy leaves early the next morning. She's got a yoga retreat that starts this afternoon and lasts the rest of the weekend. That means she won't be with me tomorrow when my niece arrives. But she's said she'll be at my command after that.

I head back over to the rally to make sure Harriman has made good on his promise of security. There are twice as many people here today, probably close to three hundred, with more arriving all the time. By the end of the day there will be close to a thousand. It's louder today, and not as organized. The food trucks and vendors are in a clump at one end, with a few drinks vendors set up in outlying areas near the beach. People have spread out all over with tents, RVs and vans. Theoretically, camping should be in one area only, but on this weekend the state doesn't restrict it.

The majority of the men sport heavy beards and tattoos, and the women wear as little as they can get away with and still be called dressed. There's also a second bandstand, with poles set up, and a well-endowed young lady wearing a thong and a bikini top is sliding around the pole giggling. I had thought of bringing Hailey here during the week, but seeing this I'm pretty sure it's a bad idea.

Soon I see a couple of guys wearing vests that say 'Security.' I stop and introduce myself.

'Pleased to meet you. I'm Allen Moon and this is my brother Gary.' Both tall, burly guys with substantial beards and ruddy complexions.

'Had any trouble?'

He grins. 'Nothing we can't handle.'

His brother says, 'If they give us too much trouble, we throw a Bible at 'em.' They both laugh. After what Harriman said I expected them to be tough guys, but they seem good-natured.

'Is it just you two?'

'No, sir, my daddy and our brother are somewhere around here.'

Glad that security is under control, I head back to town to visit the town's businesses to see if anybody has gripes about the curfew. I stop by the Two Dog Bar, our only real bar, which is nothing but a shack with blue lights strung around it that come on at night and beer signs in the windows. It's only big enough to accommodate two-dozen people, but they often spill out onto the covered patio in back that is also strung with blue lights.

I tell the owner, Wolf Goodnight, who bought the bar from Oscar Grant a couple of years ago, that I'm exempting him from the curfew. Wolf gets his nickname from his shaggy eyebrows, intense gray eyes and pointed nose.

'I appreciate that,' he says. 'We don't get too many bikers in here anyway. But I hate for regulars to go away disappointed.' He'd also hate to lose a dollar. He has the reputation of being less generous with his pours than Oscar was.

I also stop by the Quick Stop to see Amber. Ever since the town meeting, I've worried about her. She seemed desperate and I wonder if the business is making it.

The Quick Stop models itself on Seven-Elevens in bigger towns, except without a glass front. It's right in the middle of town on Highway 36, near an intersection, a rectangular box of a store that sells a little bit of everything. It usually stays open until eleven, while the big grocery store closes at nine.

'Hey, Cal,' I say to the young guy manning the cash register. He looks like a young James Dean with his blond hair flopped over and a lazy grin. He's Ralph Tyson's son. 'I saw your daddy over at the rally yesterday afternoon.'

'Yeah, but don't tell Mamma.'

'Why not?'

'She'd kill Daddy if she knew that's why he left her to run the post office by herself.'

I laugh. 'Amber here?'

'She's in the back doing bookkeeping.' He pokes his head into the adjoining room and says something, then comes back and tells me I should go on in.

Amber was pale at the town meeting, and I assumed it was because she was angry, but she's still lacking color and she's hunched over her desk like it's pulling her in.

She straightens when she sees me and gives me an attempt at a smile. 'Hey, Chief, you coming to see if I've lost my damn mind?'

I smile back. 'Among other things. Have you?'

'Just about.' She gives a dismissive wave to the papers, stacks of receipts on one side and bills on the other with a laptop computer open in between. 'I wasn't cut out to be a businesswoman. I hate paperwork like I hate copperhead snakes.'

'I'm stopping by all the businesses in town to see if the curfew is going to work for you.'

'Has to, doesn't it?'

I've been thinking about this. 'Mind if I sit down?' It's a small space, but there is another chair.

'Of course! Let me get you a cup of coffee.'

I wave her off. 'Don't get up. I'll just be a minute. Look, I know you count on late-night people for your customers, and I think we could make the case that Quick Stop is an exception to the curfew, for the sake of the folks who live here. You and the Two Dog and the gas stations. Would you like that?'

Her smile is more genuine this time, showing dimples. 'That's so sweet of you, but I was sort of looking forward to a mini-vacation. Three hours a night for a week sounds like bliss. I haven't had a vacation since the accident.' She raises her eyebrows. 'Besides, what would Lily say? She'd probably organize a boycott.'

'You two still on the outs?'

'Let's just say we're not best friends. She laid into me again after the meeting was over. I tried to apologize, but she wasn't having any of it.'

'I hate to have people feuding over something like the rally.'

'I don't know where she gets the idea that she has the right to close us down. I mean, I'm sorry for what I said about her son, even if it's true, but I'm not sorry I said that about her keeping her nose in her own business.' She grows more agitated as she speaks. She's a good-looking woman, and somehow being riled up makes her dark eyes flash and she looks even more attractive.

'Who was minding the store that night so that you could go to the meeting?'

She nods toward the front of the store. 'Cal. He's terrific. Dependable. I don't know what I'd do without him.'

'Mike not able to work at all?'

When I say her husband's name, her face closes up. 'Looks like that's never going to happen.' But she seems to catch herself and forces a smile. 'Maybe. Never know. He has those back spasms that come and go.'

'And the doctor can't give him relief?'

'He had an injection that helped for a while, but they say they can't inject him too often, that to really get some relief he has to have another operation. And that . . .' Her voice trails away.

'Wouldn't insurance pay for that? The other guy's?'

'No, the guy was uninsured, so our insurance has to cover it and they're putting up a fight about it. I don't know whether Mike wants to do it anyway. He's scared. They tell him there's a risk that he'd be paralyzed. And I don't blame him for being scared of that.' She bites her lip, her eyes anxious. 'He says he'd rather put up with pain than not be able to walk at all.'

When I leave, Cal gives me a cheerful wave. I'm almost to the door when I spy a rack of candy and stop to buy some M&Ms. When I get back to the counter, Cal is gone. I hear him and Amber laughing in the back room.

'Hello?' I call out.

Cal comes back out, his face flushed. 'Sorry about that. I didn't realize you were still here.'

The only business that gives me any grief about the curfew is Palmer's, the general store that sells dry goods – from fishing

equipment to shoes. Bud Palmer claims he has to be open in case somebody plans an early morning fishing trip and needs worms late at night. I almost can't keep a straight face, because I know he's just being stubborn. 'Bud, you usually close at eight anyway.'
'Yes, but I don't like being told that I have to,' he says.

I roll back to my place at five o'clock and see a familiar Chevy pickup sitting outside. It's filthy, which makes sense, since it's probably just come back from west Texas. I don't see the vehicle's owner anywhere around, but I know where he is.

I stop inside the house to grab a couple of beers and head down to the pasture. 'Come and meet my friend Truly,' I tell Dusty.

Sure enough, Truly Bennett is in the pen with my cows as if he's here to visit old friends. He comes out of the pen and accepts the beer. We shake hands.

'You got yourself a dog,' he says, bending down to ruffle Dusty's ears.

'Mutt,' I say. 'At least he's learned not to bark at the cows. Truly, what brings you back here? You finish the job?'

'Not yet. I needed to visit my daddy. This is a quick trip. But you don't need me anyway. Your herd looks good.'

I'm struck by a new confidence in his manner. He's always been a wary guy, a Black man who learned early on to kowtow to white people. We have a long history going back to the first time I was chief of police, and we've been good friends ever since. But I could never breach that barrier of wariness, and his sense that he owed me something. Being hired as honcho for a big outfit seems to have given him strength.

'How's everything going out there?'

'Good, good.' He nods and sips his beer. 'Mr Brixton is a good boss. Hands off. Gives me free rein. Pays well. And the herd is coming together.'

'I've missed you,' I say.

He nods toward my little herd that are crowding up to the fence. 'You're doing all right on your own.'

'Truly, I don't just mean the cows. I mean I miss having a conversation with you.'

We go up on the porch and sit down. I ask him how his daddy is doing.

'Oh, you know, age creeping up on him.'

'Tell me about it,' I say. Truly's only ten years younger than me, but looks lean and fit.

He chuckles. 'With Daddy, it's like he's gotten more ornery as he's gotten older. Lorraine tells me he about drives her crazy.' Truly's daddy got remarried a few years ago and Truly moved out of his house, which caused a little tension.

'Things better between you and her?'

'Oh, yeah. If Daddy hadn't been with her, I wouldn't have felt good about taking that job so far off.'

'How long you think you'll be gone?'

He hunches over and shakes his head. 'You know, I like it out there. I didn't think I would, but I'm thinking it might be permanent.'

I sigh. 'I hate to see you go, but I guess everybody has to find their place.'

'It's not just that.'

It takes me a second and then I realize what he means. 'A woman.'

'Yessir. I never thought I'd find anybody. Seemed like it just never got around to happening for me. But Angelina and I . . . well, when we met it just seemed like we'd always known each other.' He tells me they're getting married in the fall. 'I'll be letting you know when it happens. I'd like you to be there. Like you to meet her.'

I bring out another beer and ask him to stay for supper, but he says his daddy and Lorraine are expecting him, and we have a pleasant talk until he has to go.

FIVE

I've barely closed my eyes when my cell phone wakes me. I fumble for it on my bedside with one hand while rubbing my face with the other. 'Yeah? This is Craddock.' It's just past midnight.

For a few seconds all I hear are whispers.

'Hello?'

'Sorry. Is this the police chief?' A young man's voice, nervous.

'Yes, how can I help you?'

A sigh. 'We have a situation here.'

'Where is here?'

'Oh yeah, at the rally. The motorcycle . . . the Jubilee Rally.' He sounds like his teeth are chattering, but that doesn't make sense in this heat. Even this late at night it will still be in the 80s.

'What's the situation?'

'Dead lady. Woman. Behind the . . .' He pauses again and I hear someone say, 'Just tell him we're at the music pavilion. How hard can that be?'

'I heard,' I say. I've already stood up and grabbed some jeans and a T-shirt. 'Did you call for an ambulance?'

'No, sir.'

'Well do that. I'll be there in ten minutes.'

I go into the kitchen and start the coffee pot that I'd set up for tomorrow morning. By the time I've thrown on my clothes and boots, the coffee is ready. Dusty is staggering around behind me, staying close. 'You're going to have to stay here, boy,' I say. He disappears into my room, presumably glad to go back to bed.

I pour the coffee into a stainless-steel mug and head out to my pickup. The air is heavy with humidity.

On the way over, I phone Maria, my chief deputy, to tell her what's happening and that I'll call her if I need her.

'No, I'll come over now.' She sounds wide awake. Probably hasn't even gone to bed yet. She's young.

I show my badge at the gate and drive inside and around the perimeter of the grounds, back to the music pavilion. There's still a lot of activity, people standing around in clumps drinking and talking, some huddled over bikes. Others are strolling around, a lot of women dressed in scanty clothing, a lot of raucous laughter.

I get out of my pickup and stick my badge on my shirt, then I pull my Colt and gun belt out of the glove compartment and strap it on.

When I arrive at the music tent at least twenty people are hanging around near the area, talking in low voices, looking curiously in the direction of the stage. I suspect they know something's happened, but they may not know what.

The temperature hasn't cooled down. There's a smell of dust and motor oil and rancid food in the air and a hum of people talking. Down by the lake children are squealing and someone is strumming chords on a guitar.

The music tent is a canvas structure open on three sides with a stage up against the back canvas wall. On the stage, guitars, fiddles, and cases rest against big amps. There's a portable piano shoved to the back.

Three men are waiting for me in front of the stage. Two of them are scrawny guys in their twenties wearing jeans and fringed vests over T-shirts, long-haired and hollow-eyed. The other one is older, beefy with a bushy dark beard and small eyes, but dressed the same. All three are covered in tattoos. Off to the side two women are sitting in chairs, one slumped over with her head in her hands, the other one staring at the men. The older guy steps up. 'You the law?'

'I'm Chief Craddock. And you are?'

'Chuck Oakley. That's my sons, Johnny and Tucker.'

I nod to them. 'Where's security?'

'We talked to them first and they said to call you. They didn't want nothing to do with this.'

'Did you call an ambulance?'

'Yessir, they said they had to come from Bobtail. Should be here soon.' That's the older guy again.

'How about the Bobtail police? Did you phone them?'

'No, we figured you'd tell us what to do.'

'OK, let's see what you've got.' I need to make sure the woman is actually dead before I do anything else.

The three men lead me around the back of the stage where it's pitch dark except for the dim light that seeps through the canvas. I flick on my flashlight and see the body, up close to the back of the stage, in a heap. Behind me, I hear one of the younger men moan.

'Tucker, take it easy,' his daddy says.

The woman is facedown with her knees huddled up under her. Her long, dark hair has fallen forward over the sides of her face. There's no sign of an injury, but I flash the light around and see a trail of blood behind her. I slip on gloves and step close and reach down to check for a pulse, but I can't find one. Normally

I'd pull the hair back to see the face, but I don't need to. I recognize the blouse she's wearing. It's the same one she was wearing earlier when I talked to her in town. It's Amber Johnson.

I stay still for a minute while I get my bearings, thinking of all the ramifications of this death. I motion the guys closer, aware that their footprints could contaminate the scene, but they've no doubt already trampled any evidence, and as dry as it's been I don't expect we'll find footprints anyway. I pull her hair back. 'Take a look,' I say. 'Any of you know her?'

They say they don't.

'Did any of you touch her?'

'I did,' Chuck says. 'I thought she was just drunk. I called out and she didn't move, so I went to shake her and that's when I realized she was, uh, deceased.'

I stand up. 'I'd like you to get somebody on that stage to pull back the canvas so we can see a little better. And get some lights positioned for me.'

'Sure,' the older guy says. 'Johnny, you want to take care of that?'

'Yessir.' But he doesn't move. He's staring at the body. 'Shouldn't we cover her up or something?'

'No. We need to leave the scene as is. Which one of you found her?' I ask.

'That was me,' Tucker says, his voice miserable. Even in the dim light I can see he's pale and sweaty. He can't seem to keep himself still. He looks at the body and takes a couple of steps to the side and back, the whole time wringing his hands.

'Tucker, let's go around into the light so I can ask you a few questions.' On our way to the front of the tent I call Bobtail PD and tell them what's happened. They say they'll send a team out right away.

I hear a car, and see Maria drive up and park next to my pickup. I tell Tucker to stand by, and I signal Maria to join me so I can tell her the status of things.

'Amber Johnson? What in the world . . .? Who would have killed her?'

'I was just about to talk to Tucker here. He's the one who found the body. As soon as those fellows get the lights set up, we'll go back around there so you can get a closer look. Meanwhile, ask these bystanders to disperse and put up some tape so nobody will wander back there.'

The two women who were sitting near the bandstand are still there, though now one is standing next to the one still leaning over in her chair.

'Is she all right?' I ask.

'Yeah, she's just had a little too much to drink,' the woman standing says. She shakes a cigarette out of her pack and lights it. She's in her thirties, good-looking in a hard way, with fluffy blonde hair and a muscular body, in white short shorts, a sequined tank-top and cowboy boots. She nods in the direction of the stage. 'Is there really a body back there?'

I tell her there is. 'We're asking everybody to clear the area. She able to walk?' I nod toward the woman in the chair, who's groaning.

'She will be. Give us a minute.'

Johnny and his daddy are on the stage rolling up the canvas and I steer Tucker off to the side away from big ears. 'Tell me how you found the body,' I ask.

He shoves his hands into his back pockets. 'I went out back to take a piss,' he says. 'We'd been playing for a while and the portables are too far away.'

'You're in the band?'

'Yeah, my daddy and my brother and April over there.' He indicates the woman in the sequined top. 'We're the Oakley String Band. Bluegrass.'

I glance at the easel announcing band names and times. The Oakley String Band was apparently the headliner. Their name is bigger and they went on at 10:30.

'Tucker, did you find the body before or after you did your business?' I'm hoping he didn't urinate on the body.

'After. But I didn't piss close to her. I went further back. It was dark back there, which is why I didn't see her at first.'

'You said you didn't touch her. How did you know it was a body?'

He blinks. 'Oh, Jesus,' he says. He shakes his head and shivers like he's trying to throw off the memory. 'I thought somebody had thrown something away back there, like maybe a pile of clothes or something. Didn't make sense because it wasn't there when we set up tonight. I walked over and almost kicked it, but there was something about it . . .' He trails away. His eyes are darting everywhere. He might be under the influence of drugs. He's got that skittishness.

'What did you do then?'

'I come back around here and spoke to my daddy. We was getting ready to have another set. He went back there with me with his cell phone and used the flashlight. That's when he tried to wake her up and found out . . .'

'You didn't play any more music after that?'

'Hell, no. We told everybody we had to call it a night. Johnny ran to find security and they said to contact you.'

'Do you know if security is still being handled by Gilly Moon and his sons?'

'No, sir, I don't know.'

I walk back to the two women. The woman in the chair still hasn't budged. 'April, did you go back there and see the body?'

'No, sir, I did not. That's the last thing I need.' Her voice is husky.

By now the canvas is rolled up and Chuck and Johnny have positioned stage lights to shine in the back. I hear the sound of a siren in the distance.

April gets up and tugs her friend's arm. 'Come on, Lulu, let's get out of here. We're in the way.' Tucker grabs Lulu's other arm and they haul her up.

'I don't like seeing bad stuff going on,' Lulu mumbles, but staggers to her feet and lets April lead her away.

Maria has succeeded in getting people to back off. She has set up folding chairs around each side of the tent and strung yellow tape along them. I take her behind the stage to the scene. The lights are bright and I see something that makes me grit my teeth. Several feet behind the body there are trampled weeds and a trail of blood. 'You see that?' I say to Maria.

She groans softly. 'She dragged herself toward the stage.'

We both know there was probably no help for her, even if she had managed to alert people. But somewhere deep in her brain there was the instinct to go toward light, because people would be there and maybe they could save her. I shine my flashlight on her and don't see any kind of wound on her back. She couldn't have been shot, or somebody would have heard it, depending on how loud the music was. I suspect when the medical examiner arrives, he's going to find she's been knifed.

'Wait a minute. I don't see a purse,' Maria says. She reaches her hand out toward my flashlight. 'Let me use that. I left mine in the car.' She crouches down next to the body and shines it all over, moving Amber's blouse aside so she can peer under her where her position makes a little cave of her body. 'No purse. Now where could it be? Could this be a robbery? Maybe somebody followed her and attacked her for her purse.'

'I suppose. It seems odd, though. What was she doing back here anyway?' We flash the light around looking for a weapon, but we don't want to mill around too much in the dark and trample the area any more than it already has been.

'Shine that light on her belly again.'

She does, and we see blood matted at the front of her shirt.

Chuck and Johnny Oakley are walking toward us.

'Stay back,' I say. 'The whole area is a crime scene. We need to keep it clear.'

I see Chuck looking at the drag marks. 'Oh my Lord,' he says. 'That poor girl tried to get to us.'

The ambulance has arrived with the mournful moan the siren makes as the crew silences it. I hear voices as people come to see what the fuss is about. Maria goes back to shoo them away and to bring the EMS personnel back here.

I tell Chuck and Johnny it would help if they'd ask people to keep back. They seem grateful to have a reason to leave the scene.

The two ambulance drivers, young but at least not teenagers, come around the corner of the stage and I go over to meet them. 'I'm sorry you got called before Bobtail PD and the ME. We'll have to wait for them to come and take care of forensics.'

They nod. They're used to this. One of them lights a cigarette. 'Let us know.'

My phone pings and I see it's from Bobtail County Sheriff Alvin Hedges. 'Craddock, I heard about your body. I called the DPS. The rally's on state property and they're going to want to handle it.'

I tell him I understand and hang up, stifling a sigh. The Department of Public Safety is the umbrella agency for the Texas

Highway Patrol. If a small town suffers a major crime, the highway patrol usually catches it first, since most small towns don't have the personnel or the equipment to cover it. I've only had them step in once since I became sheriff, and that was a no-brainer bar fight between strangers who were in transit through town. I was glad for them to deal with it.

Hedges is right. This is state property, and even if I want to take on the investigation because I know the victim, I don't have the manpower to handle it. They'll have to question a lot of people – how many, and how they'll identify who, is up to them. Still, I hate to give it up altogether. They're notoriously slow to get to small-town crimes.

But even knowing it might fall to them doesn't mean I shouldn't question some people now. They'll get the benefit of anything I find out that could help. I tell Maria my thoughts on how to proceed.

She nods. 'Sheriff Hedges is right. This one is too big for us.'

'Stay here and make sure nobody approaches. I want to talk to the Oakleys a little more.'

Before she steps away, she takes in her surroundings. I know her. She'll be making a mental note of anything that might tell us something. She's that kind of officer, into details.

The Oakleys are fending off people trying to wheedle information out of them. 'Go on, folks. It will be a while before there's anything to tell,' I say.

A few grumble, but Chuck Oakley tells them he'll let everybody know as soon as he can. He seems to command respect.

I notice that the older guy who was in the near-brawl with the younger man yesterday is part of the crowd. His girlfriend is hanging on his arm, chewing gum like she's in a contest to see who can chew fastest. He gives me the stink-eye. I ignore him and turn back to the Oakleys.

'I don't know how this music thing works,' I say, waving my hand at the stage area. 'Do you all hang out in the area before you go on, or do you hang around in back, or what?'

Chuck says, 'We don't normally go back there, unless like Tucker there's a call of nature. We're usually mingling with the fans. We know a lot of folks here. We've performed at every rally at the lake for the last ten years.'

'I'd like to hear you play sometime,' I say. I don't tell him that his gigs most likely start past my bedtime. I'm starting to feel the effects of being up late now. 'I know this is a long shot, but did any of you notice anybody hanging around that made you wonder what they were up to?'

'A suspicious person, you mean?' Chuck says. He shakes his head. 'I wish I could tell you, but my mind was on the set we were about to do. April was being a little temperamental. Nothing new there, but I had to soothe her feathers. Boys? You see anything unusual?'

They both shake their heads.

'How about when you were back taking a leak?' I ask Tucker. 'You see anybody back there?'

Tucker seems to have calmed down a little. He frowns. 'Well I'll be damned,' he says. 'I did see somebody, but I don't know who it was. It was further back, down by the lake. I don't even know why I noticed him.' He runs his hands through his scraggly hair. 'No, that's wrong. I do know why. I couldn't see his face or anything, but I felt like he was watching me.' He shudders. 'Kinda like maybe he was, I don't know, queer or something. I just don't roll that way, you know?'

'Did he say anything to you? Was he by himself?'

'He was too far away to speak to without hollering. And I didn't see anybody with him. I think if he had been with somebody, I wouldn't have been spooked. Sort of gave me the creeps.'

Johnny snickers. He's standing with his hands in his back pockets. 'Tuck, everything gives you the creeps,' he says.

Tucker ducks his head. 'Not like that.'

Although I'd like to have Tucker take me down to where he saw the person watching him, I don't want to trample around in case there are footprints closer to the lake that might be useful. 'How far back was he?'

He squints. 'Lemme think. About the same distance as here to that white pickup yonder. The four-by-four.'

'So about thirty yards?'

'Something like that. It was sloping down toward the lake so it's hard to judge.'

'That's close enough. You have a cell phone?' I ask him.

He gives me his number and I tell him I'll call him in the

morning. 'I'd like you to show me where the guy was in the daylight.'

After I dismiss them I go back and tell Maria what Tucker said. 'It would be a miracle if there are footprints.' I look down to where the drag marks stop. 'That must have been where it happened, but the ground is hard as rock. You know how the clay is.' Our soil is clay, and if we have a week without rain it gets like a concrete floor.

'Speaking of rain,' I say. I nod toward the west where clouds are boiling up, obscuring the stars. The half-moon is hidden behind them. 'If there are prints, they aren't going to be there after tonight.'

It's almost two o'clock by the time the highway patrol officers arrive and take charge of the scene. I send Maria home, telling her there's nothing more for us to do tonight.

The patrolman in charge, Dan Weinman, is well over six foot, with a salt and pepper shock of hair and a strong jaw. He's wearing pointed-toe cowboy boots and a tan suede Stetson that puts my old straw one to shame.

After we introduce ourselves, I say, 'That's a fine hat. If I was inclined to covet a man's hat, it might be that one.'

He grins. 'I just turned fifty and my wife said I ought to have a hat befitting my advanced age.'

'I hope my lady friend doesn't see it. She's been after me to retire this one.' I take mine off and we both eye it.

'I can see her point,' he says. He's got a friendly laugh.

I tell him the details of what I've seen so far and he says he'll have a crew out as soon as it gets light. 'Not much we can do tonight.' We could set up an elaborate crime scene with a tent and lights, but by the time it got set up, it would be daylight.

The medical examiner drives up and I introduce them. It isn't T.J. Sutter, but his assistant, Mary Lou. Mary Lou's a solemn women in her thirties with a long face and a dry sense of humor.

Weinman and I go back to Amber's body with Mary Lou and stand aside while he examines the body. 'You got a knifing here,' he says. He shines a powerful light on Amber's belly where there's a lot of blood. 'At least two entry points for the knife.' He points to two places where the fabric of her blouse is torn.

'It also looks like there was a tussle.' He shines the light onto her shoulder where the fabric is pulled to one side and torn.

'Any idea about when it happened?'

'Blood's still tacky, but it's so humid out that it wouldn't have dried fast. I'm thinking at least two hours, maybe three. Don't quote me.' Which puts it sometime inside eleven o'clock.

I tell Weinman I'm going to leave him to it. He tells me he'll keep me up-to-date on what they find. He follows me back to my pickup. Before I climb in, he says, 'Chief, I find that some of you old boys do better than we can in a local investigation, so I'll be glad to have your input.'

'I appreciate it. But if somebody at the rally killed her, I don't know that I'm going to be a lot of help finding out who it is.'

I tell Weinman that I know the victim and that I'll contact the family. 'It's a tough situation and Mike's health isn't the best. I'll wait until the morning. Give him a night's sleep anyway.' I'm not looking forward to having to tell Mike Johnson that he's on his own now, with a business to run and two pre-teen kids to raise, and him on disability.

SIX

Maria and I decided to wait until six a.m. to inform Mike Johnson of his wife's death. He's likely to be facing a few sleepless nights, and I hate to wake him too early. But any later and the gossip mill might already have spun his way.

We meet at headquarters and Maria doesn't look like she slept any better than I did. Even though we have a lot on our minds about what has to be done today, we don't make small talk on our way over to deliver the news.

The Johnsons live a few blocks from the high school in a tree-lined neighborhood of older homes, most of which have been remodeled. Theirs has gray vinyl siding that looks ghostly in the morning light. The yard is as minimal as you can get without being graveled. The grass is a little long, but somebody keeps it mowed. No flowerbeds or pots in sight. Amber had her hands full enough without keeping a showy yard.

We mount the steps and have to ring the doorbell twice before it's opened by a sleepy pre-teen girl still in her pajamas. She's got her mamma's pretty brown eyes. 'What?' she says, irritated.

'Your daddy home?'

'They're not up yet,' she says.

They. She thinks her mamma is inside with her daddy.

'I'm Chief Craddock, and this is my deputy, Maria Trevino.'

'I'm Brittany,' the girl says. 'I know you,' she says to Maria. 'You're giving those self-defense classes. I wish you'd give one for kids my age.'

'I'll think about it,' Maria says. 'Right now, we need to talk to your daddy. Can you get him up for us?'

The girl looks back and forth between us. 'He doesn't like us to wake him up. Can you talk to my mamma?'

A young boy appears behind her, yawning. He's taller than his sister, gangly, with that skinny look of a kid who's just getting a growth spurt. 'Hey, Brit, what's going on?' His voice is not changed yet.

'They want to talk to daddy,' she says, her eyes worried.

He frowns. 'Not a good idea. He, uh, he doesn't sleep too good.'

I tell him who we are and ask his name.

'I'm Jimmy.' He sticks his hand out and I shake it. Then he shakes Maria's hand, too, which clutches at my heart. What's going to happen to these two kids without their mamma?

'I'm sorry, Jimmy,' I say. 'I understand your daddy is laid up, but we need to talk to him. It's important.'

The boy searches my face for clues and then nods. 'I'll get him,' he says.

The girl watches him go down the hall. She doesn't turn back to us, but I notice her shoulders tighten as she watches her brother tap on the door at the end of the hall. Then he opens it and goes inside.

Within a few seconds we hear, 'What the hell! You know you shouldn't wake me up. What do they want? Where's your mamma? Is she already gone?' His voice lowers and we don't hear the rest of his words. In a minute the boy comes back down the hallway, looking dejected.

'Daddy says he'll be here in a minute,' he says. His cheeks are flamed up. He knows we heard.

'So Mamma already left?' Brittany asks.

He shrugs. 'I guess. She wasn't there.'

Maria and I glance at each other. I'm tempted to sit them down in the living room and give them the hard news. It's terrible to think that they're proceeding as if she's alive.

'What time is it anyway?' Jimmy asks.

I tell him it's just after six. We four stand waiting, and after a minute Maria starts talking to Brittany about the self-defense course. Jimmy shifts from one foot to the other, glancing down the hallway every few seconds and sighing. Neither of them suggests going back to bed.

It takes a good ten minutes before Mike Johnson comes limping down the hallway. Barefoot, he walks as if he's treading on thin ice. I've seen him around but don't know him. He's as tall as me but weighs thirty pounds less, and I'm lean. His shorts and short-sleeved shirt hang off him. The bones in his face are prominent and his shoulders are hunched. Meeting my eyes with his angry ones, he looks like he's going to lay into me.

'Mr Johnson,' I start, before he can say something he'll later wish he hadn't, 'I'm sorry to bother you, but we need to talk.'

He flinches and, like his son, searches my face for a clue.

'Can we sit down?' I suggest. 'Maybe it's best if I talk to you alone.'

'What's this that my kids can't hear?' He's testy.

'It's fine if you want them to stay.' They'll have to hear soon anyway. 'Your living room in here?' The living room is wide open to our left, so my question is just meant to get us moving in that direction. I walk ahead of them.

The room is small and dominated by a recliner chair, where it's obvious that Johnson normally sits. It has a table next to it with an arm on it that can swing over in front of him for reading or eating. Magazines are stacked on the table along with a soda can and a glass with a little liquid in the bottom.

'Why don't we sit down?' I say again.

Johnson eases over to the chair and sits with a groan. 'Jimmy, will you get my pills and some water please?'

The boy darts down the hallway. Maria and I sit on a big,

flower-patterned sofa and Brittany perches on a footstool near her daddy's chair.

Jimmy comes back with pills and a glass of water and after handing them to Mike Johnson, he stands by his chair.

Johnson downs the pills and wipes his mouth. His eyes are wary. 'OK, what's this about?'

'Mr Johnson, Jimmy, Brittany, I have bad news. It's about Amber. She was killed last night.'

Johnson freezes for a minute, staring at me.

'What?' Jimmy yelps, his expression stunned.

'Daddy?' Brittany whimpers. She hugs herself as if trying to make herself small. Maria goes over and puts a hand on her shoulder.

As what I've said sinks in, Johnson's eyes get panicky. 'No, that can't be. It's gotta be a mistake.'

'I'm afraid it's true. I identified the body myself.'

'What are you talking about?' Jimmy says. 'She's—'

'Where was she?' Johnson asks. He's gone pale. 'Was it an accident? What happened?'

'She was attacked out at the motorcycle rally. Somebody found her about midnight.'

'Attacked.' Johnson's voice is high and scared. 'You mean, like, murdered?'

'I'm afraid so.'

'Daddy, no.' The boy turns stricken eyes to Johnson, who holds his hands out and the kids lean into him. He flinches, shutting his eyes tight and gritting his teeth. He lays his free arm over his daughter's back. 'Kids, we're going to be all right,' he says. He looks toward me and his eyes say otherwise, but I admire him for holding it together for the children.

'Mike, when did you last see your wife?' Maria asks.

He's stroking his daughter's hair. She's sobbing quietly. 'She was here at dinner last night and then she said she had to go check to make sure Cal locked up the store.'

Jimmy stands up and stares at me with resentful eyes. He bites his lip, trying not to cry.

'What time was that?'

'Maybe eight o'clock. We eat supper early. Jimmy, you remember?'

'No, sir.' His voice cracks.

'Did you worry when she didn't come back?'

'I went to bed when she left. The kids were up watching TV or whatever. But let me ask you, do you know who did it? How did they . . .' He looks down at his daughter, who is sobbing on his chest. 'Honey, you need to let me talk to these officers alone. Can you go to your room for a few minutes?'

'No, I want to stay with you.'

I glance at Maria and she reads my mind, as usual.

'Kids, come into the kitchen with me so Chief Craddock can talk to your daddy. It won't take long.'

Johnson looks like he's going to protest, but I catch his eye and shake my head. Jimmy notices, too. 'Come on, Brit.' He leans over and pats the girl's shoulder. She sits up and grabs his hand and climbs off her daddy's lap. The kids go with Maria and she closes the door behind them.

'We don't have any suspects yet.'

'How was she killed?'

'She was stabbed.' I tell him where she was found.

'I can't believe this. Who would do something like that?'

'We'll get to the bottom of it. The highway patrol is on it.'

'Why not you?' he says.

'I'll be helping them. We'll work together.'

His face, already ravaged by pain, has sagged further. 'I just can't believe this,' he says again. 'She was our rock. What are we going to do without her? Who would want to hurt her?'

'Mike, did Amber tell you she was going out to the motorcycle rally?'

'No, but I'm not surprised.'

'Why not?'

'You know, before this happened,' he gestures to his legs, 'we were in a motorcycle club. We used to ride all over with our group. She probably went out there to see if any of the members came this year. She might have wanted to arrange to ride somebody's bike. Ours were totaled in the accident and we didn't replace them. She says she doesn't miss it, but I know she does.'

'Do any of your friends, members of the club, come by and visit?'

He chews his bottom lip. His eyes are gloomy. 'I asked them not to. It's too hard for everybody. They feel sorry for me and I feel sorry for myself and then I feel bad because I snap at them. I try to stay positive, but it's hard.'

'Anybody in particular she might have been there to see?'

'Probably Jack and Emma Cassidy. She's kept up with them.'

'What's the name of the club?'

'It's called the Rough Roaders. You know, after the Rough Riders. Humph. Silly, I guess, but we thought we were clever.' He looks toward the kitchen door. 'Is she going to be good with the kids?'

'Officer Trevino is professional. She'll do fine.'

He nods, but his eyes look anxious.

'Mike, do you know anybody who might have wanted to hurt your wife?'

He rubs his hands along his thighs. 'No. She was a sweetheart. Everybody liked her.'

'Did she tell you she got into a tangle with Lily Deverell last week at the city council meeting?'

'Yeah.'

'Was she worried about it?'

'Not at all. It was just a spat. She and Amber aren't friendly, but it was nothing serious. Amber felt bad about what she said to Lily.' He moves restlessly. 'Maybe it was a robbery. Our Rough Roaders were good folks, but some of those bikers are shady.'

'It's possible it was a robbery. We didn't find your wife's purse. Do you know if it's here?'

'Usually she leaves it on the hall table or in here. Sometimes in the bedroom.' He scans the room. 'I don't see it. If you go get Jimmy, he can look for it in our bedroom.'

I go into the kitchen and ask Jimmy to look for Amber's purse. 'You know what it looks like?'

He says he does and trots off down the hallway. He comes back in a minute and says he doesn't see it. His daddy sends him to check the kitchen, but it isn't there either.

'She might have left it in her car,' I say. 'What did she drive? It's likely still out at the rally.' Unless somebody stole it along with her purse.

'She drives a 2012 Honda CRV. We have to have a good-sized car because sometimes she has to haul merchandise.'

'And your car?'

'The CRV is our only vehicle. I can drive if I have to, but it isn't easy and I don't tend to.'

I stand up. 'Do you have a spare set of keys? Don't get up. Just tell me where they are.'

'They're on the hall table in a bowl.'

'I'll look for the car and get it back to you. That's all I need for now. Is there anybody you want me to call?'

He moans. 'This is terrible. I'll have to call . . . oh Lord, I'll have to call Amber's sister and she'll have to tell her folks. It's gonna kill them.'

'Where are they?'

'Down on the Gulf Coast, near Corpus. My folks are there, too. They loved Amber.'

'Can I call a neighbor? Somebody to open the store for you?'

'I'll do all that. Can you ask my kids to come in here?'

They're sitting in the kitchen drinking chocolate milk. Maria always claims she's not crazy about kids because she has so many siblings, but she knows how to deal with them. They jump up when they see me. 'Can we go to Daddy?' Brittany asks.

I tell her yes and we follow them back.

'Mr Johnson, I made some coffee for you and if you want me to I can make some breakfast,' Maria says. That's going above and beyond for Maria. She lives on hamburgers and frozen dinners.

'No need. We can manage. Son, would you go get my cell phone? I left it in the bedroom.' The boy is off like a shot.

'We'll leave you to get yourself together. If you need anything at all, you call me.' I hand him my card.

Normally, I'd be asking a husband where he was last night when his wife was killed, but it's clear that Johnson is in no shape to have attacked his wife.

On the way out, I find the set of keys, take the vehicle key off the keychain and leave the rest in the bowl.

The sky is still clouded over and it's likely to rain before the day is out. We got lucky last night that the clouds blew over and there wasn't any rain. I wonder if Weinman's crew managed to get any footprints.

'Let's go on over to the rally,' I tell Maria. 'We can check out the area in daylight and look for Amber's car.'

As we're getting into the squad car, my cell phone rings. I see that it's Vicki and my stomach plunges. Last night's events have pushed out of my mind the fact that Vicki is bringing Hailey here today.

'Samuel,' she says. Her voice is subdued. 'I thought we'd get off early, but I'm having some trouble getting Hailey packed. We probably won't leave until this afternoon. I expect we'll be there around four.'

She sounds so tense that I don't tell her what's going on here. 'No hurry. You have my number. Just keep me in the loop.'

When I get off the phone, I tell Maria that Hailey arrives this afternoon. She gives me the big eyes. 'How in the world are you going to manage a teenage girl with all this going on?'

'I thought I'd turn her over to you,' I say with a chuckle.

'That's not funny. No way.'

'I'll have to figure it out.'

On our way to the rally, I swing by Loretta's to tell her what happened. She's ready for church, and I find her clipping flowers in the garden to take in for the altar. When I tell her about Amber, for a few seconds she's speechless.

'I don't know what to say. That's the worst thing I've heard in . . . I don't know when. Who could have done such a thing?'

I shake my head. 'I had to go over just now and tell Mike and the kids what happened.'

She puts a hand to her throat, where there's a locket that she wears a lot. It has tiny photos of her and her husband when they were young. Her eyes have clouded over. 'That's terrible. What are they going to do? That woman did everything for her family. There is such evil in this world.'

'Do you know if Amber was a church-goer?'

'I don't, but I can find out. And whether she was or not, we'll be taking care of that family.'

I have no doubt of that.

SEVEN

Maria and I go straight to the rally parking lot. It's early enough so that it isn't too crowded and we spot Amber's CRV right away. We find her purse in the trunk.

'We'll take a look at this before we turn it over to DPS,' I say. We drive up to the music stage. There's a highway patrolman staked out to keep people away, but he's the only police presence. There aren't many people up and about right now, and only a few standing at the crime scene tape talking in hushed tones about the murder.

As soon as I open the door, Dusty jumps out of the truck and takes off for the lake. I call him, but he doesn't pay any attention. I hope he doesn't go in the water or the squad car will be a mess.

I ask the officer if the forensics crew have been back to look for footprints.

He says he relieved somebody at seven this morning. 'Nobody has been back there yet. They should be here soon.'

He has no problem with Maria and me entering the crime scene. We parallel the path where Amber dragged herself toward the tent, which is even more obvious in the daylight. Where the drag marks end abruptly, there are no clear footprints, but the ground in one area is scuffed up, and there are rusty-looking blood spatters in the dirt and on the dead weeds. We look closely at the area surrounding the assault scene, but it's impossible to tell what direction anyone took when they left.

We walk down the slope approximately where Tucker Oakley said he saw a man watching. Even though the crime scene tape extends down to the water, there are lots of footprints in the soft clay on the shore. Whether they were there before or after the murder is anybody's guess.

Maria wants to take a closer look at everything, so I leave her and head over to Walter Dunn's repair trailer. They're already up and at 'em. Walter's working on an oversized orange and black Harley, decorated with flames and a busty woman. Standing and watching is a guy who matches the Harley in bulk and even in looks, with a flame-red beard. He's got a red bandana around his head. He's looking on like a father watching his child being operated on.

Walter nods at me. 'Heard you had a little excitement last night.'

'Yeah, it's a bad one.'

'This about that chick that got killed?' the biker says.

I nod.

'Do they know who done it?'

'No, sir. The highway patrol will be investigating.'

He spits a stream of tobacco. 'Good luck with that. All these people around here, could have been anybody.'

Walter looks up, his intense blue eyes concerned. 'I'll be done here in about ten minutes. Then we can talk. Go on in the trailer. I've got coffee on. I know you won't say no to that.'

I smile. He knows me well.

I bring my coffee outside, and when he's done with the motorcycle he gets a cup and brings it out. 'Let's walk away for a minute,' he says. 'Somebody will be after me to take care of their bike *yesterday* if they see me here.'

We stroll down toward the lake. It's gray and murky because the sky is cloudy. The humidity is so high that even walking slowly, my shirt is sticking to me. All of a sudden Dusty comes running up, tongue lolling.

'Hey, Dusty,' Walter says. He crouches down and scratches Dusty's ears and Dusty is in heaven. When Walter stands up, Dusty runs back in the direction of the lake.

'Rumors are flying about that woman found last night,' Walter says. 'You want to tell me the facts?'

'I'm curious to know what they're saying.'

'My favorite is that it was a satanic ritual. There were supposedly messages carved on her arms and legs.'

I shake my head. 'Where do people get that stuff? And no, there was nothing like that.'

'And then somebody said she was killed because of that accident she and her husband had a couple of years ago.'

'Really?' This sounds more realistic. 'What about it?'

'Somebody said she milked that guy who was responsible for

all he was worth. I don't know why anybody would feel sorry for him. I heard the guy was drunk.'

'I don't think she got anything from him. She said he didn't have any insurance and their own insurance company was taking the hit. She and her husband were part of a motorcycle club called Rough Roaders. You know if they're here?'

'Yeah, I know a couple of them are here, but I don't know where they're located. Some of the clubs camp together, but I don't know if they do. If I run into any of them you want me to ask them to call you?'

'I'd appreciate it.'

'There's one more rumor, that the woman who died was turning tricks and one of her johns killed her.'

'That's not likely,' I say. 'Amber was run ragged trying to raise her two kids and keep their little store running. I don't know how anybody thinks she'd find time to prostitute herself. Anyway, the fact is we don't know anything except that she was attacked with a knife. We assume that's what killed her, but we won't even know that for sure until the autopsy.'

'She lived in Jarrett Creek?'

'Yeah, I had just talked to her Saturday afternoon. She was a nice person. Her family is devastated. Listen, I want to ask your help. That guy whose bike you were repairing is right. I don't know how we're going to investigate this. You got over a thousand people here, and any of them could have killed her. Walter, you're one of the hubs of this event. Keep your ears open, and if you hear anything that isn't crazy, I'd like to know about it.'

'I'll sure let you know, and I'll ask my boys to pay attention, too. Speaking of which, I'd better get back up there.'

On the way back to his truck, I tell him that Hailey is coming to visit for a while.

He snickers. 'A teenager? That should be fun.'

'Not just a teenager. Her folks are having trouble with her and in a foolish moment I said I'd take her off their hands for a few days.'

Walter laughs. 'You're asking for it. Bring her over here to the rally. That ought to give her an eyeful.'

'Probably not the best idea.'

'Maybe not. But I expect she's not going to want to sit around at your house tending to cows and watching TV. She's going to want some action. If you'd like to, bring her over and I'll have one of my boys take her for a ride.'

I tell him I'll think about it. I go back to round up Maria. A couple of guys from forensics have arrived and they're talking to her. She's in her element.

I greet them and ask if they found anything useful.

'Not yet,' one of them says, 'but we're just getting started.'

'No sign of a weapon,' the other one says.

'Maybe T.J. can tell us what kind of knife we're looking for,' I say. They look puzzled. 'T.J. Sutter is the medical examiner in Bobtail,' I explain.

He nods toward the lake. 'Could be we ought to poke around in the mud along the shore here.'

I don't say anything but I can sense Maria perking up. She'd like nothing better than to drag a rake through the mud looking for it. That's the kind of thing she loves.

We go back to the office, Maria driving the squad car, me driving Amber's car. We need to check it out before I take it back to Mike. In fact, I probably ought to turn it over to Dan Weinman, but Maria is as good at forensics as anybody.

It's ten o'clock and the message machine is lit up with phone calls about the attack. I ask Maria to call them back. 'Tell them the highway patrol has charge of the case and we'll be assisting. Also, ask if they have any information that might be of help.'

Maria groans. 'You know how that's going to go. Half of them will tell me it had to be one of their neighbors who's been acting suspicious.'

I laugh. 'I know it, but we have to ask. And then take a look at the contents of the purse.'

'What are you going to do?' Maria doesn't like to miss out.

'It's too early for people to be back from church, so I'm going to do a preliminary examination of her car and you can go over it for prints later. Then I'm going back over to the rally to hunt down the Oakleys again. The guy who found Amber's body was pretty shook up, and I want to make sure he's telling the same story today. And I'd like to see if I can get hold of that girl who was with the singer, April. She was drunk but she said something I'd like to follow up on.'

That's not all I want to do. Sometime last night I remembered
seeing Amber coming out of a big RV on Friday when I was
breaking up the fight. I'd heard the guy selling the motorcycle tell
Ralph Tyson that the RV belonged to somebody named Grant
Butler. I'd like to find out what Amber was doing there.

Amber's CRV is full of the kind of junk you'd expect from a
family car: Dairy Queen cups and napkins on the floor in the back,
a tube of lipstick under the driver's seat, a folder with purchase
orders that pertain to her store, and a baseball. In the trunk there
are folded grocery bags and totes, a half-drunk bottle of water, a
paperback book, and a wadded-up beach towel. I bag all of it.

The glove box contains the usual car papers, which indicate
that the car is in Amber's name. There's a half-pack of gum, an
empty candy wrapper and a hairbrush. The only odd thing is a
scrap of paper with what looks like a phone number on it. I bag
that and take it inside.

I call the number and get an answering machine that just says
no one is available to talk and to leave a message. I start to leave
a message, but decide to try again later.

I'm in a hurry to get back to the rally to talk to the Oakleys. I
call Mike Johnson and ask if he needs the car right away and he
tells me he doesn't.

In the last hour the rally has come to life. It's Sunday, and there's
a large gathering of people in one of the open-air tents. I walk
over to see what's happening, and they're listening to a preacher.
Nobody seems to have dressed up, but there are lots of people
seated on folding chairs, and a guitar player is standing off to
the side.

Although I can hear the preacher loud and clear, I can't see
him for the crowd, but a sign out front advertises: 'Jubilee Rally
Revival, Reverend Gilbert Moon.' So the man who pitched in for
the security crew really is a preacher. I listen for a minute.
Reverend Moon has got the fire-and-brimstone down pat.

I walk on past the general area where I saw Amber Johnson
leaving the RV on Friday. The problem with identifying the vehicle
is that by now the place is crammed with RVs, tents, and vans. I
finally see what I think is the right one, a big silver vehicle with
a black stripe, one of several I've seen with similar markings. I

knock on the door, wait and knock again, but there's no answer. A guy in a smaller RV next to it pokes his head out. 'Oh, I thought somebody was knocking on my door.'

I walk over to talk to him. 'You know the people who own this?' He steps down onto the ground. He's wearing cutoffs and a wife-beater bearing a Harley logo. He glances over at the RV with a frown. 'Seen him, but don't know him. He was off early this morning. Not real friendly like most of the people here.'

'Did he leave on a motorcycle?'

'I don't think he has one here. I just saw him walking that way.' He nods in the direction of the entrance.

'You know his name?'

'Butler's his last name. He has a girl with him named Becky. Like I said, not real neighborly with me, although he has people coming in and out.'

'Was he here last night?'

'Yeah, he had a party in the RV.'

I thank him and go over and leave a card stuck in the door of the RV, asking Butler to call me.

Next, I go back to the bandstand tent where Amber's body was found. There are a half-dozen people sitting inside the tent on folding chairs drinking beer, paying no attention to a muscular young woman who's doing acrobatics of a sort on a pole near the stage to a country and western song. She seems as oblivious to them as they are to her. I ask if anybody knows where I can find the Oakleys.

A man with a long white beard and bloodshot eyes says, 'Chuck is right yonder. That blue tent. His boys' tents are around there, too.'

I go over to the tent and call out. Chuck pokes his head out and when he sees me he climbs out, zipping the tent behind him. He's dressed in cutoff jeans and a vest. He pokes his paw out for me to shake. 'How you doing today?' he asks. 'That was some bad scene last night.'

'I appreciate your cooperation. I just wondered if you or the boys had thought of anything new that we didn't talk about last night.'

'I don't know anything else, but you could ask them. Tucker was pretty shook up and he might be more clear-headed this morning.'

'You going to do any more performances?'

'As a matter of fact we're on tonight and Tuesday afternoon.'

He points out his boys' tents close by. I go over and find them sitting outside facing the lake.

'Hey boys, how you doing?'

They both get up. They're looking as bleary-eyed as I feel. I ask them if they've remembered anything that they didn't tell me last night. Tucker is not as jittery today, but he's as bleak as he was last night. 'I hope I never find another body,' he says. 'Poor lady.'

'You recall anything more about the man you saw watching you? Can you describe him?'

He scrunches up his face. 'Tall, rangy. No belly on him, so maybe not old. He was just standing there.'

'I know it was dark, but could you tell anything about his clothes? Was he wearing shorts? T-shirt? Hat?'

'No hat.' He shakes his head. 'Seems like if he'd been wearing shorts I would have seen pale legs, but the only pale thing I saw was his arms.'

'You didn't mention that his arms were pale.'

'I guess it didn't seem important.'

'And you only saw him briefly.'

'That's right. I didn't stick around. I wanted to get up to the tent and tell my daddy I'd found that body. Sorry I can't help more than that.'

The guy Tucker saw might not have had anything to do with Amber's death. Still, Tucker noticed him. Sometimes instincts kick in and you don't even know why you take interest in something.

'You did good. I appreciate you making the effort. You happen to know where the girl who was with your singer is located?'

'You mean Lulu? I imagine she's sleeping it off. She was pretty drunk last night.'

He's right. It's probably not the best time to approach her, as drunk as she was. I can come back later. It's getting on toward noon. People will be getting home from church, and I want to stop in and have a chat with Lily Deverell. I haven't heard from Vicki again. I hope she doesn't have too much of a fight on her hands getting Hailey in the car.

EIGHT

I don't for one minute think the little set-to the other night at the town hall meeting was enough to spur Lily to kill Amber. If Lily had in her mind to murder Amber, it isn't likely she would have picked the rally as the perfect spot. I'm here to talk to her son, Steve, who's working at the rally. Maybe he saw or heard rumors about what went on last night.

Lily's husband answers the door still dressed for church. 'You're lucky to catch us. We're going over to Bryan to have Sunday dinner at my sister's house.'

'If you and Lily could spare a minute, I'd like to have a word.'

'Come on in.' He holds the screen door open wide. Inside, he says, 'If you're here to tell us about Amber, we already know. Lily is broken up about it. She feels bad that they had that argument the other night.'

Sure enough, when Lily comes in her eyes are red and her face splotchy. 'Oh, Chief Craddock, I don't know what to say. The poor girl. What is her family going to do?' Even dressed up, Lily's color combinations are eye-popping. She's wearing a bright blue skirt and a blouse with big orange flowers on it.

We sit in their living room, a pleasant room with comfortable seating but more knick-knacks than my friend Loretta has, and I thought she had set a record. There are Hummel figures, ceramic animals, brass bells of various sizes and shapes, and glass globes mixed together on every surface.

'Lily, did you talk to Amber again after that little spat you two had?' According to Amber, they'd had more words outside, but I want to get Lily's side of the story.

She bites the side of her lip. 'I wish I'd been nicer to her. She was waiting when I came outside after the meeting and said she wanted to apologize. I told her it would take . . .'

She gasps and tears leak out of the corners of her eyes. She whips a tissue out of her pocket and dabs at them. 'I said it would take more than an apology. That she needed to make it up to me.'

I wondered what she had in mind.

'You can't blame yourself for that,' Harold Deverell says. 'She was rude, and she was right to apologize, but that doesn't mean you had to kiss and make up. It's not the first time she's gotten out of line. And besides, you couldn't know something like this was going to happen.'

'Was that the last time you saw her?'

'Yes.' She frowns. 'Why are you asking that? You don't think I had anything to do with her getting killed, do you?'

'I'm just trying to get some idea of her movements before she was attacked. Harold, you said this was not the first time she'd gotten out of line. What did you mean by that?' Harold looks how I imagine Steve will when he's grown. Same blond hair, but a little thin in front, ears that stick out a bit, and alert brown eyes.

He looks over at his wife. She picks at the necklace at her throat and looks away from him. 'It wasn't anything important,' she says.

'It might help me get to know a little more about her, though,' I say.

'She accused our son of shoplifting,' Harold says, his voice raised. He sets his lips in a firm line.

This is a tough one. Their son Steve is perfectly capable of shoplifting. I don't think he's a bad kid, he just seems to gravitate to low-level trouble.

'I don't recall her making a police report,' I say.

'No, but she called Harold and told him we needed to teach him the Ten Commandments,' Lily says. 'As if she ever goes to church.' She groans. 'Oh, wash my mouth out. I don't want to speak ill of the dead. It wasn't a big deal. Really.'

'Was Steve upset?'

Harold snorts. 'Upset that he was caught. We made him offer to spend an hour helping her out – cleaning up or doing something like that. He wasn't happy about it, but he did it and Amber said she was satisfied, so that was the end of it.'

'Is Steve here?'

'He's supposed to be. He said he was going up to the rally to talk to somebody and he'd be back in time to go to his aunt's house. I don't even know why he's going. He has to turn right around and go back to work at four.'

'I know why,' Lily says. 'It's an excuse to tear around on that motorcycle.'

The front door bangs open.

'Speak of the devil. Steve! Come on in here.'

Steve ambles into the room. He's fairly presentable, dressed in jeans and T-shirt, except he's got big scratches down one cheek.

'What in the world happened to you?' Lily jumps up and goes over to him and touches the scratches.

'Ow! Cut it out. I just got scratched.'

'How?' she demands.

I don't like the look of it.

'I was with some kids and one of the girls got mad and raked her claws over me. Bitch.' He's usually an upbeat kid, and I'm surprised at the bitterness in his voice.

Lily's mouth falls open. 'You are not to say that word in this house, do you hear me?'

'Well she is.'

'Son,' Harold says, 'I don't know if you're showing off in front of Chief Craddock or if you've temporarily lost your mind, but I want you to apologize to your mother and the Chief for your language and get yourself ready to go to your aunt's house. We leave in ten minutes.'

Steve's face has turned deep red during his father's outburst. 'I am ready,' he says through gritted teeth.

'No, you aren't. I want you to put a real shirt on. But first the apology. Now.' His father stands up. I'm getting a lesson in how a defiant kid behaves and one way to handle it.

'Sorry,' Steve mumbles. He doesn't look at me.

'Not good enough.' Harold has his hands on his hips.

'Harold . . .' Lily says. She's also blushing.

'I'm sorry, Mom. Sorry, Chief.'

'That's better. Now get dressed.'

'Apology accepted,' I say. 'And I'd like to talk to you privately after you've changed clothes.'

A young girl comes into the room. Younger than Steve, she's got Lily's features, cute with blue eyes and brown hair, but the comparison ends there. The teenager has a nose ring, hair cropped close on one side and longer on the other, and a swirl of tattoos on her left arm. I remember Amber's comments about her. She was right. The girl is quite a sight. It may be something you see in cities, but I don't remember seeing girls dressed this way in town.

'Hey, loser,' she says to her brother, 'somebody got you pretty good, didn't she?' She snickers.

'I've got a few words for you, Baby Sister, but I'm too polite to say them in company.'

'Right. Hey, 'rents, when are we leaving?'

Lily's smile is forced. 'Chief Craddock, I'll like to introduce our daughter Ashley.'

'Pleased to meet you. I call myself Ash,' she says, prancing over and holding out her hand to shake.

'Suck up,' Steve growls and leaves the room, taking his cloud of anger with him.

'We're leaving in ten minutes, Ashley.'

'I'll be out front.' She's holding a phone and sticks earbuds into her ears, then goes out the front door.

'Sorry about that,' Harold says, sitting back down. 'They're not bad kids. They just need a little prodding sometimes.'

'Not a problem,' I say. 'Now let's go back to where we were. You said Amber had gotten out of line when she accused your son of shoplifting. Were there any other instances?' I don't point out that she wasn't out of line if the boy actually did do what she accused him of.

'That was all,' Harold says. 'We had no reason to be angry with Amber. We were grateful that she didn't make a big deal of the shoplifting. And I know Lily appreciated her apology the other night.'

Lily nods.

I get up. 'I'll wait outside for Steve. I just want to ask him a couple of questions.'

'We'll send him out,' Harold says, but Lily frowns at me. She's protective.

'What do you want to talk to him about?'

'He's working the rally and I'd like to know if he saw anything unusual Saturday night.'

'Oh.' She perks up, liking the idea that Steve might be of help to the police for a change.

Ashley is sitting at the end of the porch in a swing, listening to her music. She doesn't acknowledge me. It's five minutes before Steve comes out. Pushing the limit on the dress code his daddy insisted on, he's still got his T-shirt on, but now has a short-sleeved shirt over it. Just enough to appease his father without bending. I steer him off the porch and under the shade of a big pecan tree, out of his sister's earshot.

'Steve, I want to ask if you were working at the rally last night.'

'Yeah.' Surly. He's mad because his daddy made him apologize to me.

I ignore the attitude, hoping he'll lose it if I don't give it any attention. 'How late did you work?'

'Midnight.'

'So you were there around the time Amber was killed.'

'Yeah.' His head whips up. 'What of it?'

'Did you see her at the rally?'

'No, man. How could I? There are a lot of people there.'

'I know there are. That's why I'm asking you. I'm trying to find anybody who might have seen something to help figure out who murdered her.' My language is deliberately blunt. He needs to understand that Amber didn't just die – she was murdered, brutally.

He blinks and his expression eases. 'I get it. No, I didn't see her last night, but . . .'

'But what?'

'I saw her there on Friday.'

'Was she by herself?'

'No, she was with some guy. Not from here. At least I didn't recognize him. They were walking down by the lake.'

'What time was this?'

He blows out a breath. 'I wasn't on the job yet, so it has to have been before four o'clock. That's what time I start work. Maybe three o'clock?'

'Can you describe the guy? How tall was he?'

He shrugs. 'You know Amber wasn't that tall, and he was a head taller, so maybe five ten?'

'Big? Thin?'

'Medium.' His face brightens.

'How was he dressed?'

'I don't think he was a biker. He was dressed regular, you know, like jeans and a T-shirt. And his hair was short. But I guess you can't always tell. It's just I don't see a lot of bikers that look like him.'

'Did he and Amber seem friendly? Were they walking close together? Talking?'

'I don't know. Just regular. You know, like, just walking.' He makes an impatient sound. 'I didn't pay any attention to them. They weren't close by, so I didn't say hello or anything.'

'Were you with anyone when you saw them?'

'Yeah.'

'I'd like to get their names, and also the name of the girl who scratched you.'

He turns his head away and shoves his hands into his pockets. 'Why do you need that?'

'To question them and find out if they saw anything.'

He sighs. 'Sophie wasn't there.'

'Sophie? I need her full name.' I want to check out his story and make sure she was the one who scratched him. It's hard to imagine the boy killing Amber, but I like to tie up all the loose ends.

He tells me the names of the three people he was with when he saw Amber, two boys and a girl. And Sophie's last name: Rodriguez. I wonder if she's Momo Rodriguez's daughter. He's the owner of the Mexican restaurant I go to often.

NINE

When I return to headquarters, Maria tells me that the mayor, Lester Pierce, has called twice. 'I tried to get him to tell me what was on his mind, but he said he wanted you in particular.' She tells me he made a point of making clear to her that his insistence had nothing to do with her being a woman, that he had to talk to me about something that had happened at the town meeting.

I give him a call and the girl who answers the phone puts me right through. When he isn't being the mayor, Lester is proprietor and pharmacist of our drugstore, a small adjunct to the big grocery store, the Quick Mart, at the other end of town. 'What's up, Lester?'

'Samuel, I need to talk to you. Can you come to the store? I can't really get away and it won't wait.'

'I'll be right there.'

When I hang up, I ask Maria if she found anything interesting in Amber's purse.

'I found two hundred dollars cash. It was loose in the purse. No wallet. But she did have her driver's license in a side pocket.'

'Maybe she just went to the ATM.'

'Probably. What's more interesting is what I didn't find.'

'What do you mean?'

'You know, it was a little purse. And she had no cell phone and the bare minimum that any woman would carry. Driver's license, a few dollars and tube of lipstick. Most women carry all kinds of stuff in their purse. This means she changed purses. Traveling light, I'd guess you'd say.'

'What's significant about that?'

She shrugs. 'I don't know. But I'd like to get a look at the purse she usually carries. If it has her cell phone, we might get some idea of why she was at the rally.'

'Jimmy said he didn't see it this morning.'

'She might have tucked it away somewhere. Or he may have the blindness that males get when they go to look for something.'

She's always ragging me about not seeing things that are right in front of me. I'd worry that it was a sign of encroaching senility, but my wife Jeanne told me the same thing for thirty years.

Looking for the purse is going to take a trip back to Mike Johnson's, which I'll do when I return the car. Right now I need to get to Lester.

It's only a five-minute drive to his drugstore, and I'm parking in front when my cell phone rings. It's Vicki.

'We're on our way.'

'Good. I'll look forward to seeing you in a couple of hours.'

I hang up, a quiver of nerves arcing through me. She sounded grim. They'll be here by four o'clock. I'm trying to look forward to Hailey's visit, but the tenor of Vicki's voice has me on edge.

Lester must have been watching for me, because he steps out

the door of the pharmacy and comes over to my pickup. I get out to greet him.

'Let's go in the coffee shop,' he says. 'I need to get some lunch.' The Quick Mart has a little coffee nook inside the front door. We grab coffee and sandwiches and sit at one of the two tables. The other table has a couple of local women I know by sight. Their eyes linger too long on me, so I know they've heard about Amber's death. Lester looks nervously toward them and sits with his back to them. I guess he's afraid they'll overhear whatever it is he has to impart.

'OK, Lester,' I say quietly, after I've wolfed down half my sandwich. 'Enough of the cloak and dagger. What's on your mind?'

'I heard about what happened to Amber,' he says. 'And I know this probably doesn't mean a thing, but I overheard something the other night after the meeting that I thought you ought to know about.'

'I'm listening.' I take a sip of coffee. They're not going to run out of grounds anytime soon judging from how weak the coffee is.

'You know I stay after to make sure the chairs are put away and the trash put in the basket. Usually everybody's gone by the time I leave, but I walked out and found Bill and Maureen standing in the parking lot gabbing. I heard what they said before they saw me.' Bill Kazinski and Maureen Washington couldn't be any more unlikely a pair of friends. Bill makes no secret of the fact that he thinks females are second-class citizens, while Maureen, a high school teacher, is one of the most outspoken women I've ever met. You see them sometimes having dinner at Town Café, or having a cup of coffee somewhere. Neither of them is married, but I never got the impression there was any romance between them. They're just good friends.

'And what did you hear?' I ask. Lester needs encouragement.

'Bill said, "That little bitch better look out or she's going to get herself hurt."'

'You think he was talking about Amber?'

He mulls over my question. 'I guess I assumed that's who they meant because of what Amber said to Lily. People were pretty shocked that she spoke out that way. But now I think about it, I suppose they could have meant Lily, since she's the one who was so intent on getting the town shut down. Speaking of which, after the meeting I had a lot of calls from merchants saying they would go along with the eight o'clock curfew but not to get any big ideas about making it earlier next year.'

'You didn't ask Bill and Maureen who they were talking about?'

'I didn't see any reason to stick my nose in. And I'll admit, I was ready to get home. My wife isn't too keen about night meetings that run late.'

His wife is a mousy woman, petite and nervous. She's friendly, but she always looks alarmed. I can imagine her being scared to be home alone after dark.

I tell him I appreciate his tip, even though I don't think it amounts to much. Before he goes back into the pharmacy he asks if I think I can keep his name out of it if I talk to them.

'Of course.' I'll tell them I'm talking to everybody who was at the meeting. Besides, it's true.

I drive back to headquarters. I had intended to get Mike Johnson's car back to him this afternoon, but Maria has left a note saying she wants time to dust for fingerprints, so I leave it and take the squad car to the Johnson's place to get somebody to find that purse.

By now there are half a dozen cars outside the house, parked both in the driveway and on the street.

When I ring the doorbell, a woman who looks like Amber, a few years older and with a few more pounds on her, opens the door. Her eyes and nose are red. Inside I hear hushed voices.

I introduce myself and she says she's Amber's sister, DeeDee Crane. 'I just got here. I came as soon as Mike called me. I can't believe what happened. I keep telling myself it can't be true. Do you know anything more? Made an arrest?'

'I'm afraid it's too early for that,' I say. 'Is Mike here?'

'He's laying down.'

'Can you do something for me? Can you see if you can find Amber's purse and her cell phone? Also, if she has a computer at home, I'd like to take a look at it.'

DeeDee looks around the room, as if the purse and cell phone might leap up. 'Let me see if the kids might know. I'm just so flustered I don't even know where to look.'

She goes down the hall and taps on a door across the hall from Mike Johnson's room. I walk into the living room and see a couple of women I know – friends of Loretta's. They look at me with alarmed expressions, as if somehow I've brought this tragedy with me.

'Chief, can I get you something?' one of the women asks. 'There's pie and coffee.'

I thank her but tell her I'll take a raincheck. In a minute DeeDee comes back with twelve-year-old Jimmy. His face is bleak. 'Aunt Dee says you're looking for Mamma's purse? I couldn't find it this morning.'

'Honey, let me go with you,' one of the women says, jumping up from her seat. She has a deep east Texas accent. She's about Amber's age and her eyes are red from crying. She's a well-built woman, leggy as a colt. Her brown hair is short and curly. She grabs Jimmy's hand.

'Daddy's resting. I don't like to disturb him.'

'Well, I'll go by myself,' she says, 'but we have to get that purse. We have to find out what happened to your mamma.' She notices that Amber's sister is taken aback by her offer. 'Dee, I think we're out of coffee. Can you make some more? I'll bet there are going to be a lot of people coming. Your sister was so loved.'

DeeDee is mollified and heads off to the kitchen.

'Jimmy, let's go get that purse.' The woman looks at me and shakes her head sadly.

They go down the hall and after a few minutes they come back, Jimmy holding a big shoulder bag. He brings it to me, cradling it to his chest like it's precious cargo.

'Thank you for finding this,' I say to the two of them.

'I'll do anything I can to help. I'm Lisa Hedgepeth, Amber's best friend. I loved her to pieces. If there's anything I can do . . .'

'I appreciate it. I'll come by and talk to you. You home during the day?'

'Here . . .' She goes over to the chair she was sitting in, grabs her purse and rummages through it, coming back with a business card. 'Call me anytime. I'll drop what I'm doing.'

I put on gloves to handle the purse, and Jimmy's eyes widen. 'You have to do that so you won't get fingerprints on it?'

'That's right. Is this the purse your mamma usually carried?'

'Yes, sir.'

I open it and look inside. Maria was right. It's crammed full of things. I don't want to rummage around in it in front of her son, but I want to know if the cell phone is here.

'Did you see her cell phone?'

'No, sir, but it's usually in her purse.'

I take it over to a side table next to the sofa and pick around in it gingerly until I find the phone. When I take it out, I see Jimmy look at it with longing, as if it somehow holds the identity of his mamma. I slip it back into the purse. 'How about a computer. Does she keep one here at home?'

'She keeps one at work. And we have one here that we all share. She doesn't use it much. Just for emails.'

'You mind if I take a look at it?' The women in the living room have fallen quiet, watching me as intently as if they're watching a crime show on TV.

'It's in my room.'

I follow him back. The computer is a desktop model. I imagine Weinman's officers will impound it, but I'd like to take a look at it before they get their hands on it. 'Can you fire it up and get me your mamma's emails?'

He sits down and in a minute her email list comes up. He gets up and I sit down. I look through the last week's correspondence and see nothing remarkable. There are a few exchanges between her and Jack Cassidy, the man from the motorcycle club that Mike said had remained friends with them. Interesting that she emails with him and not his wife, but the emails are casual, not suggestive. They talk about when they'll be getting together, and Jack says that he and Emma are looking forward to seeing Amber. In the last one Jack asks how Mike is doing. I look through the 'Sent' emails, and only one catches my eye. It's to an email address for somebody called 'HonchoBen.' In the email, Amber says, 'I'll be there. Can't wait.' I look back through incoming emails to see what the arrangements were, but I don't find anything from that address. Maybe there was one and she deleted it. I look through the Trash folder and it's not there either.

'Jimmy, is there anything else on this computer that would be something your mamma was involved with?'

'She has some files.' He goes into a Word program and I see a short list of her files. They're all business-related.

'You don't happen to have a thumb drive that I could upload

these onto so I can look through them, do you?' I don't want to take their computer unless I have to. And if the highway patrol gets around to it, they'll impound it soon enough.

He opens a drawer. There are a couple of thumb drives. He picks one up, slips it into the slot on the computer, and scans through the contents. 'I'm going to copy these to the computer and then you can have this drive.'

I envy the way young people seem so relaxed with computers. Within a few minutes, he's copied the files that were on the thumb drive to the computer, erased them from the thumb drive, and copied Amber's files onto it.

'You sure that's all?'

'Yes, sir. Brittany and I use the computer for school and games mostly. Mamma doesn't . . .' He stops and takes a deep, shaky breath.

'How about your daddy? Does he use it?'

He frowns and steps back. 'Not really. He's not into computers. Sometimes, though.'

I stand up and we go back into the living room where his aunt DeeDee is chatting with Loretta's friends. She gets up when she sees us. 'Why don't you go in the kitchen and get yourself some pie, Jimmy. It won't do any good to brood, will it, sweetie?' She puts her arm around his shoulders. He's almost too tall for her to do it.

'I guess,' he says.

'When should I go get your sister from her friend's house?'

He looks surprised. 'Oh, she'll walk home. She's just down the block.'

'OK.' She watches as he trudges toward the kitchen.

When he's out of earshot, she says, 'I don't know what this family is going to do. I'm just glad the kids are old enough to pitch in. But the store! I don't know how they're going to run it. I'm going to work down there for a few days, but I've got my own family to get back to.' She tells me she has three kids and that her husband works in IT at a chemical company. 'Mike ought to think about moving down there to be near us. His family is there, too. It might be hard on the kids, but we'll make them welcome.'

TEN

I'm running out of time to get things done before Vicki turns up with Hailey. After being with Steve and Ashley Deverell, I'm beginning to dread Hailey's arrival. But I remind myself that I didn't get a lot of sleep last night and tomorrow I'll be in better shape.

I run by headquarters and take the purse and thumb drive to Maria. She says she'll go through the purse and see what she can find out from the cell phone. She turns it on and finds it isn't password-protected. 'And I'll take a look at the files on the thumb drive. You seem a little tense. Everything OK?'

I tell her that Hailey will be arriving soon. 'I'm getting nervous.'

She laughs. 'You should. What are you going to do in the meantime?'

I tell her what Lester said to me. 'I thought I'd go see Bill Kazinski and ask what he and Maureen were talking about.'

'Better for you to be out and about than bugging me. I'll get these things done.'

'Oh, by the way . . .' I go to my desk and paw through the box of things I found in Amber's car. I find the phone number and hand the plastic bag to Maria. 'See if she called or texted this number at all, and trace who it belongs to.'

Bill Kazinski runs a general repair shop and, although he isn't technically open on Sundays, I know he's usually puttering around at his place of business because it's also his home.

The house is a ramshackle wood-shingle with peeling paint, out on the highway north of town, close to a gas station and a second-hand store that advertises 'Antiques.' It's set way at the back of a large yard. A hand-lettered sign in front, near the road, says 'REPAIRS.' The yard is an eyesore to some, and a world of interesting curiosities to others. Bill repairs everything, and because the shop is small, he keeps a good many of the items out in the yard. It's all protected from the rain by a collection of tarps strung up on metal poles and canvas walls. There is some organization to it. One tarp-covered area contains TVs and radios – some of the radios are in big cabinets, and are old enough to be called antiques themselves. I wonder if somebody actually owns them and brought them in to be repaired, or if Bill just collects them. Another area is stacked with every kind of small kitchen appliance – boxes of mixers and microwaves stacked on top of each other, and a couple of mini-refrigerators. There are lawnmowers and bicycles, and another area full of mangled furniture – chairs listing to one side, tables missing legs or with chunks gouged out of them.

His pride and joy is a collection of hubcaps that are used to delineate the areas. If people are looking for a hubcap they can wind their way through the yard. There must be two hundred of them.

I spy Bill hunkered over a table working on some kind of contraption that he has taken apart. 'Hey, Bill, what have you got there?'

He steps back and scratches his head. 'It used to be a hairdryer, but I can't figure out how it ever worked.' He gives me a sly smile. 'It's old enough that it might be the first hand-held hairdryer ever made. Belongs to Maureen Washington's grandmamma.'

I step closer and it still doesn't look like much of anything. 'Is it really worth fixing?'

He snorts. 'No, but we're talking about Ida Washington. Most women are stubborn, but Ida wins the prize. 'Bout drives Maureen crazy. She told her grannie she'd buy her a new one. Oh, heavens no. She'd rather spend thirty dollars for me to fix it than spend fifteen on a new one.' He puts down the screwdriver he was holding. 'Not to mention that I'll probably end up not charging her, so I'm the one who will be out.' Bill is only mid-forties, but he has the mannerisms and speech of an old man. He's never married and I can imagine him driving a woman crazy with his laconic speech and gruff manner.

'Bill, I don't think of you as soft-hearted. Why won't you charge her?'

He guffaws. 'She's about a hundred years old, and sharp. I get a kick out of her. Besides, she hates it when somebody does something nice for her. Especially if he's white. It'll drive her crazy. Now, what do you need? Can you use a beer? It's hot as the inside of a bear out here.'

'Sounds good, but I'm expecting company and I probably shouldn't. I'm here about Amber Johnson.'

'What about her?' He looks startled.

My heart sinks. I'd assumed by now, with the grapevine as it is, that everybody would know. 'Bill, I hate to tell you, but Amber is dead.'

It takes him a beat to react. He blinks as if he thinks he misheard. 'Dead? What happened? She have an accident? She drives that car of hers like she's in the Indy five hundred.'

I tell him how she was found. He wipes his hands on a rag and says, 'Let's go sit down on the porch.'

The porch is almost as cluttered as the yard, but in the shade of the overhang there are two battered wicker chairs that we sink into.

'I'm talking to everybody who was at the meeting the other night to see if they know of anything that happened after that set-to between Lily and Amber.'

'You don't think Lily had anything to do with Amber's death, do you? I know Lily and Amber didn't get along, but I don't believe Lily is a violent person.'

'I'm just checking off the boxes.'

'I'll be right back.' He gets up and goes inside, coming back out with a beer for himself and a soda water for me. He sits back down. 'As it happens, I do have one thing to add. I saw Amber waiting after the meeting for Lily and I saw them talking. But I didn't hear what they were saying.'

'Did they appear to be friendly?'

'Not so's you'd notice. Tense. That's what I'd say.'

'What did you think of what happened between them earlier in the evening?' I ask, trying to get to the part where he told Maureen that something was going to happen to Amber. If it was actually Amber they were talking about.

He takes a swig of beer and smirks. 'Somebody overheard me talking to Maureen, didn't they? Was it Lester?'

'He did say you and Maureen were talking, but he wasn't sure what about.'

'I bet. He's got ears like a fox. Anyway, Maureen told me that

Amber has a reputation at school for jumping on teachers if she thinks they aren't doing right by her kids. I said I thought Amber ought to watch herself or somebody was going to get mad. I guess I was right.'

Somehow this explanation doesn't quite ring true. Why would he call her a little bitch?

'Did Maureen say that Amber upset anybody in particular?'

'Pshaw! It's summer. School's not even in session. You should ask Maureen, except she's gone up to Austin today. Some church thing.' He stops and looks off into the distance. 'I probably ought to call her and tell her about Amber. She'll want to know. How was she killed?'

'Looks like a knife.'

'You got any witnesses? Any idea who did it?'

'Not yet.' I keep thinking about Hailey and Vicki coming, and I'm too restless to sit here and gab with Bill any longer, so I get up and thank him for his time.

On my way home I think about what I've heard about Amber today. I don't know her well, except that I go into her convenience store sometimes and then I'll have a chat with her. She always seemed like a good-natured person, but it sounds like she had another side to her. And then there's Steve's description of her walking by the lake with some man. I wonder if it was the same person whose trailer I saw her coming from.

I wish I had time to talk to the teenagers Steve told me about, but I'd better get home and wait for Vicki. It's after three. She and Hailey might already be there.

I call to get an update and Vicki says they'll arrive in thirty minutes. On my way home, I stop by the Quick Stop to talk to Amber's employee, Cal Tyson. I pull into the gravel parking lot out front and a couple of motorcycles pull in right after me.

The door jingles when I walk in.

'Hey, Cal, I see you came to work today.'

'Yes, sir. Mr Johnson said I didn't have to come in, but I wanted to.' His expression is downcast.

'So you heard what happened to Amber.'

'Yessir, it was a shock, I'll tell you. I don't know how anybody could have hurt her. She was so great.' Clearing his throat, he blinks back tears and looks away, embarrassed.

I hate to ask him this, but it has to be done. 'Cal, how late did you work last night?'

'Eight o'clock, like we're supposed to do this week. Usually it would be ten o'clock.'

'What did you do after you got off?'

'Went home. Played video games.'

'Anybody at home with you?'

'Mamma and Daddy. No, that's not true. Daddy wasn't there when I got home.'

'You know where he was?'

He shakes his head. 'I didn't ask. I was supposed to sign on and play a game with another couple of guys online.' His eyes narrow. 'Why are you asking me this? You don't think I had anything to do with what happened to Amber, do you? That's crazy.'

I start to say something but the door jingles again and the two bikers amble in. They're hard-looking guys in leather, with shaved heads and wearing leather gloves with spikes at the wrists. I recognize one of them, but they ignore me and come straight to the counter. 'Amber here?'

Cal's eyes widen. 'No, she's—'

'When will she be back? We need to talk to her.'

'Fellas,' I say. 'There's been a—'

'This ain't nothing you need to poke your nose into,' the guy says. The other one eyes me as if he's trying to place me. He looks me up and down like a stray dog who just wandered in. The first guy leans his arm on the counter like he owns the place. I feel like I've walked into a saloon scene in an old western. 'Any way you can call Amber?'

'Only way anybody can call her is at the morgue,' I say.

The guys both turn and give me a hard look. 'Who the hell are you and what are you talking about?' the chatty one says.

'I'm Chief Craddock, chief of police here in town. And I'm talking about Amber Johnson being found dead last night. Either of you know anything that might help me find out what happened to her?'

The spokesman throws up his hands. 'Oh, no sirree. Not me. I don't know a thing about that.'

'What did you want to talk to her about?'

'Nothing important,' he says, backing away slowly. 'Sorry to hear about her death. We'll be on our way.' They turn and make for the door. I remember who the other guy is. He's the one who was selling the motorcycle that Cal's dad was looking at on Friday.

After they're gone, Cal blows out a breath. 'I'm glad you came in when you did. They looked like they wanted trouble.'

'They were a little rough around the edges, for sure, but they won't be back. You working until eight tonight?'

'Yes, it's a long day. When Mr Johnson called me and told me what happened, I told him I'd come in first thing and open up. This business runs on a thin thread and I know Amber wouldn't want to lose the money from the morning. I was here by ten.'

I remember Amber telling me she was glad to be closing at eight this week, sort of a mini-vacation. 'Did Amber work alongside you at night?'

'She usually came in after supper to work on the books. And she was sometimes here until ten.'

'Tell me, did Amber ever have any trouble with anybody?'

'Oh, no sir. She gets along with everybody.' He shrugs. 'You know, people could sometimes be grumpy, but she'd talk 'em right out of it.' He shoves his hands in his pockets and looks gloomy.

I give him my card. 'If you think of anything I ought to know, give me a call.'

'I will, but I don't know what I can think of that I haven't already told you.'

'Well, in case any bikers give you trouble.'

'I can handle 'em, don't you worry.' Despite his bravado, he casts a nervous eye at the front door.

'I'd like to take a look at Amber's office. Maybe see if there's anything on her computer that might tell us who she was supposed to be with yesterday.'

He glances back toward the office, looking uneasy. 'Is it legal for you to do that?'

I'm surprised that he asks the question. 'I'll call Mike and get permission.' I pull out my cell phone and call Mike Johnson. He says of course I can do whatever I need to do.

I tell Cal I got the OK. 'Does the computer have a password?'

'Yeah. I know it because she sometimes needed to know

something and would call and ask me to look it up. It's 04050714. That's her kids' birthdays.'

The first thing I do in the office is search the desk for notes that might tell me what Amber was up to out at the rally. I'm grateful that she's neat, because I quickly see that what she has is piles of receipts and piles of bills. No personal notes of any kind. There are only two drawers in the desk and they're used for office supplies. No notes.

The computer is old and, after going through the files, I see that it's clearly used only for business. There are emails about orders and questions about stock.

Back out front I thank Cal and head off to prepare for Hailey.

ELEVEN

I'm home only ten minutes when I hear a car honk outside just before four. I've faced some tough situations in my life, but this feels more daunting. I look out front to see Vicki parking the car. She gets out of her gray Acura and pokes her head back inside the car to say something to Hailey, who has made no move to open her car door. Dusty and I go out on the porch to greet them. He starts toward the steps, but I tell him to stay with me, and for once he listens.

Vicki slams her door and walks toward my porch with the grimmest expression I've ever seen on her face. She's always been slim, but she looks like she's lost weight. Her brown hair is messy, as if she didn't bother to comb it this morning, and either the color of the gray dress she's wearing doesn't suit her or she's ashen.

I try to put cheer in my voice. 'Hey, Vicki, y'all come on inside.' Dusty's tail is thumping. The sun makes a glare on Hailey's window, so I can't see whether she's watching us.

'She says she's not coming in,' Vicki says, when she gets to the steps.

'I guess you can't make her get out of the car. Come on in and let's talk.'

She starts to say something, but shakes her head and trudges up the steps. I sit her down with a cup of coffee. 'Did you have lunch?'

'No. Hailey isn't speaking to me, and I wasn't hungry.'

In anticipation of Hailey's arrival, I've gone to the grocery store, so I have the makings for a ham sandwich. I tell her I'm going to feed her. 'Mayonnaise or mustard or both?' I ask.

Vicki shrugs. 'Mayo, I guess.'

'Pickles?'

'Dill, if you have it.' She's watching me as if I'm doing brain surgery.

I set the sandwich down in front of her. 'Eat. And no excuses.'

She smiles and I notice a glimmer of pleasure in her eyes. 'I'm not really hungry.' She picks it up and takes a bite.

'You better not leave any of it, after I went to all that trouble to slap it together,' I say.

I'm rewarded with a bigger smile. 'It's good,' she says.

I sit down across from Vicki. 'Let's talk details.'

She glances toward the front door. 'I don't like to leave her sitting in the car. It's so hot.'

'She's sixteen. If she gets too hot, she knows how to open the door.'

She grimaces. 'You're right. Of course she does. I've lost my perspective.'

'It sounds like you've had a lot of aggravation. Tell me.'

She sets the sandwich down. 'We found out that the last few weeks of school, she'd been cutting classes. Her grades had slipped, but we didn't know it until final grades came out. And now she's sneaking out at night. Tom followed her last Saturday night and saw her get into a car with some guy and they went to Sixth Street.' She crosses her arms and leans back. 'She must have a false ID to get into a club.'

'False ID? That's nothing new,' I say. 'Kids have been doing that since IDs were invented. I'll bet you did it.'

She shrugs. 'Probably.'

'Tom followed her?'

She takes a sip of coffee. 'She didn't come in until three o'clock in the morning. Tom confronted her the next morning, and at first she lied. And when he told her he'd followed her, she went ballistic.' She puts her head in her hands. 'Her language. Her defiance. It's gone too far. Plus, I'm afraid she's going to start getting into serious drugs or get pregnant if she isn't careful. And I can't talk to her about it.'

'You said you were thinking of sending her away to school. Would she go?'

She draws a shaky breath. 'This is a different kind of school. We'd take her, and they'd meet us, and there's no way she could get away from them. I don't want to do it, but we're out of options. I'm afraid she's going to get into real trouble.'

'Some kids take the hard road. I know you're worried. Why do you suppose she's sneaking out? Do you let her date?' I'm trying to think of practical questions. Hailey's older sister is off to college in a few weeks, and I wonder if they are holding on to Hailey too tight.

'That's what we can't understand. We've never hovered. I mean, June is two years older so we're used to the idea of letting them go out with friends.'

'What does June say?'

Vicki groans. 'The girls fight all the time. June told me she can't wait to go off to college because Hailey has been so hard to live with lately.'

I was tickled to death when I found out that June had decided to go to Texas A&M. It's my alma mater, and it means she'll be close by. Not that I'll see her much, but she might like a meal out at a nice restaurant every now and then. And I'll be available if she needs something. I'm over in Bryan all the time anyway, since Wendy lives there. 'Do you suppose Hailey is reacting to her sister going away?'

Before she can answer, the front door opens and Dusty leaps up and runs to greet Hailey. For the barest second, I see her expression of pleasure at the sight of him, but then she scowls. 'Get down,' she says. Dusty blinks in surprise. Not everyone appreciates him, but he's always startled when they speak harshly to him.

Hailey is dressed in shorts and a halter top with a bare midriff. Her figure is more filled out than I remember from when I last saw her six months ago. Like Vicki, she's pretty, with brown hair and almond-colored eyes. But she isn't taking good care of herself.

Her complexion is pasty, and her shoulder-length hair is stringy, as if it hasn't been washed recently. And she's got a ring in her nose and heavy eye makeup.

'Hi Hailey. Come on in. You remember Dusty,' I say. 'He was a pup when you saw him at Christmas.'

She ignores him. 'Have y'all gossiped about me enough?' she says. The look she sends her mother would shrivel a plant.

'Why don't you come on in and sit down and I'll make you a sandwich,' I say.

She looks at the sandwich on her mother's plate and sneers. 'I'm not hungry.'

'Well, when you get hungry you know where the food is,' I say. I suddenly realize I'm going to have to take the situation in hand. 'I'm happy you're going to be here for a few days. We'll figure out some things to do.'

'Like what?' I don't know how she can infuse the words with such contempt.

'I don't want to tell you in front of your mamma because she might not approve. Now go get your suitcase and let's get you settled.' I haven't actually thought of any activity that might interest her yet. I'd give anything for Wendy to be here.

She blinks, torn between curiosity and rebelliousness.

Vicki jumps up. 'I'll help you get your stuff,' she says.

'No,' I say. 'You sit down. Hailey is old enough to take care of her own business. Right, Hailey?'

'Whatever.' She marches toward the door. Dusty cocks his head. I know he's waiting to be asked.

'Go with her,' I say to Dusty. 'Keep her out of trouble.' He doesn't have to be told twice. He scoots out the door just before she slams it.

'You see?' Vicki says.

'She's not happy, that's for sure. Listen, not that I don't want a visit from you, but I think it's best if you head on back home as soon as she gets her stuff in here.'

I think I've said the wrong thing, because she tears up.

'That's not an order. You can stay as long as you like.'

'It's not that,' she says, her voice quivering. 'It's that I felt such relief when you said it. What kind of mother am I to be glad to get rid of my daughter?'

'Not that I know much, but it seems like all of you could use a vacation from each other. And it will give you a chance to spend a little time with June before she flies the coop.'

She wipes her eyes. 'You always know how to make things better.'

'Looking at it from the outside, I see that you're struggling, and sometimes it's best to step back.'

She looks toward the door and her eyes are anxious. 'What should I do? Should I just walk out or tell her goodbye or what?'

The question is a sign of how far off the rails they've come. 'I'd say act like it's normal. Act like there's nothing going on, that you've dropped her off and now you're headed home.'

'I don't know if I can do that.'

She goes in the bathroom and stays for a while. Meanwhile, Hailey comes in dragging a suitcase the size of a trunk. Dusty follows close on her heels as if it's his job to keep her corralled. I tell her to put the suitcase in the room she and her sister usually stay in.

Right then my old cat, Zelda, ambles into the living room to see what all the fuss is about. She freezes when she sees the suitcase and casts a look at Hailey. Dusty has learned not to mess with Zelda, but he inches in her direction. She hisses a warning and flies out of the room toward my bedroom.

'She doesn't like having me here,' Hailey says.

'She doesn't even like having *me* here,' I say. 'The only thing she thinks I'm good for is to feed her.' I gesture toward the suitcase. 'That's big.'

'There's more,' she says.

'You need a hand?'

She shakes her head, but her expression has lightened and she pets Dusty as she goes back outside.

Vicki doesn't reappear while Hailey brings in the last of her goods, which looks like enough for a lifetime. I don't remark on it, though, having a strong suspicion that anything I say in that vein might be taken as criticism. Hailey closes the door to the room she'll be staying in, and Dusty trots back to my side. Vicki finally emerges from the bathroom, her eyes red, and picks up her purse from the table. She hugs me and whispers, 'Thank you.'

Then she looks down the hall to Hailey's room, takes a deep breath, gives me a 'here goes nothing' glance, and heads down there. I hear her rap on the door and sing out, 'Hailey, I'm on my way.' Silence, and then she says, 'Have a good time.'

When she leaves, she's dabbing at her eyes.

I follow her to the door, holding the sandwich I've wrapped up. 'You'll be hungry on the way home. Listen, it's going to work out,' I say. 'You know I've always enjoyed Hailey and we'll get along fine.'

'Samuel, if she acts out too much, call and we'll come get her. No blame.'

'That's not going to happen.' At least I hope not. Dusty and I watch her drive away, and I wonder if his heart has sunk the way mine has.

I call Wendy. I know she's not back from her yoga retreat yet, but I leave a message: 'Hailey is here. If you could see your way to have dinner with us, I'd really be glad. We can come there if you'd like.'

It's after five. I call Maria to see how things were at head-quarters today. I tell her what Lester Pierce overheard and what Bill said they were talking about. I also tell her I'm not sure it means anything. Then I tell her about Steve Deverell's scratched-up face and his shoplifting. 'I didn't get the impression from him that he held a grudge against Amber for accusing him of shoplifting, but I do want to check out his claim that Sophie Rodriguez scratched him.'

'Sophie is in my self-defense class.'

'Steve Deverell's sister said she's in the class, too.'

'Yeah, she's a potential troublemaker. I think she's like her brother, only tougher.'

She also tells me that none of the phone calls that came in with 'hints' about who killed Amber were worth anything. 'Like I said, it was the usual.'

While we're talking, I hear Hailey's door open.

'Maria, let's talk tomorrow. I may ask you to interview the kids that Steve was with on Friday when he saw Amber walking with somebody. Depends on my timing tomorrow.'

'You mean how much babysitting you have to do?'

'Something like that.'

I get off the phone and find Hailey lurking in the hallway. 'You get settled?' I ask.

'I guess. What are we going to do now?'

'I thought we'd go out to dinner. I called Wendy to see if she wants to come. Or we might go over to Bryan.'

'My boyfriend told me there's a motorcycle rally here this week. Can we go there?'

I remember that Chuck Oakley said his band was playing tonight. I'd like to hear them, and it might appease Hailey. 'That could work too.' I tell her about the band.

'What kind of band?'

'It may not be your kind of music. Bluegrass. What kind of music you like?'

She shrugs. 'I like country and western. So I guess that's OK.' She doesn't seem to want to meet my eyes, which is not her usual way.

'Good. I'm going down to check on my cows. It won't be long before Wendy calls and then we can go get some food and head over to the rally.'

'Why can't we go now?' There's a glint to her eye. This is her first challenge.

'You don't want me to take care of my cows? I thought you liked them.'

'I guess.'

'Come down with me.'

She follows me down to the pasture and steps onto a fence rail to watch while I make sure the water level is good. One of the tamer cows goes close to her and she scratches the cow's head. 'Can I get something to feed them?'

'Sure. There's celery and carrots in the refrigerator.'

She runs back, and I'm reminded of her as a little girl, excited about helping me. She comes back soon and we stand at the fence while she feeds them, laughing when one of them licks her hand. 'I'd forgotten how scratchy their tongues are.'

When we're walking back, Wendy calls and begs off. 'I'm worn out. I wouldn't be good company.'

I realize she doesn't know that we had a murder in town. I'm hesitant to say anything in front of Hailey, but she'll find out sooner or later. 'Honey, we got called out at midnight last night. Someone was killed at the rally.' I sense Hailey's attention.

'What do you mean? Was it a fight?' Wendy says.

'No. It was a local woman. Owns a convenience store here in town. We don't know whether it was a robbery or what. It's been a tough day.'

'Oh dear, and you have your niece.'

'That won't be a problem.'

'If you need me, I'll come over now.'

I tell her it's all right. 'Hailey and I are going to the rally to see one of the bands.'

She laughs.

TWELVE

For somebody who was in a hurry to get to the rally, Hailey takes her time getting dressed. I'm ready to knock on her door and ask if she's fallen asleep, when she walks out of her bedroom.

'You can't go like that,' I blurt out before I can catch myself. She's wearing the shortest shorts I've ever seen and what looks like a bikini top that covers only the essentials. And high heels. She's got makeup on that makes her look like a floozy. Does she even know what that is?

'Like what?' Her brazen look tells me this is exactly the response she was hoping for.

'What you're wearing isn't appropriate for the motorcycle rally.'

'Why? This is the way I dress.'

'Not while you're with me, it isn't. The rally is not a place for a girl your age to show off her body. Some of the bikers can be pretty rowdy, and I don't want you to be on display.' Even as the words leave my mouth, I know I'm asking for trouble.

Hailey's chin tilts. 'I live in Austin, and I'm around all kinds of rough crowds. I can take care of myself.'

'That may be,' I say, 'but it's not going to work for you to wear those clothes.' Hailey starts to interrupt, but I put up my hand to stop her. 'I'm the chief of police here in town and I don't want you dressing like that. I'm sure you have something to wear that will work. Now, if you want to go, you need to get changed.'

She looks daggers at me. If it was possible for steam to come out of her ears, it would.

'And you have to wear flat shoes.' I point to her high heels. 'There aren't any sidewalks. You're going to break your neck in those shoes. That would be hard to explain to your folks.' I'm trying for a light note, but Hailey shoots me another murderous look before she flounces back into her bedroom, slamming the door. I glance down at Dusty, who is looking off toward the front door, for all the world as if he wants to be elsewhere. So do I.

Hailey doesn't reappear for fifteen minutes. She has changed clothes, but it's clear she's testing. The shorts are a little longer, but not much; the halter top is a little less revealing, but not much. At least she has put on sneakers.

'You look very nice,' I say. 'Now, let's get on over there before all the barbecue is gone.'

It's so hot and humid you'd think people would be listless, but there's an electric atmosphere in the air. A lot of people are drinking, and a good many bikers seem to think it's a good idea to sit on their motorcycle and rev the engine. I'm not sure what that accomplishes, but it gets Hailey's attention. I notice her catch the eye of more than one biker. They grin at her and one even whistles.

'Wow, this is so cool,' she says.

'I could eat half a side of beef,' I say. 'How about barbecue?'

We order our barbecue, and I order a beer.

'Can I have one?' she asks.

'Now what do you think?'

She sighs. 'I think you don't know me,' she says, like it's a line from a movie.

'We're likely to find out a few things about each other,' I say.

We find a table that has a little room at one end and slide in. We're about halfway through when I see a familiar face. 'Steve Deverell!'

He whips his head around and grins. He's wearing a loud checkered vest over a T-shirt with his name on a tag on it. He has on plastic gloves and is about to empty the trash barrel. He strips off the gloves and comes over to the table.

'Hey, Chief.' He looks Hailey up and down. 'And who's this?'

'This is my nephew's daughter. She's visiting. Hailey, this is Steve.'

'Hi,' she says in a small voice. I don't know what I expected, but her shyness surprises me.

'How long are you here for?' he asks her.

She shrugs and gives me a side-eye. 'Until my bitch of a mother decides I can come home.'

Before I can react, Steve chortles and says, 'Uh-oh, trouble at home. 'Course I wouldn't know anything about that, would I, Chief?'

'No comment,' I say.

'I gotta get back to work,' he says to me, and then to Hailey, 'I'll see you around.'

I decide to keep quiet about what Hailey said about her mother until the other people at the table leave – they pick up and move on a few minutes later.

'Hailey, I need to talk to you about what you said.'

Her face is crimson. 'I know, I know. Don't call my mamma a bitch.'

'She isn't, you know.'

'Yeah? You try living with her.'

I'm not going to give her the old line about her mamma loves her. She knows it. 'You're getting old enough to know not to act like a little kid,' I say. 'Calling names and whining about your folks. I bet you know you've got a part in the problem, too.'

She blinks, like I've slapped her. 'Maybe I act like a little kid because they treat me like one.'

This is an unwinnable circular argument, and I'm ready to call it quits with the conversation. I want to change the subject, and I have an inspiration. 'Let's get going,' I say. 'I want you to meet a friend of mine.' We throw our trash in the freshly emptied bin and head for Walter Dunn's repair truck.

Walter's still there, working on a motorcycle under a strong lamp.

'When do you quit?' I ask, after I've introduced them to each other.

'My brain quit about two hours ago, but we make a lot of money at this event and I have to stick with it until we're done every night.'

He asks Hailey when she got in and how long she's going to stay. This time her reply is, 'I'm not sure.'

'I'm hoping she'll stay a while,' I say. 'A week or two. Before I know it, she'll be grown and off to college and I'll barely ever see her.'

She glances at me with a funny smile on her face.

I hear music tuning up. 'Listen. The band's about to start playing. Hailey and I need to get on down to the stage.'

'Y'all stop by Wednesday,' Walter says. 'Maybe Hailey would like a ride on a motorcycle and we'll have some time then because there's a road rally that day. I can get one of the guys to take her out.'

'Really?' She squeals.

The Oakleys put on a good show and we both enjoy the music. I guess bluegrass doesn't lend itself to pole dancing, and I'm glad I don't have to be embarrassed with Hailey seeing that. April is a good singer. I keep an eye out for her friend Lulu, but don't see her in the crowd. Even if I did, I wouldn't want to leave Hailey to her own devices while I question her.

The band is done at midnight and so am I.

'Can I meet the band?' Hailey begs.

'Hailey, I know you heard me tell Wendy about the woman who was killed. I was out here until two this morning and had to be up before six, so I need to get home and get to bed. We'll come back later in the week.'

'I could stay and get a ride home,' she says. 'Maybe that guy Steve would take me home.' I'm impressed that she's ready to work every angle, and she just got here.

'I imagine he'd be thrilled. But I want you to come with me. This is your first day here. How about if you try to be on your best behavior for at least one day.'

'Oh, all right.' She sounds grumpy, but goes back to the car with me without any more complaints.

Back home, I'm happy when she disappears into her bedroom and I hear her talking on her phone. Dusty follows me into the bedroom and flops down on his bed.

'Dusty, it's been a long day, and I have a feeling it's going to be a long week.'

THIRTEEN

The next morning I'm up early to see to my cows, and when I get back I heat up some of Loretta's coffee cake and have it with eggs.

I don't know exactly what I'm going to do with Hailey today, so I need to get as much done as early as I can. I call the coroner's office to find out when they're going to do the autopsy on Amber. They say they'll have a preliminary report by this afternoon. Then I call the highway patrol lead, Dan Weinman.

'You're at it early,' he says.

'Have to be. I wondered if your officers had a chance to question any of the rally-goers yesterday?'

'Not yet. I thought I'd get a couple of fellows out there tomorrow. We had a bank robbery of all things. Over in Bobtail. Not exactly the brightest guys in town.'

'You caught 'em?'

He chuckles. 'They caught themselves. On the way to one of their girlfriend's houses they decided to put the icing on the cake by robbing a liquor store. They didn't count on the owner being on the premises in the back doing some inventory. He heard what was going on, called the police and came out with a shotgun. Held the two guys there until the police got there.'

'Why were you involved?'

He laughs harder. 'That's the rich part. This wasn't their first holdup. Turns out we'd been looking for them and the sheriff in Bobtail knew about it so he called us. Very tidy and satisfying all the way round.'

'Doesn't happen often, I'll bet.'

'Of course that doesn't help figure out who killed your citizen,' he says. 'At least the rally is going on for the rest of the week, so we have time to question people.'

This is what happens when we turn things over to DPS. They don't prioritize small-town crime, and we get shoved to the back of the line.

It's eight-thirty and Hailey still hasn't made an appearance, so I leave her a note to call me when she gets up.

Next on my agenda is to talk to the teenagers who were with Steve to find out if any of them can give me a better description of the man who was with Amber on Friday afternoon. I strike out. Two of them don't remember seeing a thing. And one left for a fishing trip on the coast with his dad this morning. I get his cell number and call him, but he's no more helpful than the first two. Then there's Sophie Rodriguez. I want to get her version about how Steve got the scratches on his face.

There's no one home at Sophie Rodriguez's house and no one is answering the phone. The next-door neighbor says she saw Sophie and her mamma leave early this morning. 'I expect they're going to Houston to go shopping. I never saw anybody who loves to shop the way those two do,' she says.

I'm headed to the lake when Hailey calls. I tell her to get her breakfast and I'll be by to pick her up in an hour or so.

'Where are you?'

'Going to question a couple of people about the woman who was killed. I won't be long.'

'What should I get for breakfast?'

'I have bread for toast, and eggs. There's orange juice. But you can eat anything you find that appeals to you. You drink coffee?'

'Eww, no.'

I laugh. 'I'll be back in a bit.'

Out at the rally, it's easy enough to find the Rough Roaders because they have a flag planted in the middle of a circle of tents set up next to their pickup trucks. The rectangular red and blue flag says 'Rough Roaders Ride.' There are people sitting around outside their tents, many with folding tables set up, eating breakfast of one kind or another. Someone points out the Cassidys to me. They're sitting with a few other folk, their chairs positioned so they're looking out over the lake.

I introduce myself and tell them I'm here about Amber. Jack Cassidy puts down his empty plate, stands up, wipes his hands on his napkin and shakes my hand. 'This is my wife Emma.' A sturdy-looking woman with short hair, wearing shorts and a T-shirt that matches Jack's, stands up too. 'You want some coffee?' she says. 'I was just about to get some more.'

The three of us walk over to a communal coffee urn set up on a big table with a selection of mugs, sugar and creamer. The Cassidys are a little older than Mike and Amber Johnson, mid-forties, and seem to be in good shape, wholesome-looking. They aren't dressed in traditional biker gear. They're both wearing cargo shorts and T-shirts with the Rough Roaders logo, which consists of a fresh-faced couple sitting astride motorcycles, grinning and giving a thumbs up. In small letters at the bottom it says, 'Bikers for Jesus.' It takes me a second to realize that the couple on the T-shirts is them.

'You probably noticed we're a little bit different from some of these hard-core bikers,' Jack says. 'Not that they aren't good people – most of them – but we like to keep a clean profile. And we like to make ourselves comfortable while we're here, kind of combine vacation and celebration of our enjoyment of our bikes.'

I tell them I'd like to ask them some questions about Amber.

Jack sighs and his wife puts a hand on his arm and looks at him with concern.

'We loved that woman,' Jack says, wiping his eyes. I notice he doesn't say that they loved both the Johnsons.

Emma shakes her head. 'I just don't know how anybody could have done that to Amber. It must have been a stranger. Somebody who didn't know her.'

'Did you see her at all this weekend?'

'Yes, sir,' Jack says. 'She came by Friday afternoon. And we were supposed to go for a bike ride yesterday after church. We had a bike all lined up for her. One of the women was going to let Amber use her Yamaha.' He looks away, his face empty.

'When did you find out what happened to her?'

Jack takes out a handkerchief and blows his nose and Emma says, 'Amber's sister called about noon yesterday. She said Mike had asked her to let us know.'

'So Friday, what time was she here?'

Jack turns to his wife. 'What time did she get here?'

'Sometime in the afternoon. We arrived at the rally about noon and had just gotten set up.'

'How did she seem? Was anything bothering her? Did she seem afraid of anybody? Somebody who wanted to do her harm?'

'No,' Emma says. 'When she was here with the two of us, she seemed OK, maybe a little down. But Jack went for a walk with her and he said she told him she was having some problems. Tell him, Jack.'

Before he can get started, I say, 'Did you by chance walk down by the water?'

'Yes, why?'

'That clears one thing up. Someone saw her walking with a man and I wondered who it was. Emma, you didn't go?'

'It was too hot for me. I can't stand hot weather. And besides, Jack and Amber have always been as close as brother and sister. I figured they might like a little time to themselves.' I remember that the email conversation was between Jack and Amber. I don't get any sense that Emma is jealous.

'Jack, tell me what she was worried about.'

Jack crosses his arms. 'She was concerned that her store wasn't going to make it. She said it did a good business, but apparently one of the gas stations was thinking about putting in a convenience store. She said if she had that kind of competition, she'd be sunk in no time.'

That's the first I've heard that she might be getting competition.

'You said she was worried about Mike, too,' Emma says.

He nods. 'She said he's always in pain.'

'Those poor people. They didn't deserve what happened to them,' Emma says.

'Emma, you know the Lord works in mysterious ways.'

She snorts. 'Mysterious to me, for sure.'

'I never heard the details of the accident. Were you there when it happened?' I ask.

'Yes. It was horrible,' Emma says.

'You mind describing it to me?'

'Let's go sit down.'

We go back to the folding chairs facing the water. The lake looks serene this morning, ducks paddling just beyond the beach, the sun lighting up the treetops on the far shore. It won't be long before it fires up the day, but right now it's pleasant, no more than eighty degrees.

'Here's how it happened,' Jack says. He's hunched over with his forearms on his thighs. 'There were about twenty of us. We'd gathered in Marble Falls at the lake at seven in the morning. Most of us spent the night at one of the hotels there. We do this ride two or three times a year. There are lots of good country roads out there that aren't well-traveled. Anyway, we rode through the hill country out to Ink's Lake and had a picnic. We were on our way back, out on Route 2342, riding two by two, when all of a sudden this old boy came barreling along in one of those big pickups.'

Emma makes a distressed sound. Her hands are knotted in her lap.

Jack sighs. 'We could see he was going too fast and I guess somebody motioned for him to slow down. Well, sir, he didn't like that one bit. He started weaving back and forth like he was going to hit us. And I guess he lost control because next thing we know we hear these brakes squeal. I looked back and I'll never forget that sight. He plowed right into the middle of the pack. Two of the cycles went airborne. That's how fast he was going.' He pauses and takes a sip of his coffee. He shakes his head. 'Lonny Tibideaux was killed outright. He and Mike Johnson were riding on the outside, with their wives on the inside. The women were lucky, you could say. They were hurt, but not as bad as Lonny and Mike.'

He pauses and Emma rubs her hand over his back.

'Was there any sense that the guy hit them deliberately?'

'It's possible, but more to the point, he was drunk. Stupid fool tried to get away. Couple of our riders took off after him and we called the highway patrol. They caught him in fifteen minutes. Anyway, the rest of us did what we could to help the ones that got hit until the ambulances arrived. We have a doctor in the club, a cardiologist. And his wife is a nurse. I have to say she was more use than he was.'

'The other woman who was hurt, the one whose husband was killed. She was all right?'

'Last I heard, she recovered. She and Amber had scrapes and bruises. As I recall, Amber had a couple of broken ribs and Cathy broke her arm. She dropped out of the club and I haven't seen her in a while.'

'What happened to the driver?'

'Charged with drunk driving and he'll be in jail for a while. Though he wasn't sentenced to as much time as we think he should have been.'

'How common are accidents when you ride in a group like that?' I ask.

'Not too common. You get people who aren't safe riders, or something goes wrong, like an oil slick or a gravel spill. Guy in our group broke his leg once when his cycle went down. People get skinned up and what-not.'

'Like that?' I point to a couple of scratches along his left arm.

He looks at his arm as if he didn't realize he'd been scratched. 'Yeah, I guess. But usually we don't experience anything so extreme. I never saw anything like it before and I never want to again. It was a terrible scene.'

'Amber told me the club was helpful to her after the accident.'

'We tried. People live all over, so it isn't easy to make a trip for some of them. Emma and I live in Houston, so we came over a few times. Until Mike told me it was too hard for him to see us, you know, going about our regular lives. Not that I blame him. He's too proud to let on that's he's in pain.'

'What kind of insurance did they have? Does the club have insurance as a group or does each person have their own?'

Jack glances over at his wife and a look passes between them. 'The club has the insurance, but we encourage people to get their own. The club has a big deductible and it only covers you when you're actually on a ride with the club.'

'Tell him the rest of it,' Emma says.

Jack grimaces. 'One of the things Amber was upset about is that a doctor says Mike needs another operation to set things right, but their insurance company doesn't want to pay for it. She was thinking about suing through the club's insurance. But she was worried that if she did sue, we'd lose our coverage.'

'Would you?'

'Maybe. But I told her, the important thing was that she and Mike get what they were entitled to. I gave her the name of a lawyer I know.'

'I'll tell you this,' Emma says. 'It's not right for people to have such trouble getting insurance. She told Jack that they tried to get insurance through the ACA and they couldn't afford it.'

'Now, Emma, don't get wound up.'

'I am wound up,' she says indignantly. 'For that man to suffer because the insurance company is so stingy, and then there's the deductible, and premiums so high. It's not right.'

'Anything else you remember that Amber told you on your walk?'

'I don't think so.'

'When Amber was here on Friday, did she visit with others in your group?'

'No, just us,' Jack says. 'Emma and I are the ones who have kept up with her. We knew her and Mike better than anyone else did.'

I thank them for their time, and tell them that if they think of anything more to give me a call.

It's time for me to get back to Hailey. I want to stop by the RV where I saw Amber last Friday and see if they can tell me anything, but I'll have to come back later for that.

FOURTEEN

When I get back home, Hailey's in her room with her door closed, talking to somebody on her phone.

I have to figure out a way to entertain her. Unfortunately, my options are limited, which I probably should have thought of before I had the bright idea to ask her folks to bring her here. But of course that was before the complication of Amber Johnson's murder. There are things we could have done if that tragedy hadn't struck – driven down to the coast, gone over to do the River Walk in San Antonio, maybe spend a couple of days in Houston.

With Amber Johnson's death hanging over me, today my time is not my own. I can take Hailey with me to headquarters, leave her to her own devices for the afternoon, or call Wendy to come and run interference. As much as I'd like to see Wendy, I decide to do what I would normally do, but with a tagalong. Maybe police work will interest her.

I tap on her door. 'Get dressed and we'll go down to head-quarters. I've got work to do.'

She opens the door and glares at me. 'What do you mean get dressed?' She's still in her nightgown, an oversized shirt with baby sheep on it, which is an amusing contrast to the tough exterior she tries to project.

'I'm taking you with me to work down at the police station. You can't go in your pajamas.'

She rolls her eyes. 'All right.' She closes the door, but not with any force.

Again, it takes longer than I think it should, but eventually she comes out of her room.

'You look nice,' I say. She's changed into knee-length shorts and a T-shirt with wild colors on it in a jagged pattern. It'll do fine.

'How long are we going to be there?'

'It depends on how much mayhem is going on in town.'

Her lip curls. 'Ha! What can be going on in this . . . town?' I'm pretty sure she was going to say hick town, and it's a small comfort that she decided that was one step too far.

'You'll be surprised. And if you get bored, I can always run you back here.'

'Can I help you find whoever killed that woman?'

'Like I said yesterday, that's mostly up to the highway patrol. But I might let you go with me when I question somebody, if you promise to keep quiet.'

She makes a zipped-lip motion.

When we get to headquarters, I introduce her to my deputy on duty, Connor Loving. Connor is blond and fair-haired and blushes easily. He's the youngest member of my team, and although he's green, he has good instincts. He has stepped up since my previous deputy Bill Odum and his wife decided to pull up stakes and move to Houston.

'Nice to meet you,' Hailey says in the sweet voice that I remember. It makes me think she's going to be OK. She's saving her bad behavior for her family.

Connor says we're getting complaints about rally-goers speeding through town, gunning their engines and cutting off motorists. I put him in charge of handling complaints because he has a gift for soothing ruffled feathers.

'If they'd just stay out at the lake, it wouldn't be such a problem,' he says.

'That's not going to happen. Do the best you can.'

I was worried that Hailey would get bored and restless with me being on duty. She's right, not much usually goes on around here. But luck is with me. We haven't been here long when we're called out to help a farmer round up some goats that have gotten out through a hole in the fence. I ask Connor to take Hailey with him to take care of it. I hope they're gone a while.

As soon as they leave, I call Maureen Washington, the woman who was gossiping with Bill Kazinski after the town hall meeting. She says she can see me, so I head over to her place. It used to be that all the Black families lived east of the railroad tracks, but gradually the old boundaries have eased. Not a huge mix, but it's a start. Maureen lives barely on the west side of the highway in a house that for years was a run-down eyesore fought over by relatives after Old Man Jamison died at the age of 102. None of his three kids wanted to live in it, but they didn't want any of their siblings to live there either. And they couldn't agree on the split they would receive if they sold it, so it sat dormant, getting more and more dilapidated, and less valuable. Our local building contractor, Gabe LoPresto, finally convinced the siblings they'd be better off selling to him.

For a year, anytime you'd drive by, a crew was always working on it. Now it's a sturdy wooden house of the old prairie style with a deep front porch. There's a porch swing and a lot of plants. The door is painted bright blue, a nice contrast to the tan wood stain and copper-colored trim.

When I knock, I hear Maureen's voice calling out, 'I'll get it, Mamma.' She opens the door and a genuine smile blooms on her face.

'Hello, Samuel. Come on in.' She's dressed in an African pattern skirt and a red blouse, with her hair done up in a kerchief. A robust-looking woman with light brown skin and liquid eyes, she has that schoolteacher way of looking at you, as if you'd best not get out of line. She says, 'Mamma and I are making peach preserves. If you play your cards right, you might be the beneficiary.'

The aroma of peach nectar fills the air. In the kitchen I hear Maureen's mamma humming.

'Come in the kitchen and say hello, and then we can sit in the living room.'

Maureen looks just like her mamma, except there's a little more silver shot through the older woman's hair.

'Mamma, you know Chief Craddock? Samuel, this is my mother, Bernice Washington.'

Bernice puts down the ladle she's using to stir the peach preserves, and shakes my hand. 'You here to arrest Maureen? She's not that bad, you know, except for having a mouth on her.'

I laugh. 'Those preserves smell good. Do you put them up every year?'

'Not always peach. Sometimes we'll do strawberry. But it's always something.'

Maureen pours us coffee and we head into the living room.

We sit down, me in a puffy easy chair and Maureen on her deep green sofa. 'Bill told me about Amber Johnson. That's a shock. He said he told you we were talking about her. It doesn't seem right now.'

'That's what I wanted to ask you about. I guess Bill told you that Lester overheard you two talking after the town hall meeting the other night.'

'He did.'

'Bill said you told him that Amber didn't get along well with some of her kids' teachers.'

'Not teachers. One teacher. Ben Holman, the math teacher. Amber seemed to think Ben was too hard on her son, Jimmy. They had a little set-to one day last year.'

'Did you see it, or hear about it?'

'Heard about it from Ben. He said he had to tell her that Jimmy wasn't doing the work. But Jimmy's work wasn't actually the problem between him and Amber. Apparently, Ben got nosy and asked Jimmy if everything was all right at home. You know, sometimes kids act out when their parents have troubles. I guess Jimmy told his mamma, and she didn't like it one bit. He told me Amber lit into him and told him it was none of his business and to stick to teaching kids.'

'Did they continue to have problems?'

'No, they patched things up between them. At the end of the year I saw them laughing together several times.'

'Well, I'm puzzled. Lester heard Bill say something about Amber being a bitch and she was going to get herself in trouble. That doesn't sound like it describes a woman who's mad at a teacher.'

Maureen rubs the back of her neck, her eyes downcast. 'I'm afraid that's my fault. I told Bill I thought Amber was flirting with Ben. That's why Bill said that.' She looks back up at me, her expression rueful.

'What do you mean "flirting"? Was it blatant?'

'It was to me, but maybe other people wouldn't notice. You know, Amber would put her hand on his arm and kind of put herself forward a little bit, if you know what I mean.' She raises her eyebrows. 'Amber had a nice figure and she liked showing it off.'

'Do you think they were involved?'

'I wouldn't go that far. You know flirting happens. Ben's a divorced man, some say attractive, although I can't see it. Not the first time I've seen a woman show interest in him.'

'Any of the other teachers ever have trouble with Amber?'

'Not that I know of. She seemed like a good mother, interested in her kids.'

'Did you know her?'

'Just to say hello to.'

Before I leave, Maureen takes me back in the kitchen and presents me with a jar of warm preserves. 'Now we haven't had time to seal this jar, so you need to eat it soon.'

'I doubt I'll have trouble with that.'

I've just gotten back to the station when the call comes in from T.J. Sutter that they've done the autopsy. 'She was stabbed in the torso four or five times, which suggests that whoever killed her was angry.'

'You know she tried to crawl for help?'

'Now it makes sense why she had dirt on her hands and knees. Wouldn't have mattered if she got help anyway. She wasn't likely to survive the attack.'

'Any sign she might have fought her killer?'

'No defensive wounds, but there was a lot of stuff under her fingernails. We'll analyze it, but it looks mostly like dirt. Whoever did this took her by surprise, and when they stabbed her they must have shoved her down, because she had a little bang on the back of her head.'

'Could somebody have hit her from behind and then attacked her?'

'Not likely. The angle of the knife tells me she was standing up facing her killer when he stabbed her.'

'Anything unusual about the weapon?'

'It was big. Like a hunting knife. The impressions were deep but also wide.'

'You find anything unusual?'

'I don't know how unusual it is, but your woman had recently had sexual intercourse.'

'Was she raped?'

'Not likely. The guy wore a condom.'

Because I've just spoken to Maureen Washington, my thoughts go to the teacher Amber was flirting with, Ben Holman. I'll have to keep that in mind and have a talk with Mr Holman.

Before I can ask T.J. anything else, Hailey and Connor walk in. Connor looks more cheerful than he usually does and Hailey is giggling.

'T.J., can you send me the full report?'

He says he will.

Through her giggles, Hailey tells me about rounding up the goats. 'They weren't running away, but they didn't want to go back inside their pen either. That meant we had to go up to each one of them very slowly with a lasso,' she says, miming the motion. 'Then you'd slip the rope over its head and lead him back inside the fence. The goats were so funny!'

'They were pretty frisky,' Connor says, grinning.

'You should have seen it. There were a couple of little ones. And one of them jumped up on a fence post and balanced. I don't see how he did it. All four of his hooves were squinched up together. It was a hoot. I got a lot of pictures and posted them on Instagram. Everyone loves it!'

I don't know exactly what Instagram has to do with it, but I'm glad she's entertained.

I send Connor off to talk to somebody about a car break-in, and Hailey says she's hungry so I take her across the street to Town Café for lunch. We dig into enchiladas. Several people stop by to say hello and to meet my niece. My friend Gabe LoPresto comes by and charms her. I think how much her folks would love to see her glowing. Today's dessert special is banana cream pie and we both order that. Hailey seems happy, and I'm relieved.

When we get back to headquarters, I tell her I need to go talk to someone. 'You can go with me or I can take you back to my place. I won't be long.'

'Can we go back to the motorcycle rally?'

'For a short time. I need to talk to somebody there, too.'

'I'll go with you then.'

Jack Cassidy said Amber was worried that one of the gas stations was thinking of putting in a convenience store, which would drive the Quick Stop out of business. I first go by the Texaco on the north end of town. Hailey says she'll stay in the car. Before I've even gotten out, her thumbs are flying across the keys of her cell phone.

Alvin Carter laughs when I ask him if he has plans to put in a convenience store at his gas station. 'Where would I get the money?' he asks. 'I'd have to build on. There's not enough room in here.'

He's right. He does stock a few basics near his cash register – gum, candy, cigarettes and lottery tickets – but that's all he has room for because the rest of the eight-by-ten room is taken up with automotive goods like oil and window cleaner.

At the other end of town is a generic gas station owned by the same East Indian family that bought the old motel. Rakesh Patel and his wife keep a low profile. They live in a house behind their gas station and as far as I know do little mingling in town. The man working at the gas station tells me I can find them in the motel. Mrs Patel, a short, robust woman wearing a traditional sari, is behind the desk and she calls her husband from the back office. He greets me with a slight bow.

'Mr Patel, have you heard what happened to Amber Johnson?'

'I did, and I'm very sorry. My wife and I are appalled at the violence in this country.'

'Raki.' It's a warning note from his wife.

'Yes, my wife is reminding me that there is much violence in India as well. It is not confined to one country.'

'I understand you were thinking of putting in a convenience store at your service station.'

'Yes, I was,' Patel says. He's a dark-skinned, solemn man, only slightly taller than his wife. He is wearing a gold and green shirt of a design that looks East Indian. 'It would be a smart business move for me. People stop at a gas station and they like to buy snacks and lottery tickets.'

'You had a conversation with Mrs Johnson about it?'

He shrugs. 'I felt it was only fair to let her know.'

'How did she react?'

'She was upset, more than I expected. You know in the United States there is much talk of the free market, but sometimes it is not so free when competition threatens an established business. She told me she would fight to deny me a business license. I told her she had no grounds.' Patel has a lilting accent.

'Have you applied for the license?'

'Not yet. I was thinking it over. Mrs Johnson told me of her family situation. I felt sorry for her, but I have an obligation to my family to make the most of the opportunity. Unfortunately, I have heard of other men like me who challenged the status quo and were punished when they upset people in town.'

'Punished how?' I ask.

'There is retaliation.'

'Have you had that here in Jarrett Creek?'

'Oh no, people here have been kind. This is just what I was told from people in my community.'

As far as I know there has been no talk of anyone being disgruntled about the two businesses that Patel owns – the motel or the gas station. Since there are only two of each in town, there's plenty of business for all. 'If you ever have any problems like that, be sure to report it to me.'

He nods.

'Had you spoken with Amber Johnson since you approached her with your plan?'

'No. At the time I told her I would have to consider her objections.'

'When was this?'

'One month ago.'

Before we head to the rally, I want to take Mike Johnson's car back. 'Hailey, do you think you can drive my pickup?'

She looks startled. 'Where am I taking it?'

'It's only five minutes away. You can follow me. I need to take Amber's car back to her family. You do have a driver's license, don't you?'

'Of course I do!' She's indignant. We drive in tandem without incident. I park and she pulls in behind me. She's flushed and looks pleased with herself. I imagine it's the first time she's had occasion to drive a pickup. I ask her to wait in the truck. 'I won't be long.'

Jimmy lets me in and says there are no visitors here at the moment. He's polite, but his whole being is droopy. I ask how his sister is doing. He says she's at her friend's house again. 'Which is a good thing. Takes her mind off stuff here.' His words are too old for his age. He's got too big a burden to bear. He leads me into the kitchen where Mike is sitting at the table. It's covered with papers.

'Excuse me if I don't get up,' he says. There's a cane parked near him.

'Stay seated,' I tell him. 'I'm just here to let you know I brought your car back. I left the keys in that bowl by the front door. I also wanted to check on you. How are you holding up?'

'It's been a rough couple of days.'

'I met your sister-in-law earlier.'

'She's down at the store. She's going to help us out there the next few mornings and she wanted to find out from Cal how things work.'

I tell him I talked to Jack and Emma Cassidy.

'They're good people,' he says.

'I think they'd come and see you if you'd ask.'

His expression closes up tight. 'I'll think about it.'

'Mike, did Amber ever have any trouble with anybody that came in the store? Attempted robbery, anything like that?'

'No. If she had, I'd have insisted we sell. I don't much like the store anyway. I don't know what I'm going to do about it now.'

'Don't rush into anything,' I tell him. I know from experience that when your wife dies, it takes a while to get your head on straight.

FIFTEEN

When I get back in the pickup, Hailey is whispering into the phone. 'I have to go,' she says, and clicks off.

'Who were you talking to?' I'm thinking she might have called her folks.

She scowls. 'A friend.' She crosses her arms and looks out the side window. Apparently, I've been too nosy.

We arrive at the rally at 3:00 and Hailey perks up, especially when we drive straight to the front and I tell the guys I'd like to park at the entrance. For thirty seconds she thinks I'm cool.

Almost immediately we come upon a small crowd gathered around a man inking a tattoo on one of the bikers. It's an elaborate tattoo featuring the ever-popular flames.

'Oh wow!' Hailey says. 'Can I stay here and watch? I might want to learn how to do tattoos.'

'That'll be all right, but I don't want you to wander off. If you leave here, call me.' I start to walk away, and come back to whisper to her, 'And I don't want you getting a tattoo.'

'Duh. As if I have the money for that.'

I'm here to question April and Lulu, the two women who were in the music tent the night Amber's body was found. Lulu said something that made me wonder if she saw something important. Surely she's had enough time to sober up by now.

I figure that since April is the singer in their band, the Oakleys will know where she is. I find Tucker Oakley outside his tent, playing a mournful tune on a mandolin. He gets up when he sees me, and says his daddy and brother have gone to the grocery store. He looks a lot more with it today.

'Tucker, do you know where I can find your singer, April, and her friend Lulu?'

'Most likely those two are together. They hang out a lot. April's going to be singing with another group tonight. The Flintstones. She might be over with them. I'll go with you to look for them.'

The late afternoon sun is trying its best to fry us before it disappears behind the low hills to the west. The crowd feels restless, gearing up in preparation for the evening. With the rally half over, it's at maximum crowd size – at least a thousand people. Wherever people have been all day, they're returning now, and the place is louder and more crowded. We wind our way through tents and trailers until we come up to a group in a picnic area near the music tent.

April and Lulu are sitting on mats on the ground, backs up against a picnic table, taking advantage of the shade it provides. April is wearing shorts and another sequined T-shirt. Lulu is short and pudgy, a belly roll peeking out between a tank-top and her shorts. She wears her light brown, curly hair long in the back and in a high pouf on top that reminds me of the mullets boys used to wear a while back. Both girls are wearing cowboy boots, but April's are showy, while Lulu's have a lot of wear and tear.

'Hey, April, Lulu, how's it going?' Tucker asks.

'It was going pretty good until Gopher ran off with my pickup with all the beer in the back,' April says with a sullen pout.

'Well, you can come over to my place,' Tucker says. 'We have beer.'

'No, I'm waiting until that son-of-a-bitch gets back with my pickup. I didn't tell him he could take off in it. I'm going to ream him a new one.'

'I'll come over to your tent and get some beer.' Lulu gets to her feet and looks at me with curiosity. So far, I've been left out of the conversation.

'Y'all remember Chief Craddock?' Tucker says. 'He's the police chief in Jarrett Creek? You met him the night that woman was killed.'

'Oh yeah,' April says. She gets up and dusts off her shorts and offers her hand to me. 'I'm sorry, I didn't recognize you. You figure out what happened to that woman?'

'I didn't. That's what I wanted to talk to you and your friend about.'

'I'll be going back to my area unless you need me,' Tucker says. 'If Daddy comes back and finds out I've left our stuff without locking up, he'll have my hide. Lulu, come on over when you want to. You know where we are.'

'I'll be there in a minute,' Lulu says. She gives me an uneasy glance. 'I'm sorry, I don't remember you,' she says.

'You weren't feeling too great that night,' I say.

'You mean she was drunk as a skunk,' April snickers.

'I had my reasons,' Lulu says, smacking April on the arm with her fist.

'You can always find a reason,' April says.

'Look, I want to ask your help,' I say.

'With what?' April says, genuine curiosity on her face.

'About the night Amber Johnson was killed. Do either of you remember hearing anything outside the music tent that night? An argument? Or has anybody mentioned seeing anything going on out behind the tent?'

Lulu's head drops and she digs the toe of her boot into the dirt.

'You mean like did we hear a scream or anything?' April says. 'We couldn't have heard anything out there. The music's too loud.'

I'm alerted by Lulu's sudden shyness. 'Lulu,' I say, 'did you by any chance go back behind the stage that night? Like maybe you were sick or something?'

Lulu looks at April. Her face is positively green.

'Lulu, what the hell?' April says. 'Did you see something?'

Lulu's lips are quivering and her eyes tear up. 'I think maybe I did.'

'What?' April is practically yelling. 'Why didn't you say something?'

'I don't know, I just—'

'Tell me what you remember,' I say. 'Where were you?'

She crosses her arms under her bosom and sighs, a shaky sound. 'Behind the tent. I felt bad and I went back there, thinking I was going to upchuck. I didn't, but I stood there for about five minutes. I was pretty drunk and I might not remember exactly what I saw.'

'Honey, you have to tell whatever it was,' April says.

'It was dark!' Lulu cries.

April gives her a stern eye.

'OK.' She looks at me as if she's afraid of being punished. 'There was a man and woman down by the water. They were talking. I don't know why I was watching. I guess they were silhouetted against the sky. Anyway, after a minute the guy shoved the woman. And then they walked up toward the tent. I

was hoping they wouldn't see me. They stopped and she . . . I
don't know exactly. She put her hand up, like, to his face or head
or something. She was kind of leaning toward him and I couldn't
hear what they were saying, but I kind of thought she was trying
to make up to him or something.'

'You have any idea what time it was?'

She looks helpless. 'I don't know. The band had been on stage
for a while, so it had to be after eleven.'

'What happened when she touched his face?'

'He jerked back and I saw him say something to her. I don't know
how to describe it. The way his chin jutted out, he looked mad.'

'Did you hear what he said?'

'Mostly not, because of the band. But just then they stopped
playing and I heard him call her a whore.' Her voice is small.

'Lulu,' April sputters, 'why didn't you come forward with this
information before?'

She hugs her arms to herself. 'I was so drunk I wasn't sure I'd
actually got it right. Besides, it's not like he hit her or anything.
He was mad, but I didn't think it was serious. You know, like a
lover's spat.'

'So what happened after that?' I ask.

'I got out of there. I didn't want her to look up and find out
somebody had heard him call her that. It was embarrassing. So I
sneaked off.'

April makes a sound like a growl.

I could shake Lulu. If she had called out or let them know she
was there, Amber might have been embarrassed, but she might
also still be alive. But that's a thought born of frustration. Lulu
is no different from most people who freeze when a situation
gets contentious.

Lulu looks like she's about to cry. 'You're thinking I could have
saved her, right?'

'There's no way to know that. You were in an awkward position.'

'And drunk,' April mutters.

I throw her a look, hoping she'll stop butting in. 'Lulu, can you
describe the two people at all? Like how tall they were?'

'The woman was short, and about my size. Not fat or anything,
like curvy, well-built. I couldn't tell how long her hair was, but it
wasn't short.'

'And the guy?'

'Tall. At least a foot taller.'

'You heard his voice. Did he sound young, old?'

'Young.'

'Like a teenager?'

'Mm, I don't know. But definitely not an old guy. Just regular.'

'Could you tell what color his hair was?'

'It was so dark outside that I couldn't see much, but I think his hair was light. Lighter than hers anyway. And honestly, that's all I remember.' She bites her lower lip. 'I know it's not much. You think this will help you at all?'

'I don't know. It might.'

For all I know the couple she saw wasn't Amber and whoever killed her. It could have been anyone.

I go back to the tattoo station to make sure Hailey is still there. She's ready to go, so I take her with me to see if anybody has returned to the RV I saw Amber coming out of on Friday.

When I get there, I see that the door is open. I send Hailey off to get a Sno-cone and tell her I'll be here.

I knock on the door of the RV. 'Anybody home?'

A woman appears in the doorway. I'm stunned. She's gorgeous. She could be a model or a movie star.

I introduce myself and she steps down out of the RV. She's almost as tall as me, five ten at least, and willowy, with long blond hair and aquamarine eyes. I've never seen eyes that color.

'Hi,' she says, and offers a firm handshake. 'I'm Becky. What can I do for you?'

'Do you know a woman by the name of Amber Johnson?'

She shakes her head.

'Are you sure?'

She shrugs. 'I suppose it's possible I've met her. You meet a lot of people at a rally like this. Everybody sort of blends together.' There's laughter in her voice and I get the eerie sense that she's mocking me. 'Who is she?'

'She was found dead here at the rally Saturday night. Murdered.'

'Oh my goodness. Poor thing.' Her voice holds not a shred of empathy. 'But I don't know why you're asking me. Like I said, I don't know her.'

'She was seen coming out of this RV on Friday.'

'Oh, maybe she knows Grant.'

'Grant Butler?'

She nods.

'Is he here?'

'No, he's out.'

'I'll come back later. I'll give you a card.' I've already left a card and no one called me back.

Hailey comes up. 'Hey,' she says, and eyes Becky.

'Anything else?' Becky says to me with a smile that would keep the lights on in a blackout.

'No, I'll check back.'

When we walk away, Hailey says, 'You thought she was hot, didn't you?'

'She's good-looking. I never saw eyes that color.'

Hailey giggles. 'That's because they aren't real. She's wearing colored contacts. And that's a wig if I ever saw one.'

I laugh. 'I'm glad I've got you to point that out.'

'Hey, Uncle Samuel?' Her expression is all innocence.

'Yes.'

'There's a band here tonight I want to see,' she says.

'We're going out to dinner with Wendy, remember?' I say.

'We could come afterwards,' she says.

'Not tonight. We're not going to spend all our time here.'

'You don't have to babysit me. I can see the band by myself and get a ride home with that guy Steve. He came by while I was watching the tattoo artist. He said he'd be glad to take me home after he gets off work.'

I'm not about to say yes, and she's not going to like my reason. 'You're not old enough to be here by yourself,' I say. 'And Steve is not exactly what you call reliable.'

She stops walking and puts her hands on her hips. 'How about that friend of yours, the guy who repairs cycles. One of those guys could take me home.'

'They'll be long gone before the music is done. They put in long hours working.'

She looks outraged. 'That means I'm stuck at your house with nothing to do,' she says.

I feel my first tickle of irritation. She has no way of entertaining herself? Maybe all teenagers are like this. 'Let's talk about it after dinner,' I say. I hope I have a chance to quiz Wendy about how to handle a situation like this.

On the way home, we stop back by headquarters so I can make sure everybody has gone home.

'You just lock up at night? No one is on duty?' Hailey asks as we drive away.

'We don't have enough manpower to have somebody on duty all the time, but the police line goes directly to my cell phone after hours.'

SIXTEEN

Wendy is waiting for us at my house. She takes Hailey under her wing right away, promising that they'll go to an outlet mall right away. 'And one day we can get manicures and pedicures. My niece is on vacation with her parents, but they'll be back soon. Then the three of us can do something together.'

I'd forgotten about her niece. Tammy is the same age as Hailey. She's as sulky as Hailey was yesterday, and always having trouble with her folks.

The local Mexican café, The Ranchero, has decent food, but more important it has a festive atmosphere. Set back from the road, surrounded by a cactus garden, it's painted in bright colors – red, green, blue, and yellow. Hailey's eyes light up when she sees it.

Tonight the parking lot is full of motorcycles. Inside, it's crowded with bikers standing out on the porch waiting to get in. I'm worried we'll never get seated but Wendy says, 'Lucky for you I called this morning and made a reservation. Momo said he'd fit us in.'

A doe-eyed teenager dressed in a colorful Mexican skirt and lacy white blouse greets us at the door. She and Hailey eye each other as she hustles us to our table. She looks frantic, and flings our menus to us so fast that I don't have time to register that this must be Sophie, the girl that Steve said scratched him.

'She's cute,' I say to Hailey, thinking they may be the right age to be friendly.

'Whatever,' she says, shrugging.

Shortly, the proprietor, Guillermo 'Momo' Rodriguez, stops by the table to say hello. He confirms that the hostess is his daughter. 'That's Sophie. She's not happy to be working tonight, but the regular girl is out sick.'

He makes a fuss over Hailey, telling her she's beautiful, and brings her a Shirley Temple on the house.

After he leaves, she says, 'I'd rather have the real thing.'

Wendy says, 'Do your folks let you drink alcohol?'

'No. They treat me like a baby.'

I pick up my menu. 'We can discuss the merits of sixteen-year-olds drinking alcohol and the sins of parents after we order. Right now, I'm starving.' To my surprise, Hailey grins.

As soon as we've ordered our food, Hailey says, 'Can I ask you some questions about the woman who got murdered?'

Wendy says, 'Do we really need to do that?'

'I'll answer a few questions,' I say. 'As long as they aren't too graphic.'

Hailey props herself on her arms and leans forward. 'Who was she?'

'A business owner here in town. She and her husband own the Quick Stop. It's a little convenience store.'

'How was she killed?'

I pause. This threatens to get to the graphic part. 'With a knife.'

She shudders. 'Was it gory?'

'Hailey!' Wendy says.

'I'm not going into details,' I say.

She rolls her eyes. 'Does she have kids?'

'Two. A boy twelve and a girl ten.'

'Oh, wow. That's so sad.' She sits back, her expression thoughtful. She's only a little older than Amber's kids and no matter how angry she is with her parents, she would be devastated if her mamma was killed.

She takes a sip of her cranberry-colored drink, her eyes unfocused. Then she says, 'What kind of knife?'

'We haven't found the weapon.'

'Why do you think she was killed? Do you think it's a drug war or something?'

I can't help laughing. 'Look, this is a small town. I think drug wars are more likely in cities.'

'Then why do you think she was killed?'

Wendy is sipping her wine, looking around the room as if she doesn't want any part of this discussion.

'Why do you want to know all this?'

She shrugs. 'I don't know. I like to watch *CSI* and I think I might like to do something like that.'

'You know that show is unrealistic, don't you?'

'No it isn't. Cops in cities have all those techniques for figuring out crimes.'

'We have them too, but most of them take a long time to process. A lot longer than an hour-long TV show. For example, did you know that bullet comparison by the state takes almost a year?'

Her mouth falls open. 'That can't be right. On TV they do it right away.'

I nod. 'Like I said, TV gets it wrong. It isn't that it's so hard to do, or takes so long, but that they have so much work that there's always a backup. I'll let you in on a secret, though. There are little tricks that small-town guys like me can use to make a rough comparison.' Even Wendy looks interested now.

'Like what? Can you show me?'

I tell her about the trick with shooting the gun into cotton batting and inspecting the bullet under a microscope or magnifying glass. 'It isn't good enough to stand up in court, but it can at least tell you if you're in the ballpark. And no, I can't show you. But you could read about it online if you wanted to.'

'It seems to me that if you know why she was killed, you might find who did it.'

'That's a good point. It works that way sometimes.'

'So how would you figure out why?'

I think about it for a minute. I want to give her a serious answer. 'Motives are tricky. Usually it works the other way. You don't know for sure why until you find out who did it. Meanwhile, you get little hints here and there about why somebody might be a target, but in this case, it's hard to say. Amber was a young woman, popular, hard-working, and her husband is disabled so she had extra burdens and everyone respected that. She didn't seem a likely target at all.'

Hailey screws up her eyes, thinking. 'Maybe she was having an affair with a married man and the wife found out.'

'That's pretty dramatic, but it's always possible.' In fact, after what the medical examiner said, I wonder if Hailey is uncomfortably close to the truth.

'Or her husband is just pretending to be disabled and he found out she was having an affair and he killed her.'

'That would make a good TV plot,' I say.

'What does that woman Becky have to do with anything?' she asks with a sly smile.

'Who's Becky?' Wendy asks.

Hailey giggles. 'She's this hot lady that Uncle Samuel went to see.'

Wendy laughs. And I'm happy that at that moment the food comes.

We've just taken a few bites when there's a loud rumble of thunder and a flash of lightning and we hear the heavens open up outside and smell the crisp scent of ozone in the air. Murmurs around the restaurant tell me everyone is as glad as I am for the rain. It was too hot today, and maybe a shower will cool the air. I don't envy people camped out by the lake tonight, though.

'Hailey,' Wendy says, 'Samuel probably has some work to do on this case so we should entertain ourselves. How about if we go to the outlet mall near San Antonio tomorrow?'

'I'd rather go back to the motorcycle rally,' Hailey says. 'We haven't had a chance to see any action.' There's a whine in her voice.

'What action are you hoping to see?' I ask.

She shrugs. 'I guess some trick riding, and different kinds of motorcycles. Different people.'

'The rally is on all week, so we'll be getting back there.'

'I don't have any money, so going to the mall won't be that much fun.'

'I can lend you some money,' I say.

'I can't pay you back, though.'

'I'll find some things around the house for you to do to earn enough to pay me back.'

Her eyes narrow. 'Like what?'

'I don't know. Paint the house. Scrub my cows. Dredge the tank. Hunt down some water moccasins that have been hanging out there. You can use a shotgun, can't you?'

Her eyes have been growing bigger as I talk, but all of a sudden, she gets it and starts laughing. 'I thought you were serious!'

'What are you good at? Which, by the way, isn't the same as asking what you like to do.'

She shrugs, frowning. 'I guess I can wash dishes.'

'Can you sweep? My front porch and my kitchen could use a good sweep.' That isn't true. I have a woman who comes in to clean every two weeks, but I've got to think of something for Hailey to do.

'I guess.'

'Can you cook?'

She brightens. 'I can make spaghetti.'

'Good. Then that settles it. I'll lend you some cash and you can go to the mall and you can work off the money you owe me. We can go back to the rally later in the week. There's plenty of time.'

'The two of us will have fun,' Wendy says. 'I'll pick you up tomorrow at ten o'clock. Is that too early?'

'I guess not.'

By the time we're done eating, Sophie is nowhere in sight. On the way out I ask Momo if Sophie is around. 'I need a word with her.'

He says she's already gone home, so I'll have to question her another time.

'Why did you want to talk to Sophie?' Hailey asks.

'Just checking something out.'

'Something about the murder?' She's on the alert.

'Hailey, don't pester Samuel,' Wendy says.

'It's OK. You're right,' I say to Hailey. 'She had a disagreement with somebody and I want to find out what it was about.' She doesn't need to know specifics, but it doesn't hurt for her to get some sense of what an investigation entails.

The rainstorm is over. I had hoped it would bring cooler air, but all it has done is make the air muggy. Hailey and Wendy complain that their hair will be frizzy tomorrow. I file that under things I didn't know anybody had to worry about.

When we get home, Hailey plunks down in front of the TV and Wendy and I go into the kitchen to drink a cup of coffee. She puts her hand on the table and I cover it with mine. Normally we'd be headed for the bedroom, but with Hailey here that's not in the cards. We'll have to change our habits for now.

'What do you think?' she whispers, nodding toward the living room.

'She doesn't seem able to entertain herself.'

Wendy laughs quietly. 'Like every other kid her age. Hormones raging, feeling restless and powerless. It's a tough time.'

'I have to figure out a way to have her meet some kids.'

'Tammy will be home in a couple of days. We'll get them together.'

Wendy doesn't stay long. She has a thirty-minute drive to get home. I walk her out to the car, Dusty at my side. We stand by the car for a while, arms around each other, making small talk.

When I go back inside, I tell Hailey I'm going to walk Dusty. 'You want to come along?'

She looks at me like I've suggested she might want to walk to Houston. 'No.' Seeing my raised eyebrows, she says, 'No, thank you.'

'That's all right. I won't be gone long. Why don't you call your folks while I'm out? That way I don't have to listen to you tell them how mean I am.'

'How you made me go to the motorcycle rally?' She raises an eyebrow.

'Uh, maybe you don't want to mention that.'

'Grounds for blackmail,' she says.

'Oh great. I have a budding criminal on my hands.'

She smirks. 'I'll call my folks tomorrow. I don't have to call them every day.'

Her phone rings and when she sees who it is, her face lights up. I imagine whoever is calling is one of the people her folks want out of her life. But at least she's here instead of there. She wiggles her fingers at me and says, 'See you in the morning,' and runs to her room, closing out me and Dusty, who comes away looking dejected.

'Never mind,' I say. 'We'll go for a walk.'

On the walk, I put in a call to Tom and Vicki. 'I'm still alive,' I say. 'In fact, we had a good day.' I describe the goats and the dinner. But I leave off the part where she got a phone call that lit up her face.

'So far so good,' Tom says. He sounds cautious. 'Are you sure everything's all right?'

'She was a little balky at first, but I think we're going to get along. There is one thing I should mention. We had a little excitement in town. A woman was killed here Saturday night and I've got some work to do. Hailey asked me a lot of questions, and I tried to be honest with her without telling her too much. She didn't seem to be upset, but I wanted you to know in case she says anything.'

'I doubt it will bother her,' Vicki says. 'She's got nerves of steel.'

'Anyway, I'm going to be busy tomorrow, so Wendy is taking Hailey to the big outlet mall on the highway to San Antonio.'

'She ought to love that, but do you think Wendy can handle her?'

'Better than I can. She raised two daughters.'

He sighs. 'She might not have one quite like Hailey.' His tone is dark. 'I hate to say this, but I want to warn you. She can be sneaky. She'll act all cooperative and pleasant and the next thing you know, she's found some way to get into trouble.'

'I don't know how much trouble she can get into around here.' Is that true? I hope so.

'I told you she's been sneaking out with this guy who's a lot older. I think he's around twenty-five. She's obsessed with him.'

'With that gap in age, he's looking at legal problems. Has he been in trouble with the law?'

'I had him checked out and no, he hasn't, but he's too old! She's a teenager!'

'Tom, he's there, and Hailey is here. I'll keep an eye on her. You need to take this time to relax.'

'You don't know how much we appreciate this. Vicki was ready to have a nervous breakdown. You're right. We just need time to take a deep breath.'

As I click off, without warning, the rain starts in again and Dusty and I have to run the last half-block and we still get drenched.

SEVENTEEN

When I go down to check on my cows the next morning, I spend some time hanging out at the fence watching them and thinking about what I have to do to investigate Amber's murder. The autopsy revealed that Amber had recently had sexual relations. Was it a one-time thing or was she seeing someone? It stands to reason she might be messing around if her husband is too laid up to perform in bed. Did whoever killed her do it out of jealousy, or maybe out of anger if she threatened to break it off?

Ben Holman's name has been nagging me. The email I found in the Johnson's computer, from Amber, saying she was meeting someone and 'can't wait', was sent to someone with an address that had 'Honcho' and 'Ben' in it. The Ben part is obvious, and Honcho could be taken from the first two letters of Holman's last name. It's possible that he was the one who was seeing Amber.

But Amber had a lot on her plate. If she was having an affair, she was stretching her time. I need to look at other possibilities. There's the matter of the Patels wanting to open a rival store. As long as Amber was alive, she was a problem. It's a long-shot, but I can't ignore it.

There's something else bothering me. When I was looking at Amber's computer, I got a sense that her son, Jimmy, was hiding something. When I asked him if his daddy used the computer, he was oddly secretive. Whatever they're hiding may have nothing to do with Amber's death, but I'd like to know what it is.

When I get back to the house, Loretta has left muffins along with a note on my kitchen table: 'I thought your niece might like some of these.' Hailey might like them, but I do too, and I eat a couple with coffee and eggs.

I don't want to be a nag, but I'd like for Hailey to be ready when Wendy arrives to take her to the mall. At 9:15, I steel myself and knock on Hailey's door. Her hair is tousled and she looks younger than her sixteen years. In the background her room looks like a tornado hit it. How is that possible? She's only been here a couple of days. 'What time is it?' she asks.

'Nine-fifteen. Wendy will be here soon.'

'Oh, I didn't get to sleep until two o'clock.' She yawns and stretches.

Was she on the phone that long? 'You want breakfast?'

She makes a face. 'Just orange juice.' She pads out into the kitchen.

I pour her a glass of juice. 'My friend Loretta made some fresh muffins this morning.' I put one on a plate for her. She sits down and takes a bite.

'Yum. These are good. You said she made them this morning? What time does she get up?'

'Earlier than anybody else I know.'

Orange juice in hand, she goes to her room to get dressed.

Wendy arrives a few minutes later. She sits down to have coffee with me. 'It's going to be even hotter today,' she says. 'Humidity must be nearly one hundred percent.'

Hailey is just coming out of her room. 'I know,' she says. 'Look at my hair!'

'Looks fine to me,' I say, and they exchange eye-rolls. There's something here I'm not privy to.

They don't seem inclined to hurry. They sit and discuss what stores they want to visit. I'm impatient for them to leave so I can get to work.

'How much money do you think you'll need?' I ask Hailey.

'I don't know. A thousand dollars?' She flashes an innocent look.

'A hundred,' Wendy says. 'It's an outlet mall. You can find some deals.'

I give Hailey the money and tell her I'll make a list of chores. 'I'll pay you ten dollars an hour.'

'That's not enough,' Wendy says. 'That's what babysitters make.'

We compromise on $15, which seems like a lot to me. Not that I mind paying that. I want to be fair, but not throw money at her like she's a princess.

*   *   *

As soon as they're gone, I head for the rally. I park near the front
and go straight to the security facility. I tie Dusty up outside so
he won't wander. Luke Harriman, the rally organizer, is in the
office. It's the first time I've seen him since Amber's body was
found. He comes around the front of his desk to shake my hand.
'I heard about the local woman who was killed. They say she and
her husband used to ride with the Rough Roaders. Anything new
on what happened to her?'

'No. And we don't have much to go on. The DPS will likely
step in since it took place on state property. Meanwhile, I'm
looking into it.'

He scratches his head. 'If I can be of any help, let me know. I
wasn't here in the office the other night when it happened. The
guy who was here was just helping out and didn't know what
the protocol was, so he told the guys who found the body to call
you. I hope he did the right thing.'

'He did.'

'What brings you here?'

'I have a question for you. You know a guy by the name of
Grant Butler?'

A shadow crosses his face. 'Yeah.'

'What do you know about him?'

'Not much. How did you come to get hooked up with him?'

I tell him I saw Amber coming out of his RV the night before
she was killed.

'Really? Have you talked to him?'

'I went by his RV, but he wasn't there. A woman was there,
though.'

'So you got a look at Becky?' He grins. 'She's a piece of work.'

'What do you mean?'

'She's damned good-looking and she knows it. Comes on all
honey and sweetness, but I've heard that if you get on the wrong
side of her, she's got a mean streak. And she has a mouth on her.
She and Butler come to these motorcycle events all around
the state. I've seen them before. Rumor has it that he deals drugs
out of that RV.'

'Really? Is it a problem?' I wonder if Amber was having trouble
getting medication for Mike and might have been there to buy
something.

'No one has ever caught him at it, and we haven't had any complaints.' He huffs a laugh. 'Not that anybody has tried too hard to catch him, you understand. It's kind of a low-yield problem. If we caught him with drugs, he'd probably get off because he doesn't have a record. But even if he did get convicted, somebody would just take his place. It's a situation we keep an eye on, but as long as they stay low profile and don't create trouble, we put up with it.'

I can sort of see that. He's right. The rallies are temporary, and by the time somebody nailed down that he was actually dealing drugs, he'd be gone.

'Ever had any trouble from him?'

His eyes shift past me. 'No, never.'

I stand up. 'If you hear anything that might have to do with our victim, Amber Johnson, I'd appreciate a call.'

I thank him for his time, but when I walk away I think about that shifty-eyed look when I asked if Butler had ever given him trouble. I'm not sure how much I trust Harriman. He's congenial, but maybe a little too congenial. I wouldn't find it surprising if he puts up with a little drug action because he gets a cut.

I head over to Grant Butler's RV, but just like yesterday there's no one around. I have plenty to do, so I'll come back later in the afternoon.

Maria has come in to work. I go over and grab an early lunch for us at Town Café and we eat at our desks while I tell her about my talk with Jack Cassidy and his wife. 'The Cassidys were good friends of the Johnsons. Jack Cassidy and Amber Johnson were particularly close.' I tell her about the emails between the two of them. 'And Friday afternoon Amber went to see them and she and Jack went for a walk.' I tell her that Steve Deverell had already told me he saw Amber with a man.

'I wonder how Jack's wife felt about that?'

'I wondered the same thing, but she seems to genuinely be sorry about Amber's death and I got no impression that she was jealous of her husband and Amber.'

I describe what they said about the accident that hurt Mike Johnson, and tell her that Amber and Mike were having money problems because the insurance company wouldn't cover the cost of Mike's surgery. 'Jack said Amber told him that Mike's always in pain. You'd think the doctor could give him something for it.'

Maria frowns and shakes her head. 'Not the way the federal government is about drugs these days. I had an uncle who was in a car accident and broke his leg and it didn't heal right. He couldn't have surgery because the insurance company wouldn't pay for it, because his doctor said he was fine. And the doctor didn't believe he was in pain so wouldn't prescribe drugs. They couldn't afford to sue the insurance company either.'

'Did he manage to get drugs?' I'm thinking about Amber's visit to Grant Butler's RV.

'Not my *tío*. He was not one to complain or do anything illegal. But my auntie said he suffered a lot.'

'There's one more thing. I don't know if you saw the autopsy report, but Amber Johnson had sex in the hours before she died. So how do I ask her husband if it was him she had sex with without letting him know that she'd had sex recently?'

Maria throws her paper plate into the garbage can. 'You don't. I mean, you have to tell him. It's possible they had an active sex life, even if he is disabled. Or maybe they had an arrangement that she could go elsewhere as long as she was discreet. We can't know unless we ask. And we can't ignore it either, because it's possible it had to do with her death. But there may be another way. If she has a close friend, she might have discussed it with her.'

'Good point. I met her best friend, Lisa Hedgepeth. I could ask her. Also, her sister is here, staying with Mike and the kids. Maybe Amber confided in her.'

I ask if Maria has had time to go through Amber's purse and to take a look at her phone and the computer files.

'The computer files were just spreadsheets and tax information for the store. And the purse, nothing different from what any woman would carry. But the phone did have a couple of text messages that might mean something. She was meeting someone Friday. A guy named Grant Butler.'

'Oh! I forgot to tell you about Grant Butler. Let me see the messages.'

Maria gets the phone. It's in a clear plastic bag, so we can read through it without touching it. The first text message, written last Thursday, says, 'Mr Butler, has Jack Cassidy been in touch with you?'

Butler replied, 'Yes, he has. When would you like to meet?'

Jack Cassidy didn't say anything about connecting Amber with Grant Butler.

They arranged to meet Friday afternoon. 'I saw her coming out of Grant Butler's RV Friday afternoon,' I tell Maria.

'Who is he?' she asks.

'I haven't met him yet, but the guy in charge of the rally says there are persistent rumors that Butler is selling drugs. I wonder if that's what Amber was there for?'

She nods. 'If Mike's doctor refused to prescribe medication, maybe she was buying them on the sly.'

'Let's get on over to Mike Johnson's and talk to Amber's sister, and afterwards we'll go out to the rally and tackle Grant Butler. Did you find out who the phone number I found in her car belongs to?'

'Someone named Ben Holman.'

Bingo. 'That's interesting.' I tell her that Ben Holman is the teacher Maureen Washington thought Amber was flirting with. 'We'll have to go see him after we get back from questioning the sister-in-law.'

We're at the door to Johnson's house when my cell phone buzzes. I ignore it and knock on the door.

Jimmy opens the door and we tell him we need to speak to his aunt.

'She's over at the funeral home picking out a casket.'

'You know when she'll be back?'

'She's only been gone a half-hour. I imagine it will be a while.'

We drive the three blocks to Landau's Funeral Home. It's in a one-story, cream-colored brick building that could be someone's house. It has a front porch where mourners who are there to view the deceased often hang out to talk. The front room is a soothing area with displays of photos of deceased loved ones. I know all this because it's where my wife Jeanne's funeral was held a few years ago. Since then, I always feel a little gloomy when I go into the place.

Belle, Earnest Landau's long-time assistant, greets us in the office. In general, you can't imagine a less likely person to work in a funeral home. She's easily irritated and has strong opinions about the way funerals ought to go. Before I buried my wife, I often wondered how the bereaved put up with her, but I found out when I was in the same position that it was comforting to have someone behave like a mother hen, guiding you to the best way to do things and protecting you from outsiders who might confuse you.

'Belle, is Amber Johnson's sister here?'

'She sure is. She's in Earnest's office. He's not here, but I set her down with some of our catalogs for selecting caskets. You want to talk to her? I'll tell her you're here.'

Belle gets her on the intercom and then says, 'Go on in. She's says she'll see you.' I know Belle didn't send us straight in, in case DeeDee was taking private time to grieve.

I introduce DeeDee to Maria and we sit down. I don't know where he gets them, but for his visitors Earnest has the most comfortable chairs I've ever sat in, armchairs with padding in muted colors.

'We need to talk to you about a delicate subject,' I say. 'Something we don't want to bring up with Mike if we can avoid it.'

'What's that?' She frowns and closes the catalog she was looking at.

'Did your sister ever talk to you about her marital relations with her husband?'

She blinks. 'You mean, like, sex?'

'Yes, ma'am.'

'We didn't really talk about things like that.' Her cheeks are getting pink.

'Then you wouldn't know if they were still having relations.'

'No, I do not. Why would you be asking that?'

'I'm sorry, but I have to ask. Do you know if your sister was having an affair?'

Her face is blazing. 'I . . . I don't know what to say. That's just not something we ever discussed. I mean, it's so personal. You think she was having an affair? And maybe somebody killed her because of it?'

'We're not sure. We're just covering all the bases.'

My phone buzzes again and I switch if off.

'Did she ever talk about anybody she had a problem with? Neighbors? Friends?'

'You know, Amber wasn't a complainer, but she did sometimes get irritated with Mike's situation. Not that she volunteered anything, but I asked her once and she said it could be a burden having to take care of the kids and the house and the store, and having to deal with the insurance company.'

'Do you know what Mike does with his time?'

She clears her throat. 'Well, that was the problem. She said she thought even if he had trouble getting around, he could help with the bookkeeping and bill-paying and what not, but he spent all his time on the computer.'

Now we're getting to the heart of the matter. I remember Jimmy acting funny about what was on the computer. 'I thought it was shared with the kids.'

'"Shared" is a loose term. I love Mike dearly, but he can be self-centered.'

'What does he do on the computer?'

She clamps her lips closed and her gaze is restless. She knows something she's not willing to say. I glance at Maria and we know to wait her out. 'I'm sorry, this is something I overheard. I swear I wasn't eavesdropping, but I heard Jimmy complaining because his dad plays poker on the computer.'

'You mean, for money?'

'I can't tell you that. I don't know anything about it. I just know I heard Jimmy say something to Mike, something like, "Yeah Daddy, you *need* the computer, but you just need it to play poker."'

Maria and I are on the way to the car when I remember I turned my phone off. I turn it back on and see that the two calls I got were from Wendy. Uh oh, I wonder if they had car trouble.

'Hold on,' I say to Maria, 'I need to call Wendy.'

Wendy picks up on the first ring. 'Samuel!' Her voice is frantic. 'Oh, thank God you called. I've lost Hailey.'

'What do you mean, lost her? Where are you?'

'At the motorcycle rally. I'm so stupid. The mall was a bust and she begged to stop back by the rally. I didn't see any harm in it. Oh, I can't believe this.'

'I'm coming right now. I'll call you from the car and you can tell me the details while I drive.' I try to keep my voice calm, although fear courses through me. Where has the girl gotten to?

I tell Maria what's happening. 'I'll run you by headquarters and then go meet Wendy.'

EIGHTEEN

As soon as I'm on my way to the rally, I call Wendy back. 'Tell me exactly what happened.'

'I didn't follow my instincts, that's what.' She sounds miserable. 'While we were at the mall, Hailey kept talking to someone on her phone. She seemed really secretive. I felt uneasy, but decided not to make a fuss. After we'd been there an hour, she said she was bored and wanted to go back to Jarrett Creek. She kept texting, and when we got close to town she begged to go back to the rally. Honestly, I didn't see how it could be a problem. I figured we wouldn't stay long. I was trying to entertain her.'

'I get it. And when you got to the rally?' I'm turning onto the road along the dam, so I'm almost there.

'When we got here, Hailey said she wanted to use the restroom, so we headed for the portables. I waited for her, and she never came back. I looked everywhere, thinking I'd missed her. It's really crowded today.'

'I'm pulling up now.'

I drive right up to the entrance, where two men are directing people to parking areas. They see that I'm in a squad car and ask how they can help me. 'I need to park right out here,' I say. 'I got word that a girl is missing.'

They point out an area behind one of the booths where I can pull in.

'Do you have a way to contact security?' I ask when I get back to them.

They have a walkie-talkie and they call Luke Harriman, who says he'll notify security. Harriman and two guards appear within minutes.

'My nephew's daughter is here and has gotten separated from our friend. She's sixteen.'

The head of security is a tall, wiry guy with a bald head covered by a baseball cap that advertises a feed store in Lubbock. 'That's Hailey, right?' he says. 'I talked to your friend Wendy. We've got the word out. She can't have gone far.'

I've heard parents say they are torn between being furious and being terrified when a kid goes missing, and now I know what that means. I'm worried that she's in trouble, and if she isn't, there's no telling how mad I'll be.

Harriman contacts the music booth and tells them to broadcast an appeal to help find her.

I text Wendy to let her know I'm here and she comes right away. She's perspiring, sweat beading her forehead. Her face is white. 'I feel like such an idiot.'

'Let's get you something to drink,' I say.

'No. We need to be looking for her. Suppose somebody—'

'Stop,' I say. 'Security is looking for her and they're putting out a call. It won't do any good for us to start running around here. First, we'll get some water.' I steer her to one of the soft drink booths. The area is a lot more crowded than it was yesterday, more vehicles set up with folding chairs and little tables outside.

We get bottles of water and stand in the shade of the booth. 'From the way you described it, she may have set up a meeting with somebody. I'm guessing her boyfriend might have come into town. Have you remembered anything else about what she was doing? Did you say anything on the phone that you remember? Anything she said that seemed odd?'

'Just that when I asked who she was texting, she clammed up. Said "nobody." But my younger daughter was always trouble, and I recognized that guilty look. You're right. I'll bet she was making arrangements to meet someone. She got antsy when we were close to town, and as soon as I agreed to take her to the rally, she seemed to settle down.' She sighs. 'It was stupid of me not to get what she was up to.'

'You aren't stupid. You got conned. Her parents warned me she might do something like this, and I should have warned you. We'll find her.'

'Do you have her cell number?'

I take off my hat and scratch my head. 'No. It never occurred to me that I'd need it. I'll call her mom.' I can't believe I didn't think to get it before.

I phone Vicki and, although I hate to do it, I lie to her. I tell her I'm meeting Hailey and that I'm going to be a few minutes late and I need to call her. It won't do any good to scare her.

'Is she doing OK? Not giving you too much trouble?'

'She's fine. Let me call you later and we can talk.'

When she hangs up, I call Hailey's number. It goes to voicemail. I leave her a message to call me and I click off. 'Not answering,' I say to Wendy.

'Oh my God. What are we going to do?' Her voice is a wail.

'Take me to where you last saw her.'

We walk to the porta-potties. She points to the one Hailey was in. 'I wasn't watching closely because I expected her to come to me. I told her I'd wait for her right here.'

'You know, it's possible she got turned around and went in the wrong direction.'

'I suppose.'

I don't believe it any more than she does. 'Let's talk to Walter Dunn. We need more people looking for her, and he can round up bodies faster than I can.'

Walter is hard at work on a huge Harley, its owner standing by wringing his hands as if it's a family member in surgery.

'I hate to interrupt but I've got a bad situation.'

Walter looks up. 'Tell me. I'm almost done with this.'

I give him the short version. I figured the Harley owner would be annoyed to have Walter's attention taken, but he says, 'Teenage kids! Damn, I've got a couple myself. They ought to be shipped off to an island and raised there until their hormones settle down and they can behave themselves in civilized society.' Then he catches himself and looks at me. 'I'm sorry, I didn't mean to make light of your situation. You think she's in danger?'

I tell him I don't know what to think.

Walter makes a couple of turns with the wrench, pats the side of the Harley and stands up. 'That ought to fix you up.'

'You're a life-saver, Walt.'

Walter turns to me. 'Maybe we can get bikers out to search the area and see if we can find her.'

I look at the rows of vehicles and suddenly I'm really nervous. What if she got lured into an RV and she's in trouble? 'That would be a start. If I have to I'll knock on every RV door to search for her.'

Walter stands with his hands on his hips, head swiveling up and down the rows of vehicles. 'You have a picture of her?'

I don't. It never occurred to me that I might need one. But Wendy says, 'I took a selfie of the two of us at the mall.' She whips out her phone and brings up the photo.

'Send it to all of us,' Walter says. 'I'll scare up some people to ride up and down looking for her.'

We hear a squawk from a PA system. 'Ladies and gentlemen, we have a lost young lady. We'd appreciate help finding her.' He gives the description and says for anybody who has information to come to the office or the music stand. He also gives out my phone number.

I try Hailey's number again, but it still goes to voicemail. I leave another message, stronger. 'I don't appreciate you running off. You need to call me right now.'

I hear a bunch of motorcycles being gunned and Walter and four other men and two women ride off in opposite directions. They'll be able to cover a lot more territory than we would on foot.

My cell phone pings and I grab for it, but it's Maria.

'You want me to come over there?'

My first impulse is to say no, but Maria has a way of seeing a situation in such a way that sometimes surprises me. 'That would be good. I'd appreciate it.'

'See you in a minute, boss.'

'What have you done with Dusty?'

'He's with me. I'll take him by your place.'

Wendy and I scout the shoreline, hoping maybe Hailey wandered off down that way. We come across a couple of women sunbathing topless and I have to remind them that there are families here and that there's a law against public exposure. Their response is predictable. Police interference with people having a good time, and all that.

We're on our way back up to the main area when I get another call from Maria. 'Found her.'

'What? Where?'

'She doesn't know I've seen her. I drove by your house, planning to take Dusty in, and I spotted her sitting outside in a car with a guy.'

'Keep her there. I'll be there in a minute.'

I tell Wendy, and ask her to stay and notify Walter and the security people that Hailey has been found. 'I need to get on home.'

'Samuel?'

'What?' I can tell my question is sharp.

She blinks. 'Don't be too hard on her.'

'We'll see.'

NINETEEN

A faded blue Chevrolet Lumina is sitting in front of my house, engine idling. Maria is standing at the driver's side window, hands on her hips. My guess is the driver started up the car and was ready to leave and Maria is stalling him.

I walk to the passenger side. Hailey is sitting in 'pouting' position, arms folded tight across her chest, eyes front. I try to open the door, but it's locked. I tap on the window. Hailey barely moves her head, but she can see me. I motion for her to get out of the car. She shakes her head.

The driver's side door explodes open and Maria yells, 'Whoa!' and jumps back. A rangy guy with a skimpy goatee and longish, pale brown hair lunges out of the Chevy. In Maria's car, Dusty starts barking sharply. The window is down and I'm afraid he'll jump out.

'Dusty, stay!' I yell, hoping for once he'll actually do it.

'Sir, please get back in your car,' Maria says. I've always admired that such a commanding voice can come from such a small woman.

'What if I don't? You going to arrest me? I haven't done a damn thing wrong.'

'I'm asking you to get back in the car. You're being confrontational.'

'You started it. All I'm trying to do is get out of this hick town.'

'Sir, I'm not going to ask you again.'

Dusty's barking is increasingly frantic and I tell him once again to stay put.

I stride around to join Maria. 'We can arrest you if you'd like, but it's better if you get back in the car,' I say.

'Arrest me for what?'

'Trust me, I'll think of something,' Maria says.

The guy looks from her to me and decides not to push it. I wouldn't either when she has that stone-cold look on her face.

As he gets back in the car, taking his time, he turns to whisper to Hailey. She shakes her head.

His window is open, so I speak across him to Hailey. 'Hailey, I'd like you to get out of the car and come into the house.'

'You can't make me.'

'I'm asking you.'

'I'm going with him,' she says.

'That's not going to happen,' I say. 'Sir, can I see your driver's license and registration?'

'What for? I wasn't driving. We're sitting here talking. This is police harassment.'

I repeat my request, hoping that this beat-up old car won't have the proper registration or his license will be expired. No such luck. They're both in order.

'Lyle Fargo. Twenty-four years of age. From Austin, Texas,' I read off. 'Lyle, what would you be doing in the car with a sixteen-year-old girl?'

Neither he nor Hailey face me. Normally I would wonder if drugs were involved in their behavior, but even though Lyle's clothes are scruffy, he doesn't have that druggy look. 'There's no law against that.'

'Actually there is, especially if you're taking her someplace without her parents' say-so.'

'He's my boyfriend,' Hailey yells. 'He came to take me back to Austin. I'm old enough to decide for myself, and I'm going with him.'

'No, you aren't old enough,' I say. 'Not legally. I get to say whether you go or not, and I'm saying no.'

'You're not my daddy!'

'Either of you know what *in loco parentis* means?'

'Crazy parents?' Lyle asks. He's serious.

'It means that in the absence of a minor's parents, they can designate a substitute. And I'm the substitute. As such, I get to make decisions about Hailey's welfare. I don't deem it good for her or any teenage girl to be going off with a man eight years older.'

'Why are you being so mean?' she wails.

'Get out of the car and let's talk, and I'll tell you why.'

'I'm not getting out.'

I can't help wondering what led to this. Hailey didn't seem miserable; in fact, she seemed fine.

I crouch down next to the car so that I can be eye level with the two of them and speak directly to Hailey. 'I'm disappointed,' I say. 'I thought you were having a good time. I like having you here. Did Wendy upset you?'

No reply.

'I'm surprised if she did. She's usually a lot of fun. She'll be sorry to hear that she upset you.'

'She didn't upset me.' Her voice is smaller.

'Can you get out of the car and talk to me? I feel like a fool hunkered down here.' To emphasize it, a car drives by. It's Jolene Ramsey. She makes no secret of getting an eyeful. She'll be calling Loretta and everybody else she knows as soon as she gets home to say that there's an incident going on in front of the police chief's house.

'Oh, all right.' She puts her hand on the door handle and then hesitates. 'You're not going anywhere, right?' she says to Lyle.

'I'm staying right here, honey.'

Maria has retreated to her car, where she's leaning against its door, petting Dusty to keep him quiet. But she's totally tuned in.

Hailey opens the door and climbs out, but stands right next to the car as if she's afraid I'm going to grab her and carry her into the house.

I approach her like I would a scared dog. 'Tell me what brought this on,' I say. 'Was I unkind to you?'

'No, it has nothing to do with you. Lyle and I are in love and we want to be together.'

'If that's the case, how come you didn't bring him to meet me? Why sneak around?'

She chews her lip and won't look at me. 'Because I knew you wouldn't let me go with him.'

'Why do you think that is?'

'Because everybody thinks that just because I'm sixteen I'm still a child. I'm old enough to make my own decisions.'

'You have to admit, an eight-year gap between your ages is significant.'

'Not if you're in love.' She meets my gaze with a glare.

'Have you introduced him to your folks?'

'No.'

'Why not?'

Lyle leans over and rolls down the window. 'Babe, you coming? I need to get back. I've got to go to work tonight.'

'What kind of work do you do?' I ask.

'Why do you want to know?'

I splay my hands out. 'I swear, you two are awfully touchy for people who think you're doing the right thing. I was asking out of curiosity.'

'I work at an industrial park.'

'I see. Lyle, can you give us another minute here?'

'Five minutes.' There's a warning note in his voice. He rolls the window back up.

'Sounds like he likes to call the shots,' I say.

'He's smart,' she says.

'So are you. Yesterday, when you were asking questions about the murder, you were thinking clearly. You noticed details that a lot of people would miss.'

She shrugs.

'Now, you want to tell me what brought this on? I can take it. Tell me if I hurt your feelings or didn't treat you right.'

Her cheeks are bright pink. 'I told you, it wasn't you. I like you.' She almost whispers the last part.

'Did Lyle call you or did you call him?'

'He told me he missed me and wanted me to come back to Austin.'

'And you were planning to skip out without even saying goodbye?'

She's looking at the ground. She shrugs.

'Where were you planning to stay when you got to Austin? With him?'

She bites her lower lip. 'I guess.'

'Do you think your folks would be comfortable with that?'

Her lip curls. 'Them? I know they wouldn't.'

'Why not?'

'Because they want to control me.' She tosses her head. 'They treat me like a child.'

'They do that because they worry about the choices you're making,' I say. 'You said you hadn't introduced Lyle to them. They probably think you're hiding something.'

'I'm not. They wouldn't think he's good enough for me.'

'Is he?'

She swallows. 'Yes. He's great. He's so good to me.'

I smile. 'I guess that's a plus on his side. But let me ask you, Hailey, do you think a man who really cares about you would want to separate you from your folks? Would you want to run off and scare people who don't know where you are? Isn't that wanting to control you in his own way?'

She takes a breath. 'Not really.'

'What do you think he'll do if you tell him you're going to stick around here for a few more days?'

'But I don't want to. I want to be with him.' She's got her hands on her hips, which oddly makes her look more like a child than a woman.

'But still, how do you think he'll react? Will he be mad? Will he find another girlfriend? Or will he be waiting for you when you get back to Austin?'

'Of course he'll wait for me! He loves me.'

'Then you don't have any reason to be nervous being away from him for a few days.' She starts to speak, but I hold up a hand to stop her. 'Listen, it's a good test of whether you care for each other. If you do, then being away will give you a chance to consider what you appreciate about each other, and to anticipate getting back together. But if not, you might realize your relationship isn't as good as you thought it was. Either way, a few days won't hurt.'

'We don't need time apart to know we love each other.'

'Maybe. Hailey, I can force the issue and make you stay here, but I'd like you to show your maturity by making the decision to stay for yourself.'

The window goes down again. 'Hailey, I'm not kidding. Get in the car and let's go.'

'What are you going to do with all your clothes?' I say. 'Are you going to leave them here? I hope you don't expect me to pack them up and bring them to you.'

She looks panicky. In the rush to go off with this man who she supposedly loves, she has completely forgotten the details.

'Lyle, I have to get my stuff.'

'What stuff?'

'My suitcase. My clothes.' She looks from Lyle to me. She's in a dilemma. She wants to grow up, and wants to do it right now. She doesn't want to wait around. But she isn't stupid.

'Hailey, Lyle will be waiting for you when you get back to Austin. And if he isn't there, then he wasn't the man you thought he was.'

She looks at Lyle. 'Samuel won't let me come with you,' she says. Her voice is trembling.

'Your choice,' he says. His voice has hardened.

'Lyle . . .' She draws his name out in a wail.

He rolls the window up and revs the engine.

I have a feeling it's best to keep my mouth shut. I can see the war on her face.

Lyle gives her one more long look and eases away from the curb. He's moving so slowly that I'm sure he's hoping she'll run after him and jump into the car.

At that moment the cavalry arrives in the form of Wendy. She gets out of her car, and Dusty has had enough. He leaps out of the window and joins us, as usual prancing with joy that he's with his people. When he leaps up on Hailey, she says, 'Down, Dusty,' but there's no heart in it.

Wendy looks to me for a signal of how to approach Hailey. But before I can say anything, Hailey makes a break for it and runs up the steps to the house. She's crying. I may have won this battle, but it doesn't feel like a win.

I tell Wendy how it went, and she says it's probably better if she goes home and gives me time to mend bridges with Hailey.

'You're right.' I fold her in a hug. 'I don't want you to feel guilty. This was fireworks waiting to go off. Tom warned me and I didn't take it seriously enough.'

'I should have known better.'

'That was my job, not yours. I'll call you tonight.'

TWENTY

I t seems impossible that it's only four o'clock. I don't want to go to headquarters and leave Hailey alone, so Maria and I sit down at my kitchen table to talk about what we heard from Amber's sister earlier and what to do next.

'Playing poker,' Maria says. 'Do you suppose he's addicted to gambling online? Maybe that's where some of their financial problems come from.'

'Or maybe he's trying to beat the odds to take the pressure off their money situation. Either way, we're going to have to ask him.'

We look at each other. We don't want to wait around, but we can't both go. 'I'd like to volunteer to talk to him, but something tells me he'd be more willing to talk to you,' she says. 'I can stay here and call you if I need you.'

I don't want to ask my deputy to babysit, but I feel the pressure of investigating Amber's murder, and I'm not comfortable leaving Hailey alone. I want to go talk to Mike, and the only other solution I can think of is to take Hailey with me. Somehow, I can't picture that being a possibility. But then it strikes me that this is exactly the thing that makes her think people are treating her like a child. If she were an upset adult, I would go do what I needed to do and leave a note.

'We are both going,' I say. And I tell Maria my thinking.

I write a note to Hailey that says: 'Gone to question someone in the case. Back in an hour. Call me if you need me.' But I do leave a babysitter of sorts. I decide to leave Dusty. I add to the note: 'Please don't let Dusty out. He tends to wander.'

Outside, Maria says, 'I'm serious. I think it's best if you talk to him alone. He's a guy who might be finding out his wife was having an affair. He's not going to want to admit it in front of me.' She says she's going back to the office.

'Wait . . .' I say. 'I have an idea. Tell me if you think it's a bad idea. Suppose Hailey comes to your self-defense class tonight?'

She nods. 'That could work. If she's OK with it.'

'I think she would be.'

'You know where it is, and it starts at six-thirty. Bring her.'

After what happened this afternoon, it seems like days since I talked to Amber's sister, DeeDee, instead of this morning. She answers the door and when she sees me she flinches.

'I need to have a talk with Mike,' I say.

I follow her inside and she trudges down the hall to Mike's bedroom door. From behind, she looks like someone headed for the doghouse.

It takes several minutes for Johnson to come out, walking slowly, with a cane. 'What is it?' he says, without preamble.

'Can we go somewhere private?'

He glares at me, but says, 'We can go in the kitchen.' I don't know why he would be annoyed with me, but people have strange reactions when they're the victim of a violent crime. As a cop, I represent the failure of the law to keep people safe.

In the kitchen, Mike sits down heavily at the kitchen table, just big enough for four people. It still contains papers, but they are in neat stacks now, so it looks like he's made progress.

I sit down across from him. 'Mike, I've got some extra questions and some things to tell you.'

'I can't sit here too long,' he says.

'I understand. First, I need to ask you what you're taking for your pain.'

'Why is . . . oh hell, you mean, am I a drug addict? Am I taking opiates? You honestly think I could be? If I was, why would I still be in pain?'

'Have you asked your doctor for help with the pain?'

'What does this have to do with Amber getting killed?'

'Mike, I'm trying to figure that out. It occurred to me that if you were hooked on drugs and she was getting them for you, it might put her in danger.'

'Are you serious?' His face is contorted with fury. 'Goddammit, you have no right to come in here and accuse me of having something to do with my wife's death. I would never do anything to put her in danger.'

'Have you been back to the doctor to get some relief?'

'No, I haven't. What's the point? The doctor says I need surgery and insurance won't pay for it. And the government has gotten so hard about doctors giving pain medication that I got tired of begging for it. So I put up with the pain.'

'I'm really sorry,' I say. I know from when my knee was damaged a few years ago how pain can annoy you and eventually drag you down. 'Have you tried getting a second opinion?'

'That's what we were trying to set up just before Amber was killed. I need to get another opinion because the doctor I saw said the surgery could leave me paralyzed. At least I can get around now. Is that all you wanted to ask?'

I wish it were. The next part is going to be tougher. 'Mike, there's no way around this question. How was your personal life with Amber?'

He squints at me. 'You mean, like . . . what?'

'Like sex.'

His mouth drops open and his eyes flash. 'I don't know what business that is of yours.'

'I need to know if you and Amber had sexual relations the day she was killed.'

He's utterly still, staring at me. And then his eyes narrow. 'Are you telling me she had sex recently?'

'The autopsy showed that she had.'

His mouth quivers and he puts his hand over it. His voice hoarse, he says, 'Was she raped before she was killed?'

'No, no. It doesn't appear to have been rape.'

He can't seem to figure out where to look. 'At least there's that.' He rocks back and forth a couple of times. 'I can't blame her. If a man can't satisfy his wife, I guess he has to put up with her going elsewhere.'

'Did you know she was having sex with someone?'

'Of course I didn't know.' His voice rises. 'You think she told me? We may have had our differences, but she wouldn't have been that cruel. She tried every way in the world to make things easier for me.'

'So you don't have any idea who she might have been with?'

He sits back in his chair, flinching, but whether from pain or from an idea coming to him of who his wife might have slept with, it's hard to say. 'No, I don't.'

'Was there anyone from the motorcycle club she might have gone to see the night she was killed, and maybe one thing led to another?'

'Anything's possible.' His tone is bleak.

'Mike, there's one more thing. Yesterday I asked your son if Amber kept a computer at home. He told me the family shares a computer. When I asked if I could see what Amber had worked on recently, he seemed reluctant to let me use it. Do you know why that would be?'

He shrugs. 'Just that he probably doesn't want her memory disturbed.'

'Maybe. Or I wonder if they're protecting you for some reason. Is that possible?'

His eyes are crazed. 'Listen here. I'm about fed up with you and your insinuations. If I knew anything that might help you find out who killed my wife, I'd be all over it. I didn't kill her and I don't know who did. And furthermore, there's nothing going on in my life that would have put her in danger. So you can just butt out.' He pulls himself out of his chair, a groan escaping him.

I get up too. 'Mike, I have to ask you. Have you got gambling debts that put you in a bad financial situation?'

'She told you that, didn't she?' He looks toward the other room, as if thinking his sister-in-law is right there. 'That nosy bitch. Acting like she's here to help, when all she wants to do is snoop in my business.'

How often people backed into a corner are angry at the messenger. But I'm not easily diverted. 'Is it true?'

His face is fiery. 'No, it isn't. You know where the door is. You can see yourself out.'

*   *   *

When I get home at five, I heat up chili from my freezer and the aroma of it brings Hailey out of her room. Her eyes are swollen and her body sags like she's lost all her bones.

She wanders to the table and plops down across from me.

'I didn't have any lunch today,' I say, 'so I'm hungry. I'll bet you are too. I hope you like chili.'

'I guess.'

'I've got cornbread to go with it. Can you grate us some cheese?' I get some Cheddar out of the refrigerator and find my ancient cheese grater.

Hailey isn't saying anything, but she does go over to the counter and begins to grate the cheese. I ask her what she wants to drink and she says a Coke. I get myself a cup of coffee. The day is a long way from over.

I wait until Hailey has eaten a bit before I tell her I have somebody I have to talk to this evening, 'and an idea for you to do something you might like.'

'Like what?'

'You met Maria. She's giving a self-defense class to a bunch of high school girls and I thought you might like to go.'

She barely glances at me. 'Whatever.'

'You don't have to go. She's doing a session on guns tonight, and I thought it might be interesting. You know, Maria is a really good cop and she knows her stuff.'

When I say the part about doing a session on guns, she perks up. 'Do I get to handle a gun?'

'I have one you can take, but Maria doesn't want anyone to bring ammunition. She's just going over the basics.'

'OK, I can do that. What time do we leave?'

'Class is at six thirty so we'll leave at six twenty. I don't know if you've noticed, but this is a small town and it doesn't take long to get anywhere.'

'Duh,' she says, but she gives a little grin.

'Good, we have time for ice cream, too. Then I'll take you over there.'

'Are you staying to watch?'

'No, like I said, I have to go talk to somebody.'

She narrows her eyes at me until they're slits. 'You aren't afraid I'll run away?'

My gut tightens. She's a tough one. 'Should I be?'

She doesn't answer right away. She butters a piece of cornbread and eats a bite, then says, 'Not tonight anyway. Lyle has to work. But I can't promise anything after that. Did you persuade Maria to let me take the class tonight? Are you just trying to be nice to me?'

'I didn't have to persuade Maria. She was fine with it. As for being nice to you, that's my aim all along.'

'Who are you going to talk to?'

I finish up the last of my chili and push my plate back. 'It's concerning the woman who was killed, Amber Johnson.'

'I thought you said the highway patrol was going to handle that.'

'The officer in charge said they can't get to it for a couple of days and he'd appreciate my input. It's best to get all the information I can while the case is still fresh.'

'Does that mean you're going to the motorcycle rally?'

I nod.

She takes a drink of her Coke. 'Whoever killed her might already be gone,' she says. 'Or it might not even be someone who was here for the rally. It might be someone from town.'

I prop my elbows on the table. 'Good observations. But I do know that Amber was supposed to meet someone at the rally, and I'd like to find out what she was meeting them about.' I shrug. 'Might not even be connected with the case, but you have to cover every possibility.'

She looks interested. 'Still, if somebody who is just here for the rally killed her, you probably won't ever figure out who it was, will you?' There's a challenge to her voice. She really is struggling to find her place.

'There are a certain number of cases that are never solved.'

'Why do you care so much about this woman anyway? Was she a friend of yours?' She is looking at me intently and I feel like the answer will be important.

'It's a good question. Not many people think about it. No, I hardly knew Amber. But as police chief, I feel a certain sense of responsibility for the well-being of the people in town.' I cringe as the words sound pompous coming out of my mouth. But she doesn't seem to notice.

'For everybody? Even if you don't know them?'

'Yes.'

'Even bad people?'

I don't know what's driving these questions, but they seem important to her. 'Hailey, sometimes people get driven into a corner by circumstances, and they end up not making good choices. Sometimes they make really bad choices and it ends up meaning somebody gets hurt or even killed. And they lose their freedom. But in a way, I feel responsible for them, too. To make sure they pay their debt to society, but also to make sure they don't suffer any more than is due.'

'What about somebody who's a serial killer?'

'I've never had to deal with somebody who's bad through and through. I hope I don't ever have to.'

'Do you think most cops feel the way you do?'

I throw up my hands. 'These are some heavy thoughts. I can't account for other cops. I do know that Maria has the same philosophy.'

'Have you ever shot anybody?'

'No.'

'Ever beaten someone up to get them to talk?'

I shake my head. 'You're getting these ideas from tough guys on TV. It always seems to me to be more useful to use my powers of persuasion and logic.'

'Sort of like what you did with me today?' If I'm not mistaken there's a hint of humor in her voice.

'Sort of like that, although I have to say most criminals aren't that smart.'

I had decided that I wasn't going to bring up the incident with Lyle, but we're more relaxed now and I really want to know more. I go and get myself another cup of coffee and sit down again. 'Can we discuss what happened this afternoon?'

It's like a door slams shut in her face. 'Why?'

'I'm trying to understand your position. Why did you want to leave? I thought we could get to know each other a little bit, have some fun. I thought you had a good time at the rally.'

She gives me a withering look. 'It was probably fun for you, but we didn't really *do* anything. I didn't get to ride on a motorcycle.

I didn't get to stay and listen to music, except that once. All we did was walk around.'

'Do you feel like you have to be entertained every minute?'

'No,' she grumbles. 'But I don't want to be stuck here with nobody to hang out with until my mom decides I can go home.' The way she says it, a little forlorn, I realize she feels like she's been banished. And maybe the only person she felt like she could turn to was her boyfriend.

'Tell me, Hailey, what do you like about Lyle?'

'He loves me.' She juts her chin out like she's ready to be socked.

I nod. I don't really know what I'm hoping for, but at least she's still here. 'You like the way he treats you.'

She hesitates. 'Most of the time.'

'And the rest of the time?'

She shrugs.

'I think you're right that he cares for you. He came to get you, and that's a good sign.'

'For all the good it did.'

'You understand why I couldn't let you go with him, don't you?'

'Everybody wants to control me.' She gets up and I suspect she's going to retreat to her room. I'd like to get us on an even keel before she storms out.

'Do you mind helping me with the dishes? We need to get out of here soon.'

She takes the dishes to the sink, but doesn't offer to wash them. I do that and ask her to dry. Dusty takes the opportunity to act silly, chasing his tail, and that makes her laugh. And then she spies Zelda. 'Look at the cat! She looks like, "Whoa, is that dog nuts!"' Sure enough, Zelda is watching Dusty from the hallway. If cats could roll their eyes, Zelda would.

After we finish the dishes, I spoon up ice cream for dessert and we go into the living room to eat it in front of the TV. But before Hailey sits down, she goes over to the wall where my Frederic Remington hangs. 'You have a lot of art, but this is the only one that's a real picture of anything. Why do you have all those other weird paintings? Do you like that stuff?'

I didn't even realize Hailey had noticed them. 'You know, when I first saw contemporary art, I felt the same way. I liked pictures of cows and bluebonnets. You remember your Aunt Jeanne, don't you?' Hailey was a youngster when Jeanne died.

'Sure. She was really nice.'

'Her family collected contemporary art and Jeanne and I inherited several nice paintings. I've come to appreciate it and we bought a few pieces of our own.' I find a pen and some paper in the drawer of a side table and write down the names of some of the artists. 'Why don't you look these up on the internet and you'll find out who they are.'

She reads off, 'Richard Diebenkorn, Vasily Kandinsky, Wolf Kahn, Ellsworth Kelly, Melinda Buie. Are they famous?'

'Most of them are.' I point to the painting of the cow in red, blue and burgundy. 'That's the newest one, Melinda Buie. She's an artist working now.'

'At least I can see that it's a cow,' she says.

We get to the high school gym five minutes early. Maria introduces Hailey to a couple of girls. I see Steve's sister huddled with another group. They turn to eye Hailey.

'How are you going to handle the gun thing?' I ask Maria.

'Each girl will keep her weapon on the table in front of her so I can keep an eye on them.'

She takes Hailey to a place at one of the tables and I head out.

TWENTY-ONE

I'm beginning to get used to the rally. The carnival atmosphere, the noise, the bawdy sights, the smell of smoke and oil and fast food. Drifting over everything is country music from the pavilion. I see more than a few people from town strolling around, stopping to admire particularly showy motorcycles. It's a louder, more raucous group. I catch snatches of intense conversation arguing the merits of the different bikes, the paraphernalia associated with them, and the best places to ride.

Before long I run into Steve Deverell doing his rounds.

'How's Hailey doing?' he says at once. 'I'll bet it's not as exciting here as it is in Austin.'

'You'd win that bet.'

'Where is she?'

I tell him she's at Maria's class.

'I don't know if she'd want to, but tomorrow me and my friends are going swimming at the lake. Maybe she'd want to come.'

'Who will be there?' I ask. Steve is a step up from Lyle, and younger, but he's still not a guy I would put my trust in for Hailey.

He names a couple of boys I don't know.

'Any girls?'

'My friend Sophie, and a couple of other girls. And my sister. She's fifteen, but she's cool.'

Cool is one way to put it.

'How about if I call Hailey in the morning?' he asks.

'Sounds like a plan. I wouldn't call too early, though. She sleeps in.' I give him Hailey's cell number and continue on my way to Grant Butler's RV.

Across the walkway from the RV, Ralph Tyson is back, talking to the guy who has a bike for sale. Ralph seems too stuffy to be a candidate for owning a motorcycle. Maybe he's having a mid-life crisis and needs a little excitement in his life. Tyson and the guy look like they're negotiating, so I don't butt in.

A man I presume to be Butler is sitting outside his RV in a folding chair fancier than most of the ones people bring, with arms and a drink holder. He's talking to a biker in jeans and a Hell's Angels T-shirt, with his hair covered by a bandana. They're drinking whiskey out of real glasses, not plastic. A bottle of Monkey Shoulder scotch is sitting on a low camp table between them. They look none too welcoming. Neither of them gets up.

'Help you?' Butler says.

'Are you Grant Butler?'

'That's right.'

'I need to have a word with you when you have a minute.'

The friend he's sitting with rises, belts back the last of the booze and sets his glass on the table. 'Something tells me you're a lawman. I can smell them a mile off.'

'Good nose,' I say.

'Hah! A lawman with a sense of humor. Like a dog with two tails. Rare. Grant, I'll catch you later.'

Grant stands up and I see that he's huge, at least six-foot-six and 250 pounds. He's handsome, with a firm jaw, a mane of dark hair shot with flecks of silver, and serious gray eyes. Around forty, he's at least ten years older than Becky. 'What do you want?' he says. His neighbor was right. Not friendly.

'Mr Butler, where you from?'

'Houston.'

'What do you do there?'

'Why are you asking?'

Suddenly the door opens and Becky steps out. 'Hi,' she says. 'You came back.'

'I did.' I turn my attention back to Butler. 'Mr Butler, I understand you know a woman by the name of Amber Johnson?'

Before he can reply, Becky says, 'Grant, I told this guy I didn't know her, but he says someone saw her coming out of our RV Friday.' Her voice sounds anxious, like she's scared he'll be mad at her for talking to me.

'Who said that?' he asks me.

'I'm the one who saw her,' I say.

Butler's voice is cool. 'Yes, I met her, but I wouldn't say I know her. What about her?'

'She was murdered Saturday night.'

'I heard that,' Butler says, his expression unmoved. 'But I don't know what it has to do with me.'

'Why was she here?'

He puts his hands on his hips. 'She came to me for advice.' His voice has an edge of impatience.

'About what?'

'That's confidential.'

'Can you at least tell me whether it's anything that might have a bearing on her death?'

'Honey,' Becky says, 'you have to help this man if you can.' She sidles over to me and puts her hand on my arm.

I see Grant smirking. He knows the effect Becky has on men. And so does she. 'Well, I can't. Is there anything else?' He's just shy of belligerent. I wish Maria were here. She has a knack for taking men like this down to size.

'You were going to tell me what line of work you're in.'

'I don't recall that I was going to, but it's no secret I'm a lawyer.'

'Was Mrs Johnson by any chance asking you about her rights in an insurance matter?'

'Like I said, it's confidential.'

I remember that Jack Cassidy told me he had recommended that Amber talk to a lawyer. 'Mr Butler, are you acquainted with Jack Cassidy?'

'I am.'

'Is he the person who introduced you to Amber Johnson?'

'He is.'

The guy rubs me up the wrong way. I'd like to ask him more questions, to prod him, but I don't know what else to ask that would get me anywhere. I give him my card and ask him to contact me if he thinks of anything relevant.

'I'll sure do that,' he says. But his tone says different.

I find Jack and Emma Cassidy hosting a cookout along with a few other families.

I tell Jack that I have a couple of quick questions for him. He's the one tending the chicken on the grill, so he turns it over to one of the other men with strict instructions, and we go off out of earshot. He grabs a beer and hands one to me.

'I found out that Amber met Grant Butler the day before she was killed,' I say. 'He's the lawyer you referred Amber to, right?'

'That's right.'

'Why him in particular?'

He takes a sip of his beer. 'Butler had a run-in with an insurance company and his client came out of it with the company paying a good chunk of change. I thought maybe he could give her some advice. Amber said they couldn't afford to hire a lawyer, but I told Butler what the situation was and he said he'd talk to her pro bono to see if she had a case.'

'The rally organizer told me that Butler hangs out at these rallies and that there are suspicions he's dealing drugs.'

Jack laughs. 'Grant Butler loves drama. He knows that's his reputation, and he plays it up.'

'Then if he's not a biker, why does he hang around the rallies?'

'Drumming up business. There are always a couple of accidents at these things and he discreetly lets them know he's a lawyer who can help them get compensation. He's not a bad guy, really, just quirky.' He grins. 'What did you think of Becky?'

I tell him Harriman's assessment – that she may be attractive, but she's a tough cookie.

'She has to be. That's why she's lasted longer with Butler than most women do. They've been together a couple of years. Most of them last six to nine months.'

I notice him looking back at the grill again, worried that the guy he left in charge will screw it up.

'We can go back over there,' I say.

'Good. I don't want those birds to be overcooked.'

We walk over and he relieves the guy at the grill and begins turning the chicken.

'There's one more question. It's important, but just yes or no.'

He meets my gaze. 'Go ahead.'

'Did you have sex with Amber last weekend?'

Whatever he was expecting, that wasn't it. 'Oh, hell no.' He gives a half-laugh. 'What made you think I did? Where would we even go?' He waves his hand at the surroundings. 'We'd have to have an extra RV set up somewhere. If we even wanted to, which we didn't. It wasn't that kind of friendship.'

'Do you know anybody she might have met secretly? Anybody she might have been involved with?'

He shakes his head. 'That's a disappointing line of questioning. And no, I don't know anybody who had designs on her.' Still, he has an uneasy expression on his face. There's something he isn't telling.

I arrive at the high school gym a little early to pick up Hailey. It's 7:45 and the class gets out at 8:00. While I wait, I consider whether to call Vicki and Tom to tell them what happened this afternoon. I decide not to worry them tonight. I can imagine Vicki tossing and turning with nerves if she hears that Hailey almost escaped my care.

But I do call Wendy to update her on my talk with Hailey.

'I'm so sorry I let her get away today,' she says. She still sounds subdued. 'It didn't occur to me that she'd try to run off.'

'Listen to me, you don't need to apologize. It isn't your fault.

I shouldn't have put you in that position. Who would have expected her to pull that kind of stunt?'

'You never met my younger daughter,' Wendy says, with a wry laugh. 'She once decided that she was going to hitchhike to California. To become a star in Hollywood. She got as far as Giddings before a truck driver picked her up and called the highway patrol. Ooo, mad? She thought that truck driver was the devil himself. How dare he spoil her great plans!'

'She was lucky she got a ride with him and not a man with a different idea in mind.'

'Damn right she was. And she was also lucky I didn't tie her up and keep her in a locked room for the next month.'

'Hollywood? She thought she wanted to be in the movies? How did she think that was going to work?'

'Hard to say. I didn't give her much of a chance to explain herself.'

I'm glad I talked to Wendy. I know her daughter is still a free spirit, but she survived.

When Hailey comes out of the gym, she's with two other girls, one of them Steve's sister, Ashley. They approach my pickup, giggling.

I thought when I met Ashley that her dress was outlandish, but tonight she's outdone herself. She's wearing black tights with holes torn in them, a black blouse that hangs off one shoulder, and what looks like a dog collar with spikes. She's wearing dark purple lipstick and makeup to match.

'Samuel, this is Ash and her friend Eva,' Hailey says. Her eyes are glittering with excitement. 'Eva's older brother is going to take them over to the rally and they want to know if I can come too.' It's interesting that as negative as Ashley's mother, Lily Deverell, is about the rally, her son is working there and she's letting her daughter go.

'Ash, does your mamma know you're going out to the rally?'

'It'll be fine,' she says. 'My brother works out there.' That didn't exactly answer my question.

'Who is your older brother?' I ask Eva.

'Shelby Holman.'

I haven't heard of Shelby, but that's a good thing. It means he either hasn't done anything illegal or is smart enough to have gotten away with it. 'And how old is Shelby?'

'He'll be a senior at JC High this year. He's over there.' She points to an older Jeep Wrangler.

'I'll come over and say hi.'

Hailey and the two girls give each other the side-eye, disgusted with me.

I stroll over to the Jeep. As soon as the driver sees me, he opens the door and steps out. He doesn't look old enough to be in high school, much less a senior. He's short like his sister. He immediately makes a good impression when he sticks his hand out and introduces himself. And he also looks familiar.

'Are you by chance Ben Holman's son?'

'Yes, sir.' He scowls, which tells me something about Holman's relationship with his family.

'Your daddy in town?' I'm planning to go question Holman when I get a chance.

'I couldn't tell you. We live with our mamma.'

'Your sister tells me you're going to be a senior this year. Thought about where you're going to college?'

'Yes, sir, I got into UT. I'm going into engineering.'

'Good for you.' That's why I don't know him. The only high school boys I know play sports or get into trouble, or both. It may be a stupid prejudice but I'm inclined to think that a boy who's smart enough to get into the engineering department at UT is also smart enough not to put the girls in danger. 'You going to stick around with these girls while they're at the rally?'

'I hadn't planned on it. I'm just giving them a ride.'

'Are you going to pick them up?'

He shrugs. 'If I have to. They told me Steve Deverell would bring them home.'

'Steve brought my mamma's car to work so he could take us home,' Ash pipes up.

'All right, Hailey, I guess you can go.' All my better judgment is telling me it's a bad idea to give in after the stunt she pulled this afternoon, but I hope she'll respond positively to me not trying to keep her on a leash. Also, I like the idea that Hailey will get to hang out with kids around her age. It might give her reason to stick around. 'Let me talk to you for a minute.'

I pull her off to the side. Before I can speak, she says, 'I know, you think you shouldn't let me out of your sight, but I'll stay with them.' She doesn't sound contrite.

'That isn't actually what I was going to say, but now that you mention it, I don't want any more disappearing acts, you hear?'

She nods, chewing the side of her mouth.

'How was the class tonight?'

'It was OK.'

'I'd like to get my gun back. It might surprise you to know that I'd just as soon you not take it out to the rally with you.'

She rolls her eyes. 'Maria heard us saying we were going out there and she kept our guns. She said she'd drop them off at our houses.'

'That's good. If you have any problems at all at the rally, you call me.'

'I'll be fine,' she says. 'You know, these girls are a lot younger than I am. I almost feel like I'm babysitting.' Ashley is a year younger.

'Well, if you get bored, I'll come and get you.'

She starts back to join the others, but I hear her say, 'God!' under her breath.

I watch them leave. At least while he's in sight, Shelby drives cautiously.

After this afternoon's fiasco, my trust in Hailey's goodwill is gone. I think of what I can do to make sure she doesn't bolt. Follow the car to confirm that they're really going to the rally? For the first time in my life, I think positive thoughts about a car tracking device. Looks easy enough on TV. I'm beginning to understand what Tom and Vicki are going through.

TWENTY-TWO

Next morning I'm all the worse for a restless night. Intending to trust Hailey, I went to bed at ten, but I was still wide awake when she rolled in at close to one o'clock. I heard her tiptoe past my room and close her door quietly.

When I get back from the pasture, Loretta is waiting in a rocking chair on my porch.

'I left you some coffee cake on the counter.'

'Let me get some coffee and I'll sit down with you. You want anything?'

She doesn't. Hailey isn't stirring. I pour myself a mug of coffee and go back out and join Loretta.

'You look tired,' she says.

I describe the excitement yesterday.

'I knew something went on. Jolene Ramsey had it all over town that there was a strange car in front of your house and some kind of standoff.'

I tell her that we worked it out and that I let Hailey go to the rally and come home with Ashley Deverell.

'You're braver than I would be. Those Deverell kids are wild. Why Lily lets Ashley have those tattoos and that nose ring is beyond me.'

'Maybe she hopes she'll get it out of her system. Anyway, Hailey got home in one piece, so it ended up okay.'

'Have you found out anything more about what happened to Amber?' she asks. 'People are getting restless. They don't like knowing something happened and nothing coming of it.'

'Not anything to tell. If it was a random attack by somebody at the rally, we may never know who did it. The highway patrol said they'd be on it, but I don't know how they're going to find out anything unless somebody saw what happened and comes forward.'

'Ladies have taken some dishes over to Mike Johnson and the kids. He's a sad case. Those poor kids are going to have it rough having to depend on him.'

'His sister-in-law is there for now anyway.'

She cocks an eyebrow. 'The way I hear it, Mike and his sister-in-law are barely speaking. The only reason she's staying around is to help with the store until he finds somebody to work in the mornings. And I heard that Ralph Tyson doesn't want Cal working there anymore, so Mike is going to have to hire two people.'

That's news. 'Why doesn't Ralph want Cal working there?'

'Apparently some kind of rough bikers came by and Cal called his daddy to come down to the store in case they came back.'

I'm surprised Cal did that. He seemed to be fine when I left. I wonder if he had more trouble. 'So Cal wants to quit?'

'I don't think it's him. I think it's his daddy.'

'I'll go have a talk with Ralph. I was there when the guys came in. I don't know why Cal was worried that they'd come back. They wanted to talk to Amber. Once the rally is over, things will calm down.'

'I'll be glad when those motorcycle people are gone, I'll tell you that.'

When Loretta leaves I go in to call Dan Weinman, but before I can dial the number, a call comes in from Walter Dunn.

'I told you I was going to get one of my guys to take Hailey for a motorcycle ride. You think she'd like to do it this morning? We have a little break.'

'She's not up, but I'll bet she'd like it.'

I have to tap on Hailey's door a couple of times before she opens it, yawning. 'What time is it? Feels like it's about six o'clock.'

'You up for a bike ride?'

'Bicycle?' She's not awake yet.

'Motorcycle.'

That wakes her up. 'Yes! I'll get dressed.'

'Walter said you have to wear jeans and they'll have a jacket and a helmet for you.'

She's dressed in record time and gobbles down some coffee cake and milk.

When we pull up and park at the rally, she's subdued. I wonder if she's embarrassed that she created such a fuss here yesterday. But more likely, it's just early for her.

We're at Walter Dunn's booth by 8:30. Walter greets her, grinning. 'Come on and meet Rod.'

Rod Cantrell is a wiry twenty-year-old who's working on a motorcycle. When he sees us, he stands up and wipes his hands on a rag. 'You ready to go tear up the countryside?' he asks, winking at Hailey.

She glances at me but speaks to Rod. 'I don't think *he* wants us to do anything crazy,' she says.

'Hey, what he doesn't know won't hurt him, right?'

She giggles, but her eyes are wide and her hands are clutched together. I suspect she's more nervous than she wants to let on.

Walter gets her squared away with a leather jacket and a helmet. She looks increasingly anxious, but Rod and Walter either don't notice or pretend not to. Rod gets her positioned on the back of the motorcycle, a green Yamaha, relatively tame-looking compared to some of the monsters I've seen here.

While they're gone, Walter says, 'Let's walk for a minute. Our repair load is light this morning with everybody being out on the road rally.'

He brings us mugs of coffee from the trailer and we walk down to the water, which is still and clear today. 'I heard a little scuttlebutt yesterday I thought you might be interested in. Couple of guys brought a bike in for a repair and they were talking about the woman whose body was found. You know when you work on bikes, you're more or less invisible, so people say things not thinking you're paying attention.'

'You've got my interest. What'd you hear?'

'One of them said they knew her from when she was in the Rough Roaders. He said she was a hot little number. And the other guy said, "Yeah, but that little gal was looking for trouble." And the first one said, "I guess she found it."'

'Looking for trouble. I wonder in what way?'

He shakes his head. 'It may be nothing. You know how guys love to gossip. They say it's women, but men are just as bad. They seemed to think it was funny.'

'Do you have the name of the guy whose bike you were working on?'

'I do. His name was Elvis Garrison. He's one of the Rough Roaders. They're a pretty clean-cut bunch, so I was surprised.'

I thank him for the tip, although I don't quite know what to make of it, and we head back to wait for Hailey and Rod. I'd like to go round up Elvis Garrison right now, but I have to wait a while until I can turn Hailey over to Steve for their trip to the lake. I sit and watch Walter's crew tackle the Harleys and Yamahas and Hondas, big and small, with repairs of every part imaginable. I'm impressed by how many parts they carry in their truck.

'Does anybody ever give you any trouble? Some of these guys are pretty rough. I expect they have more than their share of guns. Knives, too, for that matter.'

Walter laughs, hefting a wrench. 'You're right about that, but they don't give me any trouble. Everybody has sense enough to be nice to the repair people. We can make the difference in whether they get to ride home or have to be towed.'

Rod rides up with Hailey on the back of his cycle. Her grin lights up her face.

'I take it you had a good time,' I say.

'Wow, it was the coolest.' She glows when she looks at Rod.

'You want to hang out here a while?' I ask. 'I've got a couple of stops to make.'

She makes a face. 'I'm supposed to go swimming with Steve and them today.'

'Let's get you home to change clothes then.'

In the pickup, I ask if Hailey likes Steve's sister.

'Ashley? Oh, please,' she says, her voice dripping with scorn. 'Such a wannabe goth. She doesn't even know what that means.'

I'm not sure I do either, so I figure I'd better not comment on it. 'I hope you have a good time with them today.'

'It's better than sitting around here doing nothing.'

'Did Steve behave himself when he brought you home?'

She lifts her lip in a sneer. 'Of course he did. I wouldn't have put up with anything from him. He seems like a nice enough boy, but I prefer older men.' She tosses her hair.

When Steve honks out front, Hailey rushes out of her room in a short dress over her bathing suit. I want to tell her she needs to take something longer to cover up in case they wander up to the rally, but suddenly I'm too exhausted by the drama to make anything of it. I'm going to have to trust that Steve will take care of her. She tells me she needs a towel and I tell her where to get one.

I go outside to Steve's car where he's sitting with the window down looking like he has the world by the tail. I go to the window and lean down, startling him. He jumps. 'Whoa! I didn't see you there.' A second of fear sparks in his eyes.

'Sorry about that.'

His sister and Eva are in the back seat with a boy Steve's age sitting between them. He's dark-haired and wearing a scowl, but he brightens when he sees Hailey walk out of the house.

Before she can get to the car, I say quietly, 'Steve, I don't have to tell you to behave yourself, do I? I need to hand her back to her folks in one piece.'

He grins and salutes me. 'You can trust me, Chief. I'm a working man now, and I have to maintain my good reputation.'

I can't help laughing. I slip a $20 bill out of my billfold and hand it to him. 'For gas and snacks.'

He puts his hand up. 'You don't have to do that.'

'Go ahead. It won't take care of everything, but it will help.'

TWENTY-THREE

This time I manage to get a call into Dan Weinman. He tells me he plans to send a couple of officers out this afternoon to question people at the rally. 'Lot of folks there. I don't expect to have much success, but we have to try.'

I tell him that I questioned the women who were in the tent the night Amber's body was found. 'One of them saw a man and woman arguing down near the lake. She didn't know Amber, but the description sounds like her. But no idea who the guy was. Did you get a chance to go over the autopsy report?'

'I haven't had time.'

'Amber Johnson had sex with somebody within a few hours of her death.'

'DNA?'

'They used a condom, but T.J., the medical examiner, said they'd see if they could get samples from her clothes. Also, she had a lot of dirt under her fingernails, but they're going to see if she might have tried to defend herself and got some skin.' Telling him reminds me that I need to check Steve's story with Sophie about how he got his scratches.

I also tell Dan about Grant Butler. 'I'm getting mixed messages about him. Harriman says he has a reputation for dealing drugs, but one of Amber's friends in the Rough Roaders Motorcycle Club said he's a lawyer and doesn't have anything to do with drugs.' I don't have any reason to think that Butler is involved with Amber's death, but his reputation and his nasty attitude have drawn my attention. I'd like to know the reason for both.

'Did you look him up?' Weinman asks.

'Not yet. I'll do that today. See if he has a record of any arrests.'

When I hang up I head for the station, but on the way I stop by the Quick Stop to have a word with Amber's sister, DeeDee.

DeeDee is busy. With so many folks in town for the rally, the store is swarming with people buying chips, beer, and anything else that strikes their fancy. DeeDee is efficient and friendly. It's ten minutes before there's a let-up. Her face immediately settles into an expression of gloom.

'How you doing?' I ask. 'You've barely had time to mourn your sister's passing.'

'I don't know why Amber thought it would be so great to have a convenience store,' she says, her eyes sweeping the shelves. 'It's non-stop work.'

'When we don't have the rally in town, it's a lot quieter,' I say.

She sighs. 'You're right. And I have to say most of the bikers are polite and friendly, even the ones dressed like they're going to a Halloween party.'

'Has anyone been rude or demanding?'

'Oh, you always have that. People who think they ought to be treated "special."' She makes air quotes.

'Anybody asking for Amber?'

'Asking for her?'

I tell her about the two bikers who came in wanting to talk to her. 'They kind of bothered Cal.'

She rolls her eyes. 'Oh, yes, Cal. Well, you can't be sure what somebody said to him. He's a complainer.'

'I was here when it happened, so it was real.'

'Oh, I see. Well then . . .' She has to ring up some items for a couple of customers.

When they're gone, I ask her what Cal complains about.

'I shouldn't say complain. He was mostly moping around about Amber. He said they were simpatico. I guess that means they got along well.'

'I heard that his dad wants him to stop working here.' I figure it's better that she knows now than that it gets sprung on her.

'He told me that. He told me no way was he going to quit, that he owed it to Amber.'

'Good, that's one thing you don't have to deal with,' I say. Nevertheless, I wonder why his daddy is so intent on having him quit. The guys who came in were surly, but not threatening. Maybe there's more to it than I saw.

'Speaking of stuff that has to be dealt with,' DeeDee says, 'I don't know how Mike is going to cope. He seems lost. Doesn't know the first thing about keeping the store going. To tell you the truth, I don't know what the problem is. It's not that complicated. Money comes in from customers, money goes out to pay for the goods to stock the store and to pay for rent, taxes, insurance, and employees. It isn't easy, but it isn't rocket science either. I honestly believe Jimmy could do it.'

'So Amber did all that work in addition to keeping hours at the store?'

'Every single thing. Mike doesn't lift a finger. You can't tell me he's too disabled to take care of paperwork.' She leans across the counter. 'In fact, I'm not so sure he's all that disabled at all. He gets around well enough when he wants to.'

'What do you mean?'

'Well, he found out he was out of beer last night and he didn't seem to have any trouble getting in the car to come down here to get some. Not that he drinks too much, mind you,' she adds quickly. 'I don't mean to imply that. I just mean that he wants what he wants, and he's not too disabled to get it. It's a good thing they had that life insurance policy on Amber. That ought to make things easier for him.'

That's the first I've heard of a life insurance policy. I didn't think to ask because they seemed so strapped for cash that it would be unlikely they'd pay for such an expensive item. 'Life insurance policy? You know how much it was for?'

'I sure do. It was for one hundred thousand dollars. The reason I know is because it was me that made her get it after the accident. I told her she ought to be glad the two of them weren't killed riding around like teenagers. And what would have become of her kids then? I would have taken them, of course, but it would have about killed me. So, after the accident, since she was the main breadwinner, I told her she ought to get some insurance in case something happened to her. Well, I was right. Not that I'm glad I was.'

One hundred thousand dollars can go a long way to help Mike. If he has gambling debts, that ought to pay them off. And it might even be a start toward the surgery he needs.

DeeDee seems to enjoy chatting. She tells me she needs to get back home to her kids before too long. She says she has three teenagers. 'I hate to admit I don't mind staying away a few extra days to help out here. They flat wear me out. But my husband is up to the task, no problem. He doesn't take any guff. And they're good kids.'

I tell her about Hailey visiting. 'Maybe I ought to hire your husband to come set her straight.'

'He would, too. Although I tell him that one of these days he's going to get his butt kicked by our middle boy. He's the sassy one, and I have a feeling he's saving up to be trouble. He's fourteen.'

A bunch of people swarm in all at once and I leave her to it.

I stop by headquarters. Maria is off today, and Bo Murray is on duty. He tells me that one of the local church ladies called to tattle that Wolf Goodnight wasn't abiding by the eight o'clock curfew out at the Two Dog Bar.

'Call her back and tell her the city council gave Goodnight a special dispensation to keep the bar open his usual hours.'

'What if she wants to know why?' Bo is a diligent worker, but not much of a self-starter.

'Tell her because he's outside the city limits.' Which he is, but that doesn't mean anything. He pays taxes here and is subject to our laws.

I'm thinking about DeeDee's hint that Mike isn't as disabled as he seems. Amber told me his pain came and went, which would account for his sudden ability to drive, but I'd like some verification of his condition.

I call the two doctors in town to find out if Mike Johnson is a patient of either of them. He isn't, but Dr Lipton's receptionist tells me she thinks Johnson's doctor is Mark Tanick in Bobtail. I call Tanick's office and tell the receptionist I'd like a few minutes to talk to the doctor. She says to come in at twelve-thirty and she'll carve out a few minutes for him to speak to me.

I have just enough time to stop in on Cal's daddy, Ralph Tyson, at the post office where he works. I call him and he says to come on down and we'll talk.

Tyson was a mail carrier for a number of years until he got promoted to postmaster. People have complained that he doesn't always take the mail seriously, that he doesn't seem to worry if a package doesn't show up. He always blames 'the sorting center', whatever that is.

As postmaster, he not only oversees the mail delivery by our two mail carriers, he also mans the desk. 'We don't get much traffic until about four, so I have some time,' he says, leaning with his elbows on the counter.

'I saw you out at the rally last night,' I say.

He straightens. 'You did?'

'I was out there to talk to somebody and I saw you looking like you were ready to buy that bike.'

'Don't tell my wife I was there. She'd have my hide. If I did buy a bike, I'd have to rent somewhere to keep it and drive it on the sly.'

I laugh, but he doesn't join in. He asks what I want to talk to him about.

'I understand your son told you a couple of bikers showed up the other day and wanted to talk to Amber and they made him nervous.'

'Yes, I went down there, even though it was inconvenient. I had to get my wife down here to man the post office. She doesn't like it because every time she works here somebody comes in and wants something strange. Like somebody wants to ship something off to France or something. The kind of thing that never happens when I'm here. She seems to attract trouble.' He laughs.

'Did Cal ever have trouble at the store before?'

'No, not that I know of. He likes working there. I don't like it, but he's stubborn.'

'Why don't you like him working there?'

'He could make better money somewhere else. I thought Amber was taking advantage of him. Him being younger.' He sniffs.

'Do you know if Amber was ever hassled?'

He shakes his head. 'Never heard anything like that. But the way Cal told it, she could have handled anything that came up.'

'How old is Cal?'

'He just turned twenty-one.'

'No plans for college?'

'Cal's a good boy, but he's not really college material. I'm trying to convince him to take the state Civil Service Exam. There are good jobs to be had for the state.'

'Live at home?'

'Yeah, he keeps talking about moving out. He's like every other kid his age, wants to be footloose and out from under his folks, but he likes to have a square meal at our house and get his laundry done. So far, that has been more important than having his own place. My guess is when he gets a girlfriend, he'll be quick enough to move out.'

When I leave, I see a text message from Dan Weinman: *Looked up Grant Butler. He is a lawyer. An ambulance chaser. Doesn't mean he isn't a dealer.*

When I arrive at Dr Tanick's office, his receptionist, Louise Barrett, says Tanick will see me soon, but he's running a little late. If he wasn't running late, he'd be the first doctor in history not to. I've known Louise casually for years. She lives in Jarrett Creek, and as far as I know she's never worked for anyone but Tanick.

Tanick only keeps me waiting fifteen minutes, but five minutes after that, I'm back out on the street. No matter how I phrased the question of how bad Mike Johnson's back problem actually is, Tanick, a man who looks to be near retirement, insisted that he couldn't tell me anything. 'Patient confidentiality is sewed up tight,' he said. I don't know how to find out Mike's real condition if I can't get it from his doctor. I could get a court order, but I don't know that it would be worth the trouble. Despite the insurance money and the hint that Mike is gambling, I simply find it hard to believe that Mike killed Amber. It would mean getting up after the kids were in bed, driving to the rally, walking a long distance to the music tent, and then attacking her. Even if his back isn't as bad as he says, it's still a stretch to think of him going through all that.

TWENTY-FOUR

t's time I went to see Ben Holman. Besides Maureen Washington's observation that he and Amber seemed cozy, there's the matter of finding his phone number in Amber's car.

Holman's a teacher, so he has the summer off, although he may have another job. I decide to go to his place and try to catch him at home rather than calling first. He lives in a duplex in the area of town back behind the Best Value, our fanciest motel. The duplex looks tired, its gray siding green in spots from moss, and the shingle roof is looking sparse. I wouldn't want to live here in a rainstorm. There's a white Kia parked in front. I park behind it and go up the walkway, dodging broken parts of the concrete slabs. I go to the left-hand door, open the screen, and knock.

The man who comes to the door is about forty, tanned and muscular. Maureen Washington said women find him attractive, but I think he looks a little like a weasel, with a pointy nose and eyes set too close together. But his smile is warm and softens his face. 'I know you,' he says. 'You're Chief Craddock. What brings you here?'

'You're Ben Holman?'

'That's right.'

'Mr Holman, I'm investigating the death of Amber Johnson, and I'd like to ask you a few questions.'

'About Amber? Why sure, come on in.' If he's nervous, I don't catch a glimpse of it. 'That was a hell of a shock,' he says.

He shows me into a sparsely furnished place. The living room has a two-seater sofa and two easy chairs, all some version of brown and tan. The carpet is worn, but looks clean. I'm always interested in what kind of art people have. It tells me something about them. The art on Holman's walls tells me he isn't much interested in art. There's a framed poster of a rock concert from fifteen years ago and some photos of his kids. Above the fireplace is a painting by a hand that I think I recognize. 'Nice picture.

You get that from Ellen Forester's gallery?' Ellen and I used to go out together. She has an art gallery and workshop in town where she gives lessons. She paints what I think of as the Texas trio – cows, cactus, and bluebonnets.

'I did buy it from her. She painted it. I like bluebonnets and I think she does a good job.'

Holman tells me to sit and asks if I want some coffee, which I accept. He brings out two mugs.

I sit in one of the easy chairs and he takes the other one. 'I was really broken up about Amber,' he says. 'I can't imagine anybody attacking her.'

'How long have you known Amber?'

'I met her about a year ago when her son Jimmy was in my math class.'

'I understand you had a little trouble with her.'

'Trouble?' He cocks his head. 'Oh, you mean when she scolded me for giving Jimmy a bad grade?' He laughs. 'I wouldn't call that trouble. If that was the worst trouble I ever got from parents, I'd be grateful. We got it sorted out pretty fast.'

'Did you have a relationship with Amber outside of school?'

He takes a sip of coffee. For the first time he looks uneasy. 'I'm not sure what you mean.'

'Did you see Amber Johnson privately outside of school?'

'I might have once or twice.'

'Can you tell me the nature of your meetings?'

Holman runs his hands down his thighs. 'Am I in trouble?'

'I'd appreciate it if you'd answer the question.'

'I don't understand why my private life is of any interest.'

'Anything pertaining to Amber Johnson is of interest to me at the moment. So let me rephrase it. Were you having a sexual relationship with Amber Johnson? Yes or no.'

He gets up so abruptly that I'm startled. His expression is panicked, but he doesn't move, just stands there as if unable to decide what to do next.

I stand up too. 'Were you?'

'We might have gotten together a few times. But I swear I had nothing to do with her getting killed. We just had some good times, that's all.'

'When was the last time you saw her?'

He blows out a breath and runs his hand across the top of his head, ruffling his smooth hair. 'I guess it was last week.'

'What day?'

He's breathing hard and suddenly looks like he's going to cry. 'I saw her last Saturday afternoon. It was just before she was killed. But I did not kill her. I never raised a hand to her.'

'Was it a serious relationship?'

'Oh, hell, no. We were just . . . seeing each other from time to time.'

'Did either of you want to be more serious than the other one?'

He meets my eyes, but looks away quickly. 'Nothing like that. I'm telling you, it was casual. We enjoyed each other's company. You know, her husband . . .' His words trail away. He looks ashamed.

'When did it start?'

'Not that long ago.' He sets his mug on the side table, but remains standing. 'Sometime after Christmas. In the spring.'

'Did her husband know?'

He looks stricken. 'We didn't talk about her husband. Poor bastard. I hope she didn't tell him.'

'She came here?'

He nods.

'So she was here that Saturday. Did she say anything about going out to the rally for any reason?'

'Not a thing.'

'What time was she here?'

'I don't know. She got here about eight thirty or nine, after she fed her family supper.'

'And when did she leave?'

'Ten? A little after?'

'How did she seem?'

He thinks about it. 'She kind of seemed in a hurry. But she often was, so I didn't think much of it.'

'She didn't say where she was going after she left here?'

He shakes his head. He looks tortured. 'No. I assumed she was going home, so when I heard . . .' He stalks around like a caged man.

'Did you leave your house after she left?'

'No, of course not, I was right here.'

'Can anybody vouch for that?'

'It's possible the couple next door heard me watching TV. Walls are thin.'

'All right. That's all for now, but if you think of anything she said that might be of interest, call me.'

'I will. I'm really sorry about everything.'

I want to go out to the lake to check on Hailey. Make sure she's where she said she would be. I'm still not ready to trust her. While I'm there I'll stop by and talk to Gilly Moon. He and his sons provided security for the rally the first couple of days, and I want to ask them if they saw or heard of anything unusual the night Amber was killed, or if they know anything more about Grant Butler. The way Harriman mentioned them the first day, I get the feeling that Gilly Moon likes to keep his eye on things.

Before I go to the lake, I stop by headquarters to check in. Bo Murray is there and he shuts his computer so fast I'm pretty sure he's either playing computer games or looking at porn.

'Ever played online poker?' I ask.

He looks relieved at the question. 'A few times. It's the same as regular poker.'

'Not exactly. For one thing there's no one at the table with you. When you play online do people see each other sitting around a table, like it's real time?'

'Well, no. But other than that it's the same. Like I said, I only played a couple of times.'

'Tell me how it works.' I could read about it, but I want to see if he can explain it to me. I'm trying to bring him along as a deputy and sometimes I get the feeling that he doesn't have a good grasp of how to communicate. He tends to mumble if he doesn't know something. He's a nice-looking kid, built rangy like his daddy, with brown eyes and sandy blond hair. He played football in high school.

He opens his computer as if he needs a refresher. He punches in a few words. 'You look up what sites there are for playing.' He turns the computer so I can see the screen. 'See all those sites? You choose one. I've heard they're all pretty much the same, but some are more popular than others.' He chooses the one at the top of the list and the site pops open, all bright colors and visuals of chips and slot machines and cards. And it's got the sound of bells ringing with jackpots. 'You sign on – you know, give them your name and basic information. Then you find out which poker games they play. I like Texas Hold 'Em, but there are lots of games. You choose the one you want, put money in the bank, and then bingo, you start playing.'

Couldn't be clearer. 'What makes a site popular?'

'I can't tell you that. I only played on a site that one of my buddies played on.'

'How much do you have to deposit in order to play?'

'Totally up to you. Some sites allow you to play with five or ten bucks. Others have a higher minimum. I'm on the low side.'

'Did you win?'

'Won a few bucks. That's fine with me. I won't play much. Usually just if there are other guys I know into it. I have to admit, playing poker makes me itchy. I hate to lose money.'

'Good to know.' I laugh. You never know what people are like, and sometimes you find out more about them when you start talking about money. I wouldn't take Bo for a miserly type. He's good-natured and quick with a joke. Of course, you don't have to be a miser to be careful with funds.

My thoughts go to Mike Johnson. I wouldn't wonder whether he'd lost a lot of money playing poker, except he was defensive when I asked about it. I wonder what kind of stakes he plays for? And how I can find out?

I didn't have time for lunch so I send Bo to the Dairy Queen to get us hamburgers so that I have time to think by myself. I need to address the questions of the case. Instead of just a few loose ends, it seems like there are nothing but loose ends. People loose ends. I jot them down:

1) Mike Johnson. Is his gambling habit a problem, or just a diversion? Is he as disabled as he seems to be? The life insurance pay-out – $100,000. Enough to kill for?

2) Grant Butler. Amber supposedly met him for insurance advice, but is that true? Drug related?

3) Rakesh Patel. With Amber's death, his plans to open a store like hers are freed up.

4) The bikers who came to the Quick Stop asking for Amber. Why were they there?

5) Amber herself. Did she tell her husband she was having an affair? What was she doing at the rally Saturday night after she left Holman's house?

6) Ben Holman. Was he telling the truth about the relationship?

7) Cal Tyson. Why was he so upset about those two bikers who came by that he called his daddy for help? Doesn't seem in his nature.

8) What happened to the knife Amber was stabbed with?

Hints of drugs, hints of gambling, hints of competition, and none of it enough to lead to real clues. It's about as sparse as any information I've ever had about a case.

TWENTY-FIVE

Despite the blistering heat that still hasn't let up, people are out and about, drinking beer, gathered around motorcycles deep in conversation, and watching girls pole dance at the two music venues. It's as if they want to grab every minute because the rally will be ending soon. It's the same reason I'm anxious. It's been almost four days since Amber was killed, and in four more days people will scatter back to where they came from, and the chances of finding out who killed her will plummet.

I stop by Luke Harriman's trailer. He's going over figures at his desk. It's ten degrees warmer inside his trailer than outside. His face is slick with sweat.

'What happened to your air conditioning?' I ask.

'On the blink. Typical. I feel like this rally is snakebit.'

'What do you mean?'

He gestures to the papers. 'We're losing money. We always have a slim margin and this year we don't have as many people here. I heard that people were mad because your town tried to ban the rally, so they said if Jarrett Creek didn't want them, they don't want to be here.'

'Sorry to hear that. You know the curfew was a compromise.'

'I know that, and I expect next year it'll be back to normal. Some of these people take offense easy, but they'll get over it.'

'Anything else?'

'You mean besides the woman getting killed and having to pay extra for security because of the strike? I guess not.' He snorts.

'Speaking of security, you know where I can find Gilly Moon?' I ask.

'Let me text him.' He punches in a text. After a minute his phone buzzes.

'He's at his camping site. I'll take you over there.'

On our way over, Harriman asks me if we've gotten any leads on Amber's death.

I tell him I haven't. 'Having someone killed here doesn't seem to have slowed anybody down,' I say.

He glances at me sharply. 'Should it? She's local. Not one of our bikers. I know she belonged to a club a few years ago, but it has nothing to do with anybody here that I know of.'

He's right. Most of the rally-goers wouldn't consider the death of an anonymous woman a reason not to have a good time. And something else. If she's local, there really is more of a chance that someone local killed her.

I look toward the lake and see Steve Deverell with a few youngsters, including Hailey, walking along the shore toward the boathouse. I wish she wouldn't wear such skimpy clothes, but she's no different from the others.

I point Steve out to Harriman. 'He's the one wearing the shirt. I appreciate you hiring him. Is he doing a good job?'

Harriman squints and puts his hand to his forehead. 'Oh, right, Steve.' He chuckles. 'He's OK. Not always on time, and he abandoned his cart a time or two, but he's cheerful. Now if he'd stop hitting on the ladies, he'd be golden.'

I laugh. I doubt that's going to happen.

We stop in front of a group of four small camper trailers that look like overgrown pill bugs hooked up to pickups and SUVs. They're all blue and white. A big man gets up from the shade of an awning jutting out from the top of one of the trailers. I've only seen Moon from a distance. Up close, I see he's in his fifties, with flowing gray hair, a well-trimmed gray beard, and piercing blue eyes. He's wearing a brown and green plaid shirt and shorts that come to his knees. 'Reverend Moon,' he says, sticking out his hand. 'Not the Korean Moonies Reverend Moon. I'm the Woodland Fellowship Reverend Moon.' He's got a firm grip and intelligent eyes.

I chuckle and introduce myself, and Harriman says he'll get on back. 'I hate numbers and I've got nothing but numbers to deal with.'

'I hear you, Brother,' Moon says. He invites me to sit in the shade with him and provides a plastic glass of iced tea. 'My wife doesn't come on these little jaunts, but she loads me up with enough iced tea to last the week and then some. Now how can I help?'

'I'm looking into the case of the woman who was found dead here around midnight Saturday night. I understand you did a little security work at the beginning of the week, and I'd like to ask a couple of questions.'

'Fire away, but you have to understand I don't know anything that might help you with that poor woman's death. If I did, I would have contacted you.'

'This is sort of a side issue. Do you know a fellow by the name of Grant Butler?'

'Oh, yeah. Arrogant son of a gun.' He takes a tin of chewing tobacco out of his shirt pocket. 'You mind?' he says.

I shake my head and he offers me some. I tell him I don't indulge.

'Nasty habit,' he says. 'But keeps me focused.'

I've never heard that as an excuse to chew tobacco. He puts a big wad into his cheek.

'I'm getting mixed signals about Butler,' I say. 'He's a lawyer and he either is or isn't here to drum up business if somebody has an accident. And he either is or isn't mixed up with drugs.'

Moon works on his chaw and spits a stream of juice to one side. 'About the same thing I've heard. But tell you the truth, I never saw any evidence of the drug thing. Still, it's peculiar. He sits in that trailer and never comes out to mingle or be neighborly. I don't know why somebody comes here if they aren't going to be part of the festivities. But you know, people don't always open up to me. They think because I'm a preacher, I'll look down on them if they don't toe the straight and narrow. They don't understand that a preacher sometimes knows more personally about sin than his people do.'

'So you don't know anything about Butler?'

'Let me ask my son. He's likely got a little more gossip under his hat. He's in his trailer communing with God, or as I think of it, taking a nap.'

I laugh. I hadn't expected to like Reverend Moon, but I do.

He hauls himself up and pounds on the door of one of the other trailers. A man who looks like Reverend Moon might have looked twenty-five years ago opens the door, scratching his belly. He's not one of the two men I met Saturday.

'Daddy, what the hell do you want?'

'Is that anyway to talk to your beloved Daddy?' Moon says.

'It is when you wake me up out of a good dream.'

Moon tells his son what I'm here for.

'Hold on, let me get my sandals on.'

He comes over wearing flip-flops and shorts and a short-sleeved button shirt. His daddy puts a plastic cup of iced tea in his hands. We introduce ourselves. His name is Mark, but he says to call him Junior.

'I met a couple of your brothers, Gary and Allen. How many of you are there?'

'Just three of us. Plus we have a couple of sisters, and we're all married, but the women and kids don't come with us to the rallies.'

'Sounds like quite a gang,' I say to Moon.

'There's enough of 'em,' he says, grinning. He turns to his son. 'Junior, the Chief here wants to know what we can tell him about Grant Butler. Is he into drugs or is he a real lawyer? Or is there anything else that sets him apart?'

Junior takes a long drink of tea and wipes his mouth with the back of his hand. He looks at Moon. 'I can tell him something, but are you sure you want to know? You being a preacher and all?'

'Son, I've heard every sin in the books. You can't surprise me.'

To me, he says, 'This one lives in Lubbock. I don't see him often, so he doesn't know that I'm not a delicate flower.'

Their eyes meet and they snicker. It sounds like an old joke between them. 'OK,' Junior says, 'well, you know that woman he has with him?'

'Becky?' I ask.

'That's the one. She's his latest. They usually don't last as long as she has. She has a lot of *enthusiasm* for the job.' He lifts his eyebrows. He's speaking in code.

'What job?'

Mark grimaces and takes a pocketknife out of his back pocket, opens it and starts cleaning under his fingernails. He's stalling. Regardless of his daddy's insistence that he's heard it all, he's embarrassed by what he's got to impart. Finally he shrugs and snaps the knife closed.

'Good ol' Grant is pimping out his woman. And she isn't the only one.'

The hairs on my arms prickle. 'You mean he's got a little prostitution business here?'

He nods. 'I hear he makes a killing at it, too.'

'You say it's more women than just Becky. How many?'

'I can't tell you from first-hand experience, but I heard it's half-dozen over the course of the week. Not that I've been in the RV, mind you, but rumor has it that there are three very nice bedrooms set up. One of them is his, and the other two are used for his ladies.'

'Why didn't I know that?' Moon asks.

'Well, Daddy, I don't know. Are you thinking of visiting his trailer? Is that what's on your mind?'

Moon snorts. 'Your momma would know by mental telepathy if I visited that trailer. She'd be here in two hours – and we live four hours from here.'

Junior guffaws.

'Who are these women he gets to do this?' Moon asks.

He shakes his head. 'I can't tell you that. I imagine you have biker chicks who like to make an extra few bucks. Maybe a couple of locals.' He shrugs. 'You'd have to ask Butler.'

'Are you sure about this?' I ask Junior. I can't believe nobody has told me this.

'No reason for the guy who told me to lie about it. He says that Butler covers his tracks by putting out that he's a drug dealer. And I think people keep quiet about it because they like having the service at the rallies, and they know if Butler gets run in, they're screwed . . . so to speak.'

'You take your clever mouth and get on back to your nap,' his daddy says, laughing. When his son disappears back inside, Moon says, 'I guess you got what you came for. Question is, what are you going to do about it?'

'Probably nothing. Still, I met the guy and I didn't much care for him. And when I asked if he knew Amber Johnson, he lied at first and said he didn't. Got my curiosity going.'

'You don't think he had anything to do with her death, do you?'

'Anything's possible. But if not, I'll let the rest of it slide. He'll be leaving here soon anyway.'

'Good man. Know when to hold 'em and when to fold 'em.'

I don't tell him that I'm likely to put in a word to Dan Weinman about the prostitution. The highway patrol can do what it wants with the information.

After talking with Ben Holman yesterday and now hearing what Junior Moon had to say, I want to have a long chat with Amber Johnson's best friend, Lisa Hedgepeth. Something isn't adding up. Or rather, it's adding up to something that makes me uneasy.

Before I leave, I go down to the lake and find Hailey with the two girls she was with last night, and Sophie Rodriguez. Convenient for me. I still haven't managed to catch up with her. 'Hey, how's it going?' I ask.

Hailey sits up and yawns. 'Lazy. We went swimming and now the guys have gone off to get a boat for us to tool around in.'

I look at my watch. It's almost 4:00. 'Doesn't Steve start work at four?'

'Yes, but he'll be back in time.'

'How many can get in the boat?'

'It's just me and a couple of the guys. These girls don't want to go.'

'What guys?'

She rolls her eyes. 'Just some guys. You can stay and check them out if you're so worried.'

'I might just do that.' I turn my attention to Sophie Rodriguez. 'I know your daddy and we saw you at the restaurant the other night. I need to have a chat with you soon.'

She gets up, looking uneasy. She's short, like her folks, with deep brown eyes and long, curly black hair. 'What about?'

'Just a quick word. When you get home later, how about giving me a call.'

She hesitates.

'I'll need to have one of your folks there.'

She brightens. 'Sure.'

I ask Hailey if she'd like me to come get her later, but she says after she goes out in the boat with the boys, one of them will drive her home.

I wait impatiently for the boys to get back, and when they do Steve introduces them. They're his age, both awkward at meeting me. I'm relieved to hear that I won't have to argue with Hailey about whether she can go out in the boat, because the boats were all rented. I tell the boy who will be driving her home, Teddy Ronan, to say hi to his daddy for me. I figure that will be enough to let him know that I know who he is and I've got my eye on him.

Steve acts as if he's the emcee of the whole gang. It occurs to me that despite his tendency to be the 'bad boy', Steve has a good way with people.

As I get in my pickup, I realize that no matter how much gossip I've picked up today, it's just that. No hard evidence.

TWENTY-SIX

Lisa Hedgepeth wheels into the driveway just as I'm parking. I've driven the squad car so she knows the police are in front of her house. She gets out of her SUV and meets me at the sidewalk.

'Hi, Chief Craddock.' She has a deep east Texas accent. She would look cheerful in her sundress with apple and oranges splashed on a green background if you didn't see the drawn expression on her face.

'Have you got some time? I need to talk to you about Amber Johnson.'

'Come on in. I'll be glad to give you any help I can. My heart is just broken. I don't know if I'll ever get over what happened.'

The house is white with blue trim and with a garden that is wilting in the heat. 'Look at those poor zinnias,' she says, pointing to the droopy heads along the front of the house. 'The heat is cruel.'

Inside, she says, 'Let me go check on my son to make sure he's here. Have a seat in the kitchen and I'll get us some iced tea when I get back.'

She shows me into the kitchen, then strides out of the room, calling out, 'Dale, are you here?' I hear a door open and muffled voices and, in a few seconds, she comes back. 'Those boys and their video games. I swear . . .' She grabs a couple of glasses out of the cabinet, fills them with ice cubes from the freezer, and pours iced tea from a pitcher on the counter. Energy pours off her. 'Sun tea. Hope you like it sweet. I think drinking unsweetened tea is a waste of good tea.'

I tell her it's fine.

She sits down across from me. 'I'll do anything to help you find out who did that to Amber. I have cried buckets over that poor girl's death. She did not deserve that. She bore the burden of that whole family and now what are they going to do?'

I'm wondering if I'll get a word in edgewise when she finally runs down. 'You said you were Amber's best friend. Is that right?'

'Well, there were four of us that were close in our club, but I think Amber and I had something special. We were like that.' She twists her first two fingers together.

'You had a book club?'

There's a hint of mischief in her smile. 'We told everybody that's what it was, but we actually got together to drink margaritas and play poker. I always asked why is it that men get to have all the fun playing poker when we women know how to play too.'

'High stakes game?'

'Well . . .' She draws it out. 'If you call a dollar limit high stakes, then I guess.' She winks at me.

I smile, but something occurs to me. 'Do you know if Amber ever played poker online?'

Her face shuts down. 'What makes you ask?'

'Nothing really. I was just talking to somebody about it the other day and it popped into my head.' I'm a liar.

She gives a little relieved laugh. 'I guess she did play a little online. I never did it, but she told me she had.'

'Did she ever mention that her husband might have an online gambling problem?'

She looks startled. 'Who, Mike? Not that I know of.'

'Lisa, I'm going to have to ask some personal questions about Amber.'

She nods, but pulls back in her chair.

'Do you know if Amber was having an affair?'

She makes a distressed sound. 'Do I have to answer that? I don't want to say anything that might get back to Mike.'

'Unfortunately, I think he already has an idea.'

'Oh dear.' She puts her hand to her mouth as if to hold back words.

'Do you know who it was?'

'I don't know how to answer.' Her cheeks are flaming.

'Mom, can we get some pizza rolls?' We both start at the young boy's voice. He looks at Lisa's stricken expression and then at me, as if I might be the cause. 'What's going on?'

'Nothing, honey, we were just talking about Amber.' She introduces me to her son and then says, 'Why don't you go on back and play with Cole and I'll bring you the pizza rolls when they're ready.'

He ambles out and she jumps up and pulls a package from the refrigerator and pops some rolls into the microwave.

When she sits down, I say, 'You were going to tell me who you thought Amber was having an affair with.' Even though I know the answer, I'm curious to find out how much Amber told her best friend.

She plays with a lock of her hair. 'I'd really rather not say.'

'But she did tell you who it was?'

She bites her lower lip. 'Yes.' But it's a hesitant sound. There's something odd about this.

'What did she say about him?'

She looks toward the microwave as if hoping to be saved by the ding. 'She said she was having fun. And that it wasn't serious,' she adds hastily. 'I know she loved Mike, but you know how things are.' She glances toward the kitchen door and lowers her voice. 'He just wasn't up to sex. And come on, Amber was thirty-two. She wasn't ready to be put on the shelf.'

'Did she say how she met her lover?'

The microwave dings and she practically catapults from her chair and rushes to take out the pizza rolls. She throws them in a bowl, grabs a big bottle of soda from the refrigerator and, as she leaves, calls over her shoulder, 'I'll be right back.'

While she's gone I think about how strong her reaction was to my question. If it's Ben Holman she's referring too, and he's divorced, why would she be so reluctant to name him? Is it because he's a teacher and she's worried about his reputation?

Lisa comes back in and sits down. 'Dale and his friends would eat us out of house and home if I let them.'

'Lisa, I talked to Ben Holman.'

'Ah!' She brings her hand to her chest and gives a huge sigh of relief.

'Why didn't you want to say who it was?'

'I just . . . I didn't want to hurt anybody.'

'I understand. Another subject. Did Amber ever tell you any specifics about the settlement they got from the insurance company after their motorcycle accident?'

'Do you mean figures? No, it would have surprised me if she had. People are funny about money things. She did say she thought it was stingy.'

'Did she tell you they were thinking of suing?'

'I don't think that's true. She said she talked to a lawyer and he said it might be more trouble than it was worth.'

I prick up my ears. 'When did she tell you that?'

'Saturday morning.' Her voice is mournful. 'We talked almost every morning and she told me she had gotten advice from a lawyer. Somebody she knew through that motorcycle club she and Mike belonged to.'

'Did Amber ever say she was harassed down at the store?'

She blinks at my sudden shift in subject. 'No. Was she?'

'When I was there Sunday, two bikers came in and asked for her. They didn't know she was dead. I wondered what they wanted with her – do you know?'

She shrugs, but drops her eyes to her hands, which are twisted tightly together on the table in front of her. Her cheeks have pink spots on them. There's something she's not telling.

'Did she ever say anybody had scared her or threatened her?' She meets my eyes. 'No, she never said anything like that.'

'Is there anything the two of you talked about that you think would help me find out who killed her?'

She shakes her head, but her evasive glance tells me another story. She's holding something back and I don't know how to get at it.

'You sure there's nothing else?'

'Yes.'

I get up and tell her if she thinks of anything to let me know. 'You know, anything you tell me will be held in confidence. Mike doesn't have to know.'

Her eyes look bleak and she's very still. She's struggling with something. I wait, but after a minute she gets up and says, 'I'll let you know if I think of anything.'

And that's that.

When I get home, I'm surprised to see Hailey, Sophie, and Ashley in the living room watching TV. They're giggling and barely acknowledge me when I walk in. In fact, they seem to avoid looking at me. But there's a feeling in the air that I'm wary of. A certain tension of their shoulders that tells me they're hiding something.

I walk into the kitchen, trying to figure out what makes me feel itchy about what they're up to. Everything is the way I left it except for a big bottle of Coca-Cola sitting on the kitchen table, half gone. I walk back into the living room. 'How about some dinner?' I ask. 'I could go get some hamburgers.'

Hailey looks at me, the picture of innocence. 'We're fine. We ate at the rally.' She sounds innocent. Too innocent. The three girls lock eyes, smirking. And suddenly I smell it. Alcohol.

'Suit yourself,' I say. I walk back into the kitchen, take the cap off the bottle of soda, and sniff. Definitely alcohol. I go to the cabinet where I keep some bourbon, gin, and tequila, which I rarely partake of. Of course I can't remember how much there should be in the bottles. I take the cap off each in turn and feel the top. Sure enough, the top of the bourbon bottle is wet.

I step back into the living room. 'Hailey, can I see you for a minute?'

'What about? We're watching this show. It's really good. I don't want to miss any of it.'

Ashley snickers.

'It's important.'

She says something under her breath. The other two girls shoot me narrow-eyed looks.

Hailey reluctantly gets up and follows me into the kitchen, where she plants herself in front of me, her arms folded. 'Yeah, what is it?'

'You've gotten into my bourbon.'

Her mouth falls open and her eyes flash with anger. 'No we haven't! God, you're so suspicious!'

I go to the Coke bottle and uncap it and sniff it. 'I can smell the booze. Don't compound the problem by lying to me please.'

Her face goes stony. 'It wasn't me. It was Sophie. She's eighteen. She can drink.'

'And blaming someone else on top of it? Hailey, I can smell it on your breath.' I'm trying to keep my temper, but she's pushing me.

'I just had a sip,' she whines.

'I want your friends to go home.'

She narrows her eyes. 'What do you mean? That I can't have friends over?'

'Another time, but not now. This evening you're staying in with me. I won't put up with you drinking and lying about it.'

'How are they supposed to get home?'

'They can call their parents, or I will. Or they can walk.'

'You're embarrassing me!'

'No, you're embarrassing yourself. You're proving that you aren't trustworthy. You keep telling me that you don't like being treated like a child, but you're acting like one. Do you want to tell them yourself that they have to go home, or shall I?'

In answer, she flees down the hall and slams the door to her room.

I go into the living room. 'Sorry, girls, but it's time to go home. And you need to tell your parents that you've been drinking. Or if you prefer, I'll tell them.'

'It wasn't us,' Sophie says. 'It was just Hailey.'

'You expect me to believe that?' I ask.

She looks panicky. 'She said you wouldn't mind.'

'Well, she was wrong. How old are you, Sophie?'

'Seventeen, but I'll be eighteen in October.'

'The three of you are minors and I'm going to have to notify your parents. Now go on home.'

'How are we supposed to get home?'

'Call your parents or walk.'

Ashley takes out her phone and calls her mom, giving me the evil eye the whole time. 'Come on, Sophie. We'll wait outside.'

They flounce out, leaving me to wonder why I ever thought I could handle a teenaged girl. But now I'm just mad enough to confront Hailey. As soon as Lily Deverell picks up the girls, I walk back to her room and knock on the door.

'Go away.'

'No. You need to come out here. I want to talk to you.'

It takes more insistence before she finally comes out, looking daggers at me.

'Let's go out on the porch,' I say. I have no idea what I'm going to say to her.

We go out and sit in the rocking chairs and it occurs to me that if she's had a lot of bourbon, she might not be in the best mental shape to have a conversation. I'll have to assess that as we go along.

Dusty has followed us out, his tail drooping as if he's expecting to be scolded.

I wait for silence to settle. It's late afternoon, and mosquitoes are buzzing around us. Hailey swats one, but doesn't comment.

'Hailey, we've always gotten along. In fact, I could say you've sort of been my favorite. You're curious – always asking questions. And you're clever. Don't forget, you pointed out that woman with the wig and the colored contacts; otherwise I might never have known it. Plus, you've got a good sense of humor. Always quick with a smile. So what's happened?'

She rocks back and forth and I'm reminded of Tom when he was a youngster, how he'd climb into a rocking chair when he was upset. Finally, she says, 'As I've gotten older I realize how lame everybody is. I mean, I like you, but your life is not my life.'

'That's true. But it doesn't mean we can't respect each other.'

'Well, you have to respect me too. You're like my parents. None of you understand that I'm my own person and I should get to decide what I do.'

'You're sixteen. There's a reason that laws don't recognize people as adults until they're older. You don't have the maturity to make all the decisions for yourself.'

She sighs, loading the sound with the burden of her life.

'Have you thought about what you want to do with your life? What you want to study in college?'

'I don't think I'm going to college.'

'That surprises me. Have you talked to your folks about this?'

'Are you kidding? They'd have a cow. That's all they talk about. College, college, college.'

'So what kind of job do you think you might want to do when you graduate?'

'God, you sound just like my daddy. I don't know what I want to do, OK? Why does everybody think I have to know now what I'm going to do two years from now?'

'Planning ahead isn't a bad idea. Is there some reason you don't want to think about it now?'

The light is fading fast, but I can see that the question stops her. She swallows. 'I've got plenty of time.'

'You don't have any dreams about how your life might go? Some image of yourself ten years from now? Do you want to have kids? You want to be married?'

'Why do you care?' she shoots back.

'I do care about you. You're lucky. You have family who care a lot about you. I don't mean to put you on the spot. I'm just wondering if you've thought about the future, that's all. Can you see yourself being a clerk in a grocery store or a department store, or maybe a bartender or waitress? A bus driver? Or a secretary?' I forgo adding that those are the jobs that will most likely be open to her if she doesn't have an education.

'I could be a singer or an actress.'

'Interesting. I didn't know you liked performing. Maybe that's why you wanted to go see the bands out at the rally. Have you ever been in a play or sung in front of people?'

'No, but my mom says I have a pretty voice.'

'So she's heard you sing. Do you play an instrument?'

'No. I tried to learn how to play the piano, but I wasn't very good.'

'What kind of music do you like?'

'I like country and western. I could sing that.'

'Ever had lessons?'

She shrugs. 'I'm not sure I need that.'

I think about Wendy's story of her daughter running away to Hollywood. What is it that persuades these girls that they can just show up and become an actress, or miraculously become a singer without ever trying it? Have they been assured they can do anything they want without being taught that it takes effort?

'I'm glad we're having this talk, but it doesn't tell me more about how to make your time here more agreeable. I can't have you drinking. You're underage. I thought letting you go out with Steve and his friends would give you some fun, even though I worry that Steve can get into trouble sometimes—'

'Oh, come on. He's a wuss. He treated me like I was a princess. He's scared to death of you.'

I chuckle. 'You know, I think he's basically a good guy. But he has poor impulse control.'

She sniffs. 'That's why I like older guys. The boys my age are so immature.'

Lyle is not exactly my idea of maturity, but I'm not bringing him into this conversation. 'Look, I'm willing to take you home to Austin whenever you feel like you've had enough. But I'd like to wait until I either figure out what happened to the woman who was killed or turn the case over to the highway patrol. Can you wait?'

'How long will that take?'

'A few days.'

'Lyle would come back and get me. I really miss him.'

'I'd like to take you to Austin so I can see your folks. And I wouldn't feel OK letting Lyle take you back unless your folks agree.'

'Huh! You know they won't.'

'Can you wait a few days?'

She sighs. 'I guess.'

'And no drinking or drugs. Can you spend time with Sophie and Ash under those circumstances?'

'I don't really even like them. But I guess a few days won't hurt. They want to go to the movies in Bobtail tomorrow night. Is it all right if I go with them?'

'Sure.'

'And I'd like to spend some more time at the rally, seeing the bands. This weekend there will be music all day both days.'

It occurs to me that April, who sings with the Oakley String Band, seemed like she had her head on straight. At least she was strict with her friend Lulu. 'I can introduce you to one of the singers, if you'd like that. She's the one who was singing with the Oakley String Band the night you got here. Remember her?'

'She was cool. How did you meet her?'

'She was there the night they found Amber Johnson.'

'Oh.' She freezes. I wait, and she says, 'I probably shouldn't tell you this, but Steve said something about Amber.'

'Really? What's that?'

'He said Amber wasn't the sweet girl everybody thought she was.'

'Did he say in what way?'

'Well . . .' She draws it out. 'He said she was a slut.'

Uh-oh. What does that mean? 'I hate to hear him say that. She's the mother of a couple of young kids. I wouldn't want talk like that to get back to them.'

'I'm just telling you what he said.'

'I understand. Look, I hope we've settled things between us. Are we good?'

'I guess.' She puts a hand to her mouth and her eyes widen. 'I forgot. I need to tell you something. I hope you're not mad.'

My heart sinks. What now? 'Go ahead.'

'You know you said you were going to talk to Sophie about an argument she had?'

'Yes.'

'Well, I sort of asked her about it.' She ducks her head. 'I didn't mean to butt in but she was saying that she thinks Steve is sort of a dick. He called her a bitch. So I asked her if she had an argument with him.'

'And?'

'She said she did, and that she got mad and scratched him.'

I'm glad to confirm that it was in fact Sophie who gave Steve the scratches on his face, but I don't want to encourage Hailey to have too much enthusiasm for intruding into the investigation. It might be dangerous if she starts questioning the wrong person.

'Look, Hailey, you're right, it's best for you not to get too involved. On the other hand, sounds like it was a natural conversation, and that does help me out, so I'm not mad.'

She blows out a breath, as if she's been worried.

'I tell you what, let's go over to Bryan tonight and take Wendy out to dinner.'

'I don't know if I want to. Is she mad at me?'

'One of the things I like about Wendy is that she doesn't hold a grudge. I expect if you apologize to her, she'll accept the apology with no strings. So what do you think? Dinner?'

She shrugs. 'I guess.'

I go inside and call Wendy. It turns out that not only is she fine with us coming for dinner, but her niece is back in town. She's exactly Hailey's age and we'll take both girls out. With any luck they'll get along.

We meet at Wendy's house and plan to go to the restaurant from there so the girls can get acquainted with each other first. As soon as Wendy opens the door, I say, 'Hailey has something she wants to say to you.'

I had reminded Hailey on the way that she needed to apologize to Wendy for disappearing on her.

'I'm sorry I ran out,' she says. She mumbles it and her cheeks are bright red.

'Thank you. I accept your apology. You two come in out of the heat.' She opens the door wide.

Wendy has put out chips and salsa and soft drinks for the girls. I told her what happened with Hailey's flirtation with bourbon and we decide at least tonight we aren't going to drink wine in front of the girls. I have coffee and Wendy has a sparkling water with lime.

Wendy's niece, Tammy, has blossomed into a pretty teenager and is less awkward than when I first met her last fall, but she's still as sulky as ever. Back then, she had an unacceptable boyfriend, like Hailey. Except that her boyfriend actually went to jail. Tammy still thinks he was wrongly accused – even though he was caught in the act of burglarizing a house.

The girls circle each other like wary cats. Wendy and I prod them with questions intended to help them get to know a little about each other, but it's tough going – until they find the subject of their mutual contempt for parents. Then it's a contest to see which set of parents is lamer. They keep that up all the way to the restaurant, Nico's Trattoria. By the time the girls discover that they both like sausage and peppers on their pizza and despise olives, they are bonded.

While they put their heads together to whisper about their boyfriends, Wendy asks me how the case is going. 'Finding out some interesting things,' I say. 'But nothing I can discuss at the moment.' I cut my eyes to the girls.

Wendy gets it and starts telling me about a trip she's planning to Padre Island. 'I was wondering if you might want to go?'

'Is it just you?'

'No, my friend Gayle is driving down there with me, but her sister lives there and she'll be staying with her. Not that I can't entertain myself, but I'd love to have you along.' I tell her that I've never been to Padre Island.

'Really? It's wonderful. You'd love it.'

'Let's see how things are going. I think I can get away for a few days and leave Maria in charge. She'd like that. My only worry would be that she'll change the locks while I'm gone.'

It turns out to be a pretty good evening all round, and the girls decide they want to do something together. Wendy says she'll pick Hailey up in the morning and take them to San Antonio. 'We can go to San Pedro Park and swim, or go to Brackenridge, to the zoo. I'll let you decide.' The girls opt for swimming.

'And we can also go to the River Walk.'

On the way home I remind Hailey that she was going to the movies with Sophie and Ash tomorrow night.

'We'll do that another time,' she says. 'They won't care.'

Hailey is in a cheerful mood when we get home. We watch TV until I fall asleep and Hailey wakes me up to tell me I was snoring.

TWENTY-SEVEN

The second Hailey is out the door the next morning with Wendy and her niece, I call Steve Deverell to tell him I need to talk to him.

'C'mon, Chief,' he says. 'I heard about the girls stealing booze. I had nothing to do with that.'

'I know you didn't. This is about something else. I'll be there soon to talk to you.'

'I haven't had breakfast yet.'

'You can eat while we talk.'

Twenty minutes later, Lily Deverell lets me in. Today she's wearing hot pink shorts and an orange T-shirt. It occurs to me that if Lily was her daughter's age, she'd probably be dressed in the same style, with her hair all wonky, tattoos and piercings.

She seems nervous. 'Is Steve in trouble?'

'Not at all. I just have a question for him about something at the rally.'

She bites her lip. 'Is it about what happened to Amber? I can't get over that. I wish we hadn't had harsh words the last time I saw her. And to not know what happened makes it worse.' She rubs her arms as if she's cold, which may be possible. The air conditioning is turned down to about fifty degrees.

It's just been a few days, but I expect Lily is voicing a lot of people's frustration, that not knowing what happened to Amber makes the scenario even worse. At first I thought it was possible we may never know. The rally is huge, and Amber could have been killed by anyone. It could have been a random attack. But as I've gotten to know more about her, I'm beginning to think she had a hidden side that might have led to her death.

Steve walks in looking like he just rolled out of bed. His hair is sticking out at all angles and he's barefoot and yawning.

'Let's go in the kitchen,' he says, 'so I can get something to eat.'

'You want me to come in and fix you some eggs?' Lily asks.

'That'd be great,' he says eagerly.

'In that case, we'll have to talk somewhere else while your mom cooks,' I say. 'This has to be a private conversation.' Both of them look shocked. Lily is worried, and Steve is nervous.

In the living room, Steve perches on the edge of the sofa, hunched over with his hands folded between his knees. 'Am I in trouble?' he says.

'Not at all. You might have information that could help me. I was talking to Hailey and she said you made a remark about Amber that I wanted to talk to you about.'

'Oh, yeah.' He ducks his head. 'I guess I should keep my mouth shut.'

'There is that. I'd hate to have her kids hear your opinion of their mother.'

Understanding flares in his eyes. 'I hadn't thought of that,' he mumbles.

'What I want to know is what you meant by it.' I want to know if her affair with Ben Holman was well-known. It had also occurred to me that maybe this wasn't the first time she'd had an affair.

His shoulders hunch higher. 'I know she was sleeping with this guy.'

'Who was it?'

'Should I tell you? I mean, I don't think he would hurt her. He thought she was hot. Not that I agree. I mean, to each his own. She seemed kind of old to me. You think he killed her?'

It sounds like Steve is talking about someone younger than Amber. Ben Holman was older. 'I have no reason to suspect that whoever she was having a relationship with killed her, but he might know something about her movements that day.'

'Right. Well, you know Cal, who was working in the store? Well, that's who it was. He was kind of into her. I mean, nothing serious or anything.'

His words slam me. I should have thought of that. I remember the day I was at the store, the day before Amber was killed, hearing Amber and Cal laughing in the back room. I'd thought nothing of it, but in my memory, there was a suggestive sound to it that I didn't catch at the time.

So that's two people Amber was sleeping with. And one of them was a kid. I wonder if the two men knew about each other.

'How did you find out?'

'He's not exactly keeping it a secret. He was pretty pleased with himself. Like he had all the moves, you know?'

'Did he call her a slut?'

He shakes his head.

'Do you know if she was having an affair with anyone else?'

His face is bright red. 'I might have heard something like that.'

'Who was it?'

'Hey, I don't know for sure, OK? Somebody just said she was pretty friendly with Mr Holman from school.'

'Look, Steve, if you hear other rumors, no matter what they are, I want you to tell me. And I hope you'll stop giving your opinion of Amber in public. Her kids don't deserve that.'

'Yes, sir.'

'Now, is there anyone else you know of who was sleeping with Amber?'

He mumbles that he doesn't know.

'Keep your ears open. It's important.'

Maria is on duty today, and I tell her what I found out from Steve. I knew that hearing the news about Amber and Cal would be hard for her. She's a prude at heart.

'What is wrong with her! She's ten years older than him. He's a kid.'

'He's young, but he's not a kid.'

'You know that if you have sex with an employee that's sexual harassment, don't you?' she says.

'It's a little late to worry about that now.'

'It gives us three solid suspects,' she says, ruffled. 'Her husband, Ben Holman, and Cal Tyson.'

I tell her about my talk with Amber's friend Lisa.

'They have a poker club that's supposed to be a book club?' She grimaces. 'It's looking like Amber had a secret life.'

'She certainly isn't who everybody thought she was. But she had a tough time. She's a young woman and her husband was disabled. She must have felt like her life was over.'

'That's no excuse,' she says.

'Maria, it's not our job to judge. It's our job to find out who killed her.'

She groans. 'I know, I know.'

'The first thing we're going to do is go and talk to Cal. And Maria, it's important that you not show your distaste for what they were up to. If you can't do that, I'll have to talk to him alone.'

'Boss, you know I'm professional. I'll be totally fine.'

The Tysons live a few blocks from the post office, in an older house with asbestos siding. Someone in the family is a gardener. The yard is a profusion of zinnias, plumbago, and sunflowers, but like most of the flowers, they're barely surviving the heat.

Cal's mother answers the door. She frowns when she sees me. 'Chief Craddock, what are you doing here?' She's a tall, bony woman with frizzy hair and skin so pale she clearly doesn't spend much time outdoors. She's wearing Capri pants and a white sleeveless blouse, and despite the frigid air pouring out the door from the air conditioning, she's perspiring. She's got a bandage on her hand and a little blood has seeped through.

'You hurt yourself?'

She looks down at her hand and winces. 'Slicing carrots,' she says. 'Happens all the time. I'm clumsy in the kitchen.'

I introduce Maria. 'Mrs Tyson, we'd like to talk to your son if he's home.'

'Call me Myra.' She invites us in. 'Is this about poor Amber? I keep wondering what she was doing out at the rally. That's no place for a wife and mother. So many vulgar people. The loud music.'

'We're investigating,' I say. 'Hoping to find out the answer to that.'

'I don't know how Cal can help you. He just worked for her.'

'Is he here?' I ask.

'He's in his room playing video games,' she says. 'The worst thing ever invented, if you ask me. A real waste of time. Go on in the living room and take a seat. I'll get him.'

The living room is right off the hallway. It's got matching nubby weave sofa and armchairs, and glass-and-brass end tables and coffee table. We sit down in the armchairs. The room has a lot of photos of Cal and a girl I take to be his sister. She looks a few years older. There are wedding pictures of her with a startled-looking young man, and in a few pictures she's carrying a baby.

'Hey, Chief Craddock, how are you?' Cal really is a guileless young man, coming across fresh-faced and innocent.

'Cal, sit down. We need to talk.'

'Sure.' He sprawls out on the sofa. He's wearing shorts, a T-shirt that says, 'Whatever', and flip-flops. Somehow in this house he looks younger than he does in the store.

Myra Tyson is hovering, casting glances between us and her son.

'Myra, we need to talk privately to Cal.'

'Oh, that's fine. I just . . . do you need anything?'

'We're fine.'

When she leaves, I get up and close the door to the hallway. Then I see another door at the other end of the room and I close it as well. When I sit back down I see that Cal's face has turned ghostly pale.

'This is about Amber and me, isn't it?'

I nod. 'You want to tell me about your relationship with her?'

He shrugs, but his shoulders stay bunched up tight around his ears. 'What do you want to know?'

'How long had you two been having sex?'

He mumbles something.

'You'll have to speak up.'

'Couple of months.'

'How did it come about?'

His face is even paler. 'I don't know. One night we had to stay late and do some inventory. And we got to talking and one thing led to another.'

'Who initiated it?'

The question sparks anger in his eyes. 'What difference does it make? Are you trying to say she was taking advantage of me because I was younger? I'm not that young. It was a mutual attraction.'

'Where did you usually meet?'

'Meet? Oh, you mean where did we hook up? Right in the back office.' He giggles. 'Wasn't always easy, but we managed.'

'Did she ever indicate that she wanted to break it off?'

'A couple of times she said she felt guilty, but she always came back.' He's preening. 'Besides, it didn't mean anything. I mean, it was just sex, it wasn't like I wanted to take her away from her husband.'

Maria clears her throat. She's most likely itching to give him a piece of her mind, but I shoot her a warning look.

'Not that I didn't like her. I did. She was great. Funny. Sexy. We had good times. And at least she didn't make me pay for it.' He smirks.

It's an odd comment. 'What do you mean?'

He freezes, looking like he's been caught in some nefarious action. 'I just mean, sometimes women get paid for sex.'

I get a jumbled picture of Ben Holman's uneasy expression when he told me he saw Amber 'from time to time', and of Lisa Hedgepeth holding something back. Throw into the mix the suggestion that she might have been one of the women Grant Butler was pimping for. Not to mention those two men who came into the store asking if Amber was in. Plus, Steve saying that Amber was a slut, and the $200 cash in Amber's purse. I don't like what the picture is adding up to. 'Are you saying Amber got paid for sex?'

'Ummm . . .'

There's a tap on the door. It opens and Myra sticks her head in. 'Can I get you anything?'

'No, thank you,' I say. It comes out harsher than I intended and she looks startled.

'Well, excuse me,' she says. I've offended her, but I've got more on my mind. She closes the door.

'Cal, tell me if Amber got paid for having sex with men.'

He's chewing his lip furiously. 'I guess maybe she did.'

'You guess?'

'OK, yeah she did.'

'Who all knows what she was up to?'

He looks wary. 'I don't know.'

'How many knew that you were having sex with her?'

'Listen, she wasn't—'

'Just answer the question.'

'A couple of guys. How did you find out anyway? Did somebody blab?'

'Something like that.'

'It was Steve Deverell, wasn't it? He never could keep his mouth shut. He was hella jealous.'

'Did he tell you he was jealous?'

'Not in so many words, but I could tell. He wanted the juicy details.' He glances at Maria and something in her face makes him add quickly, 'Not that I told him anything. That's private.' I'll bet.

'Did Amber say anything to you about where she was going the Saturday night she was killed?'

He shakes his head. 'I wish she had. It makes me feel bad. Maybe I could have stopped her.'

'You have any idea who she was meeting? Did she ever mention feeling afraid of anyone or having a problem with someone?'

'No, sir, but if I knew, I'd sure tell you.'

'I want you to tell me who her clients were.' Clients. I don't know what other word to use.

'I don't know. She didn't tell me their names.'

'Then how did you know she had clients?'

He wriggles around on the sofa. 'She might have mentioned it.'

'Why?'

His face is so bright red that he looks like he could combust. 'It was . . . I mean she . . . we . . .' His face is twisted. 'It turned me on, OK?' His voice is ragged. 'And she knew it.'

There's nothing more to get out of him. As we drive away, Maria says, 'I feel like I need to take a shower.'

TWENTY-EIGHT

I tell Maria that I'm going back out to the rally, but she says she'd rather stay at the station. 'What are you doing out there anyway? We need to be finding out who those men were that she . . . you know.'

'I'm going out to talk to Steve again. He's the one who blabbed about Cal and Amber, but I think he knows more than he said.'

When I get to the rally, first I go by to see if Jack Cassidy knew anything about this. The Rough Roaders camp is closed up except for a young woman in her twenties. 'They all went off on a ride this morning and should be back around two o'clock.'

The woman I'm talking to, Megan, is looking frazzled, with

two little ones, a boy and a girl, running around wild making zooming noises and kicking up dust.

'Y'all cut it out,' she yells. 'You're driving me crazy. What are you going to do when I'm in the crazy house and you're stuck with your daddy?'

'Yay!' they both scream. 'Daddy will give us ice cream for dinner.' They start parading around yelling, 'Ice cream, ice cream.'

I can see that although she's exasperated, she's also amused. 'Twins! Four years old. I'm putting them in nursery school in August. Let the teacher see what she can do with them.'

'Maybe they'd like Sno-cones?' I ask. 'My treat.'

'Ha! The last thing they need is more sugar. But sure, that would be great. At least it will give me a moment's peace.'

I go off and come back with two strawberry Sno-cones, having been told that whatever I get, I need to get them both the same. The kids take them from me and go sit down in the dirt.

I ask Megan to have Jack Cassidy call me as soon as he gets back.

Luckily for me, Steve is a creature of habit and I find him with his friends, including Ash and Sophie, lolling around in the same vicinity as he was yesterday. I notice he always wears a T-shirt. With his fair hair, he must burn easily.

'Where's Hailey?' Ash asks.

'She's in San Antonio today,' I say. 'She'll be back tomorrow. Steve, I need to talk to you again. Take a walk with me.'

'Uh oh, you're in trouble,' his sister says.

'Oh, man,' he grumbles. 'I was just feeling relaxed.'

We walk over to a stand of forlorn trees to get out of the heat.

'I have to ask you something important, and you need to tell me the truth.'

His eyes narrow. 'If it's about your niece, she's—'

I'd love to know what he was going to say, but I interrupt him. 'No. It's about Amber Johnson.'

'Did Cal tell you he wasn't having sex with her? 'Cause he sure as hell was.'

'No, he admitted it. But he said something that brought up another question. Did you know that Amber was charging men to sleep with her?'

Steve's eyes dart one way and then another. 'I didn't sleep with her,' he says.

'That's not what I asked.'

He bites his lip. 'Why are you asking me?'

'Was she?'

He blows out a breath. 'I guess.'

'Do you know who her clients were?'

'None of my friends. They couldn't afford it.'

'She charged a lot?'

'It's not that. I mean . . . God, do I have to tell you this? Most guys I know don't have to pay for it. It's older guys who can't get a woman, or who want somebody different, that have to pay.'

'Any names?'

He sighs. 'I don't know anybody for sure. Just rumors.'

'Who?'

He folds his arms across his chest and stares down at the ground. 'You said you knew about Mr Holman.'

'That's right. Who else?'

'Maybe Joey Masters, but I don't see how that can be. His wife is a fox. Why would he want to scr . . . have sex with somebody else?'

'Are there more?' My heart sinks with every name.

'Well, somebody said she was sleeping with that Indian guy who owns the motel, so she could get a free room whenever she needed it.'

I doubt it. But Steve is having a hard time with it, so maybe he's telling the truth – at least as far as he knows it.

'Who else?'

'I don't know any more names.'

'Is it common knowledge that Amber was sleeping with men for money?'

'Guys know about it.'

'How long has it been going on?'

'I couldn't tell you. I just heard earlier this summer.'

'Steve, I appreciate your telling me, and once again, if you could tamp down the gossip for the sake of her kids, I'd appreciate it.'

When I go to see if the Rough Roaders have come back, I spot Jack right away, sitting with his wife and another couple, all drinking beer. Everybody is sweating and wearing as little as they can decently get away with. Jack doesn't look happy to see me, and he'll be even more unhappy when I get through with him.

'Hello, Jack. Did your friend Megan tell you I came by and wanted you to call me?'

His wife looks at him with raised eyebrows.

'She did. I haven't had a chance to call,' he says. 'We just got back.'

'Can we take a walk?'

He gets up, leaving his beer behind. When we're a distance away, I say to him, 'You lied to me about Butler. You knew he was pimping out women in his RV.'

He's turned sideways to me so I can't see his face. 'I suppose I did.'

'And you knew Amber was one of them.'

He looks out over the lake, his expression bleak. 'Yeah, I knew.'

'How did you know?'

'He told me that when she came to see him Friday afternoon about the insurance matter, he mentioned that if she was having money problems, he knew a way to help her out financially.'

'And she took him up on it.'

He nods.

'Why didn't you tell me this?'

'I felt bad for Amber. That's actually the reason I was talking to her the day she was killed. I wanted to ask her if there wasn't some other way for her to keep afloat.'

'Keep afloat?'

He stops walking and stares at me. 'Yes, why do you think she was trading sex for money? It wasn't just for giggles. She was desperate.'

'What did she say when you asked if she couldn't work something else out?'

He grimaces. 'Told me it was none of my business and she'd do what she had to do. I was shocked, to tell you the truth. Amber was always a party girl, but I know she loves Mike and I just couldn't understand why she would turn to . . .' His voice trails off. He sounds really unhappy.

'Did your wife know?'

He gives me a swift sidelong glance. 'No, it would be awful if she found out. She loved Amber like a sister, but she's a devout Christian woman. It would be hard for her to hear that.'

'Did any of the men in the Rough Roaders take advantage of the opportunity to sleep with her?'

'Amber told me she wouldn't sleep with any of the club members.'

'Did any of them complain about that?'

He's silent for a few steps. We've made it down to the lake and he keeps his eyes fixed on the water. The afternoon sun shines bright off it. People are drifting around in the water on floats, too hot to swim. It occurs to me that the water ought to be tested for algae. Every year at this time it's dangerous to swim in it because the heat breeds bad algae in the water.

'One guy. Randy Woods. He's always had a thing for Amber and I think he saw this as his opportunity to have sex with her, so he checked in Saturday and she said nothing doing. At least he told me she said no.' He squares off with me. 'You're not thinking he got mad and killed her because of this, are you?'

'I have to consider it. I need to talk to Randy Woods. He around?'

'Yeah, he was on the ride this morning.'

We find Woods with some others gathered around a fancy Suzuki. Jack introduces us.

'Mr Woods, can I have a word?'

He comes away readily enough. I thank Jack Cassidy and he goes on his way. Woods watches him, frowning. He's a paunchy man with a receding hairline and pockmarked skin.

'Randy, I wanted to ask you about something. You knew Amber Johnson?'

'I sure did. She was a sweetheart. Damn shame what happened to her.'

'You also know a man by the name of Grant Butler?'

A shadow crosses his face. 'I've met him. Wouldn't say I *know* him. Not a particularly friendly person.'

'You know that he runs a little side business here at the rally, pimping out women?'

He sneers. 'Oh, well, that's a little harsh. He provides a service.'

'You know that Amber was one of the women working out of his RV?'

'I don't get your point.'

'I'm asking if you knew that.'

He puts his hands on his hips, legs spread apart in an aggressive stance. 'Suppose I did know? What of it?'

'I want to know if you were one of the men who slept with Amber?'

'No, sir, I did not.' His face falls. 'I'm not saying I wouldn't have liked to, but she said she wouldn't have anything to do with Rough Roaders and I respected that.' He looks off in the distance. 'Tell you the truth, I felt bad that she had come to that.'

But apparently not bad enough that he didn't try to take advantage of it.

TWENTY-NINE

I head for Grant Butler's RV and arrive in time to see a man coming out, looking sheepish.

'Is Butler in?' I ask him.

'Who?' The guy glares at me.

'This is Grant Butler's RV.'

'I don't know who it belongs to. You're gonna have to ask somebody else.'

I bang on the door and wait. Eventually it opens and Grant Butler's girlfriend Becky is standing there in a dressing gown right out of a movie from the 1940s. She could be Ava Gardner. Her smile is lazy. 'Hi, Sam. What brings you here?'

'Couple of questions. May I come in?'

She glances back into the bowels of the RV and then back at me. 'It's such a mess in here. Why don't I make myself presentable and come out there and maybe we can have a beer and get to know each other better.' She thinks she can charm any man, and mostly she's right, but her appeal has worn off me.

'Is Grant here?'

'Not at the moment, but you can talk to me.' Her tone is husky and suggestive.

'I'll wait for you to get dressed.'

She takes her sweet time. Fifteen minutes later she comes out in short shorts and an off-the-shoulder blouse. She hands me a beer and takes a swig of one herself. 'I seem to remember that you were asking about Amber Johnson. Have you found out who killed her?'

'Not yet. When will Grant be back?'

She shrugs and bats her eyelashes. 'Grant is hard to pin down. He comes and goes as he pleases. But I'll sure be glad to help you.'

'He left you to run the business?'

She has the innocent look down pat. 'Business?'

'Ms Butler, was Amber Johnson working for Grant?'

'I'm not Ms Butler. I'm Becky Henderson.'

'Was Amber Johnson working for Grant? Or for you?'

She smirks. 'She might have been doing a little of this and that.'

'Ms Henderson, Becky, I'm getting tired of your obstruction. I'm not here to make trouble for whatever activities you have going on in your RV here. I'm just interested in finding out who killed Amber Johnson. If she was prostituting herself I need to know who she might have hooked up with that night, in case somebody had a problem with her.'

'Obstruction?' Her voice is suddenly icy. 'That woman has nothing to do with me. I don't know what you think is going on in here, but it has nothing to do with prostitutes. How dare you!'

I chuckle. 'Yeah, I heard you could get feisty. But I have it on good authority that performing sexual services is exactly what's going on here. And if you continue to refuse to cooperate, I'll have no qualms about shutting you down.'

Her aquamarine eyes meet mine in a stare-down. But I'm reminded that Hailey told me the woman's eyes and hair were fake, so I'm unimpressed with her stare. She seems to read it right. 'I don't want trouble,' she says. 'But the women who work for Grant are adults and they can do whatever suits them. It has nothing to do with Grant or me. He just lets them use his space.'

And no doubt charges them for the privilege. 'Has Amber done this before at the rally?'

'I couldn't tell you. I wasn't with Grant at the rally last year, so I don't know whether she was here or not. I'll tell you this for free, though. She didn't want to be doing it. She said she needed the cash.'

'I appreciate that. But I need to know who she was with. Do you keep a record?'

'No, sir, we do not. It's strictly cash and carry. Men let us know what time they'll be here, but we don't ask questions.' Her face changes subtly. She licks her lips and frowns. She knows she's talked too much. 'That's all I have to say, though. I'd appreciate it if you didn't tell Grant what I told you. He doesn't take kindly to people knowing about his business.'

I'll bet he doesn't. I've gotten all I can from Becky. Walking away, I'm not sure I believe that they don't know who their customers are. It doesn't seem like a reasonable business model.

But my conversation with Becky has got me no closer to knowing who killed Amber. Did Mike find out what she was up to and follow her here and confront her? Did she get into an altercation with one of the men she had sex with? I can't believe I'm even thinking of her in those terms. I'm not so naïve that I don't know women sleep with men for money, but for a wife and mother in my town, a woman who is a well-known, well-liked member of the community to be driven to it surpasses my understanding.

'You think Randy is telling the truth?' Maria asks when I tell her he said Amber wouldn't sleep with members of the Rough Roaders and he was OK with it.

'That he never slept with her? Probably. But if he isn't telling the truth, I don't know how we'd prove it.'

'Did you ask Steve if he knew who was sleeping with Amber?'

I tell her what he said and she groans. 'That opens up a whole new bunch of suspects.'

'It does. I'm going to question Amber's best friend, Lisa Hedgepeth, again tomorrow. I'll bet she knew about this.'

'Maybe she's in on it too.'

Nothing would surprise me at this point.

You'd think that when Wendy and the girls got back from San Antonio at nine o'clock, they'd be worn out, but the girls are clamoring to go to the rally.

'It's almost the end of the week,' Hailey says. 'Tammy has never been to the rally, and then it will be over. And there's a band we really, really want to see tonight.'

I glance at Wendy and she crosses her eyes at me. 'Girls,' I say, 'this is going to have to wait until tomorrow night. Wendy's tired, I'm tired.'

'You can take us and leave us. We'll get a ride home,' Tammy says.

Wendy laughs. 'Yeah, I know how well that would go over with your folks.'

'But this is the only time this band is going to play,' Hailey says. 'And it's one we both love. Right, Tammy?'

'I can't stand it that we'll miss it,' Tammy says. She's even more dramatic than Hailey. 'It may be my one chance, ever.'

The fact is that I don't mind taking them. I'm tired, but I'd like to get a feel for how busy things are at Butler's trailer. 'All right, look. Can Tammy spend the night here?'

'I have clothes she can borrow,' Hailey says. Her eyes are shining. She sees victory. 'And she can use my toothbrush.'

'Eww,' Tammy says.

'That won't be necessary,' I say. 'I have an extra, But Wendy is going home now and I'll take you to the rally. But only if you promise to behave yourselves.'

Of course they promise.

'Do you think Tammy's parents will mind?' I ask Wendy.

'If I tell them the girls are with the chief of police, how can they object?'

The girls squeal and run off to Hailey's room to get dressed, even though it seems to me what they're wearing is fine.

I see Wendy out to her car. 'You didn't really have to do this,' she says.

'You've been putting up with them all day. And I've got something I need to check on at the rally anyway. The bikers will pick up their tents and be gone in a few days and it won't kill me to stay out late.'

I tell Dusty he has to stay at home. He's used to going to bed early, and he doesn't seem to mind.

When we get to the rally, the girls are in high gear, chattering and giggling, so giddy that I wonder if I've made a mistake.

There are two band stages in full swing, and although they're crowded, some people seem to be content to sit around in their groups talking bikes and drinking. I go with the girls to the stage where the band they want to see will be playing, the same one the Oakleys were on the other night. The band is setting up, and we manage to squeeze through close to the front. By now I'm beginning to see familiar faces, even though the crowds at the rally have grown. I tell the girls not to wander away if they get bored, and to wait for me after the show.

I head off to spend some time keeping an eye on Grant Butler's RV. I want to know who goes in and out, especially if there are any men I recognize.

It's easy enough to disappear into the background with the number of people moving back and forth. I position myself in the shadow of a trailer across the walkway that's closed up tight. I don't have long to wait. A man comes out of the RV. I can't see his face at first because the door is in shadows, but he walks in my direction, staggering a little, and I see that he's grinning. Shortly afterwards another man knocks on the door and disappears inside. But almost immediately another man walks out. He's tall and slender, with light, spiky hair, and wearing regular biker gear of jeans and T-shirt with a leather vest and a bandana. I can't see his face, but as he walks away from me, toward the music stage, there's something familiar about his stride. I try to think which of the numerous people I've met this week he could be.

It's a busy night at the RV, men arriving and leaving within fifteen minutes. Occasionally a woman walks out, and others go in, but I don't recognize anyone. It stands to reason that out of a couple of thousand people, mostly men, it would be hit and miss for me to see someone I know in the hour or more that I'm there. But at least I confirm that Butler has a brisk business going.

At one point I see Steve Deverell go by with his cleaning cart. He doesn't notice me. He seems cheerful, greeting a couple of people while he empties a trash can nearby. Someone has left a cardboard box and he strips it down to shove into his cart. He doesn't pay any attention to Butler's RV, and I wonder if he knows what goes on in there.

At midnight, I hear the deafening lack of noise that means the bands have stopped. People are streaming by in hordes, and I'm just leaving my post to go find the girls when I think I see the same tall man I saw earlier. He comes back to the RV and goes inside.

I'm afraid I'll never find Hailey and Tammy in this crowd. I text Hailey and she says she'll come to me. I tell her to meet me at the Sno-cone stand, and ten minutes later they show up. They're giggly and excited about the show. Although I'm tired, I catch a wave of their energy and I enjoy listening to them whisper and giggle in the back seat on the way home.

Dusty staggers from his bed to greet us, while Zelda glares down from her night perch on the post I set up for her in the living room after I got the dog.

The girls ask if they can raid the refrigerator and I tell them booze is off-limits, but they can have anything else. I've never been so grateful to climb into my bed.

THIRTY

I should have paid attention to the weather forecast. It's raining when I get up, the kind of slow, steady rain with dark, low clouds that signal we're in for a day of it.

I'm back at the house from the pasture by 7:30. I want to catch Loretta when she comes by with baked goods. As hard as the subject will be for her, she's the one person I can talk to who's likely to have gotten wind of Amber's activities in town.

She comes in with a plate full of blueberry muffins. 'Thank you, the girls will like that.'

'Girls?'

I tell her that Hailey and Wendy's niece, Tammy, seem to have bonded.

'Isn't Tammy the one with the bad disposition?' She whispers it, as if the girls would be awake at this hour.

'One and the same.'

She nods. 'I suppose it stands to reason. Two rebels. What are they going to do in this rain?'

'I guess they'll stay in and watch TV. At some point I'll have to take Tammy back to Bryan.'

She looks anxious. 'Do you suppose they'd want to make cookies at my house?'

A ray of hope. 'I don't know, it's hard for me to read these young girls. I'll ask when they get up. But, you know, that might be noon.' I tell her what went on last night.

'Samuel, you have no business traipsing around at the rally 'til all hours.'

'I had some undercover work to do.'

She blinks. 'Have you joined the FBI?'

I laugh. 'No. Look, the rally is almost over and after that I'll sleep for a week. But now I've got something delicate to talk to you about.'

'What is it? Girl stuff?'

'In a manner of speaking. Loretta, did you ever hear any rumors about prostitution here in Jarrett Creek?'

Her mouth falls open. If she was wearing pearls, she'd clutch them. 'You mean like women getting paid for sex?'

'That's what I mean.'

'Well, you do hear about girls being fast and loose. And I suppose money might change hands. You know, over at the Two Dog you sometimes hear about shady business.'

'I'm talking about regular customers.'

'I never.' She picks up a brochure from a pile of mail on my kitchen table and fans herself. 'Who are we talking about?'

I sigh. I'm torn. Loretta loves to know everything that goes on in town. She also knows how to keep her mouth shut about important matters, but this is a heavy burden. 'Loretta, are you sure you want to know?'

'It's Amber Johnson, isn't it?'

'How do you figure?'

'Who else would you be asking questions about? You're in the middle of the investigation. I can't think it's a random idea. But what makes you think that was going on?'

'I'm not going into it. The reason I asked was to find out if everybody in town knew but me.'

She raises her eyebrows. 'My guess is there's a certain type of man that knows. And if I had to do your job I'd think it might be one of those men who killed her.' She pauses and cocks her head. 'Or one of their wives.'

She may be right, but Lulu described seeing Amber with a man just before she was killed. Not that someone couldn't have been waiting in the dark for the opportunity, but for now I'm going with the man Lulu saw. I wonder if he's the same man Tucker Oakley saw in the shadows down by the lake around the same time.

When Loretta leaves, it's almost eight-thirty. I scribble a note for Hailey to call me when she wakes up, and head for work. There, I call Lisa Hedgepeth.

'I'd like you to come down to the station. I have a few more questions.'

'Am I in trouble?'

'No, we just need privacy. Last time your son needed your attention.'

'You can come here. He's gone off to his friend's house for the day. Thank goodness.'

'Then I'll come there, if you prefer.'

She's subdued when she answers the door, so much so that I wonder if she suspects what I'm here to talk about. I gratefully accept a cup of coffee and we sit at her kitchen table again.

'I found out something I suspect you know about with regard to Amber Johnson.'

She's staring at her coffee, which has enough cream and sugar in it to be called anything but coffee. She raises her head and meets my gaze. 'What's that?' she says, trying for bravado.

'That she was supplementing her income with sexual favors.'

Her mouth twists. 'You make it sound so friendly. Favors.'

'Prostituting herself. Is that better?'

She looks thoughtful and takes a sip of coffee.

'You did know about it?' I prod.

She nods.

'Were you in on it with her?'

She gives a little grunt of pained laughter. 'No, but I thought about it. She was making good money. She told me it wasn't as bad as she thought it might be.'

'Except it likely got her killed.'

She blanches. 'That's been tormenting me. You think that's what happened?'

'It would help if I knew who the men were that she was with.'

She throws her hands up. 'I'm staying out of that. She mentioned one or two, but I don't know all of them.'

'How many were there?'

'Not that many. It's not like she had a lot of free time.'

'How many?'

'Half-dozen at the outside.'

For some reason, imagining a vague number was less disconcerting than hearing a hard number. Six men in town who found out Amber Johnson was willing to prostitute herself and took her up on it.

My disapproval must show, because Lisa's eyes fill with tears. 'Please don't judge her. She was struggling. She didn't have anywhere to turn. I tried to talk her out of what she was doing, but she said it was the only way she could avoid disaster.'

'She couldn't have asked her family for help?'

She snorts. 'Her daddy is such a tightwad, she said she'd never hear the end of it if she asked him for anything. And Mike's folks just don't have any to spare. Believe me, she thought of everything. If I'd had money, I would have given it to her.'

'It doesn't make sense to me,' I say. 'Even if she was trying to get funds to pay for her husband's surgery, that's a pretty drastic solution. Was there more to it? Had Mike piled up gambling debts?'

Lisa sticks a spoon in her coffee cup and stirs it round and round. Tears slide down her face. 'I hate this so much. I loved her. I know she would have found a way out if she could have. She was just stuck.'

'What do you mean?'

'It wasn't Mike's gambling that was the problem. It was Amber's.' Now she's sobbing, gasping in between. 'I didn't know how to help her.'

Now it's clear. Mike was secretive because he was hiding her gambling problem. Trying to keep her name clear.

I wait for Lisa to calm down. She goes to get a tissue and comes back clutching it.

'Tell me about it,' I say.

She draws a shaky breath. 'At first she thought it was fun to gamble online. She won a few times and she thought that would always be the way it went. She got the idea that it was easy money. And of course before long she started losing. The more she lost, the more she tried to recover. I kept telling her she had to quit, but it seemed like she couldn't. Sure, Mike's medication and rehab were expensive, but she could have kept up if she hadn't gotten hooked on gambling. It was like a disease.'

'And that's why she wanted to sue the insurance company? Trying to make up her losses?'

She nods.

'Lisa, I need to know who the men were that she was involved with. I'm sure you know that it's very possible that one of them was responsible for her death.'

She stalls, biting her lip, sipping coffee, but finally relents. 'I only know two for certain besides Ben Holman – Hap Murray and Dale Brownwit.'

So now I have three names. Hap Murray, Dale Brownwit, and Ben Holman. And possibly Rakesh Patel. Who else?

But Lisa doesn't know any other names. 'For what it's worth, she said Ben was really nice to her. He's the one who gave her the idea of getting money for sex. He found out she was struggling and he gave her a couple of hundred dollars to tide her over. And then the next time . . .'

'How did she hook up with the others?'

'You know. The store. She was there every morning, rain or shine, and some guy would come in and she'd flirt, and one thing led to another.'

'Did you know she was also having sex with her employee, Cal Tyson?'

Her mouth falls open. 'No way. Who told you that?'

'I'm not going to tell you.' For a moment I wonder if maybe Cal was lying. But then it occurs to me that having a flirtation with Cal must have felt to Amber like she was back in high school, carefree, sneaking around just for fun. A break from the crush of stress she was under.

Leaving Lisa's house, I think about Hap Murray being one of Amber's customers. His son is one of my deputies. I hope I can keep Bo from finding out. As for Dale Brownwit, I don't know much about him. He's a wealthy rancher who retired out east of town. Why he picked Jarrett Creek I don't know, but apparently, he got to know his way around.

I go to the station and report to Maria what I found out – that I had the wrong gambler in mind.

She sighs. 'I remember you said it seemed like Amber's son and Mike were worried what you might find on the computer, and that's why you thought he was the one losing money on poker.'

'He was cagey because he was covering for her.'

We're quiet. It's sad to think of all the things Mike either didn't know or was trying to ignore about his wife.

'Boss, I feel bad about judging her. Her husband being injured, trying to keep the store going, finding a little pleasure in playing poker, and then before she knows it she's in deep trouble.'

Maria has always been a stickler for rules, but from the sound of it she's learning that rules and justice don't always tell the whole story.

But I haven't told her the rest of what Lisa reported. And before I can, I get a text from Hailey that she and Tammy are finally awake. 'It's raining. We're so bored!'

I read Maria the text and she laughs. I tell her about Loretta's offer. 'I'm going to see if I can persuade the girls to take her up on it. It will keep them out of trouble, at least for a little while.' I tell her about the alcohol incident from yesterday evening.

'You need to lock up your booze. You know they'll go after it again.'

I don't know why I didn't think of that. I'm just not used to having a teenaged girl around with nefarious intentions.

I go home to tell them what Loretta has in mind. Not only are the girls OK with her cookie project, but they're enthusiastic. 'Loretta's so cool,' Hailey says.

She met Loretta once for about ten minutes, and what she got from that encounter that led her to think Loretta is cool mystifies me. But Maria also took to Loretta right away, so there's something these young women like about her. I call Loretta and she tells me to bring the girls down.

They go back into Hailey's room to get ready and I pour them orange juice to have with their muffins before they go. Hailey comes out first.

'You have a good time last night?' I ask.

'It was dope. And we saw Steve and talked to him. I think Tammy likes him.'

Tammy goes for bad boys, but Steve is a rung up from the boy she was interested in who was arrested for breaking and entering last fall.

'Guess who else I saw?'

'One of Steve's friends?'

'Nope. It was weird. That woman you were talking to who was wearing a wig and colored lenses.'

'Where did you see her?'

'She was talking to one of the guys in the band when they took a break. She looked hella different without the wig and the contacts. Her hair is really short and she has pale eyes. I see why she wears those lenses.'

All of a sudden I picture her. Short hair.

'Her hair is really short?'

'Yeah.'

'What was she wearing?'

She shrugs. 'Jeans. A leather vest, which I thought was stupid. It was too hot for that.'

'Ready,' Tammy says, emerging from Hailey's room. She sits down to bolt a muffin and some juice. The girls start chattering, but I'm barely listening. I'm thinking about Becky Henderson without her wig and lenses. I'm thinking about the way she walks, her long legs. I'm thinking I saw her without her wig, too, leaving the RV last night and coming back later. Looking like a lanky man.

I give the girls one umbrella and I take another to walk them down the street to Loretta's house. In her cozy kitchen I ask what kind of cookies they'll bake.

'We'll make more than one kind,' Loretta says. 'It's a good day for it. Raining and all.'

'You think you can make some of those molasses cookies?' I ask. They're my favorite.

'We sure can.' To the girls, she says, 'We'll decide what kind we want and go pick up the ingredients we need at the store.'

I insist on pitching in for the ingredients because not too long ago I realized that I'd been taking Loretta's baking bounty for granted.

THIRTY-ONE

I head straight back to headquarters, steeling myself to tell Maria the rest of what I heard from Lisa Hedgepeth this morning. We need to question several men. But in the back of my mind,

Hailey's comment about seeing Becky without wig and contacts is nagging at me. There were women working in the RV last night, so why wasn't Becky?

When I tell Maria that one of the men Lisa named was Bo Murray's daddy, she balls her hands into fists. 'Why can't men control themselves?'

'Let's try to keep Bo out of this, OK?'

'Yeah. He doesn't need to know that.' Her face is flushed. 'My papa went with other women, so I know how it feels to hear that kind of thing.'

That helps me understand why Maria is sometimes a prude. 'We have four names. I wonder who else?'

Maria thinks about it. 'I didn't find anything suspicious on her computer. My guess is that it was all cash, and nothing written down.'

'Nothing on her phone either?'

'You know, she had a lot of calls and texts. I assumed they were about the store, but now that we know what she was up to, I'll go through them again and find out exactly who she was in contact with.'

'Good thing we haven't turned it over to Weinman.'

'He hasn't asked for anything. You know, Boss, I think he's waiting for us to ask for help.'

'Yes, it looks that way. I'd like not to have to ask. I'd like to get it wrapped up before the bikers take off.'

'I'm thinking it may not have anything to do with the bikers.'

'Not so fast.' I describe staking out Grant Butler's RV last night. 'They keep pretty busy and it could very well be that Amber upset a customer.'

'Chief, you shouldn't have gone by yourself. You could have called me. Or Bo. Or even Connor.'

'I went because I needed to entertain Hailey and Tammy.'

She shakes her head, disgusted with me for being indulgent, I suppose.

'There was one odd thing.' I tell her that I saw Becky Henderson leave the RV without her wig, and that Hailey saw her at the music tent. 'She said she didn't have her colored contacts in and that she looked different without them.'

Maria frowns and I can tell she's thinking.

'I don't know what that has to do with anything, though,' I say. 'I was just surprised that she wasn't working in the RV last night.'

'Maybe she had the day off,' Maria says, but she sounds distracted.

'What's going on?' I ask. 'You've got something on your mind.'

'Just . . . did you ever read the full autopsy report?'

'No. I talked to T.J., and he told me the gist of it.'

'Hold on. Let me get it.'

She goes to a stack of papers on her desk and pulls it out. She reads through it, frowning. 'There it is. Take a look.'

She points to a paragraph about the examination of Amber's clothing. I see immediately what she's talking about and I grab the phone and call T.J. Sutter's office. His assistant, Mary Lou, tells me he isn't available, that he's doing an autopsy.

'How soon will he be done?'

'Thirty minutes. Something like that. Can I help you?'

'Maybe.' I tell her what I want to know. She says she'll look and call me right back.

I make a fresh pot of coffee and pace the floor until Maria tells me to sit down.

Ten minutes later, Mary Lou gets back to me. 'It's right here in a little plastic baggie. Do you know what it is?'

'I do,' I say. 'And I'm coming to take possession of it right now.'

Before I go I make one other call, to an optometrist in Bobtail. He gives me additional information.

I can't assume that this is the break in the case that I hope it is, so I leave Maria scouring Amber's phone for the names of men she might have been hooking up with.

When I get to Bobtail and Mary Lou hands me the baggie, I know immediately that it's exactly what Maria thought it might be – a curled up plastic contact lens, tinted blue. The optometrist I spoke with said sometimes people lose contact lenses because their eyes get dry, especially late at night. 'And the lenses curl up like little doodle bugs,' is the way he put it.

'Do you know if you can get DNA from the lens?' I ask Mary Lou.

She isn't sure. 'Let me look it up.'

She plops down at her computer and starts tapping at the keys.

Within minutes she says, 'Looks like it. There's a new technique that's been developed. We would have to send it off to the lab in San Antonio, but they'll be able to do it.'

Now to get a DNA sample from Becky Henderson.

When I get out of my squad car, I consider taking my gun and holster out of the lockbox. I generally don't find it necessary to use the show of force, but I don't know what I'll be facing when I question Becky Henderson and Grant Butler. Since the first time I met them, I sensed that they carried a whiff of danger. I thought it was my imagination, but now I'm not so sure. But I leave the weapon. I'm not here to arrest anyone. Not yet, anyway. I also think about texting Maria to come out, but I decide to wait.

You never saw a more bedraggled group than the thousand bikers camped out in the rain. As is always the case in this part of Texas, the minute you have thirty minutes or more of rain, the clay earth becomes a soggy, slippery mess. Wearing my poncho and my hat, I slip and slide my way to Butler's RV and stand there staring at where the RV was parked. It's gone.

I bang on the trailer next door and the same man I talked to a few days ago yanks open the door. I ask if he knows whether Butler will be back.

'Like I told you before, I don't know the man. Didn't speak to him before he left.'

Other surrounding vehicles tell the same tale, except one woman says, 'Good riddance. We don't need that kind of activity at a good, wholesome event like the rally.' She seems to have been attending a different rally from the one I've been at.

There's one other possibility for finding out whether Butler will be back before I call the highway patrol out to look for his vehicle.

Jack Cassidy pulls on a poncho and joins me outside his tent. 'You're the chief of police,' he says, with a weak smile. 'Can't you do anything about this weather?'

'I'm working on it.' I ask him if he knows whether Grant Butler is coming back. 'I need to talk to him.'

He lifts his eyebrow. 'That's not likely. Not with what happened last night.'

'What's that?'

'Him and Becky got into a fight and security had to be called.'

'How do you know this?'

He grins. 'You remember Randy Woods? He told me he was there and saw it. Don't ask me what he was doing,' he says. 'None of my business. But he said it was a doozy. Becky slugged Grant, and it's likely he'll have a black eye this morning.'

I can't decide whether to talk to Randy Woods or to security, but Woods's tent is closer. Jack points it out to me and I stand outside and call for him. He pokes his head out. He's looking the worse for wear, with bleary, bloodshot eyes, but he emerges from his tent readily enough.

'Jack, you got any coffee brewed?' he asks.

'We drank it all up,' Jack says.

'We can get some over at one of the food trucks,' I say.

While we walk, he tells me about last night. 'I was in Butler's RV doing this and that,' he says, with a side-eye. 'Luckily, I was dressed and ready to go, so I stepped out and saw Grant and Becky at a stand-off. She was yelling at him. Sounds like he cheated on her and she was mad! Told him she was through with him and it was his fault. You know, the usual.'

We're at the food truck and both of us get the largest size coffee they've got.

I tell him I don't know what he means by the usual. 'I need details,' I say.

He laughs. 'Well, Butler says he doesn't owe her anything, that he can do as he pleases, and she says he can go to hell and she's leaving him. He says as far as he's concerned she can get out on the highway and hitchhike. And she hauls off and slugs him. And I do mean slugs.' He laughs and shakes his head. 'You know Grant's a big man and she almost knocked him down.'

'But you don't know the particulars about what started it?'

'Just that she accused him of getting it on with one of the other girls.' A shiver runs along my spine. Could that girl be Amber?

'Their RV is gone this morning,' I say.

'I'm not surprised.'

'Seems unlikely they'll be back.'

'Well, hold on,' Woods says. 'I don't think you know that. Guy like Butler is all about the money. He won't stay away when there's a buck to be made. I bet they went into Bobtail to have breakfast. A lot of people do that.'

On our way back to the Rough Roaders area, I'm wondering whether to wait and hope Butler comes back, or to get hold of Dan Weinman and get the highway patrol out looking for the RV. But as we pass the entrance, I see, like a miracle, the RV driving in.

I stand with Woods and watch it trundle by with Butler at the wheel. Becky isn't sitting in the passenger seat with him. I raise my hand and he nods.

I thank Woods for his help and walk behind the RV as it struggles through the mud back to its designated space. The rain is starting to let up and people are coming out of their tents and trailers, blinking and stretching.

Before I knock on the door, I text Maria and tell her I need her to join me, and I give her the approximate location and description of the vehicle.

I don't give Butler time to get entrenched before I rap smartly on the door of the RV. Instead of the door opening, he says loud enough for me to hear, 'We're not open.'

I rap again and call out, 'Police!'

He opens the door, but stays back in the shadow of the interior. 'What do you want?'

'I need you to step out of the vehicle.'

'What for?'

'I have questions.'

'Unless you have a reason for questioning me, I don't have to obey.'

'I'm investigating an assault that may involve you.'

He laughs, an unpleasant sound. 'I haven't complained about an assault.'

'Mr Butler, I'm asking you to comply with my request to step out of your RV.'

People are starting to poke their heads out of surrounding vans, not all of them looking friendly.

There's a moment, and then Butler calls back something I don't hear and steps out. He's got a shiner all right.

'How'd you get that?' I ask.

'It was an accident.'

'That's not the way I heard it.'

His smile is tight. 'Whatever you heard, it has nothing to do with the law.'

'Mr Butler, has Becky Henderson ever been violent with you before?'

He licks his lips and glances around. The guy next door has stepped out of his trailer and is watching us. The woman who complained about Butler's activities has opened her door and is lurking just inside.

'I wouldn't call it violent.' He's keeping his voice low. 'She has a temper, but that's between us.'

'So you're not willing to press charges for assault?'

'I certainly am not. Is that all?'

'I need to talk to Ms Henderson. Can you call her out here, please?'

'Call her yourself.'

I step to the door of the RV. 'Becky Henderson, I need a word with you.'

'What about?' She sounds surly.

'Step outside, please.'

She comes to the door of the trailer. She's got her wig on and is dressed in shorts and a T-shirt. She looks stunning. 'You're sounding mighty serious, Sheriff.' She's using that teasing voice.

'Hey, Chief.'

I glance over to see Maria walking toward us. She made good time. 'Deputy Trevino,' I nod. 'Ms Henderson, step outside please, or I can send my deputy in to roust you out if you'd prefer.' I'm not planning to arrest her, but now that she has shown her violent side, I'm inclined to push my suspicions out in the open.

'You'd send your deputy in to get me?' She steps down one step. 'What the hell for?' She's got a black eye that matches Butler's. Quite a pair.

'Deputy, could you clear these folks?' I nod toward the onlookers.

Maria moves quickly, asking everyone to go back inside.

Meanwhile, Becky steps to the ground. Her eyes are wary. Now I wish I had brought my weapon. 'I need you to come with me. I have questions for you. I'll arrest you if I have to, but I'd rather you just cooperate.'

'She's not going anywhere,' Butler says. 'Not until you tell me why you want to question her. I'm her lawyer.'

'She's welcome to have counsel, but I'm taking her in for

questioning in a homicide. If necessary, I'll call the sheriff in Bobtail for backup.'

'Homicide! You mean that woman who was murdered here at the rally? What the hell is wrong with you?'

I pull my handcuffs from my belt. Maria is alert, next to me. 'Ms Henderson, I'm taking you in, one way or the other.'

'Grant! Do something,' Becky says.

With that, Butler seems to snap into professional mode. 'Go with him, Becky. He's just a small-town cop grandstanding for the crowd. I'll follow you to his little station. I'll have you out in no time.'

'Let me get my purse.' She starts back to the RV.

'The deputy will go inside with you,' I say.

'Not without my consent, she won't,' Butler says.

'OK, then no purse,' I say.

'All right, all right. Becky, where is it? I'll get it,' Butler says.

He comes back with a bag and I intercept it and hand it to Maria. 'My deputy will carry it. Now let's go before this gets to be any more of a circus than it already is.'

THIRTY-TWO

We install Becky in the back of Maria's squad car and I follow them to the station. On the way, I call Dan Weinman to tell him I'm going to be questioning a suspect, and why. 'She's Grant Butler's girlfriend and he's a lawyer, so we probably don't have much time to question her before he'll be whisking her out of our hands.'

'I'm thirty minutes out. Don't wait.'

As soon as I'm in the door, I get a judge to issue a search warrant for Butler's RV and an order for Becky Henderson's DNA. Small-town cops may not be as slick as city cops, but we know our judges.

Bo Murray comes into the office, and when he sees Becky, with her aquamarine eyes and blonde cascade of hair, his mouth drops open. I'm surprised his tongue doesn't flop out. I tell him to make himself scarce.

Maria gets the tape recorder going. Becky seems amused by the whole idea of being questioned in a small-town police station. I'm hoping to wipe the smirk off her face.

'Tell me about your set-to with your boyfriend last night,' I say.

'What do you want to know?'

'Why were you mad at him?'

'It was a misunderstanding.' She flips her hair back and tilts her head as if she's posing for a photograph.

'Who was the woman you were fighting about?'

'Who says it was a woman?'

I sigh. 'A witness says so. Was it Amber Johnson?'

'You mean that little bitch who got herself killed? What a lightweight!'

'We'll see.' I pull the plastic bag containing the dried-up contact lens out of my desk drawer. Normally I would draw her out more, but I don't have much time. 'You know what this is?'

'Hard to tell.'

'It's a colored contact lens. The kind you wear.'

'Lots of people wear them.'

'Not so many tinted ones, though. You want to know where it came from?'

She stares at me, her expression turning not quite so cocky.

'It was taken from Amber Johnson's clothing the night she died.'

Her eyes narrow. 'So? That doesn't prove it's mine.'

'Really? I guess you didn't know that you can get DNA from contact lenses?'

She brings a hand to her mouth and bites her knuckle.

I walk over to the fax machine and pull off the judge's order. 'I have here an order to obtain your DNA.'

'No way. Grant won't let you do that.'

'Grant doesn't have a damn thing to say about it. The judge's order prevails.' Not that the DNA test will come back any time soon. Like I told Hailey, test results can take a long time. But I'm betting Becky doesn't know that and I hope it will put her on edge.

Maria is ahead of me and she has the DNA swab ready.

Dan Weinman walks in about then. 'Carry on,' he says. He takes a seat at Connor's desk and swivels it around to watch us.

Becky eyes the DNA swab. 'Even if you find out that's my lens, it doesn't prove anything.'

'Did you meet Amber the night she was killed?'

'Maybe I should wait until Grant gets here to say anything more.' She's biting the side of her lip and her eyes are calculating.

'Suit yourself,' I say. 'But you still have to let Maria get your DNA sample.'

'OK, I'll tell you. I was with her. But I did not kill her.'

'You were with her the night she was killed, though?' I ask.

She nods.

'Where was this?'

'Here and there.'

'Specifically.'

She's antsy, her eyes darting from one to the other of us. 'We were in the RV and then we went for a walk.'

'Why?'

'I walked into our RV and caught her flirting with Grant, practically shoving those tits of hers into his chest. So I told her I wanted to talk to her. She came with me and we walked down by the water. I told her Grant was off-limits and to stop flirting with him.'

'What did she say?'

'That she didn't mean anything by it.'

'Did you end up walking down behind the music tent?'

'Maybe. I wasn't paying attention.'

'Did you get physical with her?'

She shrugs. 'I might have shoved her, but I didn't hurt her. And I swear when I left her, she was fine.'

'What do you mean, you may have shoved her? Did you?'

She looks like a trapped animal. 'I suppose I did. But it wasn't rough.'

'And did she retaliate?'

Her face is flushed. 'She slapped me.'

'And approximately what time did all this happen?'

'I have no idea.'

I glance at Maria. She has an intent look on her face. I nod to her, in case she has a question. She does.

'Ms Henderson, have you ever been arrested for assault?'

Her eyes go dead. 'I might have been, but that doesn't mean I did anything to hurt Amber Johnson.'

'Have you ever attacked anyone with a knife before?'

'No.'

'When you were with Amber Johnson, did you happen to see anyone else around?'

Grant Butler comes charging into the station, banging the door open. 'This stops right now,' he says. 'She's my client, and I want it to stop.'

'Mr Butler, have a seat. I have a question for you.'

'Forget it,' he says.

'Let me introduce you to Dan Weinman. He's with the Department of Public Safety and will be carrying out a search of your RV for any incriminating evidence in the murder of Amber Johnson.'

Butler looks like he's smelled something bad. 'Go ahead. There won't be any so-called incriminating evidence.'

'Were you in your RV Saturday night when Ms Henderson here got back from her confrontation with Amber Johnson?'

He glares at Becky. 'What the hell did you say to them?'

'She volunteered that she was with Amber Johnson the night she was killed and that they had a physical confrontation.'

'Becky, what the hell! You need to learn to keep your mouth shut.'

'Grant, I did not kill that girl and you know it. And I don't care who else knows it.'

'Shut up. Just shut up. You've said enough.'

I make a tamp-down sign with my hand. 'Cool it. I'd like to ask one more question. It might help me figure out who did kill Amber Johnson if Becky didn't.'

'Ask it, and I'll tell her whether she can answer.'

'Becky, when you were talking to Amber, did you see anyone else hanging around, either before or after?'

Becky looks scared now, and I think it's Butler she's afraid of, not me. She looks at Butler. He nods. She drops her gaze, but her stillness tells me that she's not dismissing me, she's thinking. She shivers. 'Not while I was there, but when I started back, I noticed a guy standing near the water looking back to where I had been with that woman.' Standing near the water, like Tucker Oakley said.

'Remember anything about him?'

'It was dark. I couldn't see his features, but he was a little shorter than me. I don't know, it may not mean anything but he didn't look at me.'

I know exactly what she means. Men notice her. Even in the

dark, her lanky body and long hair draw the eye. And even without her wig, she has a way of walking that catches attention. So whoever was standing there was concentrating on where she had been – and where Amber still was.

'Is there any possibility that he had followed the two of you?' She shrugs. 'Maybe.'

I ask her to try to remember details of what he looked like, but she insists she doesn't remember anything more.

We're done, but I tell the two of them not to even think about leaving without letting me or Weinman know. Weinman gets their contact information.

When they leave, Maria and I sit and stare at each other. Finally she says, 'She didn't do it, did she?'

'Even if she did, she's right. The presence of her contact lens isn't enough to get a conviction. But no, I don't think she did it. She's hot-headed, but I think if she'd killed Amber she would have been much more inclined to keep her mouth shut.'

'Then who?'

'My bet? It had to do with Amber sleeping with men for money. Somebody got possessive and she kicked them to the curb. Or she refused somebody.'

'Or somebody's wife found out.'

I nod. But there's another possibility I don't mention, a loose end that I need to look into. Amber's husband had more than enough motive to kill her, including her racking up gambling debts. Mike's disability seems genuine, but his sister-in-law hinted that he isn't as debilitated as he pretends to be. I need to clear that up once and for all.

THIRTY-THREE

Something else has been nagging at me, and every time I think about it, it seems a mystery without explanation. After we cut Becky loose, I decide I need to go find out what it was about. I'm at the Quick Stop in five minutes and find Cal is doing brisk business. I hang around until he's got a break.

'Hey Chief, what brings you here?'

'I have a question for you. Remember Sunday when those two bikers came in and asked for Amber?'

'Yes.' He's suddenly wary.

'I think they were looking for her because they found out she was a prostitute. What do you think?'

He glares at me. 'I wouldn't know.' Wanting to protect her shredded reputation.

'They didn't seem particularly dangerous to me. Did they to you?'

He shakes his head. 'Not really.'

'So why did you call your daddy to come down here and hang out with you that afternoon? He said you were nervous.'

He looks startled, but the door jingles and a couple of youngsters come in to buy popsicles. When they leave I repeat the question.

'I don't know why Daddy would say that. I didn't call him, he called me. He said he wanted to come down and talk to me.'

Ralph Tyson had lied to me. Why?

We pause for another sale to be rung up. Beer and chips. When they leave, I ask, 'What did he want to talk to you about?'

He shrugs. 'He wanted me to keep quiet about him looking at a bike. He didn't think Mamma would like it if she knew he was thinking about buying one.'

'Was that all?'

He sighs, and in a wooden voice says, 'He said he wanted me to quit working here. He didn't like me working for Amber. But he said that before.' Before what, I wonder.

'When?'

'Few days ago.'

We wait again while three groups of people come in. When we're alone again, I ask, 'Did you tell your daddy you were having sex with Amber?'

He looks startled. He puts his hands on the counter and I see that they're trembling. He's steadying himself. 'I might have.'

'I'll take that as a yes. When was this?'

'Last week. When he said he didn't want me to work here anymore. He was going on about me not having any ambition. He said I shouldn't be working here because Amber was taking advantage of me, paying me shit wages. It aggravated me, him getting all up in my business. I told him there were other perks besides getting paid and he asked me what that was. I told him that Amber and I were getting it on. I know I shouldn't have. It was private. But I was mad.'

'Would he have told your mamma?'

He groans. 'I hope not. It would about kill her.'

'Was any more said about it?'

'No, but I could tell he wasn't happy about it.'

The motorcycle Ralph Tyson was looking at is still for sale. I walk around it a couple of times like I'm considering it, wondering where the owner is. After a minute I hear a truck door slam and the owner climbs down out of an idling pickup. His face is flushed, either from the heat or too many beers.

'You looking to get yourself a motorcycle?' he asks. 'This is a good one.'

'I don't know. It's tempting,' I say, keeping my eyes on the bike.

'Good thing you happened by, I was just headed out for a beer run.'

I look up and say, 'Hey, I remember you. You came into the Quick Stop looking for Amber Johnson on Sunday.'

'I don't remember that,' he says.

'Doesn't matter. I thought you had this bike sold. I noticed an acquaintance of mine looking at it a couple of days ago. I figured he'd take it off your hands.'

He snorts. 'I thought I had it sold, too. But I guess he was just kicking the tires.'

I introduce myself without the 'chief' part. He shakes my hand readily enough. His name is Kelvin Moseley.

'When did you last see your prospective buyer? I talked to him a couple of days ago and he said he thought he was going to buy it.'

'I wish he'd told me that. He came over here Saturday night about three sheets to the wind and told me the deal was off.'

'What time was that?'

'Hell, I don't know. Late. The nights run together.' He's suddenly alert. 'What difference does it make?'

I ignore the question. 'Let me ask you something. Is Tyson the one who told you you could find Amber Johnson at the convenience store?' Although it makes me sick, I put a leer on my smile.

'Heh! Yeah.'

'When did he tell you that?'

He crosses his arms. 'You know, now that I'm talking to you, I think I do recall seeing you that Sunday, and I also seem to recall you're the law. Is that right?' He puts a jocular note in his voice, but his eyes don't have the same good cheer.

'That's right. And I need you to answer my question.'

He spits and looks off to where a group of men are drinking beer and laughing. 'I don't think I remember the answer.'

I nod. 'Well, I wonder if a night in jail might jog your memory.'

His jaw is working. I can't see his eyes behind his sunglasses, but he moves so that he's standing with legs apart, his tattooed arms crossed in a challenge to me. 'Is that a threat?'

'Call it curiosity.' I'm wearing my weapon on a belt. It isn't unusual to see weapons here, but he still notices when I put my hand on it.

'What would you run me in for?'

'Material witness. It's up to you. Small question. Big answer.'

He stands there, looking off, and I see the moment when he makes up his mind. 'No skin off my nose if I tell you. This was Friday afternoon. We were shootin' the shit and we seen this good-looking woman come down out of an RV over that way.' He inclines his head in the direction of Butler's RV. 'She's a hot little number. Tyson says he wonders what she's doing there. And I tell him that Butler runs some whores out of there. I ask if he knows her and he says yeah, and that you can probably get her cheaper than having to pay Butler's fee. He tells me she runs this convenience store and that's where I can locate her. And we make a joke about it being convenient.'

Moseley is reluctant to give me his name and phone number, but I point out that I can get it easily enough from the license plate on his bike.

'In case I need to ask more questions, when will you be back from your beer run?'

'Hour or so. I need to get beer and a few eats.'

Now I need to question Ralph Tyson.

*   *   *

When I walk into the post office, I'm surprised to see Myra Tyson on duty facing a line of three people. I rarely see three people at a time in the post office, but it soon becomes clear why it's backed up. The woman at the front of the line, one of Loretta's church lady friends, is trying to mail a package to Guatemala. Goodness knows why. Myra keeps trying to find the proper charges on the post office computer, and it keeps telling her she's trying to perform an invalid operation.

The church lady is a paragon of patience. Finally she says, 'Myra, is Ralph going to be back tomorrow? Maybe I'll wait until he's here.'

'Diane, I don't know if he will be or not.' Myra is close to tears. 'What would you think about taking the package to Bobtail? Maybe they could help you.'

'I guess I can do that. If you thought Ralph was coming back tomorrow, I'd wait. I don't like to drive to Bobtail with the motorcycle rally in town, the highway gets so busy.'

I'm tempted to tell her I'll do it for her, but goodness knows what I'd be getting myself into.

'Where is Ralph, anyway?' the church lady asks.

'His brother was in a wreck and broke his leg and Ralph went to make sure he can manage.'

'In that case, I guess I'll go on up to Bobtail. It sounds like Ralph is doing good works.'

'Thank you so much, Diane. I feel like such a fool.'

Diane picks up the package and as she walks past me she rolls her eyes.

'You want me to take that to your car for you?' I ask Diane.

'It's not heavy, but I appreciate it.'

The next two customers only want routine matters, so they are quickly out the door. When I walk up, Myra says, 'Please don't tell me you want to send money to someone in Brazil.' She has an air of defeat.

'Nothing like that. I just wanted to talk to Ralph. Too bad about his brother. Where does he live?'

'He's just over in Bastrop. I don't know what Ralph thinks he's doing. He doesn't even get along with his brother. And his brother has a perfectly responsible wife and two teenagers that can do anything that needs doing. And he leaves me with this.' She waves her hands around the post office. It's a tiny room, crammed full of flat mailers, boxes, and greeting cards. 'At least it's closing time.'

'When did he get the call from his brother?'

'Not even an hour ago. He lit out like his tail was on fire.'

An hour ago I was talking to Cal. I'm wondering if Cal called his daddy to tell him I'd been sniffing around. I wasn't sure why he would, but the timeline is too coincidental.

'I'd like to get Ralph's cell number and his brother's address, if you have it handy.'

She gives me Ralph's number and then digs her little address book out of her purse and hunts up his brother's address and phone number.

'What kind of car does Ralph drive?'

She hesitates. She looks at me closely, like she's getting a hint that things are not quite right. 'He has a van, a Chevy Express.'

'What color?'

'White.'

'How old is it?'

'Not new, but I don't know what year. Maybe five years old. Why?'

'You know the license number?'

'No, I don't. Samuel, what are all these questions about? Is Ralph in some kind of trouble?'

'I just really need to talk to him, that's all.' Before she can press me, I ask, 'Myra, how do Cal and Ralph get along?'

She peers at me. 'Why would you ask that?'

'Something Cal said made me wonder if they are having problems.'

'Well, you must be psychic. I was just thinking how it might be best if Cal finds another place to live because he and Ralph have been at each other's throats the last few days.'

'They aggravated about anything in particular?'

'Not that I can tell. But if one of them says black, the other says white. I can't seem to please one of them without the other getting mad.'

'Sounds like a hard situation for you.'

'Maybe when Ralph gets back, I'll go on a vacation all by myself.'

*   *   *

At five-fifteen I call Dan Weinman. I tell him about my talk with Cal and with the guy selling the motorcycle. 'I don't know how we're going to prove it, but I wonder if Ralph Tyson killed Amber because she was sleeping with his son and he found out she was prostituting herself.'

'Oh my lord. Could it be the son who did it, and not the daddy?'

'I suppose it's possible, but the kid seemed happy with the way things were between him and Amber. Didn't seem to take the relationship too seriously. His daddy was not happy, though.'

'You going to bring Ralph in for questioning?'

'It's not quite that easy. I think he might have flown the coop.' I tell him that Ralph's wife told me he went to Bastrop to help his brother because he was hurt in an accident. 'I called the brother's house just now and his wife said he wasn't in an accident, and even if he had been, he wouldn't have called Ralph for help. And I called Ralph's phone and it went straight to voicemail.'

'So now what? He could be anywhere.'

'I'm thinking you should put out a BOLO for him.'

'I'll do that. I don't know how effective it will be if we can't narrow it down.' Before I called Dan, I looked up the license number for Ralph's van, and I give it to him.

'It's a van? Well, at least it isn't a gray sedan, like eighty percent of the cars on the road.'

'We could try to trace the whereabouts of his phone,' I say, 'but if he has it turned off, I don't know how successful that will be. Right now my best shot is to have a heart to heart with his wife and son. Maybe they'll have some sense of where he's gone.'

I tell him I'll be in touch.

THIRTY-FOUR

I tell Maria what's going on and arrange with her to come with me to question Myra and Cal as soon as Cal gets off work. Then I go home to check on Hailey and Tammy, to tell them it may be a while before I can take Tammy back to Bryan.

When I drive up to my house, my heart sinks. I can't believe what I'm seeing. There's a familiar car out front. If I'm not mistaken, Lyle is back. I wonder if Hailey called him, or if he decided to drop in on his own. Either way, in my current state I don't have much patience for him.

It's funny how dogs seem to sense an iffy situation. When I let Dusty out of the pickup, instead of doing his usual joyful sniff around the yard and lunge for the porch in anticipation of his dinner, he walks next to me, stiff-legged and alert.

In my living room, Lyle is sitting on my sofa with his arm around Hailey, while Tammy sits in an armchair looking at them with admiring eyes. There's a plate with a few of the cookies they made sitting on the coffee table. My cookies. All three of them look up at me with guilty expressions, and then with alarm as Dusty hurls himself toward Lyle, barking in a way I've never heard before – with authority. There's no question he's yelling at Lyle to get out of his house. He must remember my reaction to Lyle when he was here a few days ago.

'Whoa, whoa, dog,' Lyle says, cringing back.

'Dusty, get over here.'

He must hear that I mean business, because with one last resentful look at the interloper, he comes to my side and sits so close that he's hugging my leg.

'What are you doing here?' I ask.

'Can't a guy come and visit his girlfriend?' Lyle says. I had forgotten how scruffy he is, with his straggly blond hair and fluff of beard.

I glance at Hailey and see a smirk of triumph on her face. I don't know how to combat this. What I do know is that I can't let her leave with this guy.

'I would have preferred if you'd made arrangements in advance,' I say.

He hugs her close. 'I wanted to surprise her. And I figured you might have had enough time with her by now, so I'm taking her back with me.'

'No, you aren't.' By my leg, Dusty lets out a low growl.

'You gonna sic that mutt on me?' Lyle has the raised eyebrow down pat.

Tammy giggles.

'All right, here's what we're going to do,' I say. 'Tammy, I want you to call Wendy and ask her to come pick you up.'

'What? I told her I was going to spend another night here. She said I could.'

'Not tonight. Call her and tell her I need you to get home. I'll be taking Hailey back to Austin.'

Hailey gasps and her eyes widen. She looks like I've slapped her. 'But I can go with Lyle.'

'No, you can't. Your parents entrusted you to me, and I'm making good on it. I can't just hand you off to anybody who comes along.'

'But he's my boyfriend!'

'Maybe so, although I tend to think a worthwhile boyfriend wouldn't skulk around behind your parents' back. He'd have more respect for you and for them. But I don't have time to play these games. I'm conducting a murder investigation and I don't have time to coddle you.' I walk over to stand in front of her to make eye contact. 'Frankly, I'm disappointed in you. If you were as mature as you say you are, you'd think about whether as chief of police my priority should be catching a murderer or babysitting. But it looks like that's not something you're willing to consider. Go pack your bags. I'll call your folks. We'll be leaving as soon as I have a bite to eat.'

I walk out of the room, my heart pounding. I can't decide if I'm play-acting or really angry. Probably a little of both. Either way, I'm prepared to drive to Austin and back tonight.

There's silence in the other room. I pour dog food into Dusty's bowl. He walks over to it, then backs away from it and sits facing the living room. A dog on duty.

Although I don't feel like eating, I want to give Hailey time to digest what I've said and to make her choice. I pull cheese, lunch-meat, and mayonnaise out of the refrigerator and start slathering two pieces of bread. There's whispering going on, but I can't hear what's being said.

I pull out my phone and call Maria. 'I may have to postpone tonight.'

'What? Why?'

'Problems.'

'Uh oh. Anything I can do?'

'There is. Maybe you can go stake out the place and watch whether Ralph comes back.'

'You can't talk, right?'

'That's right. And call me if you run into trouble. I probably won't be available, but call Dan Weinman if you need backup. Or if it's urgent notify Bobtail PD.' I look up to see Hailey standing in the doorway. There's a war going on in her face. Defiance versus shame.

'Good luck,' I say to Maria and click off. 'What do you need?' I say to Hailey.

'I don't want you to have to drive me to Austin. I don't see why I can't go with Lyle.' Her voice is small.

'I've already told you. Do you want a sandwich to take with us?'

'Uncle Samuel . . .' Her voice is pleading.

'Hailey, I'm serious. I don't have time for games. Maybe I'm asking too much of you. Maybe your folks have been asking too much of you. But I have a responsibility to carry out my job and that means I had to trust you. You've broken my trust and I can't—'

'Wait. I'll stay here. Just let Lyle stay for another hour and he'll go. I'll stay here and you can take me back after your case is over.'

I shake my head. 'I'm sorry, honey. You've shown me that I can't trust you. If I leave you here with Lyle while I go do my job and you take off with him, I'd never forgive myself.'

'Tammy?' I call out. 'Have you called Wendy?'

'No.'

I walk into the living room. 'Why not?'

'Hailey said to wait.'

'I'll call her.'

'No, wait,' Hailey wails.

I dial Wendy's number. She picks up right away. 'What's going on?'

I hate to break the sweet sound in her voice.

'We've got a situation. How long will it take you to get here?'

'I'm leaving now.' That's another thing I like about Wendy. She doesn't go for a lot of drama. She doesn't demand an answer to everything. She knows that I wouldn't ask if it wasn't important.

'I appreciate it,' I say.

I'm standing in the doorway between the kitchen and the living room. 'It'll take Wendy about thirty minutes to get here. Hailey, I'm giving you a choice. You can go home with Wendy and Tammy and I'll come get you tomorrow, or you can go to Austin with me tonight. Those are your choices.'

'That's not fair,' she wails.

'What's not fair about it?' I ask. 'Adults have to make decisions like that all the time. I have to choose between taking you back tonight or catching a criminal. Decisions are part of being a grown up. So I repeat, what's not fair?'

'Hey,' Lyle says. He's gotten up and ambled over to me and Hailey. 'If you're pissed off, I don't know why you have to take it out on her. She didn't ask me to come, I just thought it was a good idea. But since you're making such a stink about it, I can get on back.' He smiles at Hailey. 'It's not like I don't have other entertainment until you get back.'

Hailey freezes.

'Exactly what do you mean by that?' I ask. 'You mean you have a spare girlfriend?'

He gives Hailey a lazy grin. 'Nah, I was just kidding.'

'What's her name?' I ask.

Hailey's expression has turned ugly. 'You're not seeing Jonelle again, are you?'

'Honey, if she came over one night, I can't help that.'

Hailey gasps and looks stunned.

'Knock knock,' a familiar voice calls out.

I hadn't shut the front door, and the screen opens and Steve Deverell is standing there. 'What's up, y'all?' he asks.

Dusty runs out of the kitchen, where he has finally decided to gobble up his food, and charges at Steve, yelping and leaping, this time with excitement. Steve crouches down and ruffles Dusty's ears.

'I thought you had to work,' I say. I'm so glad to see him I could yell.

He stands up. 'The state won't let me work seven nights in a row. The rally has to give me one night off, and this is it.' To Hailey he says, 'Ash and Sophie are in the car. We were thinking we'd go to the movies in Bobtail and you might want to come too.' He looks at Lyle. There's no jealousy, just curiosity. 'But it looks like you have company.' He walks across the room and sticks out his hand. 'I'm Steve,' he says.

'Lyle,' he mumbles.

'What would you think about the movies in Bryan instead?' I ask Steve.

'That will work. We just want to hang out. Maybe get a burger. My buddy Ted is with us, too,' he says. I happen to be looking at Hailey and I don't miss the spark of interest that flares in her eyes at the mention of Ted.

Lyle hasn't missed it either. 'Looks like you have some new little friends,' he says to her.

She blushes. Steve bursts out laughing. 'Ooo, I've pushed a button without meaning to. I don't want to create problems for you, Hail. You coming or not? And Lyle, you're welcome. You too, Tammy Wynette.'

'Don't call me that,' Tammy says, but she grins.

'Nah,' Lyle says. 'I have to get back to Austin.'

I'm thinking fast. 'All right, here's the deal,' I say to Steve. 'Hailey has your cell number, right?'

He nods, puzzled. 'Tammy's aunt is on the way over to pick her up, to take her back to Bryan. And Hailey is trying to decide whether to go over with her or if she wants me to take her back to Austin tonight. Either way, they can call you when they get to Bryan, right?'

'Sure.' He frowns at Hailey. 'You're really thinking about leaving? Girl, you just got here.' His eyes cut to Lyle, and he seems to read the situation, at least partly. 'I see, you want to get back to your boy.'

'Boy?' Lyle sneers.

'Excuse me, maaaan,' Steve says, rolling his eyes. 'Listen, Hailey, call if you want to meet up. Tammy, you can come hang out, even if Hailey decides to head back to Austin, OK?'

She nods, flashing a guilty look in Hailey's direction.

Steve heads out and, before we can start squabbling again, Wendy comes charging in. It's only taken her twenty minutes. She must have driven like a bat out of hell. She stops when she sees Lyle. 'Hi, who are you?'

'This is my boyfriend, Lyle,' Hailey says, sounding less enthusiastic than expected.

'Hi, Lyle.' Wendy smiles, but doesn't look at me. She knows exactly what's going on.

'So, Tammy, you ready to come home?' Wendy asks.

'Wait. Just wait,' Tammy says.

'Come on in the kitchen,' I say to Wendy. 'Give the kids a minute. They have to talk something over.'

In the kitchen I pour her a glass of wine and we stand near the sink so I can tell her what's going on without being overheard.

'Poor kid,' she says when I tell her the choice.

'Poor kid? What about poor me?'

'Poor you, too,' she says, and puts her arms around me and gazes into my eyes. Dusty is looking up at us, his eyes shining. Then she giggles and he starts prancing around. 'Kids!'

She looks at my half-made sandwich. 'Yum, that looks like a great dinner.'

'It was supposed to be quick.' I look at my watch. It's now almost seven. I tell her what my plan was with Maria.

'Samuel, look, I could drive Hailey to Austin. I'm sure Tammy will come along for the ride.'

I hug her tight. 'No, it's my thing.'

I'm just about to kiss her when I hear the front door slam and Hailey says from the doorway, 'All right, you win. Lyle is going back and I'll go with Tammy and Wendy.'

'You sure?'

Her eyes are swimming with tears, but she nods. I'm not about to ask any questions. Whatever made her decide this, whether it was my lecture about adult decisions or Lyle's hints about Jonelle, I'm relieved. It flashes through my mind that Lyle might be waiting to meet Hailey in Bryan, but surely there's a limit to their sneaking around.

'Let's go, then,' Wendy says briskly. 'We don't want to keep your friend Steve waiting.' Hailey turns to go and Wendy comes to give me a kiss and to whisper, 'Tammy has a crush on Steve.'

Even though I don't think Lyle will follow them to Bryan, I tell Wendy to keep an eye out. 'Call me if you even think you see him.'

'Oh, believe me, my antennae are going to be working full time.'

I'm wishing I'd told Steve to be wary as well, but I may be putting too much stock into his good intentions.

I call Maria to tell her the plan is back on. 'I don't want to wait until Cal closes up shop. I'm going by the store to tell him he needs to close up early.'

On the way over, I eat the sandwich I made, which tastes better than I thought it would.

THIRTY-FIVE

C al is confused when I tell him I need him to lock up the store and come home, but I say I'll explain when we get there.

At his place, he shows us into the living room. His movements are jittery and he barely looks at us. He's gotten the message that something isn't right.

'Just a minute, let me get Mamma. Go on and sit down.' He points the way.

He comes back in a minute with Myra. She's wearing a cotton housecoat with an apron over it. She looks tired, but she also looks suspicious. 'What in the world is going on?' Then a subtle change comes over her face. 'Has something happened to Ralph?'

'No, we just need to talk to you for a minute.'

She asks if we want anything to drink. 'Or maybe some pie?'

We thank her, but Cal goes to get himself a beer and comes back with that and a candy bar.

'Cal, what do you think you're doing?' Myra asks. 'Dinner is ready. It just has to be heated up.'

'Just to tide me over,' he says, taking a big bite of the chocolate bar.

We sit down, the two of them on the sofa, me in an easy chair and Maria in a straight chair.

'I need to talk to you about something,' I say. 'It's about Ralph's brother.'

'Oh my goodness. Is he OK?' Myra folds her hands as if she's going to pray.

'That's the thing. You said Ralph told you his brother was in an accident, but that turns out not to be true.'

I wait while it sinks in.

'What's this?' Cal asks.

Myra tells him.

'What do you mean that isn't true?' Myra asks me.

'I spoke with your sister-in-law and she said Ralph's brother is fine, there was no accident.'

'Then why did Ralph tell me that?'

'I was wondering if you had any idea why.'

'No, I don't. But where did Ralph go if he didn't go to his brother's?'

'That's what we'd like to know. I also called his cell phone, and it's turned off.'

'Oh, well, that's because it's right here,' she says. She jumps up and hurries from the room before I can tell her not to. She comes back holding it out like it's the answer to everything. 'Silly man rushed out of here so fast that he left it on the kitchen counter.'

'Cal,' I say, 'you called your daddy after I left the store today?'

'Yes.'

'What did you talk to him about?'

He glances at his mother and back to me, raising his eyebrows. 'About, you know, what he didn't want me to talk to Mamma about.'

'What's that?' she says sharply.

'Best tell her,' I say.

'Look, Mamma, Daddy was thinking about buying a motorcycle. He didn't want you to know and he told me not to tell you.'

'That man! I swear, he thinks he's a teenager. He'll kill himself on it. Besides, we can't afford something like that.'

'What did you tell your daddy when you called him?' I ask Cal.

He looks confused. 'I just said you had stopped by and asked about those guys who came to the store looking for Amber. I also told him that you knew he'd been looking at the bike, and that if you know, a lot of people probably do, too, and he'd better be prepared for Mamma to find out.'

'Was that all?'

He shrugs. 'I told him you were asking stuff about Amber.'

Maria and I glance at each other. 'Did he seem upset when you talked to him?'

'Upset?' He blinks. 'Daddy has been a little hard to get along with lately, kind of quick tempered, and he said I should mind my own business.'

'What did he mean by that?'

'About the motorcycle.' He frowns, looking thoughtful. 'At least I think that's what he meant.'

'We need to find Ralph,' I say to Myra. 'Any idea where he might be?'

Myra has been sitting silent as a stone through all this. Her chest is heaving. She says, 'What does my husband have to do with Amber Johnson?'

'Mamma, it's not about her,' Cal says. 'Don't ask, OK?'

'Did he ever talk about Amber?' I ask her.

She smooths her apron. 'He said he didn't like Cal working for her because it was going to cause trouble.'

'What?' Cal says. 'What trouble?'

'That's what I asked him and he said it was none of my business but that I ought to try to talk you into getting away from her.'

'When was this?' I ask.

She takes a deep breath and crosses her arms. 'A few days ago. Maybe last Friday.'

'Myra, Cal, do either of you have any idea where Ralph might have gone?'

'Not the slightest idea,' she says. 'It never occurred to me that he might go off somewhere. And now I find out he was hanging out at that motorcycle rally like a teenager.'

'Does he have credit cards? Any cash on him?'

'Of course he has credit cards.' She pulls herself to her feet, looking stunned. 'Samuel, what the heck is going on? Do you think Ralph had something to do with Amber Johnson's death?'

I get up. 'I'm not sure. Does he have any good friends he might hole up with?'

'Ralph isn't very social. I can't think of anybody he might go to if he's . . .'

'Running away?' Cal says, his voice harsh.

'Can you think of anywhere he'd go?' she asks her son.

My cell phone rings. It's Dan Weinman. 'Samuel, you're not going to believe this, but Ralph Tyson's van is in the parking lot at the rally. It's going to be a job to find him in this mob, but at least he's close by and we can keep an eye on his vehicle.' My heart sinks. If he's done what I think he's done, he might not be returning to the van. But maybe it's not too late.

I get up and motion for Maria to follow me. 'I know where he is,' I say to Weinman. 'I'll be there in five minutes. Watch that entrance for a motorcycle. Hold on.' I flip through my notebook and read out the description and license number.

I punch the phone off and say, 'I'm sorry, we have to cut this short. Come on, Maria, let's go.'

'Wait,' Myra says, sounding panicky. 'Where are you going? Did somebody find Ralph?'

We're out the door and I don't pause to answer her. Maria and I jump into the squad car and squeal away. I'm not much on using the siren, but I do it now. Chances are, Ralph is already gone, but if luck is with me, maybe Kelvin Moseley didn't come back as soon as he thought he would and they're still negotiating the price of the motorcycle.

Dan Weinman is waiting at the entrance to the rally. 'I've stationed some men around the other side in case Tyson tries to get away.'

'If he's still here,' I say.

It's still light, but getting to be dusk. People are in a festive mood toward the end of the week. The crowd seems even bigger. The noise is deafening. Most people are too busy drinking beer or having their dinner to notice us, but the three of us get a few curious glances. There's something about the way law officers carry themselves that attracts a certain kind of attention.

There are all kinds of scenarios that may greet us when we get to Moseley's spot. He might not be back from his errands and Ralph may be sitting around waiting for him. Or Ralph may have bought the motorcycle and be long gone. I doubt Moseley would take a check, and if Tyson had to go to the bank to get cash for the motorcycle, that might have taken some time.

What I hadn't counted on is Tyson being so cocky that he'd hang out drinking beer with Kelvin Moseley. Which means that Moseley has kept his mouth shut about me visiting him this afternoon, and I'm grateful for that.

Maria, Dan and I walk over to the group of five men standing near the motorcycle. 'Hey, Ralph,' I say as we walk up.

He freezes and his eyes flit from me to the other two. He tries out a smile. 'How you doing, Chief? What's up?'

'Need to have a word with you.'

'About what?'

Kelvin Moseley is smirking. My guess is he's just glad it's not him being invited to have a chat with the cops.

'Let's talk in private.'

Ralph blinks, and I realize he's weighing his options. I could tell him that the best option would be to stonewall. We don't have any eyewitnesses. The only thing I have going is a good, strong hunch. If he stonewalls, our case is going to be hard to make.

But he doesn't. Like so many criminals, he hasn't thought ahead to the consequences.

He takes off running.

'Runner!' Weinman shouts, and we go after Tyson. Weinman is a good deal younger than I am, and Maria is younger than him. She takes off like a jackrabbit. It never occurred to me that she could run fast. But she catches up to Tyson within fifty yards and shoves him. He stumbles and pitches headfirst to the ground, yelling. Dan Weinman is on him in a heartbeat, pulling his arms behind him and handcuffing him.

Within seconds we've drawn a crowd to witness Tyson's protests. People are holding their cell phones, I assume taking videos of the excitement. A couple of people call out comments on their opinions of cops.

'What the hell do you want with me?' Tyson snarls. 'I haven't done anything.'

'We'll see,' I say. We haul him to his feet. He has a bloody nose, but it isn't broken.

He continues to protest as we walk back the way we came. Kelvin Moseley is standing with his arms crossed, looking amused. I suspect that means he got his money for the motorcycle before all this happened.

When I put him into the squad car, Tyson says, 'You strong-armed me out of there before I could pick up the motorcycle I bought. That guy better not make off with it or I'll sue your ass.' I have to admit I never suspected that Tyson would be such a bulldog. He always seemed mild-mannered.

Back at the station, as soon as I read Tyson his rights, he doesn't waste time and demands a lawyer right away, so we're out of luck for questioning him tonight. I tell Maria to get him into a cell while I call for a court order to search Tyson's house.

'The hell you say!' Tyson howls. 'You can't do that. I told you I haven't done anything.'

'Then why did you run when I told you I wanted to talk to you?'

With that, he clams up.

After Maria gets Tyson locked up, I tell her that Weinman and I are going back to his house to make sure Myra doesn't get rid of any incriminating evidence. 'As soon as that warrant comes through, come over and we'll start the search.'

As I suspected, Myra was too stunned to do anything but feed her son after we left. When Weinman and I arrive, I sit her down in the living room and tell her that we're getting a search warrant and that she doesn't have to stay around if she'd rather go to a friend's house while we conduct the search.

Cal says, 'Come on, Mamma, we're not going to stay here.' He's pale and nervous, but I'm impressed that he's worried more about his mamma than he is about himself. And it's just as well that he does take her away, because in a drawer in Ralph Tyson's bedroom we find a knife in a sheath on a belt. Using gloves, Maria takes it out of the sheath and holds it to the light. 'I'll bet any amount of money he washed this knife but didn't think to wash the sheath.'

And if that isn't enough, in the trash can outside, we find a bloody T-shirt. It might very well be the one Ralph was wearing when he killed Amber.

At the end of the evening, after the search is over and Ralph is snug in his cell, ready to be transported to Bobtail tomorrow, I invite Weinman and Maria to my place to have a shot of whiskey and to discuss just how stupid criminals are.

'Why didn't he get rid of that shirt somewhere?' Maria asks.

I haven't dealt with that many homicides, but Weinman has dealt with a few. He regales her with a couple of stories of crimes gone bad because the criminals were too cocky, or in too big a hurry, or too ignorant to cover their tracks.

'I don't think that's what happened with Ralph Tyson,' I say. 'My guess is, he was so shocked by what he had done that he wanted to forget it. He threw that shirt away the first place he thought of because he didn't want to dwell on it.'

'How come it was still there then? Wouldn't there have been a garbage pickup? It's been over a week,' Weinman asks.

'Boss,' Maria says to me, 'he's smarter than you think.' She refused alcohol and is drinking a soda.

'How do you figure?'

'Mr Weinman is right. The trash should have been picked up. I'll bet he hid that shirt for a few days and then threw it out.'

'Not that smart, then,' Weinman says, grinning.

'What do you mean?'

'If he was all that smart, he would have found some other place to throw it away. That's the problem with criminals. They're short-sighted. Lot of 'em never think it's possible that they'll get caught.'

'There's one other possibility,' I say. 'The shirt got bloody some other way. Maybe it isn't even his.'

'Always possible,' Weinman says. 'But it all comes back down to why he ran.'

THIRTY-SIX

After they're gone I call Wendy and tell her we have detained a suspect.

'I'm glad. Now maybe you can think about that trip to Padre Island with me.'

'Did you get Hailey and Tammy handed over to Steve?'

She pauses. 'I did. I'll tell you, I got an earful on the drive over here. I almost decided to forget about letting them meet up with Steve.'

'Oh, he's not a bad kid.'

'Maybe not, but Hailey got into an argument with Tammy about him. Tammy has a crush on him, and Hailey said he's not as good a guy as she thinks.'

'Really? In what way?'

'She said he wasn't very nice to one of the girls they hang out with. The girl told Hailey that Steve tried to put the moves on her and she told him she wasn't interested, and he got rough.'

That's got to be Sophie.

'But you decided to let them go anyway.'

'There were several of them together. I figured Hailey was still upset by the incident with Lyle and she was taking it out on Steve. By now you know how dramatic these girls are.'

'Are they still out?'

'Yes. The movie was over at 9:30, but then they were going out for hamburgers.'

'You want me to come and get her tonight?'

'Don't do that. You need to get a good night's sleep. And I like having them here. Reminds me of when I used to have fun with my girls.'

I tell her I'll come get Hailey in the morning. 'I need to have a serious talk with her.'

She chuckles. 'She's expecting it.'

I walk Dusty and think about calling Tom and Vicki, but decide to wait until tomorrow. I hit the bed at 10:30, which is early even for me.

But I don't fall asleep. As soon as I close my eyes, I think about Ralph Tyson, and how surprised I am at his change of personality. His belligerence this afternoon. And his carelessness about keeping that bloody T-shirt. He always struck me as being a careful person. Of course, he was thinking about buying a motorcycle. That's not careful. But according to Moseley, he had abandoned the idea – until this afternoon. I think back over the conversation with Dan Weinman and Maria this evening, about why somebody would keep such a damning piece of evidence. And it doesn't make sense.

I'm tossing around in bed, trying to find a position to put myself to sleep. It's usually easy. Finally I have to admit it. Something doesn't seem right. Why did Tyson tell his wife the lie about his brother being injured – a lie that was easily disproved? Why did he go back to buy the motorcycle, spending valuable time he could have used to get away? Why did he keep that bloody shirt and then throw it away – almost as if he planted it for us to find it?

I leap out of bed. There's only one reason he would do all those things. He's protecting someone. Maybe his son. Here I am, convinced that Cal really cared for Amber and doesn't seem the least bit guilty. And yet his daddy thinks he killed her.

In the kitchen I make a pot of coffee. If I can't sleep, at least I can enjoy a cup of coffee. I drink it, my mind coming back to that T-shirt. A plain white T-shirt, like anybody would wear.

I suppose for young people it isn't that late, and sure enough when I ring the doorbell at the Tyson home, Cal comes to the door still dressed. 'What do you want?' he says. 'Haven't you done enough? My poor mamma is a wreck, so I'm not letting you talk to her tonight. I hope she's asleep.' There's bravado in his voice.

'It's you I want to talk to,' I say.

'I don't know why. I don't know a thing about what's going on. I don't believe my daddy killed anybody, and I don't know what else to tell you.'

'May I come in?'

He steps aside silently. In the living room, the TV is on very low, a video game on the screen. He switches it off and we sit down.

'Cal, we found a hunting knife in a sheath in your daddy's possessions. Do you know why he has it?'

'Sure. He hunts turkey every year with his brother. Or did. I don't think he much liked it and he and his brother aren't close. I think he stopped a few years ago.'

'Have you seen him use the knife since?'

'No, sir.'

'Have you ever used it?'

'No. I don't even know where he keeps it.'

I nod. 'You know, Cal, when people use a knife and clean it up, they often don't think to clean the sheath as well, and often that's where you find traces of the victim's blood if the knife was used to kill them.' I watch carefully for his response.

He looks solemn. 'So you think he used the knife to kill her and that there will be traces of blood?' His voice gets shaky. 'I just can't picture Daddy doing that. I don't understand why he would. He hardly knew her.' If Cal killed her, he shows no sign of being worried about the possible traces of blood.

'Maybe he was mad because she was having sex with you. Maybe he told her to quit, and she wouldn't.'

'I hope that's not what happened.' He hangs his head.

'You know we found a blood-stained T-shirt in the trash can outside.'

'Blood-stained T-shirt? Did it belong to Daddy?'

'Or you.'

He shakes his head. 'No, sir, it did not belong to me. I haven't had any reason to throw away a T-shirt at all, much less a bloody one.'

'But I did,' a voice says from the doorway.

Both our heads jerk up at the same time to see Myra standing there. 'I can't believe you think that shirt proves that my husband killed somebody. That was my T-shirt. Remember I cut my hand cooking a few days ago?' She gestures to the bandage. 'Bled like a stuck pig. I threw the T-shirt in the trash.'

'Myra, it's a man's size.'

'Samuel, look at me. I am not a small woman. My husband wears one size bigger than me. You are not going to find anybody's blood but mine on that T-shirt.'

'What do you want? I just managed to get to sleep and here you are waking me up. Is this supposed to be some kind of torture procedure?' Ralph Tyson swings his legs off the side of the cot and sits hunched over.

'Ralph, I'm coming into the cell with you and we're going to talk.'

He tilts his head up and assesses me. 'I told you I'm not going to talk.'

'I am.'

'Suit yourself.'

I go in, bringing a chair from the outer office and sit down. 'I got to thinking, and I realized you're not that stupid. If you really had killed Amber Johnson, you wouldn't have let yourself be caught so easily. In fact, you practically begged us to arrest you.'

He's watchful.

'So I got to wondering why you would do that. And only one thing came to mind. You're covering for somebody.'

He snorts. 'Think whatever you want to.' He starts tapping his foot, impatient for me to get on with it.

'The thing is, your son has an alibi.'

He freezes. When he looks at me, his eyes are wary. 'What alibi? Did Myra say he was home?'

'Yes, but there's more. He was playing video games. With two other players. Real time. Now unless you or Myra were playing in his place, he was right there at your house.' I have to check it out for sure, but if it turns out Cal's lying, there's plenty of time to arrest him later. Right now, I want to get things squared away with Ralph.

He swallows and buries his face in his hands. His shoulders heave. 'I didn't know what to do. When I heard what happened I was scared Cal had done something stupid.'

'What made you think he would have killed Amber?'

He looks up at me, wiping his eyes. 'I told him I heard she was sleeping around with guys for money, and he wasn't happy about that.'

'When did you tell him?'

'Friday, after I saw her coming out of that RV where they were turning tricks.'

'Ralph, you didn't tell him anything he didn't already know.'

His face flushes. 'That kid . . .'

'Didn't kill Amber Johnson.'

'Then who did?'

'That's the question, isn't it? You could have been covering for somebody else.'

His eyes narrow. 'I don't know who you mean.'

'Your wife.'

His eyes dart away from me. 'No way.'

'But you weren't sure, were you?'

He bows his head and doesn't say anything.

'You didn't know whether she had found out her son was sleeping with Amber. And if she had found out, you didn't know what she'd do.'

'I know her. I know she wouldn't kill anybody.'

'But you didn't know for sure. She had that cut on her hand that she claimed she got when she was cooking.'

'I just . . . I was scared one of them . . .'

'Either way, it wasn't you who killed Amber.'

Could it have been Myra? It would mean she sneaked out of the house while her son was playing video games. And I tend to believe her claim that we'll only find her blood on the T-shirt. We'll know soon enough.

'Does that mean you're going to let me out of here?'

'Unless you insist that you're guilty.'

'No, I didn't do anything to her.'

'Did you talk to her Saturday night?'

He hangs his head. 'I was going to. I saw her go off with that lanky woman, Butler's girlfriend. Almost didn't recognize her without her wig. I followed them, thinking I could have a word with Amber and tell her to leave my boy alone.'

'And did you talk to her?'

'No, I chickened out. The two women were having an argument and I figured Amber wouldn't be in the mood for me to confront her, and I could always talk to her later. So I turned around and went back.'

'You see anybody else around there?'

He closes his eyes and runs his hands along his jaw. 'Nobody. Just that kid, Steve Deverell, with his cleanup cart. Seems like he manages to be everywhere at once. Good worker.'

I drive Tyson back to his house and when he goes inside I sit in my pickup and think about what he said. The more I think, the more dread forms in my belly. Which means I need to talk to Cal one more time.

I knock on the door and it takes a minute for someone to answer. It's Cal. 'Can't you let us alone now? You've about driven my mamma and daddy crazy. And I'm almost there myself.'

'It's you I need to talk to.'

He glares at me, but opens the door and we go back into the living room. We sit back down.

'Cal, when I told you that I knew you were having sex with Amber, do you remember who you said probably blabbed about that?'

He shrugs. 'Yeah. I knew it had to be Steve Deverell.'

'Did you tell anyone else?'

'Sure. There were a couple of other guys there.'

'Then why did you think it was Steve who told me?'

'Like I said, he was jealous.'

'How do you know?'

He snickers. 'After I told him, he kept coming to the store and chatting her up, like he thought he was going to sweet talk her into bed with him.'

'What was her reaction?'

'She thought it was funny. I mean, she was nice to him, but she and I laughed about it.'

'Did you tell him that?'

He looks away, jiggling his leg. 'I might have.'

'What did you say?'

'Told him he should give it up, she wasn't into him.'

'Why did you tell him that?'

'I dunno. He thinks he's a stud with girls and I just wanted to take a poke at him, that's all.'

'When did you tell him that?'

'I guess it was a couple of weeks ago. He came into the store looking for her. She was gone and I told him he had to stop pestering her.'

'Why didn't you tell me this before?'

'Why would I?'

'I asked you if anybody had been bothering her.'

He opens his mouth, but nothing comes out for a good thirty seconds, and then he says quietly, 'Shit. You don't think . . . look, she didn't take it seriously. He's a kid.'

I warn him not to tell anyone about our conversation and take off for the rally.

THIRTY-SEVEN

It's just after midnight when I roll into the Jubilee Motorcycle Rally parking lot. I have to fight the outgoing tide of people who came for the day and are leaving now the music's stopped. I head straight for Luke Harriman's trailer. It's lit up, and when I mount the steps I hear laughter coming from inside. I knock on the door.

'Come on in,' Harriman calls out.

Inside I find Gilly Moon and Harriman reared back in their chairs, a bottle of Jack Daniels on the desk where they can both reach it.

Moon tips his chair forward. 'Don't get up,' I say.

'What can I do for you?' Harriman says. He does get up, with a lurch.

'I need some information.'

'I hope I'm in a condition to provide you with some,' he says. 'After the week I've had, I'm relaxing a little bit.'

'I don't blame you,' I say. 'This won't take long. I want to ask about one of your workers. Steve Deverell.'

He puts his hands up. 'I'm sorry, I know you like the kid, but I can't hire him back. He pushed my buttons one too many times.'

'You fired him?' Steve said he had the day off.

'Sure as hell did.'

'What did he do?'

Harriman goes behind the desk and gets a folding chair that's leaning up against the wall, brings it around to the front and sets it up. 'Sit down. You want a drink?'

'Better not right this minute. So, what did Steve do?'

He sighs. 'That's the hell of it. When he worked, he was a dynamo, but sometimes he just walked away from his cart like it was a toy he was tired of playing with. I'd hunt him down and—'

'Don't tell us,' Moon says, 'you'd find him chatting up the ladies.'

Harriman points a finger-gun at Moon. 'Got it in one.' He turns back to me. 'I told him he couldn't just walk away like that, but it didn't make an impression. Finally last night I saw the cart and found him down by the lake. It was the last straw. I told him not to come back in.'

'You said he was down by the lake? Where?'

'Behind the music pavilion.'

'You mean near where Amber Johnson's body was found?'

Harriman rubs a hand across his forehead. 'Yeah. That area.'

'Luke, you mentioned to me earlier in the week that Steve had abandoned his cart. Can you recall when that was?'

He squints and peers into his glass, which is empty again. The time seems to stretch out. It's late and I'm tired and I don't like the way things are trending. 'I'm not sure.'

'Well let me ask you this. You remember when you told me you weren't here when the call came in Saturday night about somebody finding a body?'

He nods.

'Where were you?'

He leans over and pours another shot into his glass. Gilly Moon is watching him intently.

'I was having a meeting with the cleaners. There were two of them that night. Starting Monday I had three on each shift.'

'One of the cleaners was Steve?'

'That's right.'

'What was the meeting about?'

'Reminding them that they couldn't leave their carts untended.'

'So Steve had left his cart untended earlier that day?'

He snaps his fingers. 'Of course, that's why I was talking to them. Because he'd walked off and left it earlier.'

'What happened to it when you found it?'

'Oh, while I was talking to the crew, he came back wondering where it was. I told him I had kept it aside for him to clean up. Which he did. But still . . .'

It flashes through my mind what Wendy said tonight, that the girls were saying he wasn't the great guy everybody thought he was.

'Luke, when the guys clean out their carts, where does the trash go?'

'We take it to the dump. At least that's where it ends up. We put it in big dumpster bins. Then at the end of the week the dumpster crew comes and takes them all to the dump.'

'But not before that?'

'Nope. All done at the same time.' He tells me where the bins are located.

Going through the dumpsters is a job that should have been done right after the murder. One of a few missteps stemming from the murder occurring at a place where there were hundreds of potential suspects. I should have realized that whoever killed Amber would have been spattered with blood and would most likely have had to remove incriminating clothing. Now I've flailed around pulling in two suspects on the basis of wild speculation. This time I have to be sure I'm looking at the right person.

'Chief.' I come out of my reverie to see Gilly Moon squinting at me. 'I recognize a man who is beating up on himself. Don't do it. It's a waste of time and energy.' His breath exudes alcohol, but his words are firm.

I shake my head and sigh. 'I missed a step I shouldn't have missed. Maybe I'm getting too old for this job.'

'You got that young gal deputy. Did she pick up on what you missed?'

'I guess not.'

'Well, then. Move along.'

He's right. There's time for recriminations later. The important thing is not to waste any more time barking up the wrong trees.

I thank them and start back to my car, but realize there's one more stop I could make.

Grant Butler's RV is lit up. I pound on the door and sure enough Becky opens it. She groans when she sees me. 'Not you again.'

'Not for long. I have one question for you, and you can answer it right here and now.'

'That's great news.' Her voice drips with sarcasm. 'But I'll come outside. I'd just as soon not let the bugs in.' And not let the clientele know there's a lawman outside. She steps down and walks into the shadows at the end of the RV. 'All right, shoot.'

'Think about that night when you had the confrontation with Amber. I want you to really picture it.'

'OK.'

'Now you've left her and you see the man looking toward her.'

'I told you I can't describe him.'

'I know you did. I'm talking about something else. I want you to try to remember if you saw anybody else. Anybody.'

'Well, there was a couple making out. Kind of gross, really.'

'Good. Anybody else?'

She sighs. 'One of the cleaners, you know, the guys with the cart.'

'OK. Remember what he looked like?'

'Oh, Lord, they all look alike. I guess he had light hair anyway. And of course they all wear those awful vests.'

'With or without a shirt?'

'I think I would have noticed if he didn't have a shirt on. Ha! I do remember something. He had this smile. Smiled at me like he thought he was a bad boy. You know what I mean.'

'Did he say anything?'

'No. But he was sure thinking it.' She laughs, low and suggestive.

'I appreciate your help.'

'I'll appreciate it when I get the hell out of here,' she says.

It's the middle of the night, and as I walk back to my car I ponder whether to roust out people right now to question them, or wait until dawn? For sure, there's one phone call I'm going to make.

'Hey, what's up?' Wendy sounds like she's still awake.

'Have the girls come home?'

'Oh, yes. We were just watching reruns of *Girls* and eating popcorn.'

'Did things go all right?'

'As far as I know. Why are you asking these questions?'

'Just checking up. But Wendy, be sure and lock the doors tonight, got that?'

'You worried that Lyle is coming back?' She practically whispers the question.

'I just want you to be careful. And if anything odd happens, don't hesitate. Call 911.'

She gives a mirthless laugh. 'Now you've got me worried.'

'I think everything will be fine. We'll talk in the morning.'

As soon as I hang up, I make two more calls, one to Maria and one to Dan Weinman. I tell them I let Ralph Tyson go, and why, and that I'm zeroed in on Steve Deverell. I tell Maria I'll meet her at headquarters at 7:30 tomorrow morning.

'Who's Steve Deverell?' Weinman asks.

I tell him. 'Sorry about this, but we're going to need a crew out at the rally to go through the dumpsters from the night of the murder. It didn't occur to me that whoever killed Amber Johnson might have taken off their shirt and thrown it away.'

'I didn't think about it either. Half the guys at the rally don't wear anything but a vest on top.'

'Have you seen the vests the cleanup crew wear? You'd have to look close to see blood on them. But I've never seen the Deverell kid without a T-shirt. If he was wearing one, we'll find it. He could easily have stashed it in his cleanup cart, knowing it was going to be dumped after his shift.'

'All right. I'll get a few guys out there in the morning, early, to go through the dumpsters. We've got a couple of smart alecks that need to be put on a detail like that to give them something to think about.'

I laugh, though I don't feel amused.

It's two o'clock by the time I fall into bed. This time, despite being keyed up, I at least get a few hours of restless sleep.

The next morning I'm out the door before Loretta has time to come by with baked goods, but it's just as well. I'm too tied up in knots to eat. Dusty hops in the pickup with me and seems to sense my mood. He sits erect in the passenger seat, looking straight ahead. It's soothing to see him as serious as I feel.

Maria is already at the station, and has brought kolaches from the bakery. I thought I couldn't eat anything, but one goes down really well with a strong cup of coffee.

We arrive at the dumpster site at the same time as the highway patrol officers that Weinman promised. They're none too enthusiastic about their chore, but they've brought coveralls, gloves, and masks. There are six big bins in rows. The likely ones we need to look at are the two at the rear – the ones from the first few nights of the rally. The crew has also brought a portable machine with a grabber that can reach into the depths of the bins to haul out loads. The only thing they have to do by hand is pick through the piles. If they think Maria and I ought to be joining in the process, they don't say so.

The three men and one woman zip into their coveralls and start in. It's a nasty operation. We knew it would be. Maria and I stand back and watch as they painstakingly go through every item, mostly food-related trash and broken bike parts, but there are surprising items as well. A woman's purse, a large photo album, and two men's wallets. They set them aside to take them to lost and found.

We're twenty minutes in when Dan Weinman shows up. I tell him and Maria exactly what happened last night and how I came to believe Steve Deverell is the man we're looking for. I don't tell them that it hurts me. I like Steve. I thought there was a chance for him.

'We'll see pretty soon if we're on the right track,' Weinman says.

The search produces results. More results than we thought. There are three bloody T-shirts in those two dumpsters. The officers bag them in the proper containers. 'You know, this may take a few days,' Weinman says. 'We'll get samples from Amber Johnson's autopsy and see if there's a match here with any of these shirts. If we do get a match, we'll see if we can identify who was wearing it. You going to bring this kid in and question him?' I appreciate that he defers to me. He doesn't have to.

'Whoa!' one of the patrolmen says. 'Look at this.'

It's a knife. One with a wide blade. With what looks like blood on it. It's been wiped off, but not thoroughly.

'That may short-cut things a little,' Weinman says.

'Unless he was wearing gloves,' I say.

'We're going to get this guy,' Weinman says. 'Let me know if you want me to sit in on an interview.'

Maria and I discuss how and when to bring in Steve Deverell. If we question him too early and have nothing to back up our suspicions, we might have to release him, and he could leave town. But if we wait too long, he might get wind of our suspicions, and then he could also skip town. 'I have one more thing I want to check,' I say.

We move through the sparse crowd, looking for a member of the cleanup crew. It's too early for most people to be up after a night of revelry. Soon we spot one of the crew pushing his cart, wearing the multi-colored vest assigned to them.

I stop and tell him who I am. 'I have a question for you.' I nod to the knife sheath at his belt. 'Do they provide you with a knife?'

He looks down at it. 'Yeah. You'd be surprised at some of the things we find that we have to cut up to get in our carts.'

I thank him, and Maria and I head back to Luke Harriman's trailer. Luke is already in, in a manner of speaking. He looks a little the worse for wear. I tell him what I'm here about.

'Let's go on to the crew area and we'll see what we can find out.'

It turns out that there's a crew captain on both the morning and afternoon shifts. The crew area is a portable shed with lockers and shelves where people can keep their clothes if they change for the job. The captain is a kid barely older than Steve. He says he's from Bobtail, which is why I don't recognize him.

Luke Harriman asks the question. 'When Steve Deverell turned over his equipment, did he hand in his knife?'

'Sort of,' the kid mumbles.

'What does that mean?' Harriman sounds impatient.

'He handed in the sheath, but it had a different knife in it.'

'Did you give it to the guy who took over Steve's spot?'

'No, sir, it wasn't a good knife. I just threw it in the basket.'
Over in the corner of the room is a laundry basket full of junk.
The kid starts to put his hand in.

'Let me,' I say. I pull on a pair of latex gloves and rummage
through and find the sheath quickly. The knife in it is too small
for the sheath.

I show it to Maria and she nods. This could be what we need.

THIRTY-EIGHT

B ack at headquarters, we sit uneasily, not having made a
decision yet as to whether to bring Steve Deverell in now
or later. Maria usually has strong opinions, but on this one
she's as torn as I am. So I have time to think.

I can imagine how it happened. Cal bragged about his prowess
with Amber, and Steve took it as a challenge. He started flirting with
Amber, but she wasn't having any of it. He got more and more
frustrated, and to get her attention he shoplifted something.
I don't know what he thought at that point. That somehow she'd
take notice of him, be impressed by how daring he was, or how
contrite he was when he was found out? And then came the
crushing point where Cal told him that he and Amber had been
laughing at him behind his back.

I don't want to believe his attack was premeditated. He must
have seen Amber go off with Becky, followed by Ralph Tyson.
And when Ralph turned around and left Amber alone, Steve saw
his chance to make a move on her under the cover of darkness.
Maybe he begged, maybe he got cocky. Maybe she laughed
at him. But for whatever reason, he pulled out that knife and
killed her. And then he panicked. He tore off his shirt and threw
it and his knife in his cart and wore the vest. One of his unlucky
breaks was when someone reported the cart he'd abandoned
when he went off to try to seduce her.

There's one more piece to the puzzle that I want to slot in before
we go after Steve. At nine a.m., I'm at Sophie Rodriguez's door.

Her mother says she's still asleep, but I tell her she needs to wake the girl, that it's important. She sits me down in the living room and leaves, but instead of Sophie, it's Momo Rodriguez who comes in. 'Is my daughter in trouble? She told us about the incident with alcohol at your place. I have told her to apologize. Has she not done so?'

I get up. 'Not yet, but she will. That isn't what I'm here about. I think she has some information that may be important to an investigation.'

He nods, still looking wary. 'I'll get her.'

Like Hailey, Sophie looks younger when she's just awakened. When she sees me, she looks nervous and glances at her daddy. He nods to her. 'Let's sit down.'

Sophie sits down at the edge of the sofa next to her daddy, knitting her hands together in her lap. 'Chief Craddock, I'm sorry about the other day.' She bites her lower lip.

'Thank you. I accept your apology,' I say. 'That isn't why I'm here today, though. I need to ask a question, to clarify something.'

Her glance darts between her daddy and me. 'OK.' It's almost a whisper.

'You remember telling Hailey that you got angry at Steve Deverell last week and scratched his face?'

'Sophie,' Momo's voice is stern and disappointed.

I hold up a hand to stop him saying more. 'I need you to tell me if you told the truth.'

Her eyes widen. 'Well . . . I was mad at him.'

'OK.'

'But . . . I didn't scratch him.' She whimpers. 'Don't tell him I told you.'

'Why did you tell Hailey he did?'

'He asked me to back him up. No, he told me to. He said if I didn't back him up, he'd tell everybody I . . .' She looks at her daddy. 'I swear I didn't, Papa.'

'Sophie, it's important that you not tell Steve that you confessed this to me, do you understand?'

She looks uncertain, but she nods. 'Is he in trouble?'

'Do you think he is?'

'Maybe.'

* * *

I'd like to wait for DNA analysis of the T-shirts to confirm that one of them has Amber Johnson's blood on it, but it could take days, and at this point, I think we have enough incidental evidence to at least bring Steve in for questioning. I call Dan Weinman and he says the matching sample won't take as long as a lot of other processes because all they're doing is matching Amber's blood with blood on the shirts. If they do find a match, finding out who the shirt belonged to might take longer. 'But there's the knife, too. Even if the kid was wearing gloves when he killed her, it's possible he handled the knife bare-handed at some point.' He agrees that there's enough to bring him in for questioning.

'There's one more thing. The medical examiner said there was a lot of material under the victim's fingernails. Most of it was dirt, but Steve Deverell had scratches on his face. I'd like to see if any of the material matched his DNA. That would nail it.'

I tell him I'd like him to attend Steve's questioning. 'I know the kid too well. I think having somebody from the Department of Public Safety in the room will be useful. Give it some heft.'

He tells me he'll be at headquarters within the hour, and Maria and I head out to bring in Steve.

Lily answers the door. She says Steve is in the back yard and she'll get him. I hate that she'll have a terrible surprise in store.

Steve is sweaty. He's wearing a Harley-Davidson T-shirt, shorts, and flip-flops. He frowns when he sees us. 'Hey, Chief. What do you need? I got the girls back to Wendy's house in good shape, right?'

'Steve, I need you to come down to the station with us. We have some questions for you.'

'Can it wait? My bike's all taken apart out in the driveway.'

'I'm afraid it can't wait.'

'Daddy'll have a fit if I leave it like that.' His voice has a frantic quality to it.

Lily has come back and is hovering at the edge of the entryway, one arm clutched to her stomach, the other fiddling with the collar of her bright green blouse.

'Can't be helped. Come on outside with us.'

He looks from me to Maria and back, his eyes showing alarm. 'What is this?'

'Samuel, what do you need him for?' Lily asks.

'We have some questions for him.'

'About what?' she asks.

'Lily, I can't talk to you right now. Steve, let's go.' I put my hand on his upper arm, firmly, but he yanks away.

'I don't have to come with you.'

'Actually, you do. Now am I going to need to put you in handcuffs, or are you going to come along?'

'Handcuffs!' Lily wails. 'What is this? Some kind of joke?'

I glance at Maria and she steps inside and takes charge of Lily.

I hadn't thought I'd need it, but I'd put my gun and holster on, and when I put my hand on the gun, Steve's eyes narrow. 'OK, OK, I'm coming. I'll be back soon, Mamma,' he calls out.

At the station, after we're seated, I ask Steve if he wants anything to drink.

'No, let's just get this over with.' He has a note of aggression in his voice that I've never heard before.

'We have to wait for someone.'

'Wait for who?'

Just then a car pulls into the parking lot with a crunch of gravel. Weinman has brought a patrol car, which is good. The sight of the law enforcement insignia on the door won't hurt. 'Here he is now.'

Weinman comes in and I see right away he's brought attitude with him. In my experience he's been a mild-mannered guy, but suddenly he's all business.

I introduce him to Steve. He nods curtly, grabs a side-chair and sits down, straddling it backwards. It reminds me of an old cop movie.

'Steve, like I said, we want to ask you a few questions,' I say.

'About what?'

'Let me start out by clearing something up. Yesterday you mentioned that you had the day off. Is that right?'

He's jiggling his leg up and down. 'Something like that.'

'Was it your day off or did you get fired?'

He smirks. 'Harriman said he was letting me go, but I figured if I went in this afternoon, he'd reconsider. I work hard and he knows it.'

'I see. So it wasn't a day off, you were fired.'

He shrugs. 'I don't know what difference it makes.'

Weinman chuckles. 'You don't know why telling the truth matters? Is that what you're saying?'

'No, I'm just saying it was no big deal.'

'Oh, I get it.' Weinman nods to me to take the lead again.

'Let's see if we can get you to tell us the truth about another thing we talked about,' I say. 'If I recall, when you told me that Amber Johnson was having sex with Cal Tyson, you said she wasn't to your taste. And yet, according to Cal, you were after Amber to get her to sleep with you.'

'If he said that, he's lying.'

'So now you're the one telling the truth, and he's lying.'

'That's right.'

'What troubles me is I can't figure out what he would stand to gain from lying about that. But I do see what you would stand to gain.'

He's worrying his lower lip with his teeth, wary eyes darting among the three of us.

I'm leading him gently because I don't want him to ask for a lawyer. As soon as he does, the questioning is over, but I won't be able to stay away from the center of things for long.

'I need to ask you about something else. Those scratches on your face. You said your friend Sophie did it, but I had a chat with Sophie and she denies it.'

His expression goes hard. 'Well, she's lying.'

'Ah,' Weinman says. 'Another liar. Sounds like you need a better set of friends.'

'You sure it wasn't Amber who scratched you?' I ask.

'I told you it was Sophie.'

'Well, never mind. The medical examiner is analyzing the material under Amber's fingernails, so if she didn't scratch you, you'll be in the clear.'

He doesn't reply, but his face goes slack. Now is the time to press harder.

'Steve, I don't believe I've ever seen you without a T-shirt on.'

He looks startled. 'So what?'

'Well, somebody saw you last Saturday night when you were working, and you didn't have your T-shirt on under your vest. What was that all about?'

'Good question,' Weinman says, his eyes fixed on Steve as if the answer means a lot.

'I don't know. It was hot. I guess I took it off.' His leg is jiggling harder.

'You guess?' I ask. 'So what did you do with the T-shirt after you took it off?'

'I don't know. I suppose I put it on the rim of the cart. I don't remember.'

'And you put it back on after you took off your vest?'

Sweat is beading along his hairline and he brushes it off with the palm of his hand. 'Could I get a cold drink?'

'In a minute. I just want to get this straight. Is that the same night you lost your knife?'

He makes a strangled sound. Maria is faster than I am, grabbing a wastebasket and shoving it in front of him just as he loses his breakfast. 'Oh, shit. Oh, man.' He groans and wipes his mouth with the back of his hand.

'What happened there, Steve?' Weinman asks.

'I don't know. It's hot. I don't feel so good. I'd like to get on home so I can lie down.'

'Steve, I don't think lying down is going to make you feel better. The only way you're going to feel better is if you get yourself unburdened of your guilt.' Weinman sounds matter-of-fact.

I glance at Maria and see that she's studying the way he's doing this. Nothing brilliant, just good, solid cop work.

'I don't know what you're talking about,' Steve says.

'I think you do,' I say, playing the gentle cop. 'Why don't you tell us what happened last Saturday night. I know you didn't mean to hurt Amber. I expect you wanted to talk to her and things just went wrong. Am I right?'

The four of us are so quiet, it's like the rest of the world has fallen away. I hope no one comes in to break the spell.

'Steve?' Maria says. 'Now is the time to tell the truth. All of it.'

His eyes dart around the room. He's breathing heavily. I expect him to break down or to resist longer, but when he speaks his words are simple. 'It happened so fast.'

I nod.

Maria gets up and says, 'What do you want, a Coke or some water?'

'You got any Sprite?'

'I'll get some. I'll be back in a minute. Meanwhile, just keep on.'

She walks out and he looks after her as if he's seeing his freedom walk out the door.

'Steve, I'm going to have to read you your rights.' I carefully recite the Miranda warning and ask him if he understands. He nods. By now he looks like he's in a daze.

'Tell us what happened,' I say. Weinman has sat back subtly, giving the impression of more space and time to allow Steve to expand.

Haltingly, painfully, Steve tells the story pretty much the way I imagined it. It was a crime of opportunity and frustration. A young man's inability to control his impulses. And in this case his impulses were deadly. By the end he's crying. 'I don't know how it happened. What am I going to do? How is my mamma going to live this down?' He looks at me with pleading eyes. 'Can you do something for me?'

That last part wrenches me. No, there's nothing I can do for him. It's up to the law now. 'Steve, you're right. Things are bad, but they're a lot better than they would have been if you hadn't told us. That will help your case.'

Weinman and I both stand up. 'We're going to be taking you to Bobtail, to the county lockup.'

'Why not here?' He sounds panicky. Jail here is at least closer to home.

'It's the way it has to be.'

'Can I at least call my daddy?'

'Don't worry, after I get back, I'll go talk to your folks. They'll need to get you a lawyer.'

'A lawyer.' He breathes the word and looks off into space.

'I'll put him in the back of my patrol car,' Weinman says, 'and you can come with me and maybe Officer Trevino can bring your squad car.'

As we're walking out, my cell phone rings. I answer it. It's Steve's daddy. I walk away to talk to him. 'Harold, I'm going to come over to your place in about an hour and we'll talk.'

'What do you mean? Where's Steve?'

'He's got some questions to answer, and it'll be a while.'

'Questions?' He knows deep down that this is not a casual matter.

'Let me get back to you. About an hour.'

It's going to be one of those conversations that will haunt anyone who participates in it. It will tear up the Deverell family and ripple out all over the community.

On the way over to Bobtail, Weinman and I don't have much to say to each other, and Steve is in the back with his eyes closed, moaning every now and then.

I call Wendy to tell her it'll be a while before I'll be there to get Hailey.

'Everything OK?'

'Sort of. I can't talk right now.'

'If you're still concerned about Lyle showing up, you may not have to worry about that anymore,' she says. 'I'm not one hundred percent sure, but I think he's out of the picture, at least for now.'

Steve's arrest has a lot of people walking around town looking grim the next few days. He was a likeable kid, and no one could have seen this coming.

According to Loretta, Lily and her daughter have left town for a while to stay with Lily's sister. Harold Deverell is staying at a motel near the jail in Bobtail so he can be near his son.

Even Hailey is subdued and shocked by the news. 'You don't think you could know somebody who would do something so awful,' she says. 'I mean, he was kind of a dick, but he didn't seem like a bad guy.'

Hailey stays with me another few days, mostly good times. And she hangs out with Sophie, Ted and Tammy, and Ben Holman's kids. And then she starts mentioning a guy named Ricky, whom I vaguely remember plays baseball for JC High. It turns out that the kid's cooler than she thought it was possible for people to be in such a small town.

But one night she comes home from being with her friends in tears and won't say why. Instead, she says she's going to talk to Loretta. When she comes home, she says Loretta fed her dinner, and she goes straight to bed. I try not to take it personally.

The next day she and Tammy go swimming at the city pool in Bobtail with a couple of other girls. No mention of Ricky. I call Loretta and she says, 'Poor little thing found out that Ricky has a girlfriend who's been on vacation with her folks, but now she's back. I told her there was another Ricky waiting out there for her, and she'll find him.'

'Too bad. I was hoping she'd have time to forget about Lyle.'

'I don't think you have to worry about that,' she says. 'It seems Lyle doesn't quite measure up to Ricky.'

I don't know which of us is more nervous when it's time for Tom and Vicki to come and get Hailey. Hailey acts like it isn't a big deal until the car pulls up in front. Then she runs out of the house and down the steps.

'Mommy!' she cries and throws her arms around Vicki. The two hug each other until Hailey yelps, 'Mooommm.' Then she hugs Tom. They're all in tears, and my eyes aren't dry either.

'Where's June?' Hailey asks.

'She wanted to come,' Tom says, 'but she had orientation at A&M, and we had to drop her off in Bryan. We'll pick her up tomorrow on the way home. She can't wait to see you.'

Hailey chatters as her folks get their bags out of the car for their overnight stay, not pausing all the way up the steps. Tom and Vicki keep glancing at me as if I'm a magician that has blown them away with an impossible trick. I know it won't last. Hailey will have more drama for them before she lets up, but at least they've had a break.

'I've made cookies,' Hailey says. 'But first I want to show you something.' She takes them into the living room. 'Did you know that Uncle Samuel has paintings by famous artists?' Nobody is more surprised than I am when she drags them to the Diebenkorn and starts explaining.

Her parents know full well about the art, but they hang on Hailey's words and she glows.

They stay overnight and, after they leave, it takes a couple of days for me to stop feeling bereft, but I settle down when Wendy reminds me of the trip she's planning to Padre Island. She talks me into going along. Although it makes me nervous, I hire Ben Holman's son, Shelby, to feed and water my cows while I'm gone. He seems like he has a good head on his shoulders. I'd give anything for Truly Bennett to be here, but he isn't, and from the sound of it, he's going to be resettling out in West Texas.

*   *   *

On the drive to Padre Island Wendy asks me what will become of Amber Johnson's family. I tell her that it was impossible to keep people from gossiping about Amber.

'Mike decided to pull up stakes and move to the coast. Both his and Amber's families are down there and he thought it would be good for the kids to have a change.'

'Probably for the best,' she says. 'He wouldn't want to be facing Steve Deverell's family.'

'One way or the other the kids would have heard rumors about their mamma. I had to tell Mike the whole sordid story.'

'That poor man.'

'It was a tough conversation. He'll have fallout from that for a long time. But in another way, it gave him courage.'

'How so?' She's driving. She's a good driver and I like to watch the concentration on her face.

'He told me he had been afraid to have the surgery on his back because of the possibility that it would leave him paralyzed. But he said Amber paid for what she did with her life, and it left him with enough money to get the surgery. He said he'd be throwing her memory away if he didn't take the chance that the operation will work.'

'I hope it does,' she says.